Everyone in Spee
Sesquicentennial
to the House O' G

Miss Iona Flowers, the self-proclaimed custodian of beauty and truth, floridly chronicling the glorious Sesqui events in her weekly society column, "Hello There." But wait—what's that crazed, maniacal glint in her eye?

Bevo Cartwright, pimply and gawky, secretly harboring an adolescent lust for head majorette Sharon DuBois. But what are three matches doing in this pyromaniac's pocket?

And, more importantly, what is *Monica Neighbors,* a proper Speed housewife, doing behind the Sani-Flush van with a no-account actor-type like Buck Fire?

. . . and many more Lee Smith characters that have caught the imagination and the hearts of an ever-growing public. Lee Smith "has the gift of a McCullers or a Faulkner of catching the sorrow, irony, and humor indigenous to the Southern temperament."

Booklist

(more)

LEE SMITH . . .

"Has been blessed with plenty of curiosity and just the right portion of nostalgia."

The New Yorker

"Takes the cake for sheer energy and comedy and ability to transform the ordinary stuff of our lives into pungent fictions."

Spectator

"Has a sharp ear for the rapid pithy speech of her neighbors and an amused eye for the sheer oddity of small town popular culture."

The New York Times Book Review

"Creates characters so vivid they leave scents on the page."

The Charlotte Observer

"Clearly a novelist to be reckoned with."

Soho News

LEE SMITH . . .

"Is a fluent, mesmerizing storyteller."
Greensboro Daily News

"A young writer of impressive talents."
Washington Star

"Knows just when to draw back, and just when to stop."

Richmond News Leader

"Is nothing less than masterly."
The New York Times Book Review

". . . a master craftsman."

The Village Voice

"Has a perfect voice, incorporating hints of both refinement and shabbiness. Quite simply, excellent writing."

Booklist

FANCY STRUT

LEE SMITH

BALLANTINE BOOKS • NEW YORK

Library of Congress Catalog Card Number: 73-4178

ISBN 0-345-34025-6

Originally published by Harper & Row, Publishers, Inc. in 1973

Manufactured in the United States of America

First Ballantine Books Edition: May 1987

For Susan and Howell Raines

Author's Note

The idea for this book came to me while I was a reporter on the *Tuscaloosa News* and was covering parts of Tuscaloosa's Sesquicentennial celebration. All characters in this story, however, are fictional.

ONE

M ISS Iona was walking to work. Miss Iona walked to work each morning and back again in the afternoon, not deviating by so much as a block from her chosen route, the accustomed way that she had come and gone for nearly forty years. Merchants and sleepy salesgirls stood at their doors to see her pass by, head high, sailing through the morning. The small, sensible black shoes angled slightly outward from her tiny ankles and were laid precisely upon the sidewalk with rapid, mincing taps, so rapid that the overall effect was one of smooth motion, a gathering speed. Miss Iona clutched her purse squarely before her with white-gloved hands. The purse was petit-point, faded now, a design of roses and cats, and she held it out slightly before her as if she planned to present it to the very next passerby. But Miss Iona's face bore no relation to that purse or even to her body, for it was set straight ahead and unheeding, fixed upon distance. She was too vain to wear glasses, and her eyes had become myopic over the years. Large and milky blue (similar to a kind of glass which is hand-blown in West Virginia), they sat in her white face like lakes. Miss Iona's features were small and wrinkled, miniature features, perfectly regular, which proved even now that she had been a beauty in her time.

She had not modified her hair style since adopting it for life in 1934. Having withstood bubbles, pixies, and stiffened domes, this hair style of Miss Iona's had now come into its own again and appeared oddly fashionable, as if cut out of a recent magazine and pasted around the aging, doll-like face. Her silver hair was pulled tightly back into a bun which dwarfed the nape of her neck, but wisps of hair escaped the bun in front and curled about her face, forming what *Vogue* called "lovelocks." The strange juxtaposition of Miss Iona's hair style and her face caused more than one pretty salesgirl to pat her similar locks absently, troubled by fleeting doubts which passed with Miss Iona.

Miss Iona's dress was tight at the waist, long-skirted and -sleeved, and of an indiscriminate, faintly iridescent hue. She looked like an antique figurine on ball bearings, wound up and set loose, magnificently incongruous upon the modern streets.

Her house stood at the corner, that Greek Revival house with six columns and a stucco front and a frieze above the columns featuring all the signs of the Zodiac. ("I am a Scorpio," Miss Iona liked to announce, "creature of earth and fire.") Once Miss Iona's house had been at the outskirts of town, but now it stood smack in the middle of Speed. People said it was a shame to let a house like that run down. In the summer you couldn't see the front of her house from the sidewalk because of the live oaks and the camellias and the wisteria and all the vines, but anybody could look in during the winter—or even now, in early spring—and see that the paint was peeling from the frieze and the porch had begun to crumble. Strangers threw Icee cups on the lawn; a row of parking meters had been installed on the block; and everything, in general, had grown much too close to everything else. When Miss Iona grew up in that house, she could sit on the front porch for hours and not see a living soul. Right out in the country it had been, surrounded by trees and fields. But the town had crawled toward it inexorably, tastelessly. First came the filling stations, with their strings of plastic pennants and their giveaway silverware. Then came the truck stops, Earl's and the House O' Good Eats. And finally, irreparably, the sidewalk. Miss Iona used to hope that a raging fire, or some similar holocaust of appropriate intensity, would come to destroy Earl's and the House O' Good Eats. But, after the sidewalk was built, she gave up. A sidewalk is most difficult to destroy.

Miss Iona walked to work in every weather. She did not have to work but she wanted to. She always had. It was her vocation. Going now along her usual route, she passed first by the block of dentists' and doctors' offices and small stores. Some of the stores had been carved from large houses like her own, and in these cases the rest of the house was usually used for storage space. The Broadway House of Beauty stood on the corner at the end of this block, and every time she saw it Miss Iona nearly died. It was pink and green, for one thing. And years ago it had been the home of Robert and Eugenia Shepherd right after their marriage and before Eugenia was seized with the vapors and died—Eugenia, the delicate cousin.

In the next block, Miss Iona passed along a row of newer buildings with dollar stores and clothing shops on the ground floor, insurance agencies and other offices one story up. In the center of the block was a store specializing in prosthetic devices. Miss Iona had never glanced into its window and she never would. Prosthetic devices were vulgar.

The last block was the one along the square (which used to be all that there was to Speed) and she passed the old bank and the hardware store with the clock out front and then she reached the tiny *Messenger* office itself, wedged in between the laundry and the Family Shop.

Many people spoke to Miss Iona. Sometimes she inclined her head in reply, but more often she did not. Speed was growing fast; people were walking faster in the square. Something new was going on, and Miss Iona knew it.

She climbed the steps to the office, waving first to deaf and dumb Will who sat at the Linotype machine on the first floor. Will grinned and grinned. He was always grinning. He had been at the *Messenger* almost as long as Miss Iona herself, ever since her father had sent him to the special school, and he thought she was a grand lady.

Sitting behind her father's old desk, Miss Iona nibbled delicately at a slice of candied orange peel and mused upon her destiny. She saw herself as the custodian of beauty and truth in Speed, the champion of the pure and good. As society and ladies' editor of the weekly *Messenger*, she controlled the public life of Speed. She announced the births of babies in her column "Hello There." She wrote all the obituaries. In between, she took care of weddings and anniversaries and parties and club meetings, and all the other important events that marked the passing of time in Speed.

What was the good of having a party if Miss Iona didn't write it up? You might as well not have bothered. What was the good of wearing a silver lamé dress if Miss Iona wrote you up in beige lace? The truth is what you read in the paper.

Sometimes, Miss Iona was incomprehensible. Once she put Grecian urns of bougainvillea in every home and at every wedding, for months on end. Sometimes she draped everyone in mink, regardless of the season. She decorated tables to suit her fancy, and put peau-de-soie slippers on whom she chose. Owing to these penchants, Miss Iona was a figure of much controversy in Speed.

In the women's pages of the paper, everything was elegant. Brides came down the aisle arrayed in beauty and grace and light, and sometimes their dresses weren't mentioned at all, so that if you wanted to sit down on your sofa at home and read the paper and review the whole thing in your mind's eye, you had a hard time with nothing but beauty and light to go on.

Some people didn't like the way Miss Iona did obituaries, but there were others who held that they were beautiful. For one thing, the obituaries never read, "So-and-so is survived by." They read, "Left in sorrow to mourn the passing of their beloved are . . ." And there were many other differences between the style of the obituaries in, say, the Mobile paper and the Speed *Messenger*.

Miss Iona was exactly as old as the paper.

She had become ladies' editor when her father was the publisher and she herself was a young girl, all those years ago. Now her father was dead, his successor had retired, and there was this new editor, this progressive young man who was active in all the civic doings of the town. His name was Manly Neighbors; and it was a surprise to all of Speed that he kept her on. But Manly Neighbors was still a young man, and he had been taught to respect his elders. Besides, there was a gentlemen's agreement in the past. So he kept her on, and often he didn't even attempt to edit her copy. Her copy was beyond him and beyond hope, from Manly Neighbors' point of view. He wrote his pages and she wrote her pages and that was that.

Besides Manly and Miss Iona, the *Messenger* staff included Manly Neighbors' secretary, Susan Watkins; Charlie, the photographer; a man who came in to write up the high school games; two people, a middle-aged man and a married woman, who handled the advertising; various correspondents from the surrounding county; deaf and dumb Will on the Linotype machine; and a legion of newsboys and menials who were concerned with the physical aspects of printing the paper. Miss Iona held herself quite aloof from menials and physical aspects.

Manly was decent but he was progressive. He hoped Miss Iona would die or retire soon, but he never voiced these thoughts. For Speed was changing, and Manly couldn't ignore the changes either. Rows of little brick houses popped up in the lots outside town where the pecan groves had been. The Greeley mansion had been made into a library and the Bobo house had been torn down. A big neon Pepsi sign—as big as any sign in Mobile—threw its varying red light down onto the marble Confederate major in the square's center, making him blush pink all through the night. Everywhere you looked, you saw them: signs of the times.

Through the open window before her father's desk, Miss Iona watched, morosely, the happily flashing Pepsi sign (which was not reserved for the P.M. but continued its flashing even throughout the day), and beside it, the little old-fashioned Sunbeam girl, continuously eating fat slices of the shining neon bread. It was all inexpressibly vulgar to Miss Iona, who nevertheless felt that this sordid view—the Sunbeam girl and the giant, bottled cola—served a mission for which they were never intended. They did not make her crave Pepsis and tuna fish sandwiches. On the contrary: they made her abhor these things, and cleave ever more strongly to her ideals. They reinforced her vocation. Miss Iona gazed out her window each morning before beginning her work and was sickened, then strengthened, by the sight. It is somewhat like the flight of the Phoenix, she realized this particular morning in a burst of inspiration; but that thought proved difficult to follow. Miss Iona smiled, sighed, and lowered her large blue eyes to the business at hand.

She did not like the note from Manly. It said: "Get pix,

feature on local winners of state majorette contest to be held tomorrow in Tuscaloosa. Local winner, if any, will lead all Sesqui parades. Yours, M.N.''

Yours! thought Miss Iona. As if she would have Manly Neighbors even if somebody gave him to her on a platter! Yours! the very idea. And the way he always wrote "Sesqui" instead of "Sesquicentennial," not even allowing their great celebration the full measure of dignity with which the sheer historical weight of the years should endow it—I must calm myself, she thought. Faint heart ne'er won fair lady, she thought too, but she discarded this thought as inappropriate.

Miss Iona walked over to the window and looked down upon the square, upon all the ignorant hurrying people in the square. My mission is to instruct, she said to herself. *Arriba!*

She looked again at the note from Manly. I will never put a majorette on the society page, she vowed. There never has been one and there never will be one, not as long as I am alive. It would be just like putting a nigger. Miss Iona shuddered to think of majorettes. They were gross and horrid. She had seen them on television and she knew. The only girls worse than majorettes, to her mind, were the girls of the Roller Derby.

Miss Iona went back to her desk and opened the bottom drawer and pulled out a volume of poetry. The bottom drawer was filled with books of poetry, and Miss Iona often turned to them for inspiration in dark hours. She liked Tennyson, Milton, Byron, and everything in her book of *One Hundred Famous Poems*, but lately she had found herself reading Matthew Arnold. She realized that it was weird and somehow distasteful to write all those poems that took place underwater, but she could not deny their peculiar, fishy appeal. She began to read, then put her book down abruptly as Manly Neighbors entered; as conscious of her image as any starlet, she rustled her papers and assumed her role as the social arbiter of Speed.

"Morning, Miss Iona," Manly said heartily, stopping to lean on the huge desk, an action which Miss Iona detested. Manly was a strapping fellow, husky and friendly, with the look of a former high school football player going gloriously to seed. His brown hair was clipped close to his head and his eyes were like cows' eyes, large and brown and blank. The hand which rested on Miss Iona's father's desk was thick and well-manicured and tan—Manly always had a tan, and Miss Iona suspected that he played many little outdoor games with his friends. Tennis, golf; Miss Iona could just hear him shouting sporty epithets to his friends in the heat of play, and she could just see him perspiring. She was sure he perspired.

"Find my note?" Manly asked.

"Oh, yes," Miss Iona said. "But I must say I think we can do without a majorette on the *society* page. I never heard of such a thing."

"Well, then, write her up for general news and I'll stick her in on page two," Manly said, unruffled. "But I want her in there. Everything that has to do with the Sesquicentennial is getting a big play, that's the deal. Good for business, you know." Manly's deep voice trailed off as he unwrapped a stick of Juicy Fruit and estimated the extra advertising to come. If the Sesquicentennial was a success, and the advertising added up to the profit he expected, Manly planned to go biweekly in the fall.

"I think we could do without her," Miss Iona said quietly, pausing carefully between each word of emphasis.

But Manly didn't notice, or chose to ignore, the emphasis. "I reckon," he said, "but I want everything about the Sesquicentennial covered right from the start. And a pretty girl never hurt the paper's sale, anyway. I just might even put her on page one, if she's really something."

Miss Iona grew quite rigid behind the desk. "Mr. Neighbors, this is not *Playboy*," she said distinctly, but Manly had characteristically bounded away. "I said this is not *Playboy*." She raised her voice for emphasis.

"What?" said Manly, absent-mindedly pausing at the door to rub his close-cropped head. "Of course not, Miss Flowers. Yes, I'd like that feature by tomorrow, and I'll take the Sesqui cover story now if you've got it ready. I'd like to get page one laid out by noon." Manly went into the other room and closed the door behind him.

So you can go to the Country Club to play your little games, Miss Iona thought. Well, some of us have principles, at least! The overhead fan whirled gently, caressing the pages of the initial Sesquicentennial story as she read through it again, checking for errors. It was a beautiful story and it would be a beautiful celebration, just beautiful.

One hundred and fifty years ago our forefathers founded Speed, the pastoral Pioneer Settlement on the banks of the great Mongawatta River.

Today we celebrate our Roots.

A group of leading citizens, together with the cooperative efforts of Speed's civic and social clubs, have planned a great Sesquicentennial Celebration to commemorate our humble beginnings and celebrate our promising future. Every man, woman, and child of Speed and the surrounding counties is invited to participate in one or more of the myriad exciting events. There is a place for All. Each citizen should consider it his civic duty to pitch in and join the fun, and make this Sesquicentennial one to remember.

The planners of the Sesquicentennial have secured the services of the White Company, renowned professional Advisors, to advise and aid in executing all aspects of the celebration. The White Company has produced over 78 such community celebrations in its history. Speed's own Sesquicentennial producer-director, Mr. Buck Fire, will arrive shortly to begin organizing the townspeople into committees. He will also commence auditions, casting, and rehearsals for the spectacular outdoor pageant, tentatively entitled "The Song of Speed."

An actor professionally, Mr. Buck Fire has appeared in motion pictures the world over as well as on television in an episode of "My Three Sons." He will bring a wealth of wide experience to his task.

"The Song of Speed" will be the giant feature attraction of the Speed Sesquicentennial Celebration. Four performances of this spectacular will allow man, woman, and child to participate. A cast of over 250 local actors and actresses will sing the Song of Speed and the surrounding countryside, exploring the wealth of History, Industry, and Raw Materials at our disposal. Professional motion picture projection will be a part of this astounding saga as well. No pageant of such breadth has ever been planned for our locale.

The lucky, lovely maiden chosen to rule as Sesquicentennial Queen will be presented at each performance, along with her Court of Honor. She will preside also at the Sesquicentennial Ball, in addition to reigning over all festivities at the week-long celebration. Many marvelous prizes will be Hers. The tentative schedule for this Glorious Week will include:

—The Parade.

—Opening Ceremonies to feature the Speed High School Band, State and Local Dignitaries, and all Club groups. A Post-Parade Reception by Mayor Bill Higgins for visiting local officials.

—First annual pilgrimage of the Speed Historical Society, in which Gracious Hostesses will open their homes, venting their traditional Southern Hospitality upon the general public. Homes both old and new will be featured herein.

—The Sesquicentennial Ball, a return to more gracious days.

—An evening square dance in downtown Speed.

—Activities to be Announced, featuring the Bushy Brothers and the Sesquicentennial Belles.

—Ceremony announcing the selection of the Queen.

—Ladies luncheon featuring old-timey costume show. *Upper Room Cookbook*, compiled by the ladies of the First Methodist Church, to be sold.

—Agricultural fair, to be planned by 4-H Clubs and their leaders. Beef-for-Bama day.

—Townwide "Sidewalk Sale and Bargain Day," featuring a cakewalk and Greased Pig.

—Burial of the Speed Time Capsule, containing relics

of modern Speed as it is today. Matinee performance of the "Song" for School Children.

—College Day, for which a tour of historic Speed Junior College is projected.

—Judging of Beard Contest.

Any man, woman, or child wishing to participate in any aspect of this celebration should get in touch with the Sesquicentennial Headquarters as soon as it is set up. There is a place for All; All are needed. Interested ladies will join the Belles group, while the men will sport full beards, moustachios, etc., and be designated as the Bushy Brothers.

Watch the Speed *Messenger* to keep abreast of developing Plans.

Our is a strong heritage, a history of courage and dedication to the highest ideal of man. And in this ever increasing age, it is well to look to the past for wisdom to guide our steps into tomorrow.

So let us take time out from our busy lives to contemplate and Celebrate. Sesquicentennial Week is but eight short weeks hence. Let them be eventful ones of zestful preparation!

Miss Iona delicately licked the end of her Bic ballpoint pen. It was a fine story. No doubt Manly Neighbors, who had no taste, would see fit to lower-case some of the Capital letters; he always did. Manly Neighbors had no sense of theater, of the dramatic element so necessary to good journalism. One could be dramatic, ecstatic, yet refined. It was a high art, akin to that of tightrope walking. One balanced an adverb here, an adjective there, and progressed along the central strand of the story. All Manly understands, Miss Iona thought, is facts and dollar bills. Manly has no flair. The elements in the story which Miss Iona particularly liked were its patriotism; its civic call to every man, woman, and child; and its stirring conclusion.

Miss Iona shut her eyes and imagined the Pageant, for it was a project which held her passionate interest. She saw a set somewhat like that of *Midsummer Night's Dream*, yet Southern, with cornstalks rustling at the sides and Spanish moss dangling all about. She saw noble Indians come and go; gentle Negroes singing their spiritual songs; crinolined ladies curtsying to gallant officers in gray. She heard a bugle, the call to War! She—

"Have you got that Sesqui story, please, ma'am?" It was Manly Neighbors, a pencil behind his ear. "I'm fixing to lay out the page."

"So you are," said Miss Iona. She handed him the typewritten pages. Manly Neighbors turned and left her office, thanking her, but Miss Iona stared at his back with distaste. Demonstrating anew his singular lack of flair, Manly had untied his tie. Its loose ends flapped at his elbows as he hurried to his desk, scanning her story; from behind, through the open door, it looked to Miss Iona as if his elbows had sprouted obscene little tails.

TWO

BOB and Frances Pitt stayed in a bridal suite in the Ocean-Aire Autel at Fort Walton Beach, Florida, on their honeymoon, and had a perfectly all right time; but do you know what Johnny B. and Sandy DuBois did? They went to the Southern 500 at Darlington, South Carolina, and sat out in the weather on those old hard benches for three entire days, watching the cars go around and around. Three whole days they sat out there! If Frances Pitt had done it she'd never tell it. But Sandy came back acting like she'd been to Europe; that's the way she was.

Frances saw red every time it crossed her mind.

She couldn't help but be reminded from time to time, either, because she and Sandy DuBois were first cousins, and in a town the size of Speed that meant Frances just had to see her every time she turned around.

When they were little girls, their Grandfather Daniels used to give them a quarter apiece and take them into town on Saturday afternoons. Sandy carried on a lot, running in the five-and-ten, running in the Rexall, giggling and showing everybody that quarter like it was a hundred-dollar bill—and then she always bought a fifteen-cent bottle of Evening in Paris perfume for their grandmother. Which tickled old Grandfather Daniels half to death every time. He showed the little blue bottle of perfume to everybody standing out in front of the courthouse or sitting on the long green benches along the square, and they all nodded and bent and Sandy smiled back at them all like a holy angel. Then, of course, Grandfather pulled out a brand-new quarter for Sandy because she was such a good girl, and she ended up with thirty-five cents, enough to buy makeup. Her favorite lipstick at that time was Fire and Ice.

Frances saved her quarters, every one, and that was highly regarded by the entire family, but Frances could tell who her grandfather's favorite was.

And Sandy hadn't changed a bit! Now she had a daughter, Sharon, who was the spitting image of her; and Sharon was a majorette at Speed High School along with Frances' own daughter, Theresa Pitt. But Sharon DuBois was the head majorette, and you can just imagine how Frances felt about that. Of course Sharon was ten months older than Theresa (they had let on like she was premature) and that might account for it.

So Mrs. Sandy DuBois and Mrs. Frances Pitt became the official Majorette Mothers of Speed High, and on February 25th they took the majorettes up to Tuscaloosa to the annual Susan Arch Finlay Memorial Marching Contest held at the University. It was the biggest, most prestigious marching contest in all the state.

They went in the DuBoises' car, which was newer than the Pitts'. (Johnny B. DuBois had surprised everybody by making a lot of money in the fried-chicken business. He had a picture of himself, framed and hanging in his restaurant on the outskirts of Speed: Johnny B. DuBois and Colonel Sanders, shaking hands.)

The girls were like a bunch of birds in the car, twittering

and twitching, and they made so much noise that Mrs. Pitt and Mrs. DuBois couldn't have said a word to each other even if they had wanted to. Sometimes Mrs. DuBois sang along with the radio and the girls.

The Susan Arch Finlay was big. Majorettes from all over the state of Alabama had come, hundreds of them. You got a set of free tassels just for being there. A judge had come all the way from California to judge the majorettes.

Frances, shaky with excitement and sticky all over with sweat, stood in the heat with the other mothers and watched the General Group Strut, and her heart did little back flips in her breast. The Speed Rockettes were the cutest things in the world, all five of them. They put everybody else to shame. Here they came across the field, stepping high. They wore white boots with silver tassels (made from Christmas icicles by Frances herself), and silver sequined suits, and long white gloves.

Here they came across the field, looking right and left in time to the music, their brushed hair and their fine teeth and their sequined suits and white gloves glinting in the sun, those silver batons sailing, sailing through the air. For their Dance Routine act, they put on derby hats which the Majorette Mothers had ordered special from Mobile. They were the only ones in the contest with derby hats.

The Speed Rockettes won first place in the General Group Strut. They would have gotten first place in the Dance Routine too, if Mrs. Sandy DuBois hadn't put their record on the wrong side. (Sandy DuBois was up by the PA system, in charge of the majorettes' music.) I could kill her, Frances thought, I could just kill her with my bare hands! Frances was so hot from excitement and the unseasonable sun that her legs were breaking out with little red dots all over.

The Rockettes had had their batons and their brown legs in the thick leg makeup lifted, all ready to go to "Yessir,

That's My Baby,'' wearing their cute derby hats—and what did Sandy DuBois put on the turntable? ''Younger Than Springtime,'' that's what. The Speed Rockettes got the funniest looks on their faces, like they had fallen out of a boat. The Susan Arch Finlay officials swore to Frances later that such a simple mistake, a technological error, you might say, couldn't possibly have influenced the decision of the judge, but Frances had her own ideas.

She pulled herself up in her new polyester double-knit suit and poured herself out like an inflatable lady, and pursed her red lips and blew out her breath in short little spurts one at a time until she had calmed herself, and then it was time to help Theresa change clothes for the Individual Fancy Strut and she was too busy to be mad.

The girls' dressing room was full of busy mothers and daughters making such a racket that the huge airy space right up to the gymnasium rafters quivered with their high, nasal, birdlike cries. The majorettes looked at themselves in long-stemmed hand mirrors brought from home and pushed at a curl here, a camouflaged pimple there, anxiously, while their mothers did up their backs. The girls were sweet and jerky. They flashed quick bright smiles at themselves in their mirrors and at each other, their eyes shifting and shifting. All the girls were nice and they smiled a lot. (Later that day, they would elect a Miss Popularity and a Miss Beauty from among their ranks. None of the girls wanted to be Miss Popularity, but everyone wanted to be nominated. It was an honor to be nominated. It was also an honor to be chosen Miss Beauty; but Miss Popularity was usually ugly.)

When the girls, sleek and shiny and twitchy as racehorses, went out to line up across the field, the mothers stood quietly and glared at one another, because each wanted her daughter to win and each knew what a time she would have going home in the car if her daughter failed at the Fancy Strut. The Fancy Strut category was the cream of the competition, the most prestigious category of them all. The mothers shielded their eyes from the sun and waited. Their conversation was brief and went off at right angles to itself, ceasing abruptly.

"Seventy-six Trombones" blared out over the PA speakers stationed on the gym roof, rolled across the field, and here came the majorettes after the music: Alabama's best, a gay and righteous army in the sun.

"Do you reckon he can see them all?" said the woman standing next to Frances, but Frances was too moved to answer.

She told Bob later, "It was the most beautiful thing I ever saw in my life, all of them coming across that field." It made Frances proud to be an American. She was worried though, worried and proud at the same time. Theresa's strut seemed to her to be far superior to the other struts, but she just didn't know. You couldn't ever tell what somebody from California was going to think.

Oh, but Theresa was a pretty thing! So young and sassy, so strange and different from her mother, marching across the field. Frances felt like she had felt the night that Bob had almost hit a deer, and they had sat there in the car and stared at its still, wide eyes in the headlights. The headlights had hypnotized it. But that deer had been different, different from Frances. It gave her the creeps.

Then they were saying on the PA system that Theresa had won the Fancy Strut, won first place and her a year younger than most of them, and Frances was running across the field in her high white heels.

"I just knew it!" she said, panting from the run and kissing Theresa. "Oh, I just knew it!"

"Oh, Mama," said Theresa, trying to straighten the satin ribbon they had put across her shoulders and ignoring her mother as much as it was possible to do with her mother kissing all over her. "FIRST PLACE FANCY STRUT" was written in red glitter on the white ribbon across Theresa's shoulder.

The emcee with the microphone asked Theresa how she felt about winning. "This is the happiest day of my life," she said. It was the happiest day of Frances' life, too.

The Speed Rockettes, individually and as a group, won more honors than any other Grade C group in Alabama. As a group, the Rockettes took first place, General Group Strut; second place, Dance Routine; honorable mention, Improvisation to a Previously Unheard Tune; and third place, Stable Baton. Theresa had won more first places than anybody else from Speed; she would lead the Sesquicentennial Parade.

Covered in glory, the Rockettes stopped at a pay phone to call the band director and tell him the news. They talked to him one by one. Theresa was the last to talk, and while she was on the phone Mrs. DuBois pulled a Polaroid camera out of thin air and got the Rockettes to pose together with their tassels and sashes and trophies. Except for Theresa. When she got off the phone, Sandy had already taken the picture. The Rockettes circled around her, hopping from one foot to the other and stumbling and drunk with fame, while they waited for the camera to print their picture.

Standing outside the group, Frances felt plump suddenly, and alone, and hurt for Theresa. But Theresa herself didn't realize that she had been slighted. She stood in the circle around Sandy, with the others, waiting for the camera to work.

No wonder she is so popular, Frances thought. She has a wonderful personality.

When the picture came out, Sandy squealed in apparent dismay. "Oh my, we forgot Theresa! Let's make another one!" But, unfortunately, there was no more film. Dried, the picture turned out to be bad anyway: Brenda Pool's eyes were closed, and Martha Lou Renfro had her mouth squinched up.

"Well, win a few, lose a few," said Sandy DuBois, who was always saying catchy things. She wore her blond hair in a French twist and she patted it now, absently, at the bottom, before she got back in the car. Sandy didn't think about Frances too much one way or the other. Frances had been around forever, as far as Sandy was concerned, like a childhood disease you ought to get over but don't. And besides that, besides their joint childhood, she had a special reason for not thinking about Frances too much.

On the way back in the car, headed south again down 82, the Rockettes giggled and giggled, packed scientifically into the car, two sitting forward and two sitting back in the back seat, and Martha Lou Renfro up front stuck in between Frances and Sandy and not liking it particularly. The Rockettes in the back seat played a game named Curvy Wurvy, where they leaned into each other as hard as possible going around the curves, and screamed, and screamed as the night came on.

THREE

*I*F all the turquoise plastic chairs of the El Rondo Motor Hotel coffee shop were filled every morning, it was not because of the coffee. It was because the El Rondo was the place to be, between the hours of eight and ten in the morning. No man of real substance in Speed could afford to bypass the El Rondo. Located smack in the middle of Speed—on the square, across from the courthouse, back to back with the jail—the El Rondo was central to the political and business life of Speed. The curved plastic chairs of the El Rondo were the most modern chairs to be found in Speed. They didn't have arm rests like decent chairs; they curved and sprawled insanely above their wrought-iron legs. The habitués of the Rondo had bitched and bitched when the chairs first appeared but the El Rondo's owner, Miss Leola Bradshaw, thought that they added a certain tone.

Before long, she said, she was going to do over the rest of the place to go with the chairs. But the cowboy murals now on the walls, relics of a former décor, were still good for another year or so at least. Smoke hung in the air of the

Rondo in solid, undulating blue sheets like plexiglass patio roofs, so that if you could see the cowboys at all you were an exception.

Mayor Bill Higgins came into the Rondo, letting the screen door slam shut behind him, and stopped where he was to check the crowd. He was feeling fine and mean. Bill Higgins was a tall man with a crew cut and a big hard belly, who dressed every day in a long-sleeved white shirt and a bow tie. He wore the bow tie because he was the mayor, and the long-sleeved shirt to hide "Snooky," tattooed inside a double heart on his left arm.

"How's your hammer hanging, Lloyd?" Higgins asked, slapping a man at the counter so hard that he spilled about half of his coffee.

"Goddamnit, Bill." Lloyd Warner started to wipe up the mess and then thought better of it and let it drip onto his knee. What the hell. Lloyd felt awful, and here was this clown. The animosity between the mayor and Lloyd Warner was so old, dating back to grade school when Lloyd had had rheumatic fever and Bill had bullied him, that Lloyd had lost interest in it. Like most of his relationships in Speed, it bored him.

"What's the matter, boy? You got the shakes?" Higgins looked at Lloyd's hands. "I guess you haven't been drinking none, have you?" Mayor Bill leered and winked. Putting things negatively was his idea of humor.

"Hyeh hyeh hyeh." Jimmy Ted Boyd, materializing out of the smoke to stand in his regular slot at the mayor's elbow, knew when to laugh and he did, twisting his face around behind the blue-framed glasses which remained perfectly still on his splotchy nose.

Lloyd smoked a cigarette and thought about lung cancer. He stared at the Indian chief hanging over the glass showcase full of Morton's cream pies. The Indian chief stared at the moon, and pointed at a rock.

"I reckon you wouldn't give a man a cuppa coffee and some peanut-butter Nabs," Higgins said to Leola.

"Hyeh hyeh hyeh," said Jimmy Ted Boyd, convulsed.

"Oh, Jesus, who is that clown?" Lloyd said.

"That just so happens to be my assistant," Higgins said.

"What's the matter with his face?" Lloyd said.

"I've got psoriasis," Jimmy Ted answered for himself, with all the dignity he could find.

"Piss-or-i-ASS-is!" Higgins said, and after a pause Jimmy Ted said. "Hyeh," but his heart didn't seem to be in it.

"I don't recall you having any money for an assistant, Bill," said Lloyd. "Where did you appropriate that from?"

"Never you mind, boy, you just stick to your liquor and let your elders run the town," said Higgins. "I wouldn't think about it twice if I was you."

"Pitt, come on over here, boy, and get yourself a chair," Higgins yelled at a slight, nervous man twitching his way through the smoke. "I got a proposition for you, boy." He leered and winked and Jimmy Ted said, "Hyeh."

"Morning, Mayor." Bob Pitt sat nervously on the edge of his voluptuous chair, picking at his kneecaps. "Tea," he said to Leola, which caused her to start in surprise. She should have been used to Bob Pitt and his tea by now.

"What you got on your mind?" Bob Pitt asked. He stared at the mayor and then looked away in that rabbity fashion he had.

"You pay attention now, Pitt," Higgins instructed, feeling that the instructions were necessary because no matter what you said to Bob Pitt he looked like he was thinking about something else. "You know this big Sesquicentennial coming up? Well, I got a special place for you, boy. I want you to be the head of the Bushy Brothers. Now that's a very important position, Pitt."

At the counter, Lloyd was seized with a coughing fit.

"You don't smoke too much, do you?" Higgins threw out in his direction. Then he went on to Bob Pitt: "You going to be responsible for a lot of things, including the Kangaroo Court on Fridays."

Bob Pitt's eyes shot back and forth, weaving around the Rondo. He seemed ready to burst forth in some manner, to vent all his individual agitations in one final gesture, but nothing special happened. "O.K.," he said.

"Oh, hell," Lloyd said to the Indian chief.

"It will all be explained to you," said Higgins, expansive, "at this meeting we're having Friday afternoon in my office. You come on over there, now. I got to have all the community leaders present, you know, and this professional we've got is going to get the ball rolling. He's coming in Thursday night."

"O.K.," said Bob Pitt again, giving his teabag a final, compulsive squash with his thumb. He drained the rest of his tea.

"We going to put this town on the *map*," Higgins said. Bob Pitt nodded and ducked his head several times as he got up to go, scraping his chair (which had become entangled with his feet) along the floor.

Higgins said, "See you Friday."

"Friday," repeated Bob Pitt, and ducked out.

"What did you get *him* for?" whispered Jimmy Ted.

"Because that is the workingest bastard in this town, is why," said Higgins. "You watch. I guess you don't think old Bill knows what he's doing, huh?"

"Uh," said Jimmy Ted.

"Goldman," bawled Higgins, "get your Jew ass over here a minute." Manny Goldman left the men at his table and took the chair lately vacated by Bob Pitt. Manny was the drugstore king of Speed.

"This here is my assistant, Jimmy Ted Boyd," Higgins

said to Manny, and Jimmy Ted said, "Pleased to meet you, Mr. Goldman."

"Yeah, kid," Manny answered. As the only actual Jewish merchant in Speed, he felt compelled to speak in the manner of the northern Jewish comedians who often appeared on TV. He cultivated a side-mouth, staccato delivery and an occasional slow burn.

"Well, so how is the Sesquicentennial, Bill? You got everything lined up? Everything all set?" Manny asked, lighting a small cigar.

"Everything's all set, all right. I'm all set to lose my shirt if this thing don't go," said the mayor. "The town of Speed has gone and hired itself a hot-shot professional company to produce the whole thing, but if everybody and I do mean everybody in this town doesn't work like hell we are sure going to get burned."

"How's that?" asked Manny, side-mouthing.

"I had to sign this contract," Higgins said, "and what this contract says is, we are liable for any expenses the White Company incurs if the townspeople don't cooperate and this company has to quit in the middle or something."

"Has that ever happened?"

"Hell, no, not in the history of the company, the man said. He said it's just a protective clause, but you know me. I don't like to write my name on them little lines." He sprawled back and grinned. "We all going to make some money," he said. "Speed can't go nowhere but up."

"You're a sucker, Bill," said Lloyd Warner, offhand, as if he didn't care one way or the other what Bill was. He spun around on his stool, but instead of stopping to face the mayor, he spun on around.

"You didn't even say what I thought you did, now did you, Lloyd?" Bill Higgins raised his voice, which was loud anyway, and a sudden silence descended upon the Rondo. Other men at other tables put their cups down and suspended their talk of crops and cash, then self-consciously began it again, louder, straining over their own voices to hear.

"I say you're a fool, Bill. Speed is going to get took for all we've got, is what I said. You know it yourself. Every business, every man in town is going to have to donate a lot of money to this thing, and sooner or later that company is going to walk out of here with a fat wallet. Speed is a poor town. We don't have that kind of money." Lloyd went on spinning around; his hair, which was somewhat longer than the hair of most of the men in Speed, blew back from his head as he whirled.

"You're going to walk out of here with a fat lip," Higgins announced, sitting straight up abruptly among the turquoise dips and humps. Jimmy Ted appeared to be very nervous; he plucked at the mayor's white sleeve.

Higgins straightened his bow tie (it was a clip-on) and tried a new tack, one more in keeping with his position. "I should of known a liberal like you wouldn't have any sympathy with the common man. I guess you feel like having town a hundred and fifty years old isn't any cause to celebrate. I guess you think it's not much. Well, you get one thing straight, there are still some people in this town who are proud of what they come from." Higgins sat back, satisfied.

"I'm not disagreeing with that, Bill," said Lloyd, slowing down, merely coasting now on his turning stool. "I'm not denying you your patriotism, which you know, you know that anyway, you're just carrying on. All I'm saying is if you want a Sesquicentennial, you should have let the town handle it, the whole thing. We've got people out at the college that could probably even write the pageant, if you've got to have a pageant. We don't need to get some jackass company in here to tell us what to do, that's all. They're going to commercialize the whole thing."

"Well, now, Lloyd, that's more or less what I had in mind," the mayor said, grinning a long, thin grin, and the men at the other tables shook their heads at each other, stumped with delight. You couldn't get the best of Higgins.

Reveling, the mayor sank back into his plastic recesses and continued, "If you got something to say about the way I run things, you come on over to this meeting on Friday and say it."

"I'm not on your committee, Bill," said Lloyd, grinning now himself. His eyes were insolent and amused.

"Well, now, is that a fact?" said the mayor, and everybody laughed.

Lloyd shook his head—suddenly remembering, for no reason, the time in grade school when Higgins had put Noxzema in the teacher's cottage cheese—and then pushed his hair back and stood up, his seersucker suit hanging wrong. "Here you go, Leola," he said, flicking a bill on the counter. "You take care of the mayor's party too." He was gone out the door, shuffling, before the mayor had time to think of a reply.

FOUR

T HE Neighborses' house was lovely. Everyone agreed that it was one of the showplaces of the town, and it was to be the only modern home featured in the upcoming Speed Pilgrimage of Homes, part of the Sesquicentennial. Not that it was really modern. It was two years old, but it was built in the style of a more gracious past: four big white columns in front supported a balcony (Monica had always fancied balconies), and an abbreviated terrace extended the length of the front of the house. Clever French doors opened from the living and dining rooms onto this terrace, which was hemmed by a low green hedge and rose trees. Monica had always fancied rose trees, too. The house was brick but the bricks had been specially made so that they were a soft rose color—not those ordinary red bricks that you saw everywhere else. Manly, who had inherited a great deal of money, had given Monica a free hand with the house, and Monica's taste was good. The interior was a blend of inherited antiques, Oriental rugs, a few blocky pieces of contemporary furniture, several good abstract paintings that Monica had gotten in Memphis, and low convenient tables which held clusters of carefully eclectic, expensive clutter and the latest magazines. The kitchen was carpeted in a yellow floral print. The bathrooms were carpeted too.

"Why, it looks just like a page out of *Good Housekeeping*, honey," Monica's bridge club had exclaimed in one breath when it was Monica's turn to be hostess. Monica winced, having had *Vogue* in mind. But it was just as well—the house was successful, that was the thing. It was really something, for Speed.

The only problem was, Monica reflected while she dressed, that now that she had this lovely house it was impossible to live in it. Maybe it wasn't the house. Maybe it was her (or is that "she"? Monica wondered). Maybe it was she. Monica didn't know what was wrong. She pulled on her stockings, taking as long as possible, because she had nothing else to do. Somewhere in the house, Suetta was vacuuming the exquisite rugs. Monica could hear the drone. Suetta came every day and told Monica what she was going to do and then did it while Monica, cowed, crept around the house and tried to keep out of her way. There was nothing for Monica to do. She had suggested to Manly several times that maybe Suetta should go, or at least come only a few times a week; but Manly had appeared horrified, as if his wife had lost her mind. All the women in Manly's family (the Neighborses of Speed) had had maids—an endless, black succession of constant help. It was unthinkable to Manly that his wife should not have a maid, a yard boy, and extra help for parties. It was not so much a question of needing the help, Monica knew. She could probably dust as well as anybody if she had a chance. It was a matter of life style: Monica should have a full-time maid, so she did. Monica and Manly should have a fine home, so they did.

The house had occupied the first years of their marriage,

for Monica at least. First there had been the endless sessions with the architect; then the actual building of the house itself; then there had been whole months spent, it seemed, surrounded by big fat books full of fabrics and furniture; then there were all the shopping trips to Birmingham and Memphis and Mobile. It was a great challenge and Monica had risen to it. Now was the time to sit back and enjoy it, the time to live in it. But suddenly, surprisingly, it had gone dead. All the color-coordinated rooms and area rugs turned gray for Monica. There was no interest anywhere. All was finished and dead.

Monica stood in her stockings and bra and kicked the chintz-covered chaise longue in the bedroom. "Speak to me," she said. It was silent.

I am going mad, thought Monica.

She sat on a small antique rocker and brushed her dark hair. At least she had something to do today. As the head of the Sesquicentennial Headquarters Committee, she was to open the headquarters in the old Pardoe home on Apricot Road. Then she and her committee—composed of three of her friends—would man the desk, every day, until the Sesquicentennial was over. Their job was to "coordinate activities," and Monica couldn't wait. It would be something to do every afternoon for over a month. Usually she went shopping in the mornings, then lunched with one of her friends, and then of course Manly came home at night, so the afternoons were the worst times. From two to five she couldn't cope at all. It might be better in the summer, she thought. If they get the pool finished, I can go to the club to swim. So that was something to look forward to, also. Monica tied her long hair back with a blue ribbon and put on a blue linen dress. She put on beige lipstick and then she was ready—twenty-five minutes too soon.

I know, she thought suddenly. I'll water the plants. But

with what? There were a lot of plants, she would need something that held a lot of water. I'll have to buy a little watering can, she thought, delighted. With a little spout. That would fill up a morning. But right now she would use her white ironstone pitcher. Why not? Things are made to be used. She went down the thickly carpeted, winding stairs into the entrance hall, and through the dining room, where she pulled the pitcher out of the breakfront, and back into the kitchen. She filled the pitcher up to the brim and started with the philodendron in the window box. Then she watered the rubber plant in the gold-and-white downstairs bathroom. She was watering the plants in Manly's study, feeling quite useful and self-contented, when Suetta came to stand behind her. Monica didn't have to turn around to know that Suetta was there. Suetta was huge, six feet tall, a jet-black woman who had come with the marriage. Her family had worked for Manly's family for decades, so Suetta worked for Monica. Suetta had worked for Manly's mother until her death five years ago. Sometimes Monica suspected that Manly had gotten married primarily to give Suetta a job. Monica found Suetta oppressive. It seemed to her that Suetta could fill a room with unease by simply entering it as she had now, broom in hand. Suetta reminded Monica of things she had read in mystery books set in the Caribbean, awful tales of arcane rites and voodoo. Suetta was just the type. She stood now behind Monica, not saying a single word.

"*Yes,* Suetta," Monica finally said. She tried to shame Suetta with patient annoyance, but it never worked.

"I done watered," Suetta said flatly. She pronounced "watered" as if the word had an extra "r": "wartered."

"Oh," Monica said. Looking at the plants more closely, she could see they had been recently watered, after all. Now they had too much water. It was spilling over the tops of the saucers and onto the polished wood of the end table by Manly's chair. It would stain the wood, wouldn't it? At least it would leave a ring. Before Monica could tell her to, Suetta lifted the plants (one by one, saucer and all), and wiped up the excess water. She did it quickly and efficiently; one swipe of the cloth and it was gone.

"Well," Monica said, and couldn't remember, for a minute, what she was going to say. "Oh, yes, I'm going to go over to open the Sesquicentennial headquarters and I'll be gone for most of the afternoon. Here's the number, in case there are any important calls. You can have them call me over there."

"Yasm," Suetta said. She still hadn't moved, and she was blocking the study door.

She wants something, Monica realized. Now what?

"I makes mine with warter," she said. Ah ha. Suetta wants to cook, Monica thought.

"Your what?" Monica asked.

"My lemon meringue pie."

"Well, that's fine but I don't think we'll need one tonight. We still have some pecan pie left."

"Yasm." Suetta, disapproving, moved to the side and Monica went back out into the entrance hall where she picked up her purse from the settle. If I can just get out of here, she thought.

"Mr. Manly just crazy about it," Suetta offered from the study door.

"About what?" Monica asked. She was fishing for the car keys, lost somewhere down in the shoulder bag.

"My lemon meringue pie."

"Oh." I'm going to scream if I can't find these keys, Monica thought. She dumped the contents of the bag onto the settle and began pawing through the pile.

"Lot of people use milk but I use warter in mine," Suetta said.

"Well, why don't you just *make* us one then," Monica

said, pulling her mouth into a wide and drastic smile.
"Make us two!" she cried recklessly as she left. Jesus
Christ. Everybody said Suetta was such a "treasure"—that
was the exact word they used, over and over. If they only
knew! Monica drove her blue Mustang into town, but as
far as she was concerned it might as well have been a
submarine. Somehow, she had gotten in over her head.
Monica giggled and almost ran off the road. In college,
she had had a roommate who loved bad jokes. So did
Monica. But Manly didn't care too much for bad jokes or
good ones, either, for that matter. So Monica had to
restrain herself when she felt a pun or a joke coming on.
But that was all right. You had to adjust in marriage,
didn't you? Of course. So why did she often feel that her
marriage to Manly was moving along under some sort of
false pretenses? It wasn't. But it was the oddest feeling she
got sometimes. Like last night: Manly had handed her a
drink, she had smiled and thanked him and suddenly,
unaccountably, she had felt like an impostor.

Ridiculous. Monica switched on the radio. "This is
Ron-the-Mouth at twelve forty on your radio dial, one
o'clock at the sound of the gong." The gong sounded.
"Hi-YAH!" screamed Ron-the-Mouth. "A little karate at
the downtown studios of WJRB. O.K., ladies, this is your
chance. The first girl to identify this oldie but goodie gets
a big kiss from Ron the famous one and only mouth. So
call in immediately, sweetheart, and name this tune. You'll
get a big kiss right in the receiver from the wonder mouth,
plus three free cartons of Coke from Foodland, locally
owned and nationally known. Are you ready out there in
Radioland? Pucker up, darlings, here we go." There followed a clash of drums.

"My God." Monica switched the radio off and passed a
pickup truck. She was driving too fast and she didn't have
her seat belt buckled, as usual. Manly was always telling

her to buckle her seat belt but she never did unless she was riding with Manly. It was a small, secret revolt.

There were no cars now on the road ahead and Monica allowed herself to slip into her familiar daydream, the one where she was driving to meet her lover. He was waiting somewhere in a sleazy motel on the wrong side of town, the sleazier the better, smoking cigarette after cigarette and choked with desire at the thought of her driving to meet him, even now, in her sleek blue Mustang. When she entered the motel room there would be no words spoken between them, just the fierce crush of their violent embrace. He would unzip her dress and she would fling her underwear into all four corners of the tiny room, gasping, and then they would make love all afternoon: on the bed, on the floor, in the closet, in the bathtub, atop the color TV. Together, they would plumb the depths of degradation. Finally, exhausted ("spent" was a better word), they would drink pink drinks from tall chilled glasses, entwining their arms Europeanly.

Monica turned left, guilty and refreshed. She was almost there. Why did she think such things? *What is the matter with me?* After all, she loved Manly. She really did. Manly had come along at a time in her life when she had especially needed somebody like Manly. She had just returned to college for her senior year after spending the summer in Europe, a summer during which she had slept with several Italians and one Swede quite casually, just to prove that she could do it. It had all been lovely, a lark. Europeans didn't count; sleeping with a European was the next thing to sleeping with no one at all.

But, as soon as her plane touched ground at Idlewild, she had been racked by guilt. This was a fierce, consuming guilt, ridiculous. Even though she knew it was ridiculous, she couldn't help it—just as now she couldn't stop having these imaginary trysts with her fictive, furtive lover.

Then she met Manly, who for six months courted her with great gentility and finesse. "Let me take care of you," Manly had said, and Monica thought that was what she needed. She agreed and had let Manly take care of her ever since. "I married for love," she used to say. In their three years of marriage, he had been the perfect husband: courteous, thoughtful, warm, devoted, rich. But I didn't want a goddamn Boy Scout, flashed into her head suddenly. That was unfair, and she knew it. Manly was simply and naturally good. He was a good person. You ought to be thankful, Monica said to herself. But she wasn't. He was too good, too good for her or anybody else. If he knew what went on in her pretty head, he would just die.

Monica giggled as she parked. O.K., weirdo, she said to herself in the mirror. Straighten up. This will be good for you. Priding herself on her self-knowledge (astounding in one so young), Monica went up the walk and into the old Pardoe house. The very first thing we have to do is get somebody to cut these weeds, she thought. Maybe Manly would loan them Will for an afternoon.

Inside the house, Buck Fire (born John Lee Dugins in Lynchburg, Virginia) sat at a Victorian desk in the empty parlor and contemplated the back of his hands. Women who noticed hands told him that they were sensitive, tender hands, but actually they were too small. Women who read palms, or pretended to do so at parties, said that he had a short life line, a great artistic flair, and a prominent mount of Venus (you know what *that* means; titters at the party). Women loved Buck Fire. There was no escaping them even if he had wanted to. They followed him around in every town, throwing themselves at him. It was the only bright point in his job with the White Company, which otherwise was a pain in the ass. The White Company. Buck Fire gave a little snort, a cynical laugh which he cultivated, and lit a cigarette. The White Company was nothing. The White Company didn't exist. All the White Company was, was a guy named Roscoe White (of the White Finance Company) who loaned money to actors and then whammo! The first thing the actors knew, they were on the road with a White Company prepared script in one hand and an authentic White Company Indian headdress in the other. Buck Fire threw back his head and laughed at the broken glass chandelier hanging from the ceiling in the empty room. Goddamn Roscoe White. Then Buck straightened up in his chair and threw back his head again, practicing. It wasn't bad. He must remember to keep his gestures theatrical. The women would be here any minute. Besides, Roscoe White no longer bugged him. He was past that. Roscoe merely amused him, now that he had paid Roscoe off and was himself getting a piece of the action. It was not a bad deal. But temporary, of course. Just a little something to keep him in shape until the time was right to hit California.

Where were the girls? They ought to be here now. Buck Fire felt primed, a little jumpy in the pit of his stomach, the way he always felt before a performance. He would come on very heavy, all sex and ego and bitter charm. They would be afraid and fascinated; they would eat it up. Then later, after he got things moving along the familiar White Company pageant routine, he would relax a little. He would administer a pinch here, a kiss there, a locking of eyes, an occasional one-night stand. They would become his slaves, as usual. They would work like dogs, these women, neglecting homes, husbands, children, and pets to work for the good of the Sesquicentennial and the approval of Buck Fire. It happened in every town. The more sophisticated they were, the harder they fell. The Junior League was putty in his hands. Buck lit another cigarette, impatient.

He unbuttoned the second button of his shirt so that (beneath the green silk of his careless Apache tie) the hair would show black and curly but not obtrusive, just visible above the startling gold of his shirt. He heard their voices outside, their heels tapping daintily on the walk. How he loved it—the rustlings and tappings of juicy suburban women, their small hesitancies and conceits! Buck was careful to dally only with the married, the ripe and ready psychic virgins of the countless small towns which engaged the White Company's varied services. There was no risk in screwing the married. Buck's view of himself, which changed frequently according to the circumstances, had one central tenet: he was a loner. Buck Fire, the loner. Love-'em-and-leave-'em-panting, that was Buck Fire. Moving on.

"Hello, you must be Mr. Fire." The girls came in the door together, all four of them, huddling as if for warmth. The White Company's guidelines, sent in advance to each of their client towns, specified a central headquarters "coordinating committee" of four women, and it always amused Buck when the four turned up. Every town followed the White Company guidelines all the way. No town yet had suggested an innovation. The citizens were always humble and dull before the professional onslaught of the White Company.

Buck leaned back still further in his chair and slit his eyes at them, an appraisal. He looked them up and down slowly and did not rise from the chair. "Since we'll be seeing a lot of each other," he said, "call me Buck." They smiled brightly. Buck didn't smile. Buck bounded up from the chair, a human dynamo, stirring dirt on the old wood floor. The girls drew back. "Now let's get one thing straight," he said, cramming another cigarette into his mouth. "This is no game. You girls are going to work your tails off before we're through here." They tittered and looked at each other. It was exactly the way they had expected the actor to talk. Buck paced back and forth, smoking cigarette after cigarette, stomping them out with his pointed boots on the dusty floor. He was surly and businesslike, then charming, then funny. He made grandiose actor-type gestures with his hands. Since he had given this spiel before (fourteen times), Buck allowed his mind to range from the performance and he speculated upon the girls. There was no rush, of course. There would be at least 150 more women in the pageant cast or on the committees, and he would have his pick. But two of the headquarters committee looked promising.

Lucia Bream was a bleached blonde running to fat, thirtyish, his favorite type for a one-night stand. She appeared to be a little slow-witted (a definite plus); had an anxious, eager-to-please smile; and was careless about her appearance. Her bra strap showed. She pushed it back; it showed again. That was not so good—when their bra straps showed too often, they tended to get pregnant, Buck had found.

Marion Van Dusen was an organizer, a handshaking bright-smiler. She was tall and lean, obviously athletic. Probably golf. Buck looked her over. He liked them limber, too, as long as their calves weren't stringy. Mrs. Van Dusen's calves were fine. The other two girls were nothing much: Caroline Pettit was very pregnant, ruling her out, and Monica what's-her-name was thin and mousy. Buck aimed his pitch at Lucia and Marion, and sat Caroline down in his chair.

He told them what he required in the way of a headquarters, listed the furniture they would need. He listed their duties, too: answering the phone, renting out the costumes to townspeople, fitting the cast, preparing newsletters and press releases and brochures, selling Sesquicentennial buttons and bumper stickers and ornamental plates, etc. It

turned out that Mrs. Mousy was the head of the committee. She was also the wife of the local newspaper editor,
which was definitely convenient.

"O.K., sweethearts." Buck clapped his hands. "That's
it for today. Now then, Lucia, you be a good girl and see
about getting us three phones in here, immediately. Will
you do that for me, doll?"

"Three phones," Lucia repeated, mesmerized.

"Right away," Buck said. "Just hop on over to the
phone company and charge it to the Speed Sesquicentennial, O.K.?"

"O.K.," Lucia said. She fixed her bra strap and wrote
"three phones" down on a little white pad. Marion had
furnished little white pads for everybody.

"Now, Marion, I want you to get us some electricity in
here, some running water, and rent us a refrigerator because we'll be spending a lot of time here. And figure out
some coffee. Got that?"

"Right," Marion said. Marion didn't write anything
down.

Buck told Caroline to pick a bunch of women to run the
Queen Contest and set up a luncheon meeting with them
for next week. He told Mrs. Mousy to fix this old barn up
immediately. Just as he was finished with his directions in
came Luther, red in the face and looking like he needed a
drink, which knowing Luther he undoubtedly did. The
girls stared at Luther, flabbergasted. He was extremely
fat—around 250 pounds—and extremely, it appeared, angry.

"Goddamnit," he roared, pounding on the desk. Caroline heaved herself up, alarmed. "I thought you said it
was all set with the man about that football field. All set,
you told me. Don't worry, Luther, everything is all set,
you said, and now he's talking about rent. RENT! Get that.
He wants to rent us the goddamn football field to give his
own pageant on." Luther wiped his face.

Buck started laughing, a real laugh. Here was a new twist in the White Company's standard routine. Seeing that everyone looked at him strangely, Buck changed his real laugh to a deep, fakey chuckle, like the public laughter of politicians. The girls relaxed. Luther stared at him a minute longer, his near-sighted eyes screwed up, his chin sunk deep into the rolls of fat which ringed his neck. A large wet patch began at Luther's shoulder blades and went all the way down his back to his Indian belt, spoiling the effect of his new pink shirt. "Well, hell," he bawled suddenly, and whooped and wheezed with laughter.

"Girls, this is my associate, Luther Fletcher," Buck said.

"Oh," they chorused. It was exactly how they had expected Buck's assistant to look, without even knowing they expected it. So fat and theatrical, so mad.

"These ladies have volunteered to run our headquarters for us, Luther. This is Mrs. Neighbors, Mrs. Pettit, Mrs. Van Dusen, and Mrs. Bream."

"Howdy," Luther said. He had played bit parts in many Westerns, so that the cowboy manner clung to him still. He was in his fifties, happily married, with a wife and four children in Florida.

"That's ridiculous, Bill Higgins wanting to rent the football field!" Marion Van Dusen said. "That's the most ridiculous thing I've ever heard of. Why, he doesn't even own it."

Lucia giggled and Buck winked at her.

"Well, I'm going to ask John about it immediately." John Van Dusen was the Commonwealth's Attorney. "See you tomorrow." Marion Van Dusen smiled and left, flashing her calves.

"Oh, Lord, I've got car pool!" Lucia suddenly blurted. "Come on, Caroline."

"Ronald won't let me drive because I'm you know,"

Caroline said apologetically, as if confessing to a fatal flaw.

"Caroline, come on! We're already late and if they get tired of waiting on me they'll just walk off like they did Thursday." Lucia haphazardly flung a cashmere sweater around one shoulder and Caroline, arms crossed over her stomach, followed her out. "Bye," Caroline said.

The big square parlor was suddenly quiet and Luther grinned at Buck. Occasionally he felt paternal toward Buck (not that he'd let one of his own daughters even meet the guy). "So how did it go?" he asked.

"Fine," Buck allowed. "That's a good group."

"This is a pretty good town," Luther said, "if it wasn't so goddamn religious. You see all those churches? One on every corner. But I like a town this size," he went on, professionally. "You get them any bigger and you get too many groups and the pageant gets strung out. Any littler and the same people have to do everything."

"It's all right." Buck put his foot on the bare window-sill and spit on the toe of his boot, then polished it with his pocket handkerchief.

"You can stay around here all day if you want to," Luther said. "I'm heading for a beer myself."

"You go on," Buck said. "I'll be there in a minute. I've still got one of them wandering around here someplace."

"One of what?"

"One of the headquarters girls. I guess she's looking around the house." Buck polished, whistling through his teeth.

"You're starting early," Luther commented, pulling himself up. He knew Buck's habits, having worked two previous centennials with him. At the most recent, in Arkansas, Buck had had a close call. A pregnancy scare. But he always got off scot free, the bastard. Luther shook his head with a mixture of envy and disgust. If he hadn't

gotten too fat to ride a horse he might still be out in
California where he belonged instead of screwing around
with such a guy.

"Not this lady." Buck grinned. "Not Mrs. Mousy.
She's just looking things over, I guess. She's supposed to
fix this place up."

"So long," Luther said. "I'll be over at the Rondo."

"Be there in a minute." Buck finished polishing his
boot, surveyed the other boot (which was perfect), and
pocketed the handkerchief. He whistled loudly, then stopped
and listened. He couldn't hear anything moving around
upstairs at all. An occasional creak, maybe, but all old
houses creak. What the hell. Buck hated to be alone. He
also hated old houses. That was the only drawback to his
job, in fact, as far as he was concerned—he was always
having to stand around in some damn spooky historical
house which anybody in their right mind would have
condemned and torn down years ago. "Mrs. Neighbors!"
he yelled. No answer. Buck looked all around the bright,
bare room, and felt obscurely guilty. "Mrs. Neighbors!"
he yelled again. He had to take a leak.

Monica stood upstairs, on a second-story back porch
that ran the length of the house, and looked out over the
overgrown garden. It must have been beautiful once. "Pull
yourself together," she said to herself, and picked at the
flaking white paint on the rail. They must wonder where I
am, she realized, but her feet were being stupid and would
not move. It was frightening. Monica tried to rationalize,
to explain to herself why she felt the way she did. But her
usual astonishing degree of self-awareness had broken down.
Nothing that she was aware of would account for it. Buck
Fire—that egotistical, twirpy little two-bit actor with the
elevator heels—had been explaining their jobs, pacing back
and forth in the empty room. As he paced, he had walked
in and out of an oblong patch of sunlight coming in the

French window at the side. Each time he had passed through this patch of sunlight, it had seemed to Monica that he was not only illumined but transfigured. He took on a new and startling dimension. He was unlike any man she had ever known. How could she explain it? It had come on her like a flash, this realization of him. Like a damn Annunciation, she thought sarcastically, annoyed. Buck Fire's chestnut hair glowed a thousand colors in the sun: every color, from palest yellow to brightest red to black. He probably dyed it. But his teeth flashed like teeth in TV commercials. His brown eyes shone and the cleft in his chin came and went, and so did fine lines at the corners of his eyes. Buck Fire's tacky clothes had picked up the sunlight and shot it back in rays. Nobody ever had a shirt of a more astonishing gold than Buck Fire's; no tie had ever appeared so mysterious, so rich and so strange as Buck Fire's green Apache. Monica could not get over it. She had left the room as soon as possible, to calm down.

The only experience which she had ever had in her life which was in any way analogous to her vision of Buck Fire had happened one summer when she was at camp. An only child, Monica had played by herself a lot and was always packed off to camp in the summers "to be with other children." She was horseback riding at Camp Alleghany in West Virginia, riding the last horse in the line. It was a trail ride. The girls had trotted through the woods, jumping logs, and sometimes breaking into a canter in the open spaces, following their counselor's lead. The counselor rode the first horse. The horse which Monica rode that day, Martini, always brought up the rear because he kicked. Twelve-year-old Monica had been trotting through the woods, thinking of nothing in particular, when all of a sudden she had thought: "I will remember this for the rest of my life." She had, too. It was odd because there was nothing much to remember: the way the woods had looked, dusty and green and thick; Martini's black, twitching ears; the green fly on his withers; her T-shirt; how hot she was. A completely unremarkable memory. Yet it had never left her. She could close her eyes and see it all and remember herself remembering. The way she might remember Buck Fire, years from now. Someone was yelling her name. Monica let go of the rail and smoothed her hair and swallowed several gulps of air. Well, she had to go now. She had to take herself in hand, vision or no vision. Who did she think she was, anyway, Joan of Arc? If she was going to have a nervous breakdown she might as well wait and have it at home where Suetta could fix her some iced tea. At least it would give Suetta something to do.

Buck came out of the bathroom at the foot of the stairs just as Monica came down. "Watch out!" he said as they collided.

"Oof," Monica said. His head, that vibrant chestnut head, was in her stomach, had knocked the wind out of her. She pitched backward and Buck threw his arms about her (blindly, his eyes shut against her dress) to keep her from falling backward. As he did so, his hands accidentally clasped the sweetest little buttocks they had clasped in some time. Well, Mrs. Mousy! he thought, surprised and suffocating. He kneaded them a little with his hands, a quick feel.

"Oh, please!" Monica cried when she got her breath. It was hard to tell whether she meant "please stop" or "please keep it up." Possibly she didn't know herself, or realize what he was doing. "I'm so sorry," she gasped. Another ambiguity. They swayed and clutched, Monica on the second step, Buck on the ground floor. Monica gained the banister and held tight. Buck knew it was stupid but he held on for that fraction of a second too long. That could get you kicked out of a town, like it had Charlie Waters in Ohio. The premature move. The collision had been accidental, but now he had his balance and she would know. But he couldn't seem to let go of her; he felt like his arms had been welded tight in that circle around her hips. He licked her belt buckle experimentally. It had a metallic, strangely familiar taste. Buck stood back.

"Please excuse me, Mrs. Neighbors," he said. "I was just on my way up to look for you."

"Oh, Jesus," Monica said, and flushed.

Looking at her more closely, Buck could see that he had made a mistake. Mrs. Neighbors was not at all plain. She was small-boned and fragile, with cheekbones like wings. Her dark hair would be pretty if she rolled it up, or maybe if she took that ribbon off and let it fall. It would make a big difference. And there was something in her face which he hadn't noticed before. He couldn't say exactly what it was. It wasn't your typical suburban wife-face, though. She wouldn't have said "Jesus" like that, for instance. They didn't usually say "Jesus." They said "My goodness" or "Oh my." He looked sideways at Monica as they started back toward the door but she was walking straight ahead, with her eyes down.

"I'll get some people in here tomorrow to clean this place up," she said. "Actually it's in better shape than I expected."

So are you. "O.K.," Buck said. He pushed his hair back into place. Now what?

They paused while he gathered up his papers, all the White Company crap, and then paused again outside the door while she locked it. "Oh, I almost forgot," she said. "I had some extra keys made so we'd all have one." She handed him several identical keys, tied together with string. She turned a deep, deep red.

Hell, Monica thought she felt it coming on. Oh, hell. It was something clandestine about giving him a key. You've seen too many movies, she told herself. Doubly embarrassed now, she blushed because she was blushing and turned to run for her car.

Buck was delighted. She was like the others, after all. Now he knew where he stood. She really wanted it, that was it. She couldn't wait. Mrs. Hot Pants disguised as Mrs. Mousy. Buck smiled to himself but at the same time he was a little sorry; he couldn't have said why. For a minute he had almost lost his cool. Now in full control, he did a little number on her.

"Just a minute," he said in a commanding voice, deep and exactly as resonant as he intended it to be in the warm, still afternoon.

In spite of herself, Monica paused.

Stepping in front of her, Buck gently placed a hand beneath her chin, raised her head, and stared at her for a second. It was a deep, full stare, packed with charisma. Monica's eyes were blank.

"See you tomorrow," he said, a little husky. He massaged her chin gently, released it, and turned. Not looking back, he went quickly down the steps and along the sidewalk.

Monica was devastated. Automatically, she got in her car and began the long drive home. She tried to imagine her lover—he was a safe, imaginary lover and she desperately needed a tryst—but he would not come to mind. He simply would not come at all. As she drove, her mood rapidly changed from devastation to disgust. So what had happened, anyway? She and Buck Fire had run into each other on the stairs, and then he had touched her on the chin. That was probably his idea of an apology and she was crazy. Insane. Imagine letting her imagination run away with her like that. Buck Fire! A lousy little creep like Buck Fire! He was probably a closet queen. If he didn't wear those revolting boots, she would be taller than he was. He probably had a wife who wore curlers and eight terrible children with runny noses and braces on their legs. Monica turned into the driveway of her lovely house, exhausted. It had been a tiring day, and yet nothing had really happened, just nothing at all.

She didn't want the iced tea, she decided. She would go upstairs, hide from Suetta, take two aspirins, and rest until Manly came home. The thought of Manly filled her with love or something close enough. She couldn't wait until Manly came home.

FIVE

*B*EVO'S grandmother was a real card. Everybody said so. All by herself, she had turned the back yard of Bevo's parents' nice new house in Manora Estates (one of the new groups of houses outside Speed) into a cross between a jungle and a slum. First she had them build the leanto for her pots and Lord knows what all. Then she had them dig up foot after foot of the Zoysia grass until there wasn't really any yard left at all, just a wilderness of great shiny green plants with little dirt paths going through it every which way. The growth was so thick that only Bevo's Mamaw herself or her hired man, Turner, could get around in it.

Bevo's grandmother wore long, full dresses with lots of pockets and stayed outside all day long, going around and around the crazy dirt paths or yelling at Turner or sitting in the leanto drinking Coke and talking on her yellow princess telephone. She sat tilted way back in one of her folding aluminum chairs and talked to her customers on the phone, surrounded by cuttings, seedlings, boxes of bulbs, ferns in pots, hanging vines, drying cattails, and

every kind of seed and weedkiller you could think of.
Bevo was afraid of his grandmother.

"Mamaw," he said, for that was what he called her,
"isn't it about time to quit for lunch?" It was Saturday,
and Bevo's hands were hot in the big gloves she had put
on them. He picked up the dried pods of okra one by one
and slapped them against the inside rim of the tin washtub,
so that the seeds clattered into the tub. After he had
slapped them about five times each (clumsily, wearing the
gloves), the hull would be empty and he would throw it
into its pile and get another pod and start slapping it. It
was a slow job. Once Bevo had thought of a faster way to
do it but he had been afraid to tell his Mamaw, so he went
right on slapping the okra against the tin.

Bevo was hungry but he didn't mind doing the okra.
There was nothing he would rather do on such a fine
Saturday morning—in fact, if a genie had come to Bevo at
dawn and told him he could do whatever he wished for the
entire day, Bevo would have been at a loss for words.
"Well," he might have said, or, possibly, "What do you
know?"

His grandmother sat leaned back in the aluminum chair
at what seemed to Bevo to be a precarious and dangerous
angle although he did not mention this to her, and checked
her catalogue from Holland Europe against orders she had
written in a spiral notebook, and mumbled to herself.

Click. Bevo and his grandmother heard the noise and
both knew what it was and both looked up, Bevo with a
patient face and Mamaw with fire in her eye.

"What did I tell you, Anne?" said Mamaw, throwing
herself forward in her seat so that the two front chair legs
gouged the dirt, kicking up spurts of dust.

"Lunch is ready," said Bevo's mama in her low, pretty
voice. She put her Kodak Instamatic camera back in its
case, snapped the case together, and dangled it carelessly

by the strap from her left hand as she walked back to the house. Bevo knew that his mama was not as careless as she seemed, though; if she broke that camera she would have a fit. But Bevo knew his mama wouldn't break it. She never broke anything.

Mrs. Sandy DuBois from next door came over with her daughter Sharon, in through the side gate and across the dirt path to the leanto. Mrs. DuBois liked to grow things herself. She and Bevo's Mamaw were big friends.

"Our Vandevener bulbs ever come in yet?" asked Mrs. DuBois. Bevo's Mamaw had lived on a farm near Cleveland, Tennessee, for most of her life, and she was a wild old lady who would probably have been a great trial to her daughter Anne if she hadn't been such a card.

Bevo's Mamaw took the glasses which hung on a chain around her neck and placed them on her nose. "I've got you down for 50 Buckingham Palace and 25 White Pearl and 25 Sunrise. And I'll tell you what I'll do, I'll give you two of these here Yellow Emperator that Vandevener has sent me free. It's a new bulk they've got."

"Let me see that Vandevener catalogue," said Sandy. Bevo thought she was real cute, still so young and all. Sandy flipped through the pages. "I guess you mean Yellow Emperor," she finally said.

"That's it," said Mamaw. "That's the new one."

"Why, look at this Parrot Feather!" said Sandy. "It's got all colors in it."

"It's ugly as a snake," said Bevo's Mamaw decisively. "I wouldn't plant it in a graveyard." She counted the bulbs out loud into the paper bag.

Bevo went on slapping the okra and finally looked up at Sharon, whom he had loved with a great love ever since he had first seen her four years ago when she and her family had moved in next door. She stood with one leg thrust out to the side like a model in a magazine, and her full bottom lip stuck out too. She wore Red Hawkins' football jacket number 70, even though it was much too warm for a jacket, strictly speaking, and a short blue skirt and tennis shoes, and her yellow hair glistened in the sun. She was not looking at Bevo. Bevo knew that she was Red Hawkins' girl but he dreamed his familiar daydream anyway, the one which had begun this winter when Sharon had worn high bright kneesocks every day to school, and he had dreamed of pulling those kneesocks slowly, slowly down her calves and feeling with his own hands the rounded, majorette firmness of her legs. Bevo turned red and looked down and went on slapping okra, feeling guilty and slightly sick, as though his mind and the hands inside the big gloves were on fire. He would not go in to lunch until Sandy DuBois and Sharon left. He did not want to do anything that conspicuous.

"Here y'are," said his Mamaw, and handed the bags to Mrs. DuBois, along with the smaller bag. Sharon carried the little one. "There's your Buckingham Palace and your White Pearl and your Sunrise and I put you two Yellow Emperor in this little bag here so you won't get them all mixed up."

Mrs. DuBois set the bag down while she wrote Mamaw a check. "Your camellias are early, aren't they?" she asked, making conversation.

"I gibed 'em," Bevo's Mamaw said proudly. Two weeks before, Bevo had gone around the garden with her, giving the camellias a shot of acid in their growth buds. Now he watched Sharon stand with her leg stuck out, staring at nothing.

Was she thinking about Red Hawkins? About winning the Beauty Award in Tuscaloose? *About him, Bevo?*

Mrs. DuBois handed Mamaw the check and picked up her bag and started back home with Sharon.

"I hope you like your Yellow Emperor," Mamaw

yelled after them. She could still yell real loud when she felt like it, for an old lady.

Bevo watched them go and wondered, for the thousandth time, what Sharon thought of him and his Mamaw, or if she thought of them at all. Sharon had a quality about her which he deeply admired. Watching her from the stands at the high school football games, he had noticed the way in which she filled her skin until it nearly burst. It was a very attractive quality. It seemed to Bevo that something was alive and jumping inside Sharon, something that was always on the verge of breaking the skin to escape. It was exciting. Bevo thought Sharon had a real mystique.

"I reckon we can quit for lunch now," Bevo's Mamaw said: "Turner!" she yelled into the depths of the yard. "You Turner! Go on and get your lunch!"

"Yasm," Turner yelled back, still invisible behind the wall of green.

Bevo's sister Ruthie sat in a kitchen chair, rocking and buffing her nails. Her curly red hair was pulled back from her forehead with a bow, but it fell from the bow down to her shoulders, all curly and messy. Where she had her legs crossed, Bevo could see a big white patch of thigh. Ruthie never cared how she sat.

Bevo and his Mamaw washed at the special stainless-steel sink that Anne had had installed near the door, separate from the regular sink. Since the regular sink was double in the first place, that made a total of three sinks in the kitchen. The Cartwrights had plenty of money, but they had not had it for very long and nobody but Anne and Ruthie had been ready for it when it came.

Bevo sat down at the table and found that there was a thin, solid film floating on top of his tomato soup, which was no longer hot.

"I don't care if my tomato soup is freezing cold," Mamaw said nastily to nobody in particular, slurping it up.

"I had it hot," Ruthie said right back, just as nasty, "and if you'd come when we told you to, it would have been good and hot."

The toasted cheese in the toasted-cheese sandwich had gotten stringy and hard to chew. Bevo pushed the film on his tomato soup over to the side so he could get at the soup, but it kept floating back and attaching itself to his spoon. It wasn't a very good lunch.

But Bevo ate anyway, and marveled at the way Ruthie talked right back to Mamaw. Bevo was a little scared of Ruthie too, come to think of it: when she was just one year older than he was now, she had been married. Then she got a divorce. Now she was only twenty-one, but what a past! Ruthie worked nights as a hostess in the Peabody Room out on the highway.

While she rocked, Ruthie placed a long white menthol cigarette between her red lips and lit it, blowing blue smoke openmouthed at the ceiling like she was a cigarette commercial. Bevo watched nervously as she flipped the match into the big ashtray which said "Panama City, Fla." on it. Ruthie never bothered to see if the match made it to the ashtray O.K., and Bevo guessed that they were lucky that he was there to watch out for them all. But he couldn't be there all the time. Bevo worried a lot about fire.

His mother, Anne, came back into the kitchen and began to wash potatoes one by one, turning them over and over in her hands as she scrubbed them; she was very thorough. When she was through, she lined the potatoes up in a little row along the back of the sink and then washed out the sink itself.

Mamaw asked for another sandwich and Ruthie got it for her, after saying something smart. "Usually I just eat like a bird," Mamaw said, when Ruthie put it in front of her. They all laughed. It was an old remark and everybody but Mamaw thought it was funny. Mamaw thought it was true. Mamaw looks like a bird, Bevo thought, even if she doesn't eat like one. She had a pointed nose and quick little eyes and brown, scrawny hands like claws.

Ruthie leaned back in the rocker and her skirt rode up even higher than before.

"I guess you take after me, Ruthie," Mamaw said suddenly, critically, with her mouth full. "Don't she, Anne?"

"I suppose so," Bevo's mother said. She looked at Bevo with her secret look, the way she always looked at him. It used to thrill Bevo when he was younger, that look, but more and more lately it made him feel peculiar. He gave Anne the familiar old wink, but then he got up and went into the den.

The whole house was only six years old. Anne had had a decorator come and do it from scratch when it was built and the decorator had picked everything out, right down to the bathroom soap. It was a long, low, ranch-type house like all the houses out where the Cartwrights lived, and it had central air conditioning and wall-to-wall carpeting all over. When they had first moved in, Mamaw and Lomas, Bevo's father, had been very uncomfortable, afraid to touch anything since everything was so fine, but that had passed and his Mamaw had started working out in the yard and his father had gotten used to the den. The decorator had done the den in washable wall covering that looked exactly like wood. You couldn't tell the difference if you didn't feel it with your hand. There were two brass curtain rods on each of the room's two windows, and orange ball fringe on the ends of the café curtains, and a nine-by-twelve Early American braided rug. On the coffee table was a huge green porcelain fish with large sculptured scales. It held a flowering philodendron in its gaping mouth.

Despite all this decoration, Lomas had made the room his own. He kept his liquor in the bookcase, instead of books; he had worn a dark spot in the light brown reclining vibrator chair before the TV; he had even, in spite of Bevo's vigilance, burned two holes in the print on the print-covered chair.

Bevo opened the other bookcase, the one that did not hold Lomas' liquor, and took them out. One by one he put them on the couch: Anne's scrapbooks.

His mother had been taking pictures of them all for as long as he could remember. Then she pasted them in the scrapbooks and put the scrapbooks carefully away. Photography was her only hobby—if you could call it a hobby at all, considering the singular lack of joy with which she went at it. It seemed that photography was not her hobby so much as putting the pictures into the scrapbooks was. She never cared what kind of camera she had, as long as it worked; the one before the Instamatic had been a Brownie Starflash. Bevo knew that his mother could have afforded one of those fancy Japanese jobs if she had wanted it, but she didn't want it. She pasted her pictures into real leather scrapbooks, though, and she was very neat about it and she wrote a title and a date beneath each one in ink.

"The Early Days" had been gold-embossed on the red scrapbook. Bevo opened it and looked through it. There were his mother and father getting married in their funny clothes; there they were standing beside an old humped automobile. Anne had written "Our First Car" beneath this picture. His daddy, Lomas, had been handsome before he lost his hair, Bevo thought, looking at the early Lomas with a perfect pompadour. His mother had looked the same then as now: a smooth round face with no lines, calm, not showing any emotion at all. Her eyes were dark and her lips were even and pale.

After "The Early Days" came the others in chronological order. "Our Little Girl," that was for Ruthie, and separate blue leather scrapbooks marked every year of her life until she ran off and married when she was seventeen. There were so many of these that Bevo left them right where they were, in the back of the bookcase. Bevo wondered why they had stopped when she got married.

Most of the pictures of Lomas had stopped a little before that, right about when Lomas started getting rich from his chain of junkyards. There were no pictures at all of Mamaw, except in groups. All the green scrapbooks bore the title "Our Son," and that was Bevo, and there was a book for every two years of his life, continuing right up to now, when his mother had one half filled.

Bevo had bought a bugle in the fall, so that he could join the high school band. Then he would have a uniform. Bevo felt that he was under a terrible obligation to be picturesque. He turned the thick, creamy pages of the scrapbooks, looking at himself as a child in short pants and white socks, as a fat boy of seven with a big grin, holding a candy cane before the Christmas tree, as a Boy Scout with a lot of other Boy Scouts, all of them standing by their sleeping bags apparently ready for a trip. He couldn't remember where they had gone on the camping trip. He didn't think he would have remembered the trip at all if it hadn't been for the picture. Bevo looked at the most recent pictures of himself. He was big and not bad-looking, although his hair was curly. He had some muscles and a wide, expectant face. But what was he expecting? Bevo sat looking at the school picture from his sophomore year.

Smack. Ruthie had tiptoed up behind him and kissed him on the cheek. Bevo managed to grin at her as she went on through the den, but once she had her back turned he leaned down and wiped his cheek back and forth across the stiff upholstery of the couch. It was really weird the way Ruthie was always kissing on everybody, Bevo thought. It was not that he didn't like for Ruthie in particular to kiss him; he didn't like for anybody to kiss him. He did not like kissing in general. Bevo guessed he did take after his mother like they said.

He closed the scrapbook, still feeling peculiar, and was on his way back outside to slap some more okra when he saw J.T. coming up the sidewalk. Bevo went back into the den and picked up Lomas' *Playboy* magazine and opened it on his lap. *Playboy* always impressed J.T., whose mother kept it (and all other magazines featuring naked ladies) out of the house. J.T. came in without knocking and threw himself into Lomas' vibrator chair and turned it on.

"Whatcha doing?" J.T. asked. J.T. was short, skinny, and freckled, conditions which he despised. He believed that he overcame these conditions by being very much with it, one step ahead of all the other kids at Speed High. J.T. got his ideas from an older cousin with whom he had spent the past summer up in Tuscaloosa, and whom he was no longer allowed to visit because the cousin had been busted in September. Everyone at Speed High admired J.T. because he had such a cousin. Most of the cousins of the Speed High students lived in Demopolis or Reform or Gordo, or in Speed itself, and none of these cousins had ever done anything which would lead, in any way, to getting busted.

"Reading," Bevo said. He affected an elaborate cool.

"Let's see that foldout," J.T. said. Bevo opened the centerfold and held it up, lengthwise. There was Miss March lying flat out in a field, yet somehow flying a kite.

"She's not anything compared to Diana Ritter," J.T. said.

"Who's Diana Ritter?"

"Miss January, stupid," J.T. said. "You know what old Hugh Hefner does?" he offered. "He sprays those girls with makeup all over and puts lipstick on their nipples before he takes the picture."

"Watch it," Bevo mumbled, looking around to see if anybody had heard. But he was safe: Mamaw and Anne were out in the yard, and he could hear Ruthie batting around upstairs.

"Well, that's just what old Hugh Hefner *does*," J.T. said. "You know what else he does? He sleeps in a round bed with eight Bunnies every night."

"No kidding," Bevo said. He marveled at J.T., always so full of facts.

"I tell you what," J.T. said, "let's go over to Sharon's."

"I can't," Bevo said. His heart bumped, and he imagined spraying Sharon with makeup, all over.

"Why not?"

"I'm busy," Bevo said.

"Well, I'm going," J.T. said. Girls liked him, and giggled at what he said, but they almost never allowed him to take them out on a date. J.T. was strictly an afternoon man.

"Oh, yeah," J.T. said, standing. "Has Ruthie got any Darvon?"

"Sure she does." Whatever it was, Bevo felt sure Ruthie had it.

"You know what Darvon is?"

"Sure."

"You don't." J.T. was scornful and secure. "It's those pills girls take for cramps."

"I don't know if she's got any or not. What do you want to know for? Are you having a period?" Bevo laughed at his little joke.

"No, stupid. You get high on them. They're these red and gray pills and what you do is take two or three of them and drink a Coke."

"Then what?"

"Then you're floating, man. It's just like LSD."

"I don't know if she's got any," Bevo said, trying to remain unimpressed.

"Well, you see if she does and slip us some, O.K.? You have to have a prescription to get them. You get us about four, though, and we'll turn on."

"I don't know," Bevo said. "I'll look."

"Well, go on and look," J.T. said.

"I can't now. Ruthie's upstairs."

"Oh. You look after a while, then. You sure you don't want to come over to Sharon's?"

"I would but I'm busy," Bevo said.

"See you." J.T. was out the door and down the walk, cocky. Bevo watched and envied. Then he went upstairs to his room and took the bugle out of its case. He tried one or two blasts, experimenting.

"You just try it," Ruthie, still in her robe, opened the door. She got red spots on her cheeks when she was mad. "You just blow that horn one more time and I'm throwing it out the window."

"It's not a horn, it's a bugle," Bevo said.

"I don't care if it's a damn orchestra, I'm trying to take a nap." Ruthie slammed the door.

Bevo looked at his shiny bugle for a minute and then put it carefully back in its case. He had practiced enough, anyway. He had practiced all morning, practically. Besides, it was still another week until the Sesquicentennial auditions. He had time. They had advertised for a bugler along with the Indians and settlers and the rest of the cast; and he planned to be that bugler. He hadn't told anybody yet that he planned to try out. It was a secret plan. Bevo put the case under the bed and wondered what to do next.

His was a corner room at the front of the house, decorated in what the decorator thought was a boyish décor. The wallpaper featured ships and guns. From one window, he could see everything that happened.

Bevo sat at the window all afternoon and watched things happen. Ruthie went off with a man in an MGB, dressed up fit to kill. J.T. left the DuBoises'. Lomas came back after a while in his pickup, and then Bevo could hear the TV going downstairs, probably ABC's *Wide World of Sports*. That was Lomas' favorite show when there wasn't a ball game on. Bevo knew that he should go and check to see whether or not his father was burning up the sofa, but he did not want to leave the window. It seemed important for him to stay there and watch.

Mrs. DuBois went out, wearing slacks, and came back with a paper bag. Red Hawkins came into their street in his father's car, swinging wide around the corner, and screeching to a stop in front of the DuBoises'. Red got out of the car and walked up to the DuBoises' door, and from the window Bevo watched him. Red walked like all the football players walked, holding his shoulders way back and somehow turning his whole body a little with each step. Striding, Bevo thought: he is striding.

Bevo watched Red push the doorbell and saw Sharon come out, as full and bouncy as any balloon, and watched her walk to the car with Red. Sharon's hair was shining in the sunlight like it had been polished; it jumped and bounced with each step she took down the walk. Sharon's eyes, teeth, and mouth were shining too. She wore a red dress and red shoes and Red Hawkins' football jacket. Sharon seemed to skim the ground instead of walk, touching earth occasionally, bouncing back up. To Bevo, her skin looked full to bursting. He was amazed. From where he sat in his window, the woodwork around the window made a frame around Sharon, and Sharon herself moved around inside the frame like she was on TV.

Life is awful, Bevo thought, surprising himself.

SIX

M ONICA stood in the foyer of the Forest Lake Country Club with Caroline Pettit, waiting for the Queen Committee to arrive.

"It keeps kicking," Caroline said. "I think I'll sit down." She sat on a long black leather bench by an artificial palm, and stared into the red pile carpet.

Monica looked at her, failed utterly to imagine what it must be like to be so swollen up and filled with kicking feet, and shivered involuntarily. "I'll wait out here," she said. She opened the heavy door and went blinking out into the sunshine. Spring was almost here. The sweeping lawn of the Forest Lake Country Club was covered with a layer of pale straw, beneath which grass was supposedly sprouting. Forest Lake itself, as yet nonexistent, was a large shallow depression at the foot of the straw-covered slope. Right now Forest Lake looked like a large salad bowl, with a puddle of muddy water in its center. It would be filled, they said, by June. The eighteen-hole golf course had nine holes to date and several water hazards. It was coming along. Manly, who had been one of the prime backers of the Country Club—What hasn't he backed? Monica thought suddenly—had told Monica that one should not look upon a country club as snobbish, that it was a necessary part of a town. In a speech to the Town Council, Manly had noted that the Country Club would bring industry to the town, and all present had said that he had a good head on his shoulders.

Monica looked out now upon the future lake, not seeing it any more, not seeing even the scores of small seedlings which made up the future forest. She counted on her fingers. Manly supports the: Country Club, Lions Club, Little League, Boy Scouts, United Fund, Sesquicentennial, Speed Preservation and Historical Society—why, she could go on and on! Monica could not think of a single thing that Manly had ever done selfishly, or for his own profit. Until today, this had seemed to her a noble trait. Now it seemed somehow weird, but Monica couldn't have said why her attitude had changed.

What had she done, after all, these past three years of their marriage? She had planned the house, often indulging in bits of selfishness or whim or waste. She had done it all by herself, for herself. She had also helped Manly, of course, sitting on many platforms, both indoors and out, while Manly raised various funds. She had served on many committees. She had been the model wife, in all outward respects, as Manly had been the model husband. The model couple. Suddenly it all seemed fake. What had she really been doing all this time, how had she felt? Well, grateful. Extremely grateful to Manly for having married her after she had slept with all those Europeans. She had felt obliged to tell Manly about them, so ever since their marriage she had been overwhelmed with gratitude. Now that gratitude was beginning, for no particular reason, to wear thin. Guilty. She had always felt guilty, as if somehow she were using Manly. She had thought that he was too good for her, a silly idea, but she could not escape it. She leaned back against the new white column (which supported nothing, a mere touch to add some Southern splendor to the club) and felt sick. No, she was not going to be sick. It was all in her mind. But she was not in her right mind. She would like to yank her mind right out of her head and go around without it—like Caroline, perhaps, mindless and huge, capable only of gut reactions to tiny kicking feet. But what had brought all this on? Buck Fire? He was a lousy little two-bit queer. All actors were homosexual. Monica had learned that from her mother during her careful bringing-up. There are certain occupational types with whom nice girls don't associate, and actors are definitely one of those types. So are garage mechanics, for other reasons.

To Monica's mother, Manly was manna from heaven. "I'm so glad you're happy, dear," Monica's mother had said to her just before she died. Monica kicked backward at the column and hoped she left a smudge. Take that, column. Thank God Buck Fire wouldn't be here today anyway. Monica had learned that Buck was concerned primarily with the pageant, while Luther handled the rest.

Luther drove up at that moment and parked his rented car. "Howdy," he said to Monica as he came up the steps.

"Howdy," Monica said.

Luther grinned uncertainly, squinting into the sun. She wass a strange one, this thin, impassive girl. She would make a good Indian squaw in the pageant.

"Fine day," Luther said, resting at the top of the steps. "Nice place."

"Yep," Monica said.

"Well, it's about time!" Caroline opened the door and

smiled at Luther. "Come on in and sit down. The girls ought to be here any minute."

But we are not girls any more, Monica thought. Will we still call ourselves girls when we're sixty years old? Monica could not imagine being sixty years old. Two station wagons turned into the driveway from the Interstate and pulled in on either side of Luther's car. The station wagons burst open to disgorge young women who pulled at their skirts and patted their hair and aimed for Monica, smiles fixed. Monica how are you what a cute dress where did you get those shoes we went to Atlanta for the weekend Susie has colic are you letting your hair grow blah. Monica smiled and held the door. They sucked in their breaths all together at the sight of Luther, resplendent in a white shirt and a wide white tie ("Look at that, that's how they dress in Hollywood!" Luther always said he was from Hollywood, neglecting to add Florida), a red-and-white-striped jacket, and gold slacks. Around his tremendous girth was clasped a silver belt of Indian design. The belt had a flat ornate buckle on the back of which was inscribed a little note from the director of *Johnny Coyote* thanking all the members of the cast. Luther beamed at the girls. "Howdy, ladies." Girls were always ladies to Luther. They squeaked their replies in chorus.

Caroline went ahead of them into one of the private dining rooms and they seated themselves expectantly around the oval table. Luther sat by Caroline.

Caroline stood up. "Well girls"—she beamed—"you all are just wonderful to come today and I certainly do appreciate such a good turnout. I told Luther"—she blushed and indicated Luther—"that we wouldn't have a bit of trouble finding plenty of help. Let's go ahead and have lunch, and then Luther will explain the whole thing to us and tell us what we have to do. I don't know a thing about it myself. I'm just as much in the dark as you." She sat down heavily and red-jacketed waiters clattered in with carts.

"I just don't know where she is," Caroline whispered to Monica, who sat on her other side. "I said twelve-thirty."

"Who?" Monica picked up her fork.

"Miss Flowers," Caroline hissed. "Luther told me to call the paper and have somebody here, so I called and she said she's coming. Every time we do anything, Luther said—I mean *anything*, Monica—we're supposed to call the paper so they'll be sure to get it in. Of course you don't have to, you can just tell Manly. But everybody else is supposed to call. Publicity is very important, Luther said."

Monica's lettuce stuck in her throat. How ridiculous for Caroline to be impressed with this aging cowpoke. And Miss Iona! If Monica had known that Miss Iona was coming, she might have stayed home herself despite the fact that Suetta was there. Monica couldn't stand Miss Iona; she had told Manly repeatedly that the woman was insane. But Manly got a kick out of her, he said. "We have to preserve our anachronisms," he told Monica, whatever that meant. Manly had explained to Monica several times, and in detail, exactly why he kept Miss Iona. Back when he had bought the paper from the former editor, he had taken on his promise to Mr. Flowers that there would always be a job at the *Messenger* for Miss Iona, as long as she wanted to stay. "But you didn't sign anything, did you, Manly?" Monica had asked. "Of course not," Manly had said loftily, "it was a gentlemen's agreement." When Monica had pointed out that Mr. Flowers had been in the hospital for three years at the time of the gentlemen's agreement, that he was both senile and delirious, and that the agreement wasn't with Manly anyway, Manly had grown yet loftier. Any gentlemen's agreement was not to be broken, it seemed. Besides, he assured Monica, "She'll retire soon anyway. That was ten years ago. I'm still not ready to expand the paper yet, so I don't see what the rush is.''

"No rush," Monica had agreed each time, the wonder wife.

Miss Iona paid the driver, a surly man, and gave him a ten-cent tip. That was certainly all the man deserved, with such a soiled cap. She readjusted her gloves and stood before the entrance to the country club. It was actually her first visit here, although she had written up several dinners and dances which had taken place within. Seeing it now for the first time, Miss Iona was simply appalled. What a travesty of good taste! All was red and ugly; all was new and raw. There was no dignity to it at all, no sense of line or form. It did not even have a second story. Of course you had to have a second story, if there was to be any sense of proportion at all! "It possesses no beauty," Miss Iona pronounced aloud into the March sunlight. She was sorry this was so, yet in a way she felt gratified.

Miss Iona knew that she was late, but she took her time. Time is a relative condition, anyway, and watches are for lesser beings. Miss Iona believed in seasons, but not in hours. She stood before the door and waited for someone to open it for her; when they did not, she entered. Her small feet sank into the alien pile of the worst carpet imaginable. The décor of the whole entrance hall was exactly what Miss Iona imagined a Miami hotel (frequented by Jews) to look like. A smiling Negro in a red coat—this was more like it!—appeared soundlessly. He took her coat and motioned. "This way, ma'am."

Miss Iona followed him down a red hall decorated by matching gilt lavabos spilling grapes. They came to a halt before a door with a plaque which read THE WILLIAMSBURG ROOM. The Negro made as if to open the door for her, but

Miss Iona stayed his hand. "A moment," she directed. One must prepare one's mind for an entrance; entrances and exits are the key to any situation. Miss Iona squared her shoulders, composed her features, and entered. She came upon them unawares, silencing even the most loquacious. They paused to gape at her as if at an apparition— the tiny self-assured figure all decked out in clothes of another age. She made them nervous. She floated across the room to them, head high.

The silence was at last broken by a large gush from Caroline Pettit. "Miss Flowers! How wonderful of you to come!" She sounded as if she had found money. "You just come on up here and sit by Luther. We've saved you the place of honor!"

Miss Iona, looking neither to the right nor the left, swept past the seated women. Luther, a large, colorful man, graciously rose and held her chair, inclining his head. Conversation surged up and around them then, and silverware clinked again on the plates. Miss Iona allowed a small, secretive smile to tip the corners of her mouth. A successful entrance, if she did say so herself. She was so pleased that, with dessert, she allowed herself a spot of small talk.

"You're in the theater, then, are you?" she said daintily to the florid man at her side.

"Yes, ma'am." Luther bobbed his head.

"I love the theater!" Miss Iona avowed, bright spots appeared on her cheeks. "Such a blend of the real and the fantastic. Such an escape from the everyday self."

"It's some business all right," Luther said, bug-eyed. He reached into his pocket for a Rolaid and stared at the old lady, wondering where they had dug her up. A real character, he decided. She ought to be in the pageant.

"You ought to be in the pageant," he told her.

Miss Iona gave him the benefit of her disclaiming laugh,

one of the laughs in her repertoire which she seldom had occasion to use. "Oh, dear me, no!" she exclaimed. "I'm much too decrepit for that. I'll tell you a personal secret, though," inclining her head toward Luther's larger head. "Once when I was but a schoolgirl in the Presbyterian School here—many years ago, sir, such a lovely place! —when I was but sixteen, I played Ophelia. It was an experience I shall always treasure in the deep heart's core as the poet says."

"I reckon so." Luther had never heard of Ophelia but it was probably before his time. This was some old lady all right.

"Girls, girls!" Caroline cried, striking her ice-tea glass with a spoon. "Now then, Luther is going to tell us all what we have to do. She dimpled. "Luther?"

He gulped a Rolaid and stood. Miss Iona drew a small black composition book and a tortoiseshell fountain pen from her bag. "Tools of the fourth estate," she said brightly to the woman at her right. The woman nodded and smiled. Some of the young women lit cigarettes; others ripped open little packets of sugar; all eyes were fixed upon Luther.

He told the joke about the actor with the lisp, studying them. He told the one about the actress who mispronounced French. It was always difficult to explain the rules for the Queen Contest. Luther had given this spiel a dozen times, yet each time he was wary. It was tricky, real tricky; you had to present it just right. So far no town had rebelled, yet they might. The White Company stressed, to all of its road men, the importance of getting the Queen Contest idea across in exactly the right light. Luther began.

"First off, ladies, let me congratulate you on being here today. What this country needs is more fine young women like you, filled with civic spirit, young women who want to make their town a finer place for themselves and their families. I don't need to tell you ladies what a tremendous undertaking this Sesquicentennial is going to be, for all of us. It's going to be a lot of fun and a lot of work. And you ladies—this select little group—can make or break the whole thing. Before I go on, I want to get your pledge of absolute secrecy. Absolute secrecy, is that understood?''

They nodded.

"Now then, let me explain to you that the pageant is the crux of this whole thing. Speaking strictly from a business point of view, the pageant is going to make it or break it. It's a huge production; it requires a huge budget just to get it going. The place the money is coming from, ladies, is the advance sale of tickets for the spectacle.''

They began to look bewildered. What did this have to do with the Queen?

"I want to make myself perfectly clear." Luther was sweating. "The town has contracted us to run the whole shebang. The town will pay us, but unless all the advance tickets to the pageant are sold, the town will go in a hole. The town's revenue is coming from the ticket sale. Everybody got that?''

Kemo sabe, Monica thought.

"Now to the business at hand. The Speed Sesquicentennial Queen Contest is not a beauty contest. It is not a talent contest." He paused for emphasis. "The only way that the lucky young lady becomes Queen is this—she sells more tickets to the pageant than anyone else.''

Luther's next remarks were drowned in an uproar. It happened in every town. He took a drink of water and waved his hands for calm.

"Ladies, ladies, I beg you! Don't go getting all riled up. This is the White Company system. It has been tried and tested in over seventy-five towns exactly like Speed, and it works. I know what you think. You think this is not the way to pick a queen, that the Queen should be picked on her beauty and charm alone. But that's what it comes down to every time. You don't have to worry about that. The prettiest and nicest girl will sell the most tickets. That's all there is to it. And just between you and me''— Luther winked broadly—"a girl from a prominent family has never failed to be chosen yet. The ones with the best connections can sell the most tickets. Now, before I open this meeting up for questions, I want to remind you again that this whole Sesquicentennial is, in many ways, a business proposition. Just ask your husbands if you don't believe me. Thousands of dollars are being invested here. O.K. Questions?''

Miss Iona had doodled and dreamed through most of the speech, her mind going back to the centennial celebration of fifty years ago, when her cousin Eugenia was crowned Queen. The entire celebration took place outdoors, in what Miss Iona remembered as a wooded glen among the pecan trees near the Bobo place. It had been impossibly lush and green, and little children had danced about the maypole in their white suits. Miss Iona remembered the entire pageant, which was given in Latin, as suffused with a golden haze. Eugenia had reclined against a bank of flowers all in white, very pale. Of course she was tubercular, but no one had known it at that time. Selected young ladies had entered singly, bearing single flowers for her garland. Miss Iona had borne a yellow rose. It was all so beautiful and all so long ago.

"That's right," Luther was saying, "any woman, married or single, who works or lives in Speed and is over the age of sixteen is eligible to run for Queen. That's right. That's the way to sell the tickets. But you don't have to worry, the White Company system never fails. The one you want will get it; it happens every time." It had better, he thought.

Luther's last words registered, partially, with Miss Iona.

Drawing herself up, myopic eyes flashing, she inquired icily of Luther, "Am I to understand that a pregnant Negro grandmother could be Queen?"

"Well, there's no reason to say it like that, ma'am," Luther said, "but technically, of course, you're right. That won't happen though, I give you my word."

Miss Iona sniffed.

"Now then, ladies, the next step is for all of you to put your pretty heads together and make a master list of all the girls or women that you can think of who might be interested. Then we send them an invitation to a kickoff where we show them the prizes first and then explain the rules. Got it?"

Caroline handed out sheets of paper and sharpened pencils.

"Anybody?" they asked.

"Sure," said Luther.

"Well, I'm going to put down the girl that does my hair." Giggles.

"I'm going to put down that cute girl that checks me out in the Piggly Wiggly."

"Ooh, I know! Let's send a blanket invitation to all the girls in the senior class at the high school. The whole class, how's that?"

"I think that's just brilliant, Rhoda," Caroline oozed. She was enjoying her role.

"Mr. Luther," Miss Iona said in one of her haughtier tones, "this whole idea seems repellent to me. In my day, an honor such as this one was awarded on the basis of character alone. Your scheme appears bourgeois and materialistic in the extreme."

Luther blinked. "Well, ma'am," he said, "I can sure see what you mean. I am in total accord with you on the principle of the thing, but you've got to realize that if we don't do it this way we might not be able to have the pageant at all. So you see we haven't got any choice in the matter, ma'am. A fine little girl will get it. I can guarantee you on that. It happens every time." He patted Miss Iona on the back, causing her heart to flutter violently. It had been years since anyone had touched her like that on any area of her body except her hand. The camaraderie of the theater, she thought. The bohemian give-and-take.

"You think about it a little," Luther said. "But don't go away because I've got a proposition for you."

Miss Iona sat quite still and straight amid the hubbub, considering. She recalled the plaster figure of Libra on the frieze above her door, and she weighed the alternatives. No one could deny that this scheme was monstrous. Yet, on the other hand, it would bring live theater to Speed and who knew how many hearts would be uplifted and inspired, perhaps even changed, by such a pageant? She must not be unrealistic. There are times when one must sacrifice one's self for the general good, and martyrs had always appealed to her anyway. She thought of the boy on the burning deck, she thought of Androcles. Well, then. Perhaps this large actor was right. She would go along with him, for the time being.

Luther moved among the women, encouraging them. The sheets of paper filled. "One thing, ladies," he cautioned. "Don't let a word of this get out before the kickoff. It's got to be explained just right, and it's going to help a lot if they get a look at all the prizes first. All right?"

They nodded, conspirators.

Luther chugged back over to Miss Iona. "Everything O.K.?" he asked.

"I have decided to go along with you, Mr. Luther," she announced, a sprightly tone in her voice. One must be game even in defeat.

"Good, good," Luther said, and the women sitting

close to them glanced at each other, amused, from beneath the lines of liner on their lids. Luther didn't know how lucky he was. "Now here's a sample press release. You can doctor it up any way you want to. I know you know more about the English language than me."

"Of course." Miss Iona calmly folded the paper in fourths and, without glancing at it, calmly placed it in her purse. A wise man is one who knows his limitations, she thought.

"Oh, wait, I almost forgot!" Caroline appeared behind them. "Here's the list of prizes. You might want to include that in your story, Miss Flowers."

"Possibly." Miss Iona folded that sheet of paper too, exactly as she had folded the first, and placed it in her purse. The purse shut with an efficient snap. Luther and Caroline towered awkwardly above Miss Iona. Monica, watching, felt an awful urge to laugh.

"And now, dear," Miss Iona said to Caroline, "if you will be so kind as to summon a cab."

"A what? Oh, yes, certainly." Caroline hurried off, looking for a phone.

"I shall be in the foyer," Miss Iona said to Luther. "Good day. It has been a most interesting afternoon."

"So long," Luther said. "Thank you a lot, ma'am."

"It was nothing." Miss Iona, regal, made quite an exit.

When the door had safely closed behind her, the young women looked at Luther and began to laugh. Luther, who was quite a man with a gesture himself, threw up his hands.

On her way home, Monica was both amused and annoyed. Like the damn Queen Mother, just who the hell does she think she is? Monica always cursed in her private thoughts. As she stopped for a light, she had the sudden urge to turn left and drive by the Sesquicentennial headquarters, just to see if he was there. No, no, you must be crazy, she said to herself, and pushed her foot down hard on the accelerator so that the Mustang charged ahead. She could not conceive of her old lover. Hell. She would drive straight home like the loyal loving wife she really was, and give Suetta something horrible to do. Something really shitty, like cleaning out the oven. Beneath her sunglasses, Monica grinned.

SEVEN

WHEN Frances Pitt came into the Speed *Messenger* office with her Theresa, she was full of pride and righteousness. She wore an aqua knit pants suit, so tight across the stomach that you could see where her navel dipped in, and she had a whole speech in her mind. She was prepared for the worst.

But Miss Iona surprised her. There she sat, almost lost behind the big desk, a little old lady. Her gray hair was pulled back tightly into a bun; her features were the features of any little old lady that Frances had ever seen. Frances was scared of good birth but she knew the weakness of old age. Everything evened up and so she sat down in the chair next to the desk. Theresa, acting dopey, stood behind her and twisted her pearl ring around and around on her finger.

"I am Miss Iona Flowers," said Miss Iona, who avoided contractions in her speech.

"I'm Mrs. Bob Pitt and this here is Theresa," said Mrs. Pitt. "Theresa, say hello."

"Hello," said Theresa, not looking at anybody.

"I'm the one that called about getting Theresa's picture in the paper. Mr. Neighbors said for me to come in and see you. She's going to lead the parade since she won the Susan Arch Finlay up in Tuscaloosa last week. We've got her trophy out in the car if you want to look at it."

"Fancy strut," said Miss Iona dreamily. She didn't feel at all well today. "What is a fancy strut?" She was small and grave and her face was as still as stone. They said she was good-looking once, Frances remembered. But she had never married. There has got to be something wrong with somebody like that.

"It's a category in the marching contest," Frances said. Miss Iona was so calm that she made Frances fidget all over her chair.

"Theresa won the biggest thing you can get," Frances said loudly.

"Je-*sus*," said Theresa in a strange voice, apparently surprising herself. She turned red and looked away.

"I tell you, they work so hard," Frances went on, talking faster and faster to make up for the way Theresa was acting, going into the speech she had made up on the way downtown. "You have no idea how hard those little things work. It's just awful. Theresa comes home sometimes after school and she's just too tired to eat. She has to lay right down on the sofa. And somebody that works that hard, why you know they deserve a little recognition! Everybody at Speed High is so proud of Theresa they are about to die."

Miss Iona turned to look at Theresa but she was looking out the window, down at the square, pulling at the buttons on her raincoat.

Miss Iona studied Frances Pitt. She was that type of person that Miss Iona had seen much of recently, walking about the town. These people were too loud and too fat and there seemed to be more and more of them in Speed.

They were not the sort of woman who had been at the luncheon yesterday. Those young ladies had dressed nicely, at least, wearing bright little linen dresses with contrasting monograms.

Frances wrote out on a piece of paper all the awards that the majorettes had won.

Miss Iona sighed, and got to the business at hand. "How do you feel about winning the fancy strut?" she asked Theresa.

Theresa thought about it a minute. "Well, I worked real hard," she said. "I think I deserve it."

"Why, Rose Theresa!" said Frances.

Miss Iona took down Theresa's full name, her age, and her address, which almost made Miss Iona stop writing. Nigger street, she thought. They wanted to name that street after Daddy but I wouldn't let them.

"All right," Miss Iona said, "go through that door and tell Charles to make your picture. Tell him I said to," and away went Theresa, pulling her raincoat tight about her hips. There is nothing lovely about Theresa, Miss Iona thought. And she colors her hair.

Frances sat in the chair next to Miss Iona's desk and tried to think of something to say, but Miss Iona was writing in the notebook and not paying her any mind. Frances was still trying to figure out if she should be offended or not, when it came Sandy DuBois and Sharon.

"I hope we're not late," Sandy said brightly to everybody. "I guess I never would have known about the picture if Theresa hadn't come bragging around to Sharon," she said straight to Frances. Sandy wore red slacks and a silk shirt with flowers on it and dangling earrings.

"I do not know what you are talking about," Miss Iona said. She drew herself up.

Sandy turned to the big desk and held out her hand and

smiled a big smile. "I'm Sandy DuBois," she said. "I
enjoy your work so much, Miss Flowers."

I doubt it, thought Miss Iona. She barely touched Mrs.
DuBois' hand. "Please sit down," she said. "Get that
chair over there. Now, ladies, what is it?" I sound like a
physician, Miss Iona thought suddenly and remembered a
time when she had had the measles and they had put dark
curtains on all her windows and she was not allowed to use
her eyes. *But Papa came in and read to me every night.*
Miss Iona noticed that Mrs. DuBois was talking and talking, gesturing with both hands. She tried to listen, but
Mrs. DuBois' earrings distracted her.

"I think it's wonderful that you are going to put Theresa's picture in the paper," Mrs. DuBois said, turning on a
wide smile and aiming it first at Miss Iona, then at Frances. "But I think we should all try to be fair. I think if you
put one picture you ought to put them all. I think that's the
only way to do it. Otherwise, you'll have a lot of un-
happy little girls on your hands. This means so much to
them, you can't imagine. Now my daughter Sharon won
the Beauty, chosen by open voting of all the girls. I think
that's really something, don't you?"

Miss Iona made some reply, her head whirling. Mrs.
DuBois' earrings swung back and forth. "Now tell me,"
Miss Iona said, trying to concentrate, "are these the two
top winners in the competition?"

"Oh, yes," said Sandy.

"You got to understand that Theresa was picked by a
California judge, though!" Frances almost yelled. "They
flew him all the way from California."

"Bickering accomplishes nothing," Miss Iona said.

Sharon and Theresa stood in the hall outside the office,
giggling and whispering. Miss Iona glanced at them, then
quickly glanced away. "What is Sharon's full name?" she

began, and wrote down the information in her precise hand.

"Mr. Neighbors said you wanted a picture of *Theresa*," Frances said pointedly.

"If it turns out well," said Miss Iona.

That woman is a little old rock lady, Frances thought. I bet she is mean as a snake. I could just kill Theresa for telling. But she has such a wonderful personality, she just can't keep a secret at all.

Miss Iona took down all the information. She sent Sharon back to have her picture taken too. Sharon, she noticed, seemed to have on white boots beneath her spring coat. They will wear anything on the street these days. Mrs. Pitt and her daughter left, and Mrs. DuBois took out an emery board and filed her nails until Sharon came back.

Miss Iona barely heard the grating as Mrs. DuBois' nails turned slowly to dust and clogged the shaft of sunlight that fell from the window across her red knees. In the sun the dust was turning, sifting slowly toward the floor. Dust to dust, Miss Iona thought. Only that which is true and good will last when we all go back to the earth. Impulsively, she leaned across the desk and spoke to Mrs. DuBois:

"Have you ever noticed the thousand little pieces of gold in the sunlight?" she said to Mrs. DuBois. "Look there, at all the little pieces of gold."

Mrs. DuBois looked where Miss Iona had pointed, and saw her own red knee.

"Can't say that I have," she said hurriedly, standing. "Thanks so much, Miss Flowers, goodbye." Before you could say scat, Mrs. DuBois had collected Sharon and left. ("I thought I'd die," she told her canasta club later. "Little pieces of gold!" Later, of course—after the pageant—when a lot of rumors were going around, the story took on an added significance.)

When Mrs. DuBois had left, Miss Iona sat and watched the sunlight again. She was warm in the light spring breeze from the window. Sometimes she wished that her vocation had been a simpler one, but now it was too late. She thought back over the years, and thought how the sounds coming in that window had changed. If they increase by so much as a decibel over the present level, she decided, I will buy some earplugs from the hardware store. Her second cousin's daughter had bought earplugs for Girl Scout camp.

Miss Iona opened her mail. Just imagine, still opening mail at three in the afternoon! What a busy day it had been. Most of the letters were handwritten accounts of women's club activities and parties, and she began to rewrite them for the paper, adding roses and decanters and credenzas lavishly, more than ever before. She punctuated one table setting with Steuben glass, added a Limoges compote to another. As she finished the stories, she sent them down the dumbwaiter to Will at the Linotype machine.

She next devoted herself to obituaries. One was especially fine. It announced the funeral of a dentist, a former Virginian, and it began, "Son of the Shenandoah, he graced these rougher streets. . . ."

Charles tapped gently on her arm.

"You want these, ma'am?" he asked. Miss Iona stared at him. He hesitated, then put the pictures down on her desk and went away.

There they were, Theresa and Sharon, all spread out on her father's desk and neither of them wearing a decent stitch. Sequins, that's what they had on, little sequined suits of underwear. Miss Iona realized that Theresa and Sharon must have worn the sequined suits beneath their coats, right downtown and right into her office.

Their legs in the pictures were strong and muscular and the toes of their white boots were pointed and the shining suits of sequins fitted them like skin. You could see everything—every curve, every little bulge of fat. Nothing was left to the imagination at all.

Manly Neighbors came in and made inane small talk; the sun set in the window, then faded. It still grew dark early, but Daylight Savings Time would soon put an end to all that. For years, Miss Iona had refused to go on Daylight Savings Time. Now she had given up time. Anyway, it was getting dark. It was past time for her to go home. Soon the sportswriters would come in to report the games of the day. Soon Manly Neighbors would be back to "lock up the pages" and another Speed *Messenger* would go out to the people.

The light on top of the bakery had been turned on and Miss Iona could see it through her window. Miss Iona could not take her eyes off the Sunbeam bread girl, feeding herself slice after slice of neon bread, for some time.

Then she sat upright again ramrod straight in the way that she had been taught and picked up the pictures of the majorettes and got her silver scissors from the drawer and cut off all four of their legs and threw them into the trash. They still smiled, and the sequins glittered just as brilliantly—from the waist up. Immensely relieved at having solved the problem so tactfully yet so definitely, Miss Iona typed cutlines for the pictures: "SPEED BEAUTY," and "WILL LEAD PARADE." There now. She sent everything down to Will. Miss Iona relaxed in her chair for a second, reading the poems of Matthew Arnold. She moved her lips as she read and thought of a darkling plain. Manly Neighbors is young and brainless, she said to herself. If he would put such legs into the paper, Lord knows what else he would put. Ah well, how did it go? He who casts the first stone should not live in a glass house. And she herself was not in accord with the method of choosing the Queen. So be it. Yet one must believe in the general good, finally, if one is to prevail. As Mr. Luther had pointed out so succinctly. The end justifies the means, something. We must all navigate faithfully by our lights. Who had said that? Why, she had, just then. A naval metaphor, as it were. Not unpleased, Miss Iona gathered together her accoutrements, as she called them, and set forth briskly for home. The dark was coming on quickly now but it held no terrors for Miss Iona. Dark is a negative condition, she said to herself, being merely the absence of light.

EIGHT

SHARON DuBois applied Mentholatum to that special place, and writhed upon her bed. She could see herself quite well in the mirrored door of her bedroom; she had pulled the bed out slightly from its normal position by the wall so that she could see. In one book, she had read that you get red all over, with red splotches the size of an orange. Watching carefully for the first signs of splotching, Sharon continued. Watching it made it better. So did the Mentholatum, although Ben-Gay wasn't bad. There was a splotch near her navel, but it wasn't as big as an orange. Oh, there. You couldn't believe everything you read in books, anyway.

She lay flat on her back on the bed and stared up at the blazing crystal globe over her head until she couldn't see any more and she had to close her eyes. Wow. What would it be like with a real man? She flopped over on her stomach and stared into the mirror. She messed up her long blond hair, letting it fall into her face, and bared her teeth at herself in the mirror. "Grrr," she said. "Grrow." She snapped her teeth together, a tigress. The White Tigress, ladies and gentlemen! "Grrup, grrup, grrup," she growled endearingly, like the MGM lion. She wrinkled her nose like the lion.

She felt herself gently, exploring. Where was the hymen? Was it this thing or that thing? Hard to tell. Wouldn't it be awful if she didn't have one? That happened sometimes; she had read it. Sometimes you broke it and didn't even know about it like if you had a bike wreck. That would be really awful, losing it that way. Such a big deal and you wouldn't even have anything to show for it. Lots of really rich women in Europe went to doctors and had the doctors build them a new one just whenever they felt like it. Then they could be virgins any time they wanted, and in this way they made more money at their trade. They were gorgeous professionals who wore long mink coats like Elizabeth Taylor in *Butterfield 8*, on the *Late Show*. Since Sharon couldn't afford a doctor every time she turned around, she was saving it for the Right Man. She would know when he came along! Until then, she refused to be tempted by offers of money or jewels or sports cars (not that anybody had come up with any offers so far). But she expected offers, of course, since she was going to be a star. She had read in *Movie World* about a girl who had "slept her way up the ladder to the stars." That was the exact phrase. Sharon knew that the girl wouldn't last long. She, Sharon, would never go all the way, yet she would drive them wild. She rolled on her back again and practiced driving them wild.

Then she picked up the Speed *Messenger* from the small, mirrored table beside her bed, taking an incidental sip of a half-full Coke as she did so. There she was, smiling right on the front page, along with Theresa Pitt. She had a bigger smile than Theresa. Sharon looked at the paper and couldn't decide whether to be mad or happy about the whole thing. Of course, she had to have publicity. Publicity was the key to success. She was glad to be in the paper and especially glad that her picture was bigger than President Johnson's picture, which was also in the paper, but she was furious because that old woman had cut off her legs. My legs are my best feature, Sharon said to herself, and flexed them in the mirrored air. Still, having your picture in the paper was something, and something was better than nothing.

In order to get into the movies, you had to get your picture in the paper. Everybody knew that. If you got your picture in the paper, why, anybody might see it! You couldn't tell what might happen. Sharon knew that there were many avenues to stardom. One star was found waiting tables in a drugstore. Still others had won contests of various kinds. But nobody important ever came into the Rexall in Speed, and the Susan Arch Finlay was the only contest Sharon had ever been in. And now they wouldn't even put her legs in the paper. Well, she would show them! She would just up and enter the Queen Contest. And then just let them try to keep her legs out of the paper when she had won everything in town. Sharon read the article again.

She wrinkled her nose. There was something funny about that article but she couldn't figure out what it was. Something didn't read right. She went over it again, moving her lips. Why, it never said what you had to do to win! If beauty and talent didn't count, what did? What else was there?

Sharon envisioned herself in a pushup bra and a shimmering silver gown, escorted by Red. Red would be having a fit. He already wanted to marry her. He asked her all the time. But she wouldn't marry Red if he were the only man in the world. Mr. Right was older and more distinguished, sort of like Carlo Ponti; he held a gold cigarette lighter in one hand and a telephone in the other hand and had connections all over the world. But meanwhile, before she met *him*, she could practice on Red. He was a lot of fun to practice on.

NINE

BEVO didn't have any problem about what to do on school nights. He went up to his room and did his homework. After supper, Mamaw always went straight to bed and Ruthie went to the Peabody Room or had a date if it was one of her nights off, and Anne read in bed or worked on her scrapbooks or quilted in the kitchen while Lomas, invariably, watched TV in the den. Nobody ever sat in the living room, which the decorator had fixed up prettiest of all. It was too pretty to sit in. Bevo didn't want to go in there, but he couldn't think what else to do. He sat for a while on the stiff brocaded sofa, staring morosely at an arrangement of artificial rosebuds made from sea shells. They were very cleverly made and quite expensive. Finally he got up from the sofa and smoothed the pillow and went into the den to watch TV with his father.

Lomas still had handsome features although his belly had grown large and flabby and fell out over his belt. In his youth, Lomas had been the wildest boy in town. Everybody who had known him then was surprised at how far he had come in the world. Lomas himself was not too surprised because surprising things had been happening to him for as long as he could remember. He had grown accustomed to it. He never knew what he would do from one moment to the next, but so far it had all worked out for the best.

Lomas leaned back and turned everything on, the vibrator chair and the remote-control TV, balancing his beer and the ashtray on his stomach. This was the part that made Bevo nervous, the steady rise and fall of that ashtray on Lomas' gut. They watched a situation comedy involving many mistaken identities, and a movie named *The Magnificent Seven* which had Yul Brynner and six other stars. By that time the ashtray was full of butts and ashes and his father had gotten sleepy. Bevo watched the ashtray.

Fire bothered him. Once when they had been driving back to Speed from a funeral in Nashville, Tennessee, Bevo had refused to let the family stop at an old hotel in the mountains for the night because he was certain that if they stayed there it would burn to the ground. Even though he was nine years old at the time, Bevo had yelled and screamed and beat his head on the floor in the high-ceilinged lobby where Lomas was signing the register, until finally Lomas and Anne had apologized to the manager and gone somewhere else for the night. Bevo still thought that if they had stayed there the place would have burned down. The fact that they had gone on, and that the old hotel had not burned (or if it did, it wasn't in the news) seemed to prove his point.

It was the only time Bevo had ever had a tantrum in his life, although Ruthie had them all the time. He is upset about his Uncle Claude's funeral, Anne had said to Lomas. We never should have let him look at Claude. Bevo was still upset the next day, but Ruthie amused him by chanting "One-a-see, two-a-see, three-a-see," and so on up to "Tennessee" all across the state.

Anne and Lomas would have been surprised to hear that Bevo's earliest memory was of fire. Bevo was not sure whether he really remembered his earliest memory, or whether he had made up his earliest memory when he was very young, and then remembered what he had made up.

He was in a crib, standing up and holding on to the wooden slats to support himself, and looking across the river from the front room in his Mamaw's old house in Cleveland, Tennessee, in the time when his father was off in the Navy, where he went for eight years, and his granddaddy (Mamaw's husband) was working on a pipeline someplace in Virginia, and he was being raised by a houseful of women. Across the river Bevo could see the Blue Flame Theater, all lit up for Saturday night.

The Blue Flame of Cleveland was some place: for a quarter, they said, you could see two shows on the screen and a magic act right before your eyes; occasionally a revival preacher; and once every two months a lady named Fatima who came down from Memphis and unveiled the wonders of the Orient, one by one. Bevo had heard this later.

From his crib, all he could see was the outside of the Blue Flame and its reflection in the slow-moving river that flowed between his Mamaw's place and the town. The blue flames licked up at the sides of the theater building and curled around the giant blue letters that spelled out the name, Blue Flame Theater. The flames had quick, electric, forked tongues that shot out in all directions, all night long.

It seemed to Bevo that the flames must be scorching, burning, consuming everybody in the Blue Flame Theater. He thought he could hear their screams. For years, when he closed his eyes at night, he could see the flames, fast and deadly, licking at the sides of his mind. He remembered them flashing in the darkened water way beyond the land.

Lomas began to make sighing noises. Bevo took the ashtray off his father's chest, and went in the kitchen and ran cold water into it and then carefully ground up ashes, water, and all in the new disposal in the sink. It made a loud, pleasant noise.

Bevo's father was sitting up when he went back into the den. He was switching channels on the TV with the remote-control switch even though he was close enough to reach out and touch the dial.

"Why don't you go to bed if you're so sleepy?" Bevo suggested. "You were asleep a minute ago." Bevo was tired himself. He did not want to have to watch the burning cigarettes far into the night.

"I haven't been to sleep." Lomas could say anything at all in his flat voice, and no matter what kind of lie it was, everybody would believe it. Bevo had known this for years, but he could not help believing his father when he was talking to him. Lomas liked to talk and joke with people, but just when you thought he was enjoying your company, he would squint up his close-together eyes and tell a huge, preposterous lie. Bevo did not understand it. It really got to his mother, he knew. She would stare fixedly at Lomas and her large eyes would go wide and dark while she looked at him. "Why, Lomas," she would say then, and it was impossible to tell what she thought.

"I guess I'll go on to bed," Lomas said then, as if he had just thought of it. "I'm going to have to go down to the yard in the morning." Lomas turned off the chair and pushed himself slowly up and out of it, grunting. He put his hand on Bevo's head and said, "Goodnight, son."

Bevo watched him go and wondered what his father thought of him. Here it was Saturday night. He should be at a drive-in movie, getting some. He bet that was what his father thought. Everyone he knew seemed to have a secret. Bevo took out some more of the green albums and looked through them. There he was at the lake, white in the sun because he had had the flu. There he was in a red sweater that Mamaw had given him for his birthday. There was that school picture again. What did the other kids think when they looked at it in the yearbook? What did Sharon think? Bevo thought he looked like a younger, thinner Lomas. No, he didn't. He was not a thing like any of them! Bevo stared more closely at his eyes in the picture. Were they out of focus? Maybe it was just the picture. There was something funny about his eyes. They didn't have any expression in them, that was what. Bevo tried to remember what he had been doing that day when the photographer made his picture, but he could not remember. When he closed his eyes to concentrate, he saw blue flames jumping at the corners of the black. As long as Bevo kept his eyes open and looked at the picture album he was all right, but as soon as he closed them he felt funny. That had been happening more and more lately. Bevo closed the album anyway, and went upstairs to bed.

Ruthie was hung over at breakfast. Anne barely looked at her the whole time, but Bevo felt sorry for her. She looked so sick. Bevo wondered what she did when she was drunk, if she changed much or was the same old Ruthie.

Anne served them the bacon and eggs without saying a word and Lomas read the sports and Mamaw read the comics. Out of the corner of his eye, Bevo could see right downw into Ruthie's robe, the way she was slouched over the table, and then he got afraid she would see him looking and afraid because he had seen.

Lomas pushed back his chair and said, "Well, I've got to go call the newspaper," and everybody stared at him.

"The newspaper," Ruthie said thickly. "What are you

going to call the newspaper for?'' The whites of her eyes were pink.

"I saw a UFO up in the sky last night," Lomas said. "You're supposed to report them if you see them. I guess I better call the airport too."

"Oh, Lomas, not again," Anne said in the tone of voice which Bevo had never figured out, and Mamaw chuckled.

"I got hot," said Lomas, leaning back and creasing his forehead, concentrating, "and so I took my beer and went out on the patio and lay down on the rocks for a while and while I was laying there I saw this thing not more than a hundred yards away, green lights all spread out, coming in for a landing. It made a noise like a chain saw the whole time."

"What did you do, Daddy?" Bevo asked. He couldn't help it.

"I just lay there and hoped it wouldn't see me," his daddy said. "My heart was just beating away."

"I bet," said Mamaw. She picked her teeth with her fork.

"Then they went away and I came on inside the house," said Lomas, who never paid any attention to Mamaw.

Bevo came near believing his daddy even though he had watched him go upstairs to bed. Bevo stared at his daddy but Lomas was looking at Anne.

Anne poured coffee from the percolator into a blue china cup, her face smooth and rosy above a rose-colored gown. She seemed to be trying not to smile and Lomas was staring at her. Bevo got a funny feeling: he thought maybe all of them were controlled by his mother, simply because she didn't do anything. That Ruthie's habits and the way his Mamaw was and his daddy's lying all had something to do with his mother and how calm she was. Bevo thought that they were all in a moving circle with Anne at the still point. Around and around they went, and she did nothing. Nothing at all. Nothing surprised or embarrassed or pleased or shocked her, or made a dent of any sort in her face—not Ruthie's marriage, or anything Lomas could think up, or anything Mamaw could say. Not even when Mamaw had told the minister that what he ought to do with his yard was "dig it up from asshole to appetite." It seemed to Bevo that everybody except him had a mystique and that these mystiques mysteriously fed off his mother and she fed off them. She kept trying to put them in order but they wouldn't stay. It was what Bevo's chemistry teacher, Mr. Locke, called a dynamic equilibrium. Bevo wondered if his mother loved him.

"Well, I better go call Manly Neighbors," Lomas said, and then, instead of going to the telephone in the hall, he put on his jacket and went outside to his truck and drove off to check the junkyard like he did every day, even Sundays. Anne turned and watched him go out the door, and Bevo reached over and ground out the butt of the cigarette that Lomas had left burning in the ashtray.

"Did you have a nice time?" Anne asked Ruthie, who was drinking glass after glass of Tang.

"I guess," said Ruthie, "if your idea of fun is a wrestling match in a convertible with the top down at about four degrees cold." Ruthie's long red hair straggled forward onto her face. Bevo was always afraid that she would catch it on fire when she lit her cigarette. Once that had happened. Only a few hairs had been burned, but Bevo could still smell that smell: acrid and sweet and completely memorable. He remembered it and looked down the front of Ruthie's robe, which was falling more and more open, and then he was afraid and he hated all of them except Anne. Bevo excused himself from the table and went outside to see if he could help his Mamaw.

She sat tilted way back in one of the Sears chairs, the

one that had gold thread running through the plastic, reading *Life* magazine.

"Can I help you, Mamaw?" Bevo asked. He blinked at the bright sun and buried his toe in the dirt.

Mamaw put the *Life* down in the dirt and, taking a roll of dental floss from her pocket, began to clean her teeth. She had never brushed her teeth in her life, and she was proud of it.

"When you get my age, you got to watch every tooth," she told him, her dark little eyes glittering from the shade of the leanto.

Bevo felt naked, standing out there. The sun came into his eyes and made it hard for him to see his Mamaw.

"Do what?" she said suddenly. "What you want to do? All I'm doing is working on my teeth." She pocketed the dental floss, and with a big spurt of energy shot her chair forward so that the front two legs landed back in the dirt, and picked up her magazine again.

Bevo had watched her shoot herself forward with much fear. He always thought his Mamaw would go too far and land on her face but she never did. Still and all, it was a weird way for an old lady to act. Bevo thought she was the most violent person he knew.

He turned around to go inside the house but his mother was standing just inside the screen door and she called, "Hold still," opening the screen door, and Bevo stood still while she took his picture. He even tried to smile.

"I'm going to call that one 'Sunday Morning,' " Anne said. "Do you want some banana pudding before you get ready for church?" she asked him when he got inside, but he said no thank you. He could never figure out when his mother cooked or cleaned or did any of the things she did. She never looked like she was in a hurry She wasn't ever busy. Bevo tried to figure it out on his way upstairs, but it was beyond him. She even had lots of time left over to do volunteer work at the hospital and the church. When she went to the hospital, she wore a gray uniform. Bevo could just see that uniform now. She had had it ever since he could remember.

TEN

*B*OB Pitt and Sandy DuBois lay on their backs on the green chenille bedspread, letting the Magic Fingers vibrate them gently beneath the blue haze of smoke from Sandy's cigarette. The bed began to slow down and Sandy said, "Put in another quarter, honey, and see can't you find me a match." Bob rolled over and fumbled near-sightedly in the clutter on the bedside table, then put a quarter in the slot, and the bed began again to rumble and hum. He handed Sandy a pack of motel matches with "Evergreen Motel" written on them in green, and a picture of a luxurious room which looked nothing like the room they were in. It was just advertising. Sandy lit another cigarette and stretched.

"You want to hear a joke?" she said.

"Sure," Bob said.

"You sure you want to hear it? If it's kind of dirty?" She grinned over at him, teasing. She was always teasing him and he never could see why.

"Just go on and tell it," he said, slightly annoyed.

"Well, there were these two whores just sitting around

95

having a beer and sort of discussing their profession, you know, and one of them says to the other, 'Do you smoke after sex?' and the other one says, 'I don't know. I never looked.' " Sandy laughed, her hearty laugh which was not like the laughter of any of the other women that Bob Pitt knew in Speed.

Bob grinned uncertainly.

"Well, do you get it?" she said.

"Sure."

"Then spell it out to me if you're so smart."

"I'm not going to do that, Sandy."

"I knew you didn't get it."

"Oh, I got it all right." Bob was irritated to hear the disapproving note in his voice.

"I don't think you did," Sandy said. "I'm going to tell you what it means, myself." She did, laughing at him.

"You didn't have to do that," Bob said.

Still laughing, she squashed out her cigarette in the ashtray. "I better take me a bath or else the dog will have a fit when I get home." Leaving him to puzzle over that one by himself, she got up from the bed and walked, stark naked and unconcerned, into the bathroom and shut the door. In a minute, Bob heard the water gush into the tub, and a minute after that he heard her singing, "I Fell Into a Ring of Fire." Sandy sounded exactly like June Carter when she sang; on Sundays, she sang in the First Baptist Church choir.

One day she had winked at him right there in the middle of the church! Bob, sitting up front with Frances and Theresa and his son Bobby Joe, had almost died. His heart had turned to ice in the middle of the hymn. No, that was wrong. His whole body had turned to ice. What a crazy thing to do! It was the craziest thing he could think of for somebody to do in church. It was so crazy he couldn't believe she had done it even after she did it again, straight-faced in her choir robe, holding the hymnal up and out before her in a professional fashion. Bob had turned to look sideways at Frances, to see if she had noticed, but Frances was holding her own hymnal tightly in her plump little hands and singing as if Judgment Day had come: "In BEU-lah LAND!" Frances sang forcefully at a high vibrating pitch. She hadn't seen. Looking back at Sandy, Bob had not been sure that he had seen either. She could not have winked at him. Not right there in the church.

But Sandy was always doing crazy things. He never knew what she would do next. It kept his insides in a perpetual turmoil, so that he had to take a bottle of Pepto-Bismol with him wherever he went, in the glove compartment of his car. Take the time Frances had gone to the PTA convention in Birmingham and he was in the Piggly Wiggly by himself, getting some TV dinners for the kids' supper. Sandy had come upon him with her cart, backing him up into a special display of potato chips.

"Well, hi there. What a surprise," Sandy had said, moving her cart to block his escape. "You're the last person I thought I'd see in here." She had seemed delighted and mischievous, on the brink of laughter. Under the black line of eyeliner her eyes had skipped and danced. "How you doing, Mrs. Matney?" she had shouted and waved to an older lady who went to their church. Bob had turned and smiled too, his stomach coiling. What was she doing? He pushed at her cart, but she would not let him out. Behind his back Bob heard the crackle of breaking potato chips. He maneuvered and turned within his tiny space, but he could not free himself without making a scene. Sandy, gleeful, watched. The crackle of potato chips had grown louder, like a hailstorm in the store.

"Sandy, please," he had said.

"Please what?" Looking quickly all around, up and down the canned-foods aisle, Sandy had moved closer to him and, very deliberately, touched what Bob called his privates. Right there in the Piggly Wiggly. It had been crazy, crazy. The potato chips were loud as thunder at his back. Even now, lying safely in bed in the motel, Bob shivered, remembering. It had been the most exciting thing that had ever happened to him, he decided, purely in terms of how he felt. Other things had happened to him that you would have to consider more naturally exciting, like the time he was in a bus wreck, but for *feeling* straight excitement you couldn't beat that time in the store. Many nights since then, Bob had lain awake in the night and thought about it and about how Frances would look if she had seen. She would draw in all her breath until you would think there was no air left anywhere around her, and then let it out in those little puffs. "What (puff) do you all (puff) think (puff) you're doing?" was what Bob had decided she'd say. And what would he answer? Bob could not conceive of an answer, only of the startled fury of his wife's round face. He lay awake in the dark hours and thought about exactly how she would look, exactly what she would say. She would just have a fit.

Oddly, Bob felt no guilt when he thought about his wife. Even now, lying in bed at the Evergreen Motel twenty miles from Speed, he felt no twinges of remorse, no sorrow, no nothing when he thought about Frances. He loved his son Bobby Joe, whose whole face was broken out. He loved his daughter Theresa, but discreetly, awed by her style. But Frances? Bob had never dated anyone else. Frances was a fact of life. Bob, the son of a woman who ran a truck stop and a daddy who was never home, had grown up obsessed with the sense of his poverty, something his brothers and sisters didn't have. They didn't seem to care how they lived. But Bob had delivered papers, swept out the café, washed dishes, and had more jobs than he could now remember. All through grade school and high school he had had jobs. "You mark my Bobby," his mother used to say. "The others don't amount to a hill of beans but that Bobby's going to make something of himself." Bob never knew whether his mother really cared, though; there was something offhand about the way she said it. She was a big, loud woman with a frequent laugh; she was always laughing with the customers, or going to dances at the American Legion. She didn't care what her children did, and except for Bob they ran wild.

Bob had worked at all his jobs and his schoolwork. Throughout his childhood, he could not remember having a good time. One Thanksgiving the Speed Jaycees, as was their custom, gathered up about fifty of the children from the poorest families in town and took them in the back of a truck to the South Alabama Fair. Pressing quarters into the children's palms, the Jaycees had posed for photographs (first one officer and then another) with the group of ragged children. Then the children were released from the bed of the truck, and with a giant, collective whoop they had run off in all directions, hurling themselves at the fair. "Yall enjoy yourselves now," the Jaycees had yelled. "Don't none of yall eat too much and get sick." Bob had wandered among the booths by himself, drifting, starting back in fright whenever he got so close that a barker began directing his pitch at him. All afternoon Bob walked and looked at the rides and the prizes and the shows, but he could not bring himself to go in. Everything cost at least a dime, and it seemed like such a big decision, how to pick which things to do or see. All around him, the other kids shot arrows and threw baseballs and flailed through the moving neon sky. In the end, Bob did nothing. He kept his eight quarters and rode silently home, wide awake among the other kids who had fallen asleep in the straw.

It was in high school that he first noticed Sandy McDaniels. She was the most popular girl at Speed High, the queen of everything. She led every parade and gave the entertainment at civic club meetings and had her name inscribed on the Speed High Hall of Fame plaque when she was only a junior. She was plumper then, but just as blonde. The mystery about Sandy was that not only did she do all these exemplary things, like organize charitable car washes, she also had the worst reputation of practically any girl at Speed High. It was a reputation built on innuendoes, locker-room asides, and broad winks by Sandy herself. It was nothing so obvious that a person could come out and say, "Oh, Sandy McDaniels, she did *that*." It was a much more subtle type of reputation. But, in all fairness, you didn't have to do much in order to get a bad reputation at Speed High in those days.

Sandy was an object of much speculation and much discussion, pro and con. Bob hung around in the background working at his jobs, and watched her. He would not dream of speaking to her. Later, home from college on those occasional weekends when he could spare the time from work, he had continued to watch her, now in her new capacity as a teller at the drive-in window of the First and Merchants Bank. Once he drove to her booth to open a charge account, purely a pretext to get a closer look at her, but a litle sign said CLOSED. He never went back to the booth, but Sandy—seen in glimpses, seconds: running across Main Street, singing in the choir, wearing slacks at the roller rink in summer—Sandy seemed more approachable to him now. In a year, he might call her. But not until he was a Certified Public Accountant.

Then wham! Sandy had done the one thing which it had never occurred to him that she might do, the one thing he hadn't allowed for. She had married Johnny B. DuBois, that joker. For months, Bob was plunged into despair. He could not say that he had been jilted, since he had never asked her out himself. Sometime during those months of despair Bob became a certified CPA, and shortly after that he married Sandy's cousin.

Frances had been around, in his class, for as long as he could remember. Frances was the girl who always read the minutes at the meetings and played the piano in assembly. She had naturally curly hair which sprang out in wads above her ears like birds' nests. Bob saw her off and on for years and then finally asked her to marry him. She was the kind of girl he needed; he knew that by then. She was religious and serious and saved her salary. She would make anybody a good wife.

And by that time Bob was consumed with ambition and he needed a wife who would help him get ahead. Frances came from a pretty good family too, so that was a plus. Her father was from the county but he owned acres of rich, black land. Bob needed land in his background. For the first years of their marriage, both had worked steadily (Frances only taking six weeks' maternity leave to have Theresa), making the money to pay back all Bob's student loans. A CPA doesn't get rich quick in Speed, Bob found. He makes a living. And so he had gone on, making a living and going to ball games and taking two weeks' vacation every summer in Florida or the Great Smokey Mountains with his wife, and gradually he became thirty-five years old and developed a sense that life had passed him by.

Bob developed this sense just at the time when he was getting on his feet financially, and was becoming a respected member of the business community of Speed. It was an irritating and stupid idea, but he could not get it out of his head. Just when he was about to get everything he had worked so hard for, his brain went into a tailspin.

The tailspin spun into a hard bright light before he knew what had happened, and focused back on Sandy. He and

Frances had seen her and Johnny B. of course, over the years, but after getting to know her Bob had had to agree with Frances that she was stuck up. Also vain and mean to other people, also extravagant. Sandy was a bitch. It was precisely when he realized what a bitch she was that Bob realized that he had not stopped loving her at all.

It was Christmas, a party at the DuBoises' house. The DuBoises' tree was aluminum, decorated in pink. Little glass bowls sat on the tables, filled with pink Christmas balls. Pink angel hair lined the mirrors and doorways and the stair rails, and Frances was allergic to angel hair. She came panting up to Bob only minutes after they had arrived, weeping through swollen lids. Her skin had turned red all over her neck. "Take me home," she moaned, so he did.

Sandy saw them to the door, wearing a hostess skirt. The sidewalk was icy, and Frances almost fell. "Now calm down, Frances," he had said, not too alarmed because Frances often had allergies and fits. "It's a shame they had that angel hair, but they didn't know."

"She did know too," Frances spat. "I saw her today buying it in the Ben Franklin and I said, 'Oh, I wouldn't buy that stuff for anything, I'm so allergic,' and she said, 'What happens?' and I told her all my symptoms and she said wasn't that something and started fooling around with the tinsel like she was going to buy that instead. And then she must of bought it anyway!" Frances wailed.

Such meanness was incomprehensible to Bob. He looked back at the doorway of the DuBoises' house and there was Sandy, pretty as a picture in her long pink skirt, arms hugged to her against the cold, framed in the long rectangle of party light. She seemed to Bob to be absolutely evil, a true bitch. It was right then, as he helped Frances across the ice to the car, that he knew how he felt about Sandy.

He had to have her no matter what. At first she had

meant all the things he wanted and admired. Now she meant ruin. She would make him give up whatever he had worked for, he knew that, but it didn't matter. And then he had her, more easily than he had ever dreamed, and the paradox began. Instead of bringing ruin, she brought prosperity. Bob's business prospered. He added new accounts and even hired a staff. Still, probably because of his reticence, he wasn't a man of real substance in Speed, and he knew it. He wasn't the kind of man who could walk into the Rondo and sit down with whoever was there, even though he kept their books. But that was coming and it wouldn't be long. Meanwhile Sandy met him, infrequently, as now, whenever both could manage it. Often she was flagrant and foolish in her arrangements, but she never got caught. It kept Bob in a constant turmoil—running his business, keeping up appearances with his family, and making seemingly endless arrangements with Sandy. Yet, because he was the way he was, he seemed to everybody else to be the calmest man around. It was frequently, and increasingly, remarked in Speed that Bob Pitt had a good head on his shoulders. The more Bob saw Sandy, the more serious he seemed, and the more he prospered. Bob lay in bed, serious, and he seriously wondered where it all would end.

Sandy came out of the bathroom, trailing little puffs of vapor and steam. Her body was long and full and very white. Her legs were too short but so what? Her features were sharp and pretty and she was all that he had ever dreamed of in a woman, all his life. He had found that she wore padded pushup bras but he had not been disillusioned. Bob had never known a woman who would wear a pushup bra before. He found it enchanting.

"Oh my God, how does this thing work? I've got to watch *Love Hurts*." Still naked, Sandy fiddled with the knobs on the great green TV. "It's not a thing like the one in that other motel; all you had to do was punch this thing and, looky here, this thing won't even *punch* on this one.''

"Sandy, come on over here and sit down. There is something we've got to figure out.''

"Well, just a minute, I'm coming, but I want to get this thing on first, O.K., today's the day they're going to find out who gets custody of the kids." Sandy flipped the dials. Gradually, as if of its own accord, the rounded screen began to glow and babble and a large, clean-cut man appeared, opened his mouth, and disappeared.

"Come on now, Sandy, this is serious. Get something on and come over here and sit down. We've got to have a talk, I'm not kidding.''

"Well, Jesus, I'm coming," Sandy said. Her white buttocks quivered as she turned the knobs. "Look here how this thing does, Bob, see here, you get the picture or you get the sound but you can't get both of them together." Sandy switched on a tearful woman accompanied by a loud buzzing, then a pattern of disappearing stripes which said, "It's the same story, Al, over and over again." She switched back to the picture and the buzzing became a shriek.

Bob got up from the bed and switched it off. "I can't stand that racket," he said. "We got to have a talk.''

"Not so quick, Mr. Smart-Ass," Sandy said, tweaking his privates. "I think I'd rather have the sound than the picture," she continued, as if he had forced her to make a choice. She clicked the largest dial. "And then I want me a beer," she said. "And then, maybe I will and maybe I won't come on over there and sit down.''

Bob got the beers, glancing at his watch on the night table as he passed. He had to get back. He wondered at the way Sandy never asked what time it was.

"Now," he said finally, over the TV voices. Now that he was ready, he didn't know quite what he wanted to say.

"I've got something to tell you," he said, biting his lip.

"Well, for Christ's sake go on and do it then." Sandy sat in the chair, somewhat wrapped in the chenille bedspread, scarlet toes protruding. "But, Johnny," protested a horrified woman's voice which arose from a pattern of rolling cubes, "you mean you didn't tell the judge the truth? Quick, to the courthouse, perhaps it's not too late!" A prophetic organ groaned.

"I have been selected to head the Brothers of the Bush," Bob said, feeling foolish now. "Nobody knows so far but one or two people because it hasn't come out yet in the paper."

"The what? You're going to head the what?"

"The Bushy Brothers, Sandy, and you'd know what it is if you'd read the paper. It's this Sesquicentennial club for men, where everybody grows a beard."

Sandy giggled, unimpressed. Yet Bob knew how important it was, he knew what his appointment meant. It meant that he had finally arrived, socially as well as financially, in Speed. It was something that he had awaited for a long, long time. But, now that it had happened, it was meaningless. He should have been the happiest man alive and he knew it. Now he had everything. But, instead of happiness, he was overcome by doom. Suddenly he leaped up from the bed and threw himself at Sandy's painted feet. "You've got to come away with me," he said, "right after this Sesquicentennial. We can run away. Just you and me. We'll make a new start someplace else, change our names. Just you and me, O.K.?"

"Drunk, drunk, drunk! You've given my child to a drunk!" wailed a section of waving stripes.

"Bob, don't be so silly now." Sandy slapped playfully at him with the chenille fringe. "You know we can't do something like that, honey." She was calm and sharp-faced but her brown eyes gleamed. It was such a crazy idea.

"I can't go on any longer," Bob said, his stomach knotting fiercely. "I'm not kidding you, I can't. Here I am the head of the Bushy Brothers and all, I just can't."

"Well, I think you ought to be proud of yourself for getting that," said Sandy, staring over his head at a pattern of merging shadows.

"Young lady, let me understand this." An elderly, dignified voice, obviously the judge. "Are you the mother of this child?"

"Sandy, that's not the point," Bob said. "The point is that we've got to run away together, you and me, right after the pageant. That's all there is to it, we've got to go."

"Hold your horses just one minute there," Sandy said. "I just don't see why we have to go and do something like that. Why don't we just go on doing like we're doing? What's wrong with that?"

"We can't keep it up, Sandy. It's out of the question." Now that Bob had said it, he knew that he had been meaning to say it for some time. He didn't understand exactly why his appointment as Bushy Brothers head had hastened that time, but it had. There it was. He stared at Sandy's face, looking for the little quirk of her mouth which came before she did something wild; but she had pushed her lips together in a pout.

"I think you're just stupid, that's all. I don't see a thing wrong with the way we're doing." Sandy stood up and unwrapped herself and began to put on her underwear.

"I was thinking we could go to Florida," Bob said, but Sandy watched concentric circles on the screen.

The judge was speaking again. "I used to have a little daughter, just your age, who was lost in a tornado. Wait! Is that a birthmark?"

"Father?" The daughter.

"Daughter!" The judge.

"Granddaddy!" The little boy.

"Grandson!" The judge. The organ blared in triumph.

Bob stood up, clicked off the set, and grabbed Sandy by the shoulders. He knew she liked dramatic gestures of that sort. "I said we could go to Florida." He kissed her ear.

"I'd have to get a new bathing suit," Sandy said. "The one I got last summer is shot." When he drew back and looked at her, the quirk was there. He didn't know if it was there because she was fooling him or because she really was thinking about Florida. He didn't know what to think. In her black pushup bra, Sandy was very sexy. She rubbed the hard black bra tips back and forth across his chest, and then pulled him into the bed.

Sandy liked to make love. If it was up to her, she would spend a week right here in this motel room. Of course she liked Bob Pitt (she had him tied around her little finger and that was fun) but she liked her husband, Johnny B., too. But there was something sneaky about motels which made it a lot of fun. Before Bob, she had come here with a salesman from Liggett-Myers. She didn't tell Bob that. He wouldn't understand that she just liked motels. She liked the idea of going to Florida too, if she could come back. She wouldn't mind to go down there for a little while.

"Could we go to the dog races?" she said later to Bob. "I went to one at Ebro one time and won fourteen dollars on a two-dollar bet."

"Sure we can go to the dog races," said Bob, who had never placed a bet on anything in his life. Bob lay on his back and enjoyed the sense of smothering beneath his certain doom.

"Now I didn't say I was *going*, you know," Sandy pointed out. "I was just asking for information." But I might go, she thought. I just might. Just for the hell of it. It was the best reason she could think of for doing anything. Johnny B. would always take her back, but Sandy grinned to think of Frances. Frances would be so put out she'd probably have a heart attack. She'd probably break out in hives all over.

"You've got to go with me," Bob said. "You're got to." He put little kisses all over her white stomach. He sounded just like somebody on *Love Hurts*.

"You let me think it over," Sandy said.

"No hurry," Bob said. He had sealed his fate; now he felt gloomy and fulfilled.

Sandy got up to get another beer and switched the TV back on. She was still wearing her bra. And it made her mad to think of what Johnny B. had said when she bought it: "I guess it's all right if your chin itches." That Johnny B. was a card; but if he didn't work so hard and fish so much he'd be a lot more fun—the way he used to be. "It ought to be time for *Silver Lining*," she said, and sure enough, a woman's voice broke forth from the frantic snow. "Every cloud . . ." she began.

"This is the best one," Sandy said, getting back into bed with Bob. "I just love Martin Dobson; he's the one that plays Robin."

Bob put a quarter in the Magic Fingers.

Two hours later, their room was empty. The door was ajar, key in its lock; and inside, the bed was unmade, its green spread in a heap on the floor before the green TV, which sang a tummy jingle and blinked solemnly into the darkening room.

ELEVEN

Ruthie was not exactly a whore, but she was not exactly not a whore either. Of course she didn't need the money. But she liked to have a good time, and she liked presents. She also liked to be surprised. Surprise parties were her favorite kind and there was nothing she liked better than finding a red silk robe all wrapped up in the seat on her side of the car, for just no reason at all. Ruthie was not averse to money upon occasion either, if it came in a cute way. Like one time a man she had been seeing, a florist, gave her a little artificial plant in a see-through pot, but instead of leaves the plant had five-dollar bills. That was all right. That was cute. But on the rare occasions when anybody had been dumb enough to offer her a bill in its natural state—not fixed up like a leaf, or stuck inside a pair of bikini pants—then Ruthie had really raised hell, and nobody could raise hell like Ruthie when she put her mind to it. "I don't have all this red hair for nothing," she warned her friends, and if they did anything stupid they found out in a hurry that this was so.

Above all things, Ruthie hated stupidity. Her ex-husband,

Don, had been a large, slow-moving high school halfback. He was incredibly stupid. Ruthie couldn't remember any more why she had ever married him in the first place, but she could remember well enough what it was like. It was awful. They had lived in a trailer (not a luxury trailer either but a second-hand Airstream) and every night Don had come in from his job selling sporting goods in Prentice's, and had eaten up every bit of whatever Ruthie had cooked, and then had gotten in a chair and watched TV until it went off. Every night. He said they were too broke to do anything else, but he never looked for a better job. But the *main* thing about Don that drove Ruthie crazy was the way he didn't talk. Nobody in his family talked to women. They didn't believe in it. Don would talk to her daddy, Lomas, just fine if they went over to her parents' house, but just let Ruthie ask him something when they got back in the car and he shut up as tight as a big fat clam. Women are good for two things, he had told Ruthie once, but he never would tell her what the second thing was.

That remark was the only one which Ruthie could ever remember Don making in the entire course of their marriage, except for "Does a fat dog fart?" which signified yes. For instance, if Ruthie said, "Do you want your supper now?" Don said, "Does a fat dog fart?" It had been a short, terrible marriage, ending finally one night when Ruthie—tired to death of being quiet and irrationally maddened by "Honey, get me a beer," which was the only thing Don had said to her for four or five hours—Ruthie had gotten the beer, opened it with a church-key-type can opener, and then had taken the can opener and stuck it between Don's lips and pushed down as hard as she could, exactly as if she were opening a foamy Bud. Now Don had a partial plate and another wife and sold Chevrolets. Occasionally Ruthie ran into him and noticed how he was gaining weight and how his neck was wider across than the flat little brush at the top of his crew-cut head.

Right after the divorce, Anne had decided that Ruthie should go to college, and just to please her Ruthie had enrolled in an English course down at the Speed Junior night school. It didn't last long though. It lasted just long enough for Ruthie to write one paper on *The Faerie Queene* on which Ruthie got a D simply and purely because she said that Una was pregnant. Well, what the hell, it said that Una was heavy on her ass and the teacher himself had said something about the Virgin Mary who *also*, as Ruthie had pointed out in her paper, rode an ass. Then she went in for a conference and the teacher, who was a fairy queen himself as far as she was concerned, had talked all about symbols. Which aren't what they are, he said. "Well, I like to call a spade a spade," Ruthie had said, and that was that. Anne hadn't seemed too disappointed when she dropped the course, and Lomas didn't care one way or the other.

Now sometimes Ruthie wondered if they knew what was going on. Or what wasn't quite going on, to be exact. Mamaw did, but she was tickled by anything Ruthie did. Anne and Lomas were both so loopy, anyway, you just couldn't tell what they thought. They probably didn't think anything, if you got right down to it. Well, anyway, nothing was going on, so there! Nothing but a little fun. And anybody who had been married to Don deserved all the fun they could get.

Once Ruthie had gone out with a teacher for a while, one she had met during her short college career. She broke it off finally because he bugged her to death. He took to bringing little squiggly pictures along on their dates and saying, "Now what does this remind you of?" or he'd say, "Now I'm going to say a word and you say the first thing that comes into your head. Just tell me the first word you think of. O.K.? *Gun*." Then one day he said, "I give up, there's nothing the matter with you at all. You are just amoral, as far as I can see. Now pretend you're walking through a forest and tell me what it looks like." After that, Ruthie didn't fool around with college creeps. She waited until after Christmas, since it was almost Christmas anyway and she wanted to get what was coming to her, and then she said buzz off.

That was the only thing wrong with Speed: it was full of creeps. When you've dated one doctor you've dated them all and ditto with postal clerks or insurance men or anybody else. Speed was just too little, but Ruthie planned to broaden her horizons. She was thinking mainly of Atlanta, but Miami had entered her mind. Anyway she was cutting out, just as soon as she won the Sesquicentennial Queen Contest. There wasn't any sense in moving if you didn't move in style, if you didn't move up in the world. After she won all that stuff she was going to sell it, and then look out for little Ruthie!

She paused a minute before she pushed the revolving glass door into the El Rondo Motor Hotel. Looking at herself from several angles in the glass, she didn't see how she could lose. But when she stepped inside she didn't feel quite as confident. Oh, she felt confident enough, but she was surprised. It was like a madhouse in there. Every girl Ruthie had even seen in Speed was there, plus their mamas and their friends. Little high school girls were everywhere, holding each other's arms, and all the working girls with their stiff heads and their certain bearing, and even a lot of married housewives. Plus the home extension agent for the county. Plus girls with little babies in plastic carriers. The babies looked around, big-eyed at all the commotion, and huddled within their plastic slats. It was a madhouse. Ruthie had never seen anything like it in Speed.

A young pregnant woman stood in the middle of the

whole thing, working her mouth. She was obviously giving the group directions, but no one was paying her any mind at all. Ruthie was glad, because she had seen Caroline Pettit before and she thought she was stuck up. She *was* stuck up, like the time she came in the Peabody Room with her husband and some more people and all the men were kidding with Ruthie and the wives acted like she wasn't even there. They had acted exactly like she was made out of air. Women like Caroline Pettit thought they were so smart with their little spectator heels. Ruthie watched with satisfaction as Caroline Pettit clapped her hands for quiet, got no response, and nervously bit her lip.

Then something right out of Hollywood happened. The fattest man Ruthie had ever seen walking came through the doors slowly and majestically, failed to get out, and glided around a second time. Conversation had hushed. Everyone was watching the man revolve. He was really something to see, in that turquoise blue suit and those boots. You couldn't get a turquoise blue suit like that anywhere around here, obviously. Not with that weave like fish scales and that shiny mirror look.

"Howdy, ladies," the man said from behind his wraparound sunglasses, as calm as if he had meant to go around twice in that door. Maybe he *had* meant to. Maybe that's how Hollywood people went through those doors. "Let's all go into the ballroom now and get a look at some of those prizes and then I'll tell you how you can win." The girls giggled and surged, doubtful. What did he mean, the ballroom? The El Rondo didn't have a ballroom. He must mean the banquet room, where the Rotary Club met. That's the only thing he *could* mean! The girls wavered and then flooded into the hall, pulling at themselves. Ruthie put a stick of gum in her mouth and smiled at some girls she knew. They smiled back down their noses, snotty. Ruthie couldn't help it and laughed. The *ballroom*. It was just too much.

The banquet room had long tables lining three of its sides, upon which a lot of the prizes were displayed and others, like the car, were pictured. The girls buzzed around the tables.

"Look to your heart's content, look to your heart's content, little lovelies," invited a deep male voice over the loudspeaker. "See all the prizes in store for the lucky Queen. Let your eyes linger, sweethearts, over that little diamond bracelet right over there at the first table, just watch that baby *shine*. Oh, mama, don't it make you feel faint the way those little diamonds carry on? And don't miss the picture of the brand-new Buick Skylark convertible, over here at the table closest to me. Look at that thing. Just cast your eyes on those whitewall tires and all that sexy chrome and believe me there's a monster under that hood, girls. It can take you anywhere you want to go if you know what I mean. Fully automatic, power steering, power brakes—all you do is get in there and whisper and it drives itself. Would I kid you? You get your initials free on the side closest to your heart. Comes in any color of the rainbow and has the softest little Naugahyde seats this side of heaven. All you little Nauga lovers are going to love these seats, it takes fourteen little Naugas to cover six square inches of comfortable foam. Now swing your little eyes on up here, dolls, and let me flash this ring at you that I am holding in my hand. Cover your eyes, that's right, five people were blinded in the jewelry store when they took it out of the case."

"Who *is* that?" Ruthie asked the girl next to her, looking for the voice.

"Why, that's Ron-the-Mouth!" the girl exclaimed reproachfully, apparently astonished that Ruthie didn't know. Well, Ruthie had recognized the voice, but she just couldn't put her finger on who it was. She had heard him often enough. It seemed like every time she turned on the radio there he was, screaming out of it, Ron-the-Mouth-of-the-South. Ruthie knew he was some sort of hero to the high school girls. Even Bevo knew who he was.

"Well, where is he?" Ruthie asked the girl, whom she now recognized as a clerk at the First State Bank.

"Right up there on the stage with Mrs. Pettit and the mayor."

Ruthie blinked. That couldn't be Ron-the-Mouth, not that short plump man with the little round glasses and those stupid sideburns and those pointed shoes. *That's* what he looked like, a shoe salesman! Ruthie giggled. No, he didn't look like a shoe salesman either, he looked like one of Santa's little helpers. It was ridiculous. He stood by the microphone, barely opening his mouth, and the voice that came out was as full and resonant, as polished and professional, as any voice on any radio station in the country. Why, he might be talking right out of Chicago, to listen to him. It was amazing. The voice turned the whole occasion into something special and glamorous. Then, when everybody had seen all the prizes, the fat man took over the microphone.

"Now, ladies, if you will just listen to me for one second, I'll explain to you exactly what you have to do to be selected as the lucky Sesquicentennial Queen."

Caroline Pettit sat on a folding banquet chair and felt sick. This was the moment of failure, the moment when—she was sure—every last one of those girls would get up and walk out. Her whole committee would be a flop, she had known it all along. She should have stayed at home and made receiving blankets.

But Luther explained the rules jauntily, as he had done so many times before. The girls still looked around the room, mesmerized by the display of prizes. Only a few of them, here and there, were really paying attention. "So what it amounts to, ladies, is a community-wide vote, and what's fairer than an election? What's fairer than the democratic process upon which this country is based?" A certain amount of discord was running through the ranks now, but Luther quelled it. "What's better than a democratic canvass of all the people, a free referendum?" That word "referendum," dimly remembered from civics class, silenced them. After all, nobody wanted to be unpatriotic. Nobody wanted to be a Communist, for heaven's sake.

"And in case any of you are a little doubtful, we have an extra incentive." Luther paused for emphasis. "Now I've told you that for each ticket you sell to the spectacular, you win a thousand votes in the Queen Contest. For each Blue Ribbon Special ticket you sell, you win five thousand votes and the buyer gets his name printed in the program beneath the American flag. In addition to winning these thousands of votes, girls, you will also receive a bonus of one dollar for each block of tickets you sell. Whether you win or not! And, since the winner in most towns sells over five hundred blocks of tickets, you figure it out. Even if you lose, you win!"

Caroline got up and Luther sat down, wiping his forehead. It had gone over, as usual. Caroline gave more instructions and passed out more instruction sheets. The girls were filled up with instructions. "The Speed *Messenger* will print a list every week of the top ten contestants, so you will know where you stand. You are free to drop out of the contest at any time, of course, and if you do so you will still receive a bonus on the tickets you sold but if you drop out don't forget to turn back in the tickets you couldn't sell." Caroline came to a stop, muddled. "O.K., girls," she finished a little lamely, "line up at the door for your Queen Contestant badges."

"And good luck!" boomed Luther, restoring the festival air. Caroline rocked like a ship toward the door.

Ruthie stood aside to check the competition. It really

wasn't much. About thirty girls didn't line up at the door at all. Apparently discouraged, they sniffed and pushed through the others and left. The high school girls would probably drop out soon enough too. It was the working girls like herself that Ruthie had to worry about, and the housewives who needed the money, and the sorority girls from Speed Junior College who were probably filthy rich. But Ruthie liked the way the contest was set up. No Miss America shit, no piano playing and "I made this dress myself." No crappy little questions such as "Do you think a woman should be President?" Everything about this contest was cut and dried and that's the way Ruthie liked it. All the cards on the table except the ones she had up her sleeve, ha ha. And she had a few. She knew some people who would be real glad to buy one of those Blue Ribbon Special tickets from her. She bet she sold more Blue Ribbon Specials than everybody else put together.

"I like big women," said the astonishingly beautiful voice of Ron-the-Mouth, right at her elbow. Ruthie jumped. He came up exactly to her ear.

"I'm Ron-the-Mouth," he said. "That's Ron Skinner, the one and only perfect untamed untouched mouth in Speed."

"What?" Ruthie said, staring down at him. She was both mad and extremely amused, as if somebody she didn't like was tickling her.

"Ron Skinner," he said. His voice was so impressive that he might have been saying President Johnson, to judge from the tone.

"Well, I'm Ruthie Cartwright," she said, guarded. He did have quite a mouth, a fine mouth, and a good-looking face which reminded her nevertheless of a rat. But it had a certain rat appeal and actually he was attractive, an attractive face stuck on top of that pudgy little body.

He thumped her on the rear, the way you thump a watermelon. "My, my," he said.

"You can just take your hands off the merchandise," Ruthie said.

"You'll never get anyplace with lines like that." Ron-the-Mouth was mellow and suave.

"You'll never get anyplace either," Ruthie said. "Who wrote your script, King Kong?"

"The little lady is quick," said Ron-the-Mouth. "Very quick. And what a fine ass, my, my. What a delicate, double, globular ass, as firm as a baseball yet soft as a baby's cheek."

Ruthie felt like killing him right there in the El Rondo. He must be crazy, talking like that. But she was intrigued by his voice. It couldn't, absolutely couldn't, be coming out of him. It must be coming out of a tiny little transistor radio hidden someplace in his fat throat.

"Will you just buzz off and let me go get my stuff?" Ruthie said. "I've got to go to work."

"I wouldn't fool with this chickenshit if I was you," said Ron-the-Mouth, apparently taking it for granted that she wouldn't care if he used the word. As a matter of fact he was right, but it made her mad as hell to think that he *knew* she wouldn't care. What did he think she was? "You're not the Sesquicentennial Queen type anyway, baby."

"Well, just what type do you think I am?"

"I'll tell you outside." Ron-the-Mouth was practically bouncing on his elevator heels. He was enjoying himself.

"If there's anything I hate it's a little old bitty chickenshit man." Ruthie lowered her voice and pushed past him. She was enjoying herself, too.

"My, my. Flower lips," she heard behind her. Ruthie got her badge and her rules sheet and stalked out to her car, parked in front of the store that sold prosthetic devices.

"I'll pick you up after work." Little Ron-the-Mouth looked even more impossible in the daylight than he had indoors.

"You don't even know where I work," Ruthie said, "and I'm not about to tell you."

"I'll find out."

Ruthie was annoyed and fascinated. None of the men she knew talked like this. The men she knew were slow talkers, for the most part, dummies with hearts of gold.

"I wouldn't go out with you if you were the last midget in the world." She got in her car and slammed the door.

Ron-the-Mouth reached in the window and stroked her long red hair. "Now it's mad," he said. "Just look at how mad it is."

"In one second I'm going to push a button and cut off your arm. I'm telling you. There's going to be a bloody mess all over the street."

"Paul Newman wears elevator shoes," said Ron-the-Mouth.

"I'm going to count to ten. One-two-three—"

"Casanova was five two."

"So was Hitler, now fuck off."

"Can I help it if I love you?"

"Seven-eight."

"Tonight after work." Ron-the-Mouth winked at her, conspiratorial and obscene, and withdrew his arm. "It's good thing you didn't do that with the window," he said. "These cufflinks are actually small grenades."

"GOODBYE!" Ruthie gunned out into the street and almost hit a pickup truck. Christ, that's all I need, she thought. Her car wasn't even paid for. In the rearview mirror, Ron-the-Mouth looked better. From a distance you couldn't tell how short he was. Oh, hell.

Ruthie slammed into the house to dress, in a bad mood.

"Cat got your tongue?" said Mamaw from the den.

"I wish the cat would get yours," Ruthie told her.

"Too tough to chew," Mamaw said. "Haw haw." She was watching *The Beverly Hillbillies* on TV. It was a bad influence on her, Ruthie felt.

"You going out?" Mamaw said.

"You know I'm going out. I'm going to work as soon as I get dressed if I can ever get upstairs to get dressed, that is, which in this house I doubt."

"Work!" snorted Mamaw. "Well, go on. Isn't anybody stopping you that I can see."

"Oh, Jesus," Ruthie said. She went upstairs.

About twenty minutes later, as she sat in her slip putting on makeup, she saw Pat of Pat's Florist come up the walk with a huge bunch of roses. It was the biggest bunch of roses Ruthie had ever seen. She put on her gown and went downstairs and Pat, who was one of her old friends so to speak, almost fell over dead at the sight of her in her gown.

"Well, give them here," she said.

He handed them over, gawking, and Ruthie shut the door in his face.

She set them down on the newel post and looked all through them for a card but she couldn't find a thing. "I'll be damned," she said, and started back upstairs.

"Hothouse," Mamaw sniffed, pawing around in them. "Nothing but hothouse."

"Paul Newman wears elevator shoes," Ruthie said from the top of the stairs.

"What?" shrilled Mamaw.

"You can't even get dressed in peace," Ruthie said. "What a madhouse."

"Haw, look at Luke," said the granny on *The Beverly Hillbillies*.

"Haw, haw," said Ruthie's Mamaw.

TWELVE

LLOYD Warner sat slumped in his chair and stared morosely at the pieces of a wooden puzzle before him on the desk. The puzzle was intricate, polished, and very beautiful; Melissa had a gift for gifts. Arty Melissa with the inch-long fingernails and the small stone gods in her ears. Oh, well, fuck Melissa anyway. She couldn't live here, obviously, and he could not live in New York again. He was too crazy up there. Was he less crazy here? Debatable. Only a fool would come back to Speed after so many years. He felt at home here, that was all. Faulkner shit. Then Lloyd was amused by his own bloody little ego and sad because he was amused and because in the end that's what it always came back to. He was too goddamn smart. Always had been, and knew it, and knew he knew it, which made it worse. It was unbearable the things he knew about himself. He had never been able to fool himself once, no matter who else he fooled. Lloyd looked around his office again and thought: It's like a stage set. I set the stage for me and then here I come, bojangles. Dance.

A soft fur of dust covered everything, every slanted or

horizontal surface, making the whole office seem alive, a large friendly organism breathing softly in the afternoon sun. There was the dust-covered picture of Bobby Kennedy, personally signed; there was the dust-covered fake filing cabinet where everybody in town knew that the liquor was kept. It was a town joke, where Lloyd kept his liquor. In fact the whole town would have been amazed to hear that Lloyd Warner, its most outstanding young alcoholic by anybody's standards, was not an alcoholic at all. It was a myth which Lloyd himself had fostered, and which he himself maintained. By his own reckoning it was the smartest thing he had ever done. For one thing, it was easier to pretend to be an alcoholic than to pretend to be crazy, which his father had done at the end. It was especially easy since Lloyd liked to drink in the first place. Because Lloyd had learned from his father that it is not enough to be the way you are, not if the way you happen to be naturally demands an excuse for itself. Since they thought he was an alcoholic, they accepted him. If they hadn't thought him an alcoholic, Lloyd knew perfectly well that they would have sent him packing several years back. Now they said, he's right bright for an alcoholic. Lloyd cursed his lucidity and grinned at the things they thought. So what? He made a damned good living, handling all the legal work for Speed Junior College and plenty of individual cases as well. But right now it was time to cut out of this office, and if those kids didn't show up in one minute flat, they were getting left.

They showed. Theolester Hodo, the one he had met before and talked with on the phone, stuck a formidable Afro around Lloyd's glazed office door.

"Where's your secretary, man, you ain't got no *secretary?*" Theolester was grinning, jiving. "You ain't got no class if you ain't got no secretary."

"What's on your mind, Theolester?" Lloyd said. He

liked Theolester but the boy saddened him too: his determined Afro and dashiki above his brown pegged pants. They tried, Theolester and his crew, but they were always behind. "Take a seat," Lloyd said.

Theolester and the other two boys sat in a row on Lloyd's dust-covered leather couch. They were very serious. They looked like See No Evil, Hear No Evil, Speak No Evil; Lloyd suppressed a laugh.

"What's the matter, big shot?" Theolester was quick.

"Nothing, man, you go ahead and tell me what you want. And make it fast. I close up like a book at five o'clock."

The boys looked at each other. They thought he wanted a drink. Lloyd grinned. "Go on," he said.

"Well, first let me introduce you here," said Theolester. "This here is Buddy Waters; he's the first vice president." Lloyd got up and stuck his hand over the desk, shaking Buddy Waters up bad. Buddy was tall and skinny; he had the narrowest shoulders Lloyd had ever seen. "Pleased to meet you," he mumbled. He wouldn't look at Lloyd, but he shook hands hard and sat down fast.

"Now this here is the second vice president, Chall James."

"I beg your pardon."

"*Chall*," Charles said. "Very pleased to meet you." Charles was a soft, silly-looking boy, much overweight and dressed in loud, tight clothes. Looking more closely, Lloyd saw that they were expensive clothes, and that Chall wore a diamond ring on his right hand.

"That's Chall," Theolester crowed unnecessarily, caught up in some secret glee, and Lloyd looked at him but couldn't make anything out, and they all sat back down.

"I'm the president," Theolester said. "El Presidente, that is me."

"President of what?" Lloyd asked because he was expected to.

"The Afro-American Society over at the college," Theolester said, "that's what. I ain't surprised that you haven't heard of it. We's brand new, baby, fixing to roll. Watch out!" Theolester was jiving all over the couch.

"Well, that's just fine," Lloyd said, and let his attention wander as Theolester went into a long Byzantine story about how hard it was to get a charter for their group from the Student Government, and how finally the SGA agreed to let them have a charter, i.e., exist, if they didn't ask for a slice of the SGA budget. This seemed extremely unfair to Lloyd, but apparently Theolester regarded the whole thing as a victory for El Presidente.

Lloyd knew that there were only about twenty black students at the whole college in the first place. "Is that what you need, money?" he asked.

"Naw!" Theolester said scornfully.

"How many people have you got in this organization anyway?" Lloyd asked.

"Nineteen," Theolester said defiantly.

"Does that include all the blacks at the college?" Lloyd asked. It was so stupid; he wondered why they didn't go to Tuskegee or Fisk, or even up to Tuscaloosa. Expenses, probably. Here, they could live at home, and hold jobs in town. If they liked washing dishes and driving delivery trucks.

"That's all of us except Bodie Green," Theolester said. "He won't do nothing except shoot pool."

"Well," Lloyd said, and paused. He didn't know what was expected of him. Had they come here merely to fill him in? "That's fine," he said. "Is this what you wanted to talk to me about, Theolester?"

"No, man, no it ain't. We want to file a housing suit in federal court."

Lloyd looked at them, practically children, sitting in a neat row on the lousy couch. "Well, why don't you start," he said, "and tell me about it."

It took Theolester a long time, with non-sequitur assists from Chall, to tell the story. Lloyd had heard it all before, of course. That was not the surprising thing. The surprising thing was that they were ready to do something about it. Things were happening in Alabama faster than Lloyd had thought possible; in neighboring Greene County, for instance, it wouldn't be long before blacks had control of their own county government. But in Speed the blacks made up only twelve percent of the population, about enough to go around as maids and bag boys. They were a docile bunch anyway: "good niggers," Bill Higgins said. There were not enough of them to cause any trouble. Had not been enough of them to cause any trouble, Lloyd amended. Patiently, he drew out the facts from Theolester and Chall. It took him three or four cigarettes to get the whole thing straight.

Chall was not what he seemed. He seemed to be a good old boy out for some fun in his nice clothes. Those clothes and that ring annoyed Lloyd for some reason, to his own annoyance. Why? The fat body in the orange pants was annoying, frivolous in a way that Theolester's pegged pants were not. But Chall was the one who wanted to initiate the suit. He turned out to be the son of Charles T. James of Birmingham, better known as Motel Charlie, who owned a string of black motels all over the South. Motel Charlie was a millionaire; he had been written up in several magazines. Lloyd gathered that Chall was the youngest and dumbest son. He must be dumb, or he wouldn't be here at Speed Junior College. It was one of the worst schools in the state except for maybe Troy State University. And Motel Charlie could well afford to send Chall

anywhere that Chall could get in. Hell, he could have sent
Chall to Harvard. But Chall had ended up here in Speed,
and he was mad.

Why? He didn't like his room in the dormitory, he said.
He had to walk all the way down the hall to go to the
bathroom. He had to climb up three flights of stairs. He
had one electrical outlet so he had to plug all his stuff in
one at a time, plus the room was so little he didn't even
have room to turn around. Were all the rooms like this?
Lloyd asked. Do you feel that you were discriminated
against by whoever assigns the rooms? Chall blinked.

"They *all* like that," Theolester said scornfully. "Every
one of them is exactly the same. That ain't the point."

The point turned out to be that Chall had decided to get
an apartment in town. He didn't like anything listed under
"Colored Housing" in the speed *Messenger*, though. Everything he looked at was worse than his dormitory room.
"They nothing but *slums!*" he told Lloyd. Some of them
had roaches. You should see where I live, Lloyd thought.
Then Chall read in the paper that a brand-new apartment
complex, the Ivory Towers, had just been completed and
was now leasing. Chall got in his Jaguar and went over
and looked at the place. It was all closed up when he got
there, but Chall liked what he saw. It even had a swimming pool. So the next day Chall had called the telephone
number listed in the paper and a delighted voice had urged
him to come right over and look at the junior suites. Chall
went over there, right after gym class.

The delighted voice belonged to a white man named
Walter Bidgood. It was the funniest thing, Chall said, the
change in that man. He said he guessed there was some
mistake, in fact he had made it, it was his mistake! When
Chall had called up, Walter Bidgood had failed to notice
this little X that his secretary had written in his book. That
little X meant that the very last available junior suite had

just been rented out. Walter Bidgood showed Chall an X. "Son of a gun," Walter Bidgood had said.

"But," Chall had protested, and Lloyd could imagine how silly Chall must have looked, protesting, with his pink lips rounded around that "but."

"Get on out of here, now," Walter Bidgood had said. "That's just the way it goes."

Puzzled, Chall had discussed the situation with Buddy Waters, the only other black in his dorm. Then, just for the hell of it, Buddy had called up the Ivory Towers, keeping the nigger out of his voice, and Bidgood had said, oh come right over, we have a junior suite which sounds tailor-made for you. Buddy didn't have a dime anyway, but at Chall's insistence he let Chall take him over there and got the same routine that Walter Bidgood had given Chall.

"Masochist," Lloyd said, and when all three of them stared blankly at him he said, "Legal term. Go on."

Well, that was all there was *to it!* Theolester said. They wanted to sue the Ivory Towers, man, that's all they wanted to do. During the lengthy recital, Theolester had been rolling his eyes at Lloyd in a manner which Lloyd couldn't quite make out. Every time Chall opened his mouth, Theolester acted as if he and Lloyd were sharing a secret joke.

"Wait a minute," Lloyd said. "Who put you up to suing the Ivory Towers, Chall? I want Chall to answer, Theolester. You shut up."

"'Well eruh," Chall said, and stopped. He had been put up to it, but he hadn't known it. He thought he had done it all along.

"What was the first thing you were going to do after Buddy saw Mr. Bidgood?" Lloyd pressed. "What was the first thing you thought of doing? Theolester, shut up."

"I was going to call my daddy," Chall said. Theolester grinned.

"What did you expect your daddy to do?"

"Don't know." Chall shook his head as if it were all a great mystery.

"O.K. now, where does Theolester come into all this?"

"He come around and signed us up, me and Buddy, and we were just talking along and we kind of happened to mention to him about the Ivory Towers, and he said we ought to sue."

"Sue their asses!" Theolester burst out. "I'm the president."

"I got that," Lloyd said. "That's fine. But it isn't free, you know, and you just told me that your society hasn't got any money."

"We got *money*," Theolester said. "I said the Student Government wasn't going to give us any money. I never said we got no *money*. Shoot. We don't need no money, man, we got all the money you can think of. Any time we need some money, we just get out this little checkbook here."

Lloyd leaned back and lit another cigarette. "You called your daddy," he said to Chall. Chall nodded and grinned, ducking.

"After you talked to Theolester," Lloyd prodded. Chall ducked and smiled.

"Well, you all let me think about this for a minute now." It was late. Lights were coming on one by one in the square outside Lloyd's window. They burned singly, brightly; it was not quite dark enough yet for them to be needed and they looked fanciful and strange as they glowed in the dusk. Lloyd's own office was lengthened, shadowed, furred. It was the best time of day. Across from him on the couch he could barely make out the three black boys. They were a mosaic of shadow and bright patches of gleaming white: a tooth, a piece of shirt. Twilight had a particular smell to it here, Lloyd thought. He had tried to find that smell in other places but it wasn't there. It was strongest in the spring, right now: Lloyd tried to analyze it but he couldn't break it down. It had some fresh-cut grass to it, some supper cooking somewhere, something else sharp and sad. Sometimes in late summer, when the smell was weighted by too much ripeness, it was more than he could stand. Then it verged on the trite—it infuriated Lloyd and made him crazy. He was liable to do anything then. But he liked it now in early spring.

Lloyd pulled the chain that switched on the floor lamp by his desk and everybody blinked.

"All right now, Chall," Lloyd said. "If your daddy is going to finance us, I want to know how much he's willing to pay. I don't know what I'm going to stick you for either. But it might be a considerable amount. Now does your daddy understand this? And he's going to pay all costs, whatever they might amount to?"

"Thass right," Chall said. He spread his hands vaguely, as if somehow surprised.

"Maybe I ought to call him up," Lloyd said. "You got any objections if I do that?"

"You call him collect," said Theolester. "Listen, man, we wouldn't be down here if it wasn't definite. We got better things to do with ourselves than sit around in the dark."

Lloyd laughed. "O.K., boys, then you've got yourselves a deal. I'm going to check this whole thing out, every aspect, but from the way it sounds I'd say you've got yourselves a case." The boys whooped, as if they were at a ball game. They might have a good case, too, Lloyd thought, but something about the way Theolester was acting still bothered him. What? Lloyd continued, "I want you to understand from the beginning that this won't be easy. You're going to run into some hard feelings around school and certainly around town. There are cases like this all over the place now, as you are well aware, but we haven't had anything exactly like this here before. So it's going to be a little tough, a sort of a trial run for your group and for some other people too. You know what I mean?''

Theolester's eyes flickered. ''You mean cool it,'' he said.

''That's right,'' Lloyd said, ''I mean cool it. It's a good suit, but as far as you're concerned the timing is shitty.''

''Shitty!'' Theolester yelled. ''What you mean, shitty? You talking about my suit.''

''My suit,'' mumbled Chall.

''It's the Afro-American suit,'' said Theolester. ''Isn't that right?'' he asked Lloyd. ''You nothing but the plaintiff,'' he said to Chall.

''Oh, Christ,'' Lloyd said. ''Just shut up and let me tell you about the timing, which may turn out to be more important than we think. The trouble is that we're going to come up in court about the last of April, as I figure it, just at the time they're having this Sesquicentennial thing. Now what that means is that everybody is going to be singing 'Dixie' all over town, and thinking they're Green Berets. I don't know if you've had any dealings with real Alabama rednecks, Chall, but everybody with a pickup is going to be here. All I'm telling you is, watch out. I think it might be a good idea, this time, to keep all the action confined to the courtroom.'' By the time he was through, Lloyd felt like an ass. Why not let the kids do whatever they wanted? Probably everybody would be too busy to care. On the other hand it was true that Theolester had a manner that made people angry and that Chall was stupid and innocent. Or maybe it was just that Lloyd had felt all along that there was something ugly and dangerous inherent in the Sesquicentennial celebration itself.

"I'll call you, Theolester," Lloyd said, "after I get everything moving along." Lloyd stood. Theolester and Buddy moved toward the door. But Chall stood in the pool of light and looked down at his new white loafers.

"You say you think this going to come up in court last of April," Chall said.

"That's right," Lloyd said.

Chall said something which sounded like "Hyuh, hyah."

"What, Chall?"

"No way it's gon' come up faster?"

"No way, Chall. That's only about four weeks away, anyway."

"Well, I sure hate to walk all the way down that hall to the bathroom for five more weeks, I tell you." Chall shook his head.

"I can't see any way out of that unless you want to piss out the window," Lloyd said. "It's going to be three weeks at the least."

"O.K." Chall joined the others at the door; their voices rose as the door closed behind them. They clattered, echoing, down the empty hall. This building had been built in the late 1800s and it seemed to Lloyd that it always began to vibrate after dark anyway; it grew larger and vibrated, and magnified all sounds.

Lloyd laughed. It was late but nobody was waiting supper for Lloyd. He picked up the phone and dialed.

"Let me speak to Owen, please," Lloyd said when a woman answered. Owen Pettigree was one of the leading real-estate agents in town, and an old hunting buddy as well. He would know who owned the Ivory Towers.

"Mr. Pettigree is having dinner," the woman said, sounding more like a wife than a maid. Must be his wife. "Is there a number where he could reach you later?"

"Tell him I'm just passing through town and want to buy the Martin house," Lloyd said. "Tell him I'm from Memphis." The Martin house, a huge white elephant of a house on the outskirts of town, had been on the market for years.

"Oh. Just a min-ute," the woman said sweetly, almost singing.

A pause, a clink, a rustle, and Owen came to the phone. "Pettigree here," he said. "My wife tells me you asked about the Martin home?"

"Hell, no," Lloyd said. "I just couldn't stand to think about you eating your dinner in peace, Owen. It tied my stomach up in little bitty knots all over."

"Hell," said Owen. "I should have known. Anybody that said the Martin place, I should have known. Listen, do you want anything, Warner, or did you just call me up to ruin my digestion? My chicken is getting cold and if there's anything I can't stand that's it."

"This'll just take a minute." Lloyd pictured Owen with a napkin tucked at his neck. "All I want to know is, who owns those new apartments that just started leasing over by the river? The Ivory Towers. I'm just curious, is all."

"Well, it's real complicated, Lloyd, the way they've got it set up. They're owned by a thing called Speed Realty, Inc., which is owned by the hardware store, which is owned by Bill Higgins. I mean they have got a bunch of other people in it all along the way, but that's what it comes down to. Higgins owns about sixty-five percent of the whole shebang."

"Higgins, huh?" said Lloyd.

"Yeah," Owen said. "Now can I eat my chicken or what?"

"Eat your chicken," Lloyd said. "Thanks."

Lloyd hung up and leaned back in his chair and looked out at the lights. What a sweet and terrible smell. *Higgins*.

He should have known. The innumerable confrontations that he and Lloyd had had to date were all stupid and this promised to be the stupidest one yet. Not that Lloyd didn't believe in open housing or open anything. But he had spent too many years of his life working for civil rights and other things for that feeling he had once had to come back. He had seen too many slogans and sudden heroes cave in as the ideals dwindled into trivia, as the ideas were translated into the real world in terms of who ought to do what and did they need a Coke machine for the office. It was one thing to think about open housing and another thing to think about facing Bill Higgins in court. Lloyd sincerely believed that Higgins was garbage. One part of Lloyd—a hidden artistic part, that had somehow escaped damage over the years—was disgusted by the thought of taking this case and turning it into garbage. Changing it from a question of equality into something minor and scummy. Lloyd's aesthetic sense was revolted, but another part of him was revolted by his own aesthetic sense. This was the part which wanted contact, a dirty fight. Lloyd could still be, occasionally, an idealist. But he hated idealists. He grinned to think of Theolester. Theolester was about as far from being an idealist as anybody his age could possibly get.

What Theolester wanted right now was publicity. What Chall wanted was a close place to crap in peace. So Theolester had used Chall and was now using Lloyd, all in the name of justice. Chall wasn't interested in equality; he was interested in creature comforts. Theolester was amused because he and Lloyd were using Chall. Theolester probably didn't realize that he and Chall were using Lloyd as well. And there was yet another, graver sense in which Higgins and Lloyd would be using the two black boys.

Outside on the square, the dusk was soft and luminous. Lloyd thought he might run by to see his mother, then he thought he might not. It was depressing as hell to go over there. It was always the same. Lloyd walked past the barbershop looking down, watching the large square shapes of the sidewalk float up toward him at regular intervals. Christ. Lloyd wanted to take off all his clothes and run naked and yelling through the quiet streets. He wanted to visit his mother and smash cups. He wanted to steal a car. He wanted to rape a high school girl. He would do none of these things. He turned toward the El Rondo, where he would sit at the bar and order a T-bone steak.

THIRTEEN

Monica sat under the dryer and looked through movie magazines. She wouldn't have had them in her house, of course, but under the dryer it was all right. The dryer was safe and private; you could do anything under a dryer. She read what Lucille Ball thinks of nudity, what was the most moving moment in Steve McQueen's life, and why Jackie secretly despises Ethel. Then she turned to the back of the magazine and idly read through the advertisements: "Remove unwanted hair." "I weighed 326 pounds and look at me now." "If you are bothered by nagging, painful hemorrhoids." "The wrinkle cream of the stars." "Add inches to your bustline in 10 days." All the ads were obscene and optimistic. Monica wouldn't mind adding inches to her bustline, but she would never send off for anything like that. You might get put on an obscene mailing list. It happened all the time.

Monica came to a full-page ad for Frederick's of Hollywood lingerie. Round-thighed blondes with breasts like basketballs pranced all across this page, wearing the most amazing things. Bras that pushed them up and out to astounding proportions. Panties that said "Gotcha" on the crotch. Pads to improve the buttocks, attached by straps to the waist and thighs. And these are *merely samples,* the ad said. For even more imaginative lingerie, send for our full-color catalogue which comes to your door in a plain brown wrapper for only one dollar.

The strangest thing was happening to Monica. She could not stop looking at the ad and besides that she was becoming a little excited. It was ridiculous and irrational and she knew it. Imagine—under a hair dryer! But she could see herself in a see-through robe—hairless, thin, non-hemorrhoidal, bursting with new breasts—bending over Buck Fire on some anonymous bed. And Buck Fire would reach up for her. Jesus, Monica thought. I am a madwoman. Diseased. Yet, undeniably, she was excited. She had not felt like this since her return from Europe, except for that idiotic moment with Buck Fire on the stairs. Maybe I'm a Lesbian, she thought, and stared down at the impossible girls. But no, the girls didn't excite her; it was the idea of herself, Monica, in a horrible sleazy G-string which excited her, leaning over horrible Buck Fire on a horrible bed in a horrible, degrading hotel. She loved it. She might as well admit that she loved it; what was the matter with her?

Inside the roaring cap, Monica considered Buck Fire seriously for the first time in two weeks. At first, she had consciously put him out of her mind, killing him off as flatly and mercilessly as she would kill a bug. This had been fairly easy to do because in the first few days after their meeting Monica had redecorated the upstairs bathroom. But then, as her Sesquicentennial job forced her to spend more and more time at the old Pardoe house, invariably she ran into him. He was always busy, professionally distraught, with carefully messed-up hair and a pencil stuck behind one ear. Sometimes he wore tight, dirty jeans. Monica paid him no attention, kept her distance, and was even able to be amused at the havoc he was wreaking among the headquarters staff. Marion Van Dusen had taken to wearing lipstick and standing too long in doorways with her leg at a certain angle.

Lucia Bream was more frazzled than ever. She glowed with a fuzzy intimacy whenever Buck came into the room. Both Lucia and Marion were stupid and pathetic, and Monica alternated between pity and scorn as she watched. And they were not even the worst! The worst were the Queen Contestants. Monica supposed that most of them had many illusions and possibly even ambitions—they practically groveled at Buck's feet. They were servile, disgusting, and wore false eyelashes in the middle of the day. Of course Buck Fire ate it up. Coldly observant, Monica saw how he manipulated them, played one off against the other, and the results were always the same. They worked harder and harder for Buck. They had already sold an incredible number of tickets, more than anyone would have thought possible at such an early date. Initially, Monica took great pleasure in ignoring Buck Fire. She was as elaborately aloof and casual as possible. She never looked his way. But in a few days, after the novelty of being aloof had worn off, Monica realized that not only was she ignoring Buck Fire: Buck Fire was also ignoring her! He had his nerve. As if she would ever notice *him*, anyway! But it was so peculiar: the minute she realized that Buck Fire was paying absolutely no attention to her, she could not leave him alone. All day she sat at her desk and thought of things to ask him, things to offer to do. It wasn't that she cared about him. She didn't give a damn if he lived or died. She didn't know what it was. An obsession, sort of. Monica admitted it all to herself, consciously, under the dryer. She was insane and it had to stop. After all, she couldn't redecorate the whole house. The house was brand new.

The top of Monica's dryer flipped up suddenly and cut off, leaving her light-headed and exposed in the perfumed air of the Broadway House of Beauty. She looked down at her magazine, which now appeared dirty and dreadful. Frederick's of Hollywood was incomprehensible, hieroglyphic. Suddenly she didn't even want to touch it. She squirmed around in the seat until the magazine slid from her lap and fell to the floor, where she kicked at it petulantly until it grew wrinkled and torn.

"Well, are you ready?" shrilled Marge, the large beautician who did Monica's hair twice a week. Actually Monica preferred to do her own hair, to let it dry and hang straight without rolling it up or anything at all, but the Broadway House of Beauty was an acceptable place to go to get out of the house when Suetta came.

Today Monica turned herself over wholly to Marge, always a mistake. But she didn't care. Marge could tease her hair as high as she pleased today. Monica wanted to be cast in a respectable mold. She sat still and watched Marge work out her own tortured aesthetic upon her black-sausaged head. When it was over Monica looked like a statue. Grim and satisfied, she gave Marge an extra large tip and drove over to headquarters without a single daydream on the way.

Buck Fire stalked in and out all afternoon, flanked by a short square man who was some sort of a pilot. He was also a member of the Playboy Club, he said. Buck had a big camera and wore meters of many sorts strapped about his neck and shoulders. They were taking aerial movies and photographs of Speed from the Playboy member's plane, Buck said, to be used as backdrops for some of the scenes in the pageant. Buck himself was exotic in an orange jumpsuit ornamented by his equipment. Lucia Bream was nearly drooling—she leaned sideways on her desk and forgot to answer the phone. Monica thought ugly things about them all, with a smile on her face so they wouldn't know.

And then, right out of the blue, Buck asked her if she'd like to go for a ride in the plane. "We're all through except for some shots of the river," he said. "Want to go up with us?" The square man shifted from foot to foot.

"Sure," Monica heard herself say. "I'll just be a minute." At first she thought she should call Manly and then she thought she shouldn't. He might not want her to go up in a private plane. He might even forbid her to go. Monica went to the bathroom and powdered her nose and looked at her face in the mirror. "You're going for an airplane ride," she said. The face made no reply. "Ready," she said to Buck when she came back out.

Nobody talked on the way out to the landing strip. Speed didn't have an airport, but the paper mill and the dye factory and B.F. Goodrich and several individuals kept planes of their own in corrugated half-moons by the side of the grassy field. Buck was brilliant in the sunshine, larger than life. At first Monica thought that the orange of his jumpsuit clashed with the deeper orange of his hair, and then she decided no, it was just such an unusual combination that it looked funny at first, like a modern painting. Something you weren't used to seeing at large in the world. Buck was busy with his gadgets, sighting through various things. The pilot drove and smoked. Buck still paid no attention to Monica, but Monica began to sense that it was deliberate, a calculated move.

"There she is," the pilot said, as they drove over the grass and pulled up a short distance from a small green-and-white Cessna. It looked like a toy to Monica.

"That looks awfully small to me," she said. "Are you sure it's safe?"

"We've already been up in it three times today," Buck said, bored. "It's O.K."

"What?" Monica asked. The April wind was fierce now, blowing his words away. It blew Monica's skirt up like a balloon and tilted the lacquered mass of her hair to one side.

"I said it's O.K.," Buck yelled. He grinned at her and took her hand and helped her up into the plane. The pilot followed, expressionless, although he worked his gum furiously. A little bunny was glued to the plane's windshield in the left-hand corner. Monica couldn't imagine who she was, to get into an actual plane with such men. She realized that she was real in her daydreams, and real in her house with Manly. But not here. She was not at all real in this plane, with these men.

The pilot unwrapped three more pieces of clove gum and thrust them into his mouth at once. Then he started the plane, and they bumped gently across the field, not going even as fast as a car. Monica held the buckle of her seat belt tightly with one hand and pushed her heavy hair back to the center of her head. She sat in a bucket seat in the back, next to Buck. The empty seat next to the chewing pilot was filled with papers and equipment. It was all messy, in fact, the whole plane. Even the instruments looked dirty. Now that she was behind him, Monica could see a gray ring around the pilot's white shirt collar. Everything was dingy except for Buck Fire. Now Buck Fire's knee was pressed against hers, but he seemed not to notice.

The plane picked up speed. Suddenly, before she was at all ready for it, they were flying. Wind rushed at her from somewhere and the noise was terrible. The trees were right beneath them, faintly green and dangerously close. Their plane circled and shivered and Monica could see the high school and its football field, then downtown Speed, the square. Manly was right down there. She saw the cars like small, bright toys. Buck was pointing at things with his camera, leaning out; the pilot handed her a beer and she drank from the can without wiping the top. Manly always wiped beer tops and Coke necks with a handkerchief before he drank. Monica felt her hair coming down in back but so what. "Marge can go to hell," she said.

"What?" yelled Buck.

"Nothing," Monica said. She smiled at him, surprising herself and him too. It was a very special smile, a little off center and wild. Buck liked it. It meant that he had been right after all. In the past few weeks he had begun to doubt his judgment as day after day Monica ignored him. She had seemed thin and efficient and sour-faced; how could he have found her attractive? Meanwhile there had been Lucia Bream to occupy him, with short mutual trips to the costume storage room, where he clutched her close and whispered into her breasts. Lucia was coming along. So were several other prospects. So all in all there had been no rush as far as Buck was concerned, but now as he saw that smile—sweet, but with a funny glitter in the eyes—he thought he might have made a mistake to neglect her so long. That impression on the stairs was right. He ought to learn to trust his instincts every time.

"Go over by the river now," Buck yelled to the pilot, "and bank around low so I can get that bend we were looking at before."

Monica stared down into the still dark water deep in the river's bend. There was a big flat rock to the side there, where she and Manly had picnicked the first year they were married. She thought they had taken a chicken covered by a cloth, and a bottle of wine. Had they done that, or did she only think they had? Of course they had done it, hadn't they? Monica couldn't remember.

Buck leaned out while the plane circled at an impossible angle and Monica was thrown over against him in spite of her seat belt. Looking down past his shoulder, she saw the green-and-white wings of the plane, and then the deep water. She opened her mouth to cry out—why wouldn't they straighten this thing up now, the angle was ridiculous—but what happened instead was that she began to laugh and laugh. It was the hardest she had laughed in years. No, she couldn't ever, *ever* remember laughing so hard. Buck turned toward her and said something she couldn't hear. He stared at her uncertainly. The playboy righted the plane and that was funnier still, for some reason. Monica loosened her seat belt so that she could breathe. The clear blue sky was dissolving all around her; the more she laughed, the more it seemed as though someone had spilled water onto a watercolor painting of some people in a plane, and that now the whole picture was dissolving and running away. Monica pounded Buck on the shoulder.

"I can't see," she yelled.

"What?"

"I can't breathe."

"What?"

But she had started again. The whole picture liquefied.

"You just take it easy," Buck Fire said. "We'll have you down in a minute."

"But I don't want to go down," Monica spluttered, convulsed. In the mirror she saw the playboy's little brown pig eyes, squinting back at Buck. "Don't let him turn around." She pulled Buck's brilliant head down and yelled into his ear. "I don't want to go down, really. There's nothing the matter with me. Why don't you take some more pictures, O.K.?"

"WHAT?"

"I said, why don't you take some more *pictures*," Monica screamed into the wind and then fell back on the seat. Every muscle ached from laughing. She had read someplace, she remembered, that it was good exercise. If you laughed one solid hour a day, you would lose one pound a week just from that. It was called the Giggler's Diet. Even now, resting, she could feel it starting up again, building from her stomach, working up. It was so incredibly silly to be up here in the light blue sky.

Watching her, Buck had been alarmed at first. She's probably never been up in a small plane before, he realized, and he hoped to hell she wouldn't throw up on his jumpsuit. Finally he realized that it wasn't the plane after all, and it wasn't the dangerous kind of hysterics. Mrs. Mousy was simply crazy, as crazy as a loon. Look at her, going off again. Buck was getting amused himself. She was so ridiculous, this skinny girl, with her hair half up and falling down, laughing at nothing. Buck put an arm around her.

The effect was astonishing. Monica flushed all over, a deep pink, and suddenly moved her shoulder so that his hand was on her breast. Then she sat very still, staring at him with her oversized dark eyes, while the wind blew her hair into his face. It was no accident this time. Buck squeezed her breast and moved a lacquered strand of hair and kissed her ear. The ear was small and white and her earrings were solid gold. Buck could tell real from fake gold every time. His instinct was toward rich women and he was rarely wrong, even when they wore dungarees and little canvas shoes. His mind was on the earring but his hand was on her breast and he continued to play with it and then with her skirt, working his hand down toward her legs.

Monica couldn't believe it. Up in an airplane with a man in an orange jumpsuit. A man who was feeling the inside of her thigh right now, biting her neck, and she felt like she was crashing and burning, a way she had not felt for years. Who was this strange sky girl, practically wetting her pants? She stared over Buck's head straight into the sun until her eyes burned and she blinked finally and then her eyes were running again and the picture faded again. When she opened her eyes a little later it was all the same: she was in a plane, she was kissing Buck Fire. Jesus Christ, I must have swooned like a maiden of old, she thought. In the mirror her eyes collided with the pilot's pig eyes, small and pale and lustful, watching. She was impaled by those eyes.

"I have to see you," Buck was saying into her neck. "You know I have to see you."

"I want to get out of this plane," Monica said.

Bitch, Buck thought. He could never tell about this one. Whenever he thought he had her figured, she would wreck everything. Skinny little bitch. He couldn't give up now, of course. The only thing to do now was to go through with it, sleep with her once so she wouldn't tell her husband that he had made a pass at her, then drop her flat on her ass.

Monica stared through her hair into the mirror. Pig, pig, she thought, I will never forget your eyes. "Is he going to land this goddamn plane or not?" she heard herself snarling at Buck Fire. A virago. She never spoke that way to anyone in real life.

Buck was moving in for the kill now, a hand inside her bra, a hand inside her pants, a hand tickling her ear. He had at least seven hands. Monica felt herself going liquid again. She stared at the playboy in the mirror. She did things with her own tongue. She was floating, flying absolutely free because it didn't matter finally what went on in the air with a pig and an actor.

The Cessna landed, bucked, and bounced across the field.

"When can I see you?" Buck yelled, thoroughly confused.

"I'll call you."

Buck gritted his perfect teeth. She would eventually pay for that one.

Monica said nothing at all on the way back to town. She stared out the window at the fleeting trees and houses and yards, drumming her fingernails on the little chrome cover of the ashtray on the arm rest in the back. After a while she became aware of what she was drumming. "Guess what this is," she said to Buck.

"The Lone Ranger thing," Buck said right away.

She left him sitting in the car, improbably orange. As soon as the playboy-pig pulled up at the Pardoe house she was out and running toward her car. "Wait a minute," Buck said, glowing and immediate, catching her at her car door. He was too much for her to realize all at once, she saw. She could only see certain sections of him at a time: his eyes, his boots, his mouth. What a weird fragmented person, pulling at her arm.

"Can you come to my apartment tomorrow at three?" Buck felt fairly confident. Nobody had failed to show up yet.

"I don't know," Monica said simply.

Buck stared into her brown eyes and decided that she wasn't bad looking after all.

"I don't know what I can do yet," she said. It was true. She got in and started her car.

FOURTEEN

BOB Pitt adjusted the stovepipe hat as he left his house. It didn't fit right. He felt like a fool. Then he had to take off the hat in order to get into his car, and he felt like more of a fool than ever. He looked up and down at the similar houses on each side of the street. They looked sleepy and blank, each with its carved W in the gray or yellow or green wood of its respective shutters. The W stood for Woodlawn Hills. It was a new and respectable suburb which was building its own swimming pool. How about that? The time was not so long ago when Bob Pitt could not have conceived of being part of a group which argued over oblong versus kidney-shaped. Bob Pitt grinned to himself as he eased into the car and looked up and down the street again to be sure that no one had seen. He would just have to get used to wearing this hat. He would have to wear it for the entire Sesquicentennial Week so he might as well like it. Besides, it was an honor. He was the head of the Bushy Brothers, something to be proud of. Yet he was filled with something very like claustrophobia at the thought. Lately his business had been growing rapidly:

Manny Goldman had called yesterday, and Pitt Associates would take over the books for his whole chain of drugstores next month. Of course Bob Pitt knew that he was a fine accountant. Yet he could not account for this recent surge in business; it seemed to have nothing to do with business itself.

Bob drove carefully toward town. This was to be the first Kangaroo Court. He was to be the judge. Anybody caught without either a beard or a mustache or a printed "shaving permit" from the Sesquicentennial headquarters would be fined five dollars and given an additional penalty. You could buy a shaving permit from the White Company for two dollars if you didn't like the idea of hair on your face, or if your wife objected, or if your beard came in red and you didn't like it, or for any other logical reason. Bob Pitt had bought one himself. He associated beards with low life, but he kept that to himself. Now he went over the list of proposed penalties suggested by the White Company; go home barefoot, stand on your head, whistle "Dixie" while eating a cracker. Bob had three crackers in the pocket of his frock coat. He hoped they would not be crushed. He also hoped that he would be able to assign the penalties in a light, joking manner. He was very nervous.

It occurred to Bob Pitt that he felt now as he had not felt on his wedding day: excited, eager, apprehensive. On his wedding day, when Frances came down the aisle, he had thought, "Well, here comes old Frances." At the time he had been shocked by his own reaction. He had known it was not the sort of thought to have at such a time. Maybe he was just a stick in the mud, as Sandy called him. No, that was not true. Perhaps it had been true at one time but it was not true any longer. Sandy had created, or coaxed into creation, some small, wild animal which prowled quietly about, even now, in Bob's mind. Right now the animal was tame, behaving, but it had the capacity to go

mad. Bob Pitt knew it and was scared of it, but he didn't
know what to do about it. He didn't know what it might
do, in what direction it might move. The animal had made
him go on and on to Sandy about Florida, for instance.
Bob Pitt in his right mind would never throw up all that he
had worked for and go to sit on some beach. He might
look like a fool in this getup, but he was not a complete
fool. A fool could never have gotten where he was today.

He parked in the "Reserved" section of the courthouse
lot and inside, by the water fountain, met his squad of
Keystone Kops. Each wore a blue Kop suit, given out by
Luther Fletcher. They had fake billy sticks and giant badges
and giant whistles. Even though they had been asked to be
Kops, they had had to rent their Kop suits. Bob assumed
that they had been picked to be Kops because they were a
naturally funny, outgoing bunch: Lomas Cartwright, the
junk and machine-parts dealer; Harry Dulaney, the Church
of Christ preacher who always winked when he shook
hands; Ronald Pettit, who owned the department store and
had just gotten a franchise and opened that new Bonanza
Steak House out on the highway; and Gene Bigelow, one
of the town characters. Gene was always in and out of the
courthouse and the Rondo, talking, and nobody had ever
seen him inside the Western Auto store which he supposedly owned. Gene was a big, heavy man with a long,
black mustache and a black crew cut, a combination which
made his face appear pear-shaped and moronic.

"Let's get a move on," Lomas said, "I got to get on."
Then without pausing for breath he said, "Want to see
how I'm going to hit them? I'm going to hit them just like
that. Blap!" With a great flourish, he brought his billy
stick down to within an inch of Bob Pitt's shoulder. Bob
winced. Lomas grinned. "Pretty good, huh?" he said. He
hit Bob jovially across the back, whack.

"O.K.," Bob said. He smiled a little too formally at

Lomas and the others. "I'm going to stay right out here on the courthouse steps. Every time you all find somebody guilty you just bring them on here and after we get six people we'll have a trial."

"I'm going to ring the bell," Lomas said suddenly, and was gone before anyone could stop him. The rest of them looked at each other uneasily and Bigelow said he guessed that was all right. None of them could think what the bell was used for, besides telling time. It wouldn't hurt to ring it once or twice.

Bigelow said "twicet," with a "t" on the end.

Then they heard it, ringing like crazy all over town. The Kops grinned at each other. "That goddamn Lomas," they said.

"Let's go get 'em."

"Who you want to get?"

"Let's get old Higgins himself; he's done shaved his off."

"He had it Wednesday."

"Well, he hasn't got it today, I'm telling you. Said a lady objected." Laughs.

"All right, you go over there, Bigelow, and get Higgins," Lomas said, back with them, panting. "Harry, you and Ronald go over in the Rondo and see what you can find. I'm going to ring that bell again and then I'll go on out in the street. I might go over to the Pure Oil station and get somebody from out of town."

Bob Pitt went out onto the courthouse steps, where a crowd had already gathered. It was five-thirty and all the stores were closing, and everybody all around the square had come outdoors to see about those bells. Luther Fletcher was out there in a Panama hat and he already had Bob's table set up: a glass of water and a giant rubber gavel with a sign on it that said "Judge's Gavel." Bob Pitt heard a lot of yelling and carrying on and everything inside him froze.

Luther put a black robe on him and he was still frozen. ''Look how serious he is,'' Luther yelled to the crowd. ''That's the *Judge*.'' They whistled and stomped, but Bob felt that the acclaim was not for him. Already, Luther was a great favorite in Speed.

It seemed to Bob that the crowd roared. Surely there were not enough of them to roar. Bob focused on the worn stone steps and endured his frozen, roaring wait and then, mercifully, the Keystone Kops were back with offenders. The Kangaroo Court itself went by in a blur, with the Keystone Kops knocking each other with their billy sticks, and pretending to fall down and stealing the show. Lomas Cartwright was the best Kop; he brought a real vision to his role, and remembered a number of vaudeville gags. Bob sentenced the mayor to go home barefooted and could not believe it when Higgins actually got down and took off his shoes. Lomas made a remark about ''toe jam'' which set the crowd to laughing; the mayor's sentence was a success. Bob made a bank teller eat crackers and whistle, with Lomas standing behind the teller and aping him. He made the Country Club golf pro pat his head and rub his stomach at the same time. Three of the Keystone Kops got into a mock fight and had to be dragged apart. The fourth, Harry Dulaney, winked and smiled gaily at his congregation members during the fight as if to say, ''See what a fun-loving fellow I am!''

The only bad moment in the whole Court came when Bigelow dragged up Lloyd Warner. Warner went along with the opening questions, such as ''Do you have just cause for shaving?'' but when Bob sentenced him to sing a song the lawyer wouldn't do it. ''Screw you,'' he said to Bob Pitt.

''Hold on there, brother,'' said Harry Dulaney, and Warner said, ''Screw you too,'' and then the whole crowd started talking at once. Lloyd Warner turned and walked back to his office, weaving a little, and everyone turned to watch him go but no one tried to stop him. "He's just drunk," said the members of the crowd to each other. Soon it was an anecdote, then a legend among the crowd. "Did you hear what he said?" they asked each other. "That man is *all* the time drunk."

The next defendant was a man from New York—a tourist on his way to Florida—who talked so funny that the crowd got to laughing uproariously again. "Oi am pleased to be a part of your celebration," said the man from New York. "Oi am delighted to take part." He sang "Yankee Doodle" and the Kops picked him up on their shoulders and then it was over and Bob Pitt was walking again to his car.

"Hey, Pitt," somebody yelled, and he turned back and there was Luther, out of breath. "I got to have that robe," he said.

"But if I'm going to wear it next Friday, too—" Bob dwindled off.

"Sorry, pal, but that's the house rules. I've got to make sure it fits the guy who plays the preacher in the pageant. Next Friday you get it back. I'm just doing my job."

Bob stood in the street and divested himself of the great, flapping black robe, since Luther evidently expected him to do it then and there. "Just doing my job," Bob heard again through the thick black folds as he pulled it over his head.

"So long," Luther said, and Bob heard himself sing out "So long," exactly like Luther as he walked to his car. It was a semi-Western voice, careless, and, it seemed to Bob, charming in the manner of singing cowboys. Bob felt giddy, and thought of calling Sandy to see if he could meet her someplace tomorrow. That would be foolhardy, he realized, since Johnny B. was usually home on Saturday afternoons, but Bob stopped the car at the Zippy Mart and went in the phone booth and dialed the number.

"Hello," she answered herself.

"What are you doing?" he asked, meaning to tell her all about the great success of the Kangaroo Court.

"I was just taking a bath," she said. "I haven't got a thing on."

Bob gulped. "They just had the Kangaroo Court," he said. "You'll have to come the next time. It was pretty funny." He knew that he wanted Sandy to see him in his robe and hat.

"I might," she said. "Do you know what I'm doing now?"

"Look, Sandy."

"Don't you want to know what I'm doing right now?"

"Sure, but."

"I'm drying my legs, Bob, and I'm kind of thinking about you."

"That's nice, Sandy, but where is Johnny B.?"

"He's in the den watching *Animal Kingdom* on TV."

"Oh, Christ, Sandy, what's the matter with you?"

"If you were here you could dry my back."

"I've got to go, Sandy."

"No guts, no glory," she said, and hung up.

Bob came slowly out of the phone booth, drained. The post-Court euphoria had evaporated. Nothing was ever enough for her, nothing. I'll show her, he thought. I'll . . . He didn't know what he would do. He would take her to Florida and comb the beach in his long black robe, scaring birds.

As he drove home, Frances Pitt was knocking on her daughter's door. It was a new thing, this having to knock. What was she doing in there that she had to close the door? She might be smoking drugs as in *Life* magazine. Frances knocked again.

"What *is* it, Mama?"

Frances took this as an invitation and opened the door. Theresa was not doing anything that ought to make her want to close the door, as far as Frances could see. She was not doing anything at all except listening to a terrible record. "I just wanna be with you," the record screeched.

"I don't see why you listen to all that rock 'n' roll; you'll ruin your ears."

"Mama, *nobody* says 'rock 'n' roll' any more," Theresa said.

"Now don't get hateful with me, miss. I just wanted to see if you want your supper now since your father is late."

"I'm not hungry."

This was new. During football season, when the Rockettes had practiced every day and performed at every game, Theresa ate three helpings of everything. And never gained a pound! thought Frances. She is as thin as a rail. Frances liked clean plates at her house.

"You've got to eat," Frances said. "You come on and get you some meat loaf."

"Mama, I'm not hungry right now." Theresa lay on the floor with her bare feet in the seat of the pink chair and stared at her mother, looming fat and unnecessary over her head.

"I've got some new potatoes." Frances could not conceive of anyone who did not want to eat new potatoes. Bob, of course, never knew what he was eating and it was a great disappointment to Frances. If she gave him fried chicken every night he'd never know the difference. Frances could kill herself rolling out little balls of dough between her finger and her thumb for cloverleaf rolls, and Bob wouldn't know the difference between them and light bread. Men are so stupid, Frances thought, and pursed her lips and shook her head. She thought this frequently, and often discussed it at length with her friend Mrs. Eustis on the phone. Men were to be catered to, and tolerated, and secretly maligned.

"I don't think I want any new potatoes," Theresa said upside down. "All I want to do is listen to this record if anybody would let me do it."

"I don't see why you want to stay up here with the door closed," Frances said, trying to think of something to say. She could feel her daughter slipping away from her, and she grabbed at something to hold on to.

"How you doing with the tickets?" she asked.

"I quit," Theresa said, spreading her long blond hair out on the floor. "I turned the rest of them back in." Now Theresa was tapping her feet on the arms of the chair.

"Quit what, honey?" Frances had become absorbed in her long blond daughter; there had never been a time when she had bony feet like that. Frances wore size 5½-C shoes.

"I quit the contest," Theresa said, with exactly as much expression as if she were saying, "Hello there." "I got tired of selling all those tickets. Besides, I get to lead the parade anyway."

"But everybody in the Altrusa Study Club has already gone and bought a ticket from *me*." Frances stood up very straight and put a hand on her stomach as if she had been shot. "They all thought they were buying them to get you some votes, and now you say you just up and quit, and what am I going to tell the Altrusa Study Club?"

"Tell them they can use their tickets to go to the show."

"Don't you smart-talk me, young lady, you're just lying there on the floor!" Frances began to speak in her accustomed, irrational spurts. "Get your feet out of that chair."

Theresa did, and Frances sat in it and began to fan herself with a pair of pantyhose that had been lying on the bed, although the day was far from hot. "Anybody that would put their feet in a chair! You'd think you'd been raised in a barn."

"Oh, come on, Mama." Theresa sat up and turned up the record player.

"I just don't know what I'm going to tell them! I just don't know what I'm going to say! I've never been so embarrassed in my life."

"You say that every time."

"Now I've had just about enough, Rose Theresa. You go on up to your room."

"We're in my room, Mama."

"They never would of bought them if it wasn't to get you a vote."

"Well, I'm sorry, Mama, I just don't have time to go around selling tickets all the time. I'm supposed to be in school if you remember. I've got exams coming up."

"But Sharon is in it. She didn't quit, did she?"

"No, she's still in it. She's got a lot of votes."

"One quitter. One quitter in the whole bunch and it's my own flesh and blood."

"You're always so dramatic."

Frances paused to suck air. "I-am-not-dramatic!" She gasped again. "I just don't know how I can face people, is all. I just don't know how I can walk down the street and hold up my head."

"It's not that much of a big deal, Mama. About thirty other people have quit so far."

"Don't you want to keep up with Sharon? I just don't see how you can let her get ahead, if she's your best friend and all."

"I hope she wins." Theresa lay back down, blank and impenetrable, upon the fluffy rug. Oh, well, she has a wonderful personality, Frances thought. But quitting made no sense to Frances, and lately she wasn't even sure about the personality.

"I was going to make you a white organdy dress with a hoop skirt and a little black ribbon around your neck. You would of looked so cute."

"Mama, I swear sometimes I think you think I'm a Barbie doll. I swear you do."

"Barbie doll," Frances said absently.

"The way you're all the time trying to dress me up."

"I won't even be able to go to the Piggly Wiggly," Frances said, flicking the light on the bedside table off and on. "I can't even hold up my head in church. If I see that Sandy I'm not going to say a word."

"Oh, come on, you make a federal case out of everything. Maybe I want more time to study, did you ever think about that?"

No, Frances never had. She didn't associate studying with Theresa. Studying was something Frances had had to do herself, and now here was Theresa taking it up! Theresa's face would probably break out next, and then she'd start getting fat. Frances wished she could keep her daughter as she was, suspended right in the middle of time, with her silver baton in the air. Frances remembered how Theresa had looked, marching across the field in the Susan Arch Finlay, and the way that she had said, "This is the happiest day of my life." Frances had thought it would be that way again when Theresa won the Queen Contest. Only it would be better, because everybody from Speed would be there and they would all see her wear that glittery crown. That had been the trouble with the Susan Arch Finlay: there wasn't anybody there from Speed to see it except herself and Sandy, and Lord knows if you counted Sandy it would be just like counting a copperhead. But

Theresa! It ought to be the most important thing in the world to her, to be the Sesquicentennial Queen. Not to mention all the prizes she would have won. Frances felt her daughter slipping, slipping away.

"I-just-don't-see-how-you-can-do-this-to-me!" Frances said.

"Please, Mama, I'm trying to listen to the record." Theresa's voice was getting high and thin.

"Well, you come on down and eat."

"Goddamn it, Mama, I'm not *hungry!*" Theresa sat up straight and yelled. Frances just stared at her. "My daughter and me don't have any generation gap," she had told the Altrusa Study Club only weeks ago. "We always see eye to eye." Now Theresa was taking the Lord's name in vain. When Frances had been a child, she had tried to do everything she could to be good. That was her sole ambition, to be good, and her relatives often said of her, "She is as good as gold." Of Sandy they had said, "She is such a card." But Frances knew that good was better. Was it possible that Theresa did not know? Who would take the Lord's name in vain?

"Your-father-will-speak-to-you." Frances stalked out of the room. What was Theresa trying to do to her? Theresa lay back down on the floor, long and blond and catlike, stretching. She acts exactly like a cat, Frances thought— and somehow it made her furious.

"Hello, honey," said Bob Pitt. "The Kangaroo Court went fine. You'll have to come next time. There was this man from New York, you should have heard him." He walked through the house to the kitchen and Frances followed, panting.

"You won't believe it," she wailed. "After I sold all those tickets you won't believe what she's done to me!"

"Who?" Bob whirled around rather quickly in the hall.

"Theresa, my own daughter Theresa. She's quit the

contest!'' Frances leaned back against the newel post for support.

Bob Pitt surveyed his wife. She had a funny, glazed look about her, as if she had been running. She wore an aqua knit dress with a pleated skirt and a low hip belt of aqua knit strips held together by tortoiseshell rings. It was not exactly becoming.

"Well, maybe she got tired of it," Bob said. "From what I hear, it's a hell of a lot of work."

"She just up and *quit!*" Bob did not seem to grasp the significance of it.

"Um," he said, and picked up the mail and went to sit in the kitchen.

Later, while they ate, Frances stood in the utility room and ironed with her hissing steam iron. She left the door open so that they could all see her work. Bobby Joe ate everything in sight. Theresa picked moodily at her food, and Bob methodically cleaned his plate by eating one thing at a time.

"Why don't you come on and eat, Mama?" Theresa said, but Frances went on ironing. When they were through Theresa rose and took her father's plate, but Frances rushed back into the kitchen and took it from her and said, "Oh no, *I'll* do the dishes because I can just do them so much quicker!" and Theresa gave her a look and left the room.

After they had all gone from the kitchen, Frances fixed herself a plate and went into the utility room to eat it so she wouldn't get caught. The potatoes were kind of sticky, being cold, but everything else was fine. Then Frances cleaned up the kitchen and went back to her ironing. She didn't have to do it—there was no rush about the ironing— but she was generally mad at them all and when she was mad there was nothing she liked better than ironing. You could pretend everybody was in their clothes.

At about eight o'clock, Bob stuck his head around the

door. "Why don't you leave that and come on in here and watch some TV? There's a movie coming on in a minute." It made him feel bad to see her iron.

"Oh no!" Frances exclaimed. "This won't take but a minute." She smiled sweetly, putting a hand on the small of her back as if it hurt. "I don't mind a bit," she said.

FIFTEEN

SOMETIMES when Miss Iona Flowers went to bed at night in the upstairs bedroom of her father's house she would get what her mother had called the "whirlies" and she would lie still in bed while the whole world rushed by in widening circles until she put one foot on the floor to slow it down. She knew where she was, and she knew every single thing in that whole house by heart, the shape and feel of it and its age and who had owned it and where it came from, but even this knowledge did not stop the whirling once it had begun. It did not help if she opened her eyes or even if she turned on the light. She still had to put one foot on the floor to make it stop.

Sometimes this happened in the daytime too. Or right after supper when she sat by herself in the front room, alone. She would begin to move quite slowly, tracing a perfect circle in space, picking up momentum, until she was moving so fast that she was barely able to get her tiny foot from the stool to the floor to make it stop. She hated the whirling in one sense: a lady must always retain a grasp on her situation. But in another sense there was something pleasant and even restful about it. No decisions, no thoughts, just the furious whirling, which was always accomplished without a single sound. After she had brought herself to stop it—which seemed to take longer each time— Miss Iona would remain strangely strung out in time, disoriented. More often than not, her mind went back to her childhood, which now seemed to have taken place in a golden, greenish mist with iridescent overtones.

At other times her childhood seemed quite theatrical in retrospect, as if it were a stage set and she, little Iona, the star. Miss Iona sat now in the front parlor after dining alone on red beans and rice and cornbread, left by the maid, and watched the play. She watched it, yet she was in it too. It was quite odd.

Out in front of her house was a bush named baby's breath. The flowers were round, white, and very small; they crowded together on the brittle branches, thousands of them with no leaves at all, bunched together yet still somehow transparent, pure white. It looked like a cloud in the yard. The baby's breath was the only bush that you could see through. It bloomed for two weeks every year in early April, along with the azaleas. Big azaleas, Pride of Mobile variety, were planted on either side of the baby's breath, framing it in scarlet and anchoring it to earth. The rest of the yard was full of camellias: Dr. Tinsley's Pink, September Morn, Pink Perfection, every variety you could name. There was no end to the camellias, but the baby's breath was the only bush of its kind in the yard.

"The verbena needs thinning out, Lester." Little Iona would hear her mother's voice and turn to see her, tall glass in hand, out gardening in the way that she always gardened; Mrs. Flowers wore high white heels and a large-brimmed floppy hat and carried spotless green-and-white-striped gardening gloves ordered by mail from a department store in New York. Mrs. Flowers never actually wore the gloves but carried them, dangling, from one hand. They were snapped together with a concealed snap. Mrs. Flowers pointed things out to Lester, wiggling her pale finger with its fragile white nail.

"Cut me some pinks for the table," she would say, or "Pull up those old glads, I'm tired of them."

Mrs. Flowers' heels made small, round depressions in the green grass as she stepped daintily, carefully around the immaculate yard with the exaggerated care of the alcoholic. She seemed to waver slightly when the wind came up. She had been a Nashville girl and she seemed like an exotic flower herself, transplanted.

And now Miss Iona could remember her mother only through that haze, that pastel mist associated with the going-down of the sun (for her mother never ventured outdoors until the cool) and her mother seemed to her to be forever wobbling about the earth, pointing, as changeable and as brilliant as the flowers they had had then, as delicate as the baby's breath. It seemed to Miss Iona that her mother's right hand had been permanently fixed, rounded in the shape of a glass, whether she carried a glass or not—but this was nonsense, of course. Little Iona was only eight when her mother died, so these memories were unreliable.

Still she did remember the way her mother smelled, a hot soft smell like late afternoon. She clearly remembered her mother correcting her, saying, "We never say 'cut the grass.' We always say 'mow the lawn.' " Her mother had corrected her too, when she had asked a question about menstruation, which an older cousin had mentioned. "Why, you nasty child," her mother had said, shocked, her dropping eyelids suddenly flung wide open over those deep blue eyes, then veiling the eyes again. "There is a lot of blood," she had said abruptly, "and it is horrible."

"You're my little baby doll," her mother had often told

her, lifting her up, pronouncing each word distinctly. Sometimes she dropped her. Miss Iona's mother tied her long curls back with ribbons and said, "You are the child of my heart." Before her death there had been several indelible scenes, with little Iona's mother intoxicated in her dressing gown at the top of the stairs, tottering toward the chandelier, or gently screaming away in her bedroom behind the big closed door at the private nurse who had come there in the end. After her death, little Iona had never cried; and it was only recently, in her old age, that she had thought of her mother at all.

At the age of eight, little Iona had ceased to be a child. She had become a small lady. She was a small *perfect* lady, and she had—perhaps unconsciously—rid herself of all the traits which would serve to make such a small lady less than perfect. She detested blood and violence and loud voices and intoxicating spirits, and had never trafficked in any of these. She had no pets. From her father, a poet much manqué, she learned to love books and elocution and such things as "Thanatopsis," read aloud. She took piano lessons for six years despite a singular lack of talent. During those six years, she practiced for one hour every day. She worshiped her father, Franklin Flowers, yet she could not bear him—or anyone else—to touch her, and she took a great many baths every day in the summer's heat.

She whirled, remembering: one summer night, out catching lightning bugs, she had gone into the old garage at the back of the property and there had seen, stretched out full length on the filthy floor, two Negroes passionately kissing. Once she and her father had traveled down the river from Cincinnati to New Orleans on the luxurious *Delta Queen*. When they boarded the ship, she wore a blue and white polka-dotted dress. And she remembered an endless succession of afternoons with her father on the screen porch, sipping iced tea with lemon and mint.

But Miss Iona could not remember exactly when she had received her "call" or when her mission had begun. There had been nothing as outstanding as that Biblical burning bush, a fact which she often lamented. It would be nice to have something like that to look back upon. But no, it had been a gradual "call." Once she had taken a trip by bus to visit a second cousin in Little Rock, Arkansas, and the mountains along the way had seemed to hold some terrible, lovely importance although she could not at that time have said what it was. As she stood in line to leave the bus, she had seen her own white face in the driver's rear-view mirror and she had spoken aloud: "You are the child of my heart, the child of my heart; you are the child of my heart." People stared. It was an exalted, mysterious moment.

She began writing poems at the age of twelve and soon she was helping her father, and by the time she was twenty-five things had begun to coalesce. The outlines of the mission could be glimpsed. As Miss Iona became more and more dedicated to her father and his craft, the world around her grew ever more modern and sordid. Girls of her childhood married fat grocers with whom they presumably had sexual intercourse. Overnight they became gross, gaudy women with hard smiles, surrounded by hordes of savage children. The girl who had once been little Iona's bridesmaid in the annual Tom Thumb Wedding at Mrs. Grayson's School had since been twice divorced. Others had died. Now they were all dying or going to live with their children, and as far as Miss Iona could see, their grandchildren were even worse than their own children had been. Each generation seemed to shed a bit of the grandeur that made man "a little less than the angels," as it were. Miss Iona had hardened her heart and continued her mission.

Admittedly, it was difficult. After her father's death she was truly "alone in the world," as she often remarked to herself. There was no one with whom to share a passing thought or a poetic insight, no one with whom to take counsel. Miss Iona walked a lonely road. Oh, there had been advances, it was true. Many persons, both male and female, had tried to befriend her. For a while she had belonged to a women's book group. And, when she was in her forties, a male biology teacher at the high school had repeatedly asked her for dinner dates! But he was a foreigner, from out of town, and no one even knew who his people were. Of course it was out of the question. Even had that not been so, Miss Iona doubted very much that she could have forced herself to *sortir* with a man who daily dissected small green frogs. Other opportunities for social life had come her way, too, but she had rejected them all.

There had always been the First Episcopal Church, but Miss Iona had suffered a severe disaffection with the church, which dated from around her thirtieth year. If there had been a Catholic Church in Speed, perhaps she would have gone to it. Once she had seen the Pope on television. She had read enough to know that she would be drawn to the vestments and incense and chanting, and to the delightful mysteries of the confessional box. But the realities of religious life in Speed were a far cry, to put it mildly, from the pageantry of Rome. The old minister, Mr. Blake, had died when Miss Iona was thirty. And a new minister had come to town with a crew cut and a leaning toward informality. He quickly organized church barbecues and formed a bowling league. He might as well have been a Baptist! Once Miss Iona met him downtown in plaid Bermuda shorts and that was the last straw; she never darkened the door again. Not that she missed it. To Miss Iona, religion was merely a form of Art, and why bother with minor forms in the first place when one can catch it at the source so to speak, when one is in direct contact with Art itself?

Increasingly, as the outlines of the mission were made clear to her, Miss Iona withdrew from the world of man. In solitude lay splendor, for only in the quiet could the small still voices tell her best how to translate Art into the world. The nature of her mission was such, of course, that it required her to deal with real people (such as the horrid majorettes and their equally horrid mothers) every day, but this was a cross which she had long ago become resigned to bearing with a martyr's grace. One could deal with people, yet keep them abstract. Miss Iona regarded people as clay. They existed to be molded, to be awakened through Art into a finer, higher form. Most people were nothing; Art was all. Paradoxically, Miss Iona was strengthened by opposition. The sillier and more bourgeois the population grew, the greater became the surge and swell of inspiration in Miss Iona's breast. She fairly fed on ugliness, crassness, and her own self-imposed loneliness, turning them into Art. It was becoming increasingly hard these days for Miss Iona to distinguish between Art, Beauty, and Truth—if, indeed, any such distinction must be made! Very often of late, Miss Iona had felt that she was approaching some sort of breakthrough, a unique synthesis in which the hidden natures of life, Art, Truth, and Beauty would be revealed to her in a fairly blinding revelation of some sort. It was to be a step forward in human consciousness.

Anticipating it—a great deal of color and pageantry seemed to be involved with the mere idea of it—Miss Iona now allowed herself to whirl for an unknown length of time, in great prophetic swoops and ellipses, before finally, reluctantly, placing her small foot again upon the stool. The room rocked and righted itself: her parlor, the parlor of her youth and age, with the remains of her supper sitting patiently on a dropleaf table near the door. Red beans and rice? Had that been tonight? It seemed years and years ago. Miss Iona tidied up and then reseated herself in the Queen Anne chair. The antique lamp on the desk glowed faintly pink through it is fluted shade. The grandfather clock chimed ten and in its upper glass panel the moon showed its happy face. The parlor was perfectly still, so still that Miss Iona could hear the ticking of the clock. She was tempted to succumb to the whirling again, but something warned her against this course. She admired instead her parlor, a room of great symmetry and charm.

Outside in the night, Miss Iona heard the raucous noises of the street, car horns and teenage laughter. "Things are coming to a pretty pass!" she thought mechanically, yet something in the tone of the indistinct voices alarmed her. It was a new excitement, akin to lust. It troubled Miss Iona, even as closed off as she was behind her shutters and Venetian blinds. It was an ambience, if you will, which seemed to be sweeping Speed as the plans for the Sesquicentennial progressed. It was both exhilarating and menacing. She continued to have high hopes for the Sesquicentennial, viewing it as a tiny Renaissance in this new dark age. The mood of the town, whatever it might be, would find its release therein. And the day of synthesis, of revelation, approached. Who can tell the day or the hour, *après tout?* Miss Iona turned off the light, checked the doors and went carefully upstairs. She made her toilet, and then lay down precisely in the middle of her mother's canopied cherry bed.

SIXTEEN

*R*UTHIE was embarrassed to be seen with Ron-the-Mouth. He was so weird in the first place, and then he was so short. But mainly he was weird. Ruthie had never been out with anyone like him before and most of the time she wasn't sure she liked it. He did such wild things all the time, not like anybody else in Speed. One day he asked her to go out to lunch (which was weird enough all by itself; nobody that Ruthie knew ever took anybody out to *lunch*, for God's sake) and then when she got in the car he drove right out on the Interstate and she said, "Just a minute, buddy, where do you think you're going?" and Ron-the-Mouth said Brennan's. "Where the hell is that?" Ruthie said.

"New Orleans, baby; you're dumb as shit."

It was a six-hour drive to New Orleans and they didn't get back until the next morning and Ruthie almost lost her job at the Peabody Room when she didn't show and nobody knew where she was. New Orleans! How about that? They ate oysters fixed some way in their shells in a little French-looking place, with a candle and wrought-iron chairs.

Still, Ruthie could never figure out what she thought of him. Sometimes when she looked at him she thought he was real cute, a little bitty man-doll. At other times she was revolted, as if he were a freak inside a bottle at a fair. And he talked so much! He absolutely never shut up, and this made Ruthie mad as hell because, before, she was always the one who did the talking. Now she had to fight like a dog to get a word in sideways. Sometimes she couldn't shut him up when he wasn't even there, which is why she had her finger (guess which one?) in such an aluminum splint. She was driving over to the Peabody Room one night, late as usual, when here he came on the radio, babbling away. She almost wrecked four times getting to the Peabody Room, she was so mad. But still she couldn't turn him off. Something kept her from switching that lighted dial. Then when she got to work, after her customary late entrance and the dirty look from Mr. Bray, she went into the coatroom to hang up her coat and who do you think was on the Muzak, coming straight out of the wall? Ron-the-Mouth, saying, "Yeah, baby, this is Ron the one and only genuine inflatable kissable MOUTH OF THE SOUTH, sweethearts, spinning the wax until midnight for your listening pleasure. This one goes out to Rhoda and Tommy, Lyle and you know who, and to Suzy with the friendly little hands. My, my. I didn't make that up, folks. That's what it says right here. If you're not doing anything Saturday, Suzy . . . O.K., Diana, hit it!" Diana Ross and the Supremes came on. Ruthie went crazy. "Shut up, shut up, shut up," she muttered.

She threw her coat down on a chair and kicked the chair, scuffing her white go-go boots. Then she hit the fancy plate grillwork where the Muzak came out of the paneled wall. She hit it several times with her fist, not even making a dent in the grillwork, or the Supremes, or Ron-the-Mouth, who came right on with the weather when the Supremes were finished. The only effect Ruthie's attack had on anything, in fact, was her finger. She jammed the joint and it swelled up as big as a plum, but she had to be the hostess anyway and she kept it in a glass of ice and Seven-Up all night, to be able to stand the pain. "Fine hostess," Mr. Bray said sarcastically. After work she went to the emergency room of the hospital and they strapped it up in a little aluminum fence, which meant that she would be shooting everybody a permanent bird for two weeks.

But she would get the best of him yet. Meanwhile, she kept one of several little velvet ribbons tied on the cast, to match whatever outfit she wore. Since she was still ahead, she could afford to be frivolous about the finger and wear all the ribbons she liked. She still hadn't slept with him and she wasn't about to until he started treating her right (which meant until he started letting her run the show). It was really funny. Ruthie couldn't even count all the men she had slept with, and she knew it, and *he* knew it too. He wanted it real bad, but little Ruthie wasn't about to give in. Not yet and maybe never. She didn't know why she felt that way about Ron-the-Mouth, where she had picked up these goddamn *scruples*, since she usually just went ahead and did it on the first date. First dates were a lot of crap, otherwise. But Ron-the-Mouth would have to wait, and Ruthie would make him suffer, or pay, or both. Something about him made her so mad.

They sat in his apartment, drinking bloody marys on a Sunday afternoon. Ron-the-Mouth always lured her up there with promises of exotic drinks and then tried to make her. Every time he asked her to go for a ride, that's how it ended up.

"I don't know why I bother to come up here," Ruthie said idly, flicking ashes into a blue glass ashtray.

"You love me," said Ron-the-Mouth. He was wearing some kind of a short-sleeved Banlon turtleneck and looked perfectly awful. The pouch of fat beneath his alligator belt made him look older and like he was three months gone. "You can't stay away. You're just waiting, hoping that I'll try to rape you. Every morning you get up and think, maybe this will be the big day."

"You couldn't rape me if you tried," Ruthie snorted, exhaling twin jets of blue smoke. "It's physically impossible to rape somebody that doesn't want to get raped. I read that in *Family Weekly*."

"You intellectual, you," he said. He grinned at her. "You want it."

"I do not."

"Sure you do."

"Up yours." Ruthie was getting annoyed at him sitting there so smug on the end of the couch with his little fat pot sticking out. Why did he talk so much? Who did he think he was, anyway?"

"I'd like to."

"Oh shit." Ruthie walked over to the window and looked out. It was a warm, still afternoon. It was a good afternoon and a good bloody mary and Ruthie could not figure out how she had come to share the whole thing with such a creep. "I wish I was someplace else," she said.

"Liar," said Ron. He walked up behind her and put his arms around her. He pawed at her. Like a dog, thought Ruthie, and was furious at the way she suddenly began to feel. He was talking in her ear the whole time, a long string of stuff she didn't even bother to listen to. Before she knew it, he had removed her blouse and her bra, both, and was fiddling around with the stretch waistband of her slacks.

"You're a quick little old thing, aren't you?" she said.

"The fastest as well as the best." His eyes were sparkling and he looked really amused, not passionate and stupid the way they usually got at this stage. He took a tube of Chap Stick from his pocket and began rubbing it into her nipples.

"Just what the hell do you think you're doing?" Ruthie said.

"I wouldn't want you to get chapped."

Exasperated, Ruthie walked back to the couch and sat in the most seductive position she could think of. She was resolved to just sit there, and not let him make a move. It was bound to drive him crazy. "I'd like another bloody mary," she said sweetly.

"Sure, baby." Ron got her glass and fixed her drink, acting exactly like she was wearing a coat. He told her a long funny story about a friend of his who got a speeding ticket. Ruthie asked him about his family and he said he had a sister and a mother and a father who lived in Panama City, Florida. "What is this, a talk show?" he asked. "I'd like to have a talk show sometime. I mentioned it to the station manager and he said he'd think about it but I couldn't really get into anything around here. When I split, I'll have a talk show."

By this time, Ruthie was really mad. She put one of her breasts on a pillow. "What's the matter with you?" she said. "You must be a homosexual."

Then Ron came over and put his famous mouth all over her, and during a break he said, "Ten thousand girls are dying for it and look who gets it, the queen of the Peabody Room."

"Don't be ugly," Ruthie said. She was enjoying herself.

"I'm not ugly," Ron said. "Ugliness is in the eye of the beholder."

"What are you talking about? Do you mean you think I'm ugly or something?" Ruthie drew back.

"Of course not, you're not ugly, it was a joke."

"You probably think crutches are funny; that's your kind of joke."

"Come on, Ruthie."

"Come on yourself."

"Where are you going?"

"I've got to go now, Ron. I've got a date. Besides, you're out of bloody marys."

"I always knew you were the kind of girl who leaves when the bloody marys run out." Ron was grinning.

"Don't smile at me, you baboon. You couldn't keep me here if you tried."

"I'm not about to try, baby. You outweigh me by about twenty pounds."

"Oh, that's it. You've had it now." Ruthie put her bra and her blouse back on, yanking at everything.

"Your grandmother told me you had a terrible temper."

"She did, huh? What else did she tell you?"

"She told me a lot."

"What? What else?"

"She said if I had any sense I'd get out while the getting was good." Ron was still grinning. "She said you were nothing but trouble."

"She watches too much TV. She thinks she has to act like the Beverly Hillbillies all the time." Ruthie picked up her bag. "Come on, Tiny Tim," she said.

As the courtship progressed—if that was the word for it—Ron became more and more determined to get her if it took weeks or months or years. Then he'd drop her. But he had to get her first. When he went up to her in the Rondo, that's all he was after—and now, after three weeks, he had barely gotten a whiff of it. It was incredible. He had already broken most of the stud records that he had ever heard of, and it infuriated him that this one was taking so long. Who was she? Nobody, a waitress. Who was she to have such long red hair and such a nice, tight butt? But mouth—what a lip on that woman. She was the first one Ron had ever met who could keep right up with him. Ron didn't *like* her at all, he decided. Too big and too much lip. He would drop her any day, but now it was a matter of pride. He wanted a piece of it first. Ron was smart and he knew it. He knew, too, the reason he had such success with women: he could always make them laugh. Ron had found out a long time ago that a woman will forgive you, or give you, anything if you can make her laugh. But with Ruthie his tactics were useless. He kept her laughing to no avail. Nothing worked. He had never met such a girl in his life. He gave her all his lines one by one. Even the "I'm afraid I'm a homosexual, help me" line had failed. Even the one about the war experience in Vietnam.

Ruthie became an obsession. But Ron didn't let her know it, of course. That would be fatal. The only chance he had was to act like it didn't really matter to him one way or the other. Which it didn't, of course! Then she might come around. But if she knew how bad he wanted it, she would never give in. Her grandmother was right; Ruthie was one of the worst people he had ever met. He was wasting his time. He liked them big and stupid and couldn't—thinking back—figure out how he had run into this in the first place. It was the last thing he needed when he was fixing to set Atlanta on fire. He didn't need any smart women to come around complicating his life.

Still, as the days passed, Ron found that he and Ruthie were spending all their free time together. She didn't seem to like it any better than he did, and he couldn't figure out why he even bothered.

"I must be a masochist," he told her one day.

"What's that?"

"It means I eat necks," he said, "thousands and thousands of necks." He bit Ruthie's neck.

"You cut it out," she said. "I'll kill you if you make a hickey on me. I'm going to wear this low-cut dress to work."

Ron grew more determined and devious. Ruthie grew sassier, and adopted a few of his own worst habits to boot. She could be as weird as the next one, she decided. Nobody was going to get *her* down (ha, ha, joke). For his birthday, Ruthie gave Ron a live piranha. She ordered it by phone from a Mobile pet shop and had it delivered to him by REA Express, COD.

SEVENTEEN

MANLY Neighbors cleared his desk except for the letter. Working methodically, he paid bills, wrote headlines, answered two personal letters, ordered a new type face from a Washington firm. Miss Iona left, Susan left, and finally Will left, shuffling down the street. Will is almost a caricature of himself, Manly thought. Will is almost embarrassing. Manly worked on until Will had whistled away and he could tell by the feel of the air that he was alone in the office. He took off his tie and his shoes and padded back to the Coke machine and got a Coke. He sat down at his desk and stared at the smudged white envelope before him. Then he got up again and went over to sit on the windowsill. He couldn't get comfortable. He couldn't keep still. And he had already taken off all the clothes that a man in his position could reasonably take off. Manly sighed and shifted on the ledge, annoyed. This was usually his thinking hour. Usually, there was about this time of day a mellowness, an air of reason and quiet, which he liked to imagine that only a very few men enjoy today. When the people left the building, the building itself took on—or perhaps reverted to an older—personality. It went from businesslike impartiality to an air of character, where lofty thoughts were quite in place. "That's the dumbest thing I ever heard of," Monica had said, laughing, when he told her. "You know perfectly well what this building used to be, Manly. A whorehouse!"

"A public house, Monica," Manly had corrected her. "An inn."

"What's the difference? I wonder if your fine little Lady Iona knows that? She's worked in a whorehouse for how many years is it now?"

"She probably knows it, Monica." Somebody was always putting him in the position of defending Miss Iona, which he disliked to do.

"Well, if she knows it I bet she's repressed it," Monica said. "You'd never get her to admit it."

"Oh come on," Manly had said wearily. He never could handle women.

Manly crossed over to his desk and read the letter again. It was clear enough. The question was, what to do about it? In an uneven, downward-slanting scrawl, the note was penciled on cheap ruled paper.

DEAR EDITOR,
   THIS SESQUISENTENIAL AND PAGENT IS JUST A MOCKERY AND IT HAS GOT TO STOP OR A LOT WILL BE HURT AND BLOOD WILL FLOW AGAIN.

                                        THE AVENGER

Manly ran a hand through his short, shaggy hair. Now what the hell? It was clear enough, but it was odd. A lot of things about it were incongruous. The misspellings indicated that an uneducated person was the author. On the other hand, the word "mockery" implied a finer vocabulary. You don't pick up "mockery," Manly reflected, unless you have read a few books. Manly decided that "sesquicentennial" and "pageant" had been deliberately misspelled to throw him off the track. The writer had to have at least a high school education or he wouldn't have used "mockery." The word that really bothered Manly was "again." "Blood will flow again." What could that refer to? The Civil War, indicating that the writer was black? Too easy. Manly felt that he was *supposed* to think that. What he really felt was that the writer was white, a mischief maker, nothing more. A crank. Manly got weird letters to the editor all the time, but not threats. True cranks had been few in the years that Manly had edited this paper, but that didn't mean they didn't exist. There were bound to be cranks.

Back to the original question: what to do about it? Manly got up from his desk and pulled *Barlett's Quotations* from the top shelf of the bookshelf, and got the pack of Winstons stuck behind it. He had quit smoking officially, but he allowed himself one or two during his thinking hour. He lit the cigarette, inhaled, and leaned back in his swivel chair, feeling slightly dizzy. Now. The crank obviously expected to have his letter printed in the "Letters to the Editor" section of the paper. He would be disappointed. Manly would print Mrs. B. Y. Yates' annual letter on the beauties of spring, Bill Eubanks' perorations on communism, and the Rev. Tilden Parker on the evils of drink, but there was simply no point in printing a letter like this. There was a point at which editorial responsibility and freedom of the press collided, and Manly thought this was the point. Printing the note would only encourage the crank. Manly stared through smoke at the note on his desk. It was nothing, a joke, yet he felt there was something symptomatic about it. He could not consider it funny. It underlined something indefinable which had been bothering him about this whole Sesquicentennial business ever since the White Company had arrived on the scene.

Manly looked at his watch. Nearly six, but Monica was at practice. She was a squaw in the second act. Whatever that meant. Manly took off his socks, thinking back. When he had come back here four years ago, everyone had thought he was crazy and had told him so. Some of his graduate-school colleagues had gone on to become editorial assistants and reporters on the Washington *Star*, the *New York Times*, *Newsweek*, etc. Others had gone into publishing or advertising and some had gone into television news departments, at astonishingly high salaries. Nobody understood why Manly, who had done fairly well in school and had been well liked, had rejected all job offers and had bought his home-town newspaper, which no one had ever heard of. "Mental suicide," his roommate had said at the time. Yet that same roommate was now on his second wife and his fourth or fifth job and, because of alimony, having a hell of a time even making ends meet in New York. He wrote Manly a long, wry letter every Christmas. But he had recently sold a freelance article to *Atlantic*, and people knew his name.

You couldn't pay me to trade with that guy, Manly thought. Manly put his feet up on the desk and looked at them. They were big white feet with tufts of hair on the toes. Manly wondered what Monica thought of his feet. Monica herself had small, thin feet with prominent white bones. Dainty feet. Monica was dainty; sometimes it seemed to Manly that she was so fragile he wondered that she could live with him at all. Monica seemed beautiful and mysterious to Manly. He loved her, and he would tell anybody that, but he didn't understand her (and he wouldn't tell you that). Women were not to be understood anyway. They were to be reverenced and protected. For the first time, Manly wondered what Monica thought of Speed. She always seemed happy, busy. She was always rushing off. But why did she want to "wait" for children? They had waited longer already than anyone else they knew. Manly frowned and bit his yellow pencil. Was Monica altogether happy with him, with Speed? It was fantastic that he could even entertain the thought that she might not be satisfied. She seemed happy, but sometimes she got a distant look in her eye and, no matter what he said, she didn't hear him. Daydreaming. Manly smiled. But, on the other hand, what did she have to daydream about? What could she be thinking of that was not real and present and accounted for?

Manly was a satisfied man. He knew what he was doing when he bought the Speed *Messenger*. He was not brilliant, and he knew it. He didn't even consider himself particularly smart. He wanted a job that would give him plenty of time on the side for the things he liked best— golf and hunting and fishing. He didn't want to work for somebody else. He was not very ambitious. What he wanted was a solid, respectable life for himself and Monica, and, hopefully, their children. Others of his classmates who, like Manly, had taken the less glamorous jobs, had said that these jobs would give them time to "write." Manly had never fooled himself on that one. He enjoyed journalism, but he wasn't about to write a book. What would he write it about?

He chuckled. This was all you could want: your own office, your own solid-oak desk, a good living, a nice town, a pretty wife, good friends. Yet something in this catalogue rankled. It was that same vague worry he had felt when he thought about Monica's daydreams.

Now Manly was a man who believed in doing good. That is, he believed that good could be done. To this end he had devoted a great deal of effort and time. Manly believed that people are basically good, and that all things will work out for the best if people help each other. Until recently, Speed had seemed the ideal place for him to put his philosophy into practice. Manly, coming back to the town after six years, appreciated it as some of its residents perhaps did not. It seemed innocent and cheerful to him. It was at least ten years behind the times. Manly saw its average citizen as a man of good will with a color TV and a boat, who would do anything to help a buddy out. Each year Speed had a townwide Christmas lighting contest, a Fourth of July barbecue, and several parades. The football team was supported. Speed was a town with values, and values were important to Manly.

He wondered if Monica saw it as he did, if she liked it as much and for the same reasons. But there he went again—wondering about Monica. Manly was a man who never, as a rule, wondered about anything. Hell. It was just the Sesquicentennial getting him down. They would all be worn out when it was over with. Also, he had to face the fact that Speed was growing up, and he was unprepared for it. He had pushed it, of course. He was head of the industrial committee which had attracted four new industries so far to town. You had to be progressive. He had written editorials concerning the schools and the sewers and other municipal considerations. He was especially proud of several editorials which had urged people to keep calm, to go along with integration. You had to be progressive. But this Sesquicentenial, with its White Company, was going a bit too far. Oh, he had pushed the White Company too, in the beginning. He would continue to support it. But he didn't like what it was doing to the town.

It seemed to Manly that there was something feverish

and unwholesome about the whole thing. It was undeniably commercial, which he found, in a way, offensive. It was *supposed* to be commercial, but still—Manly had an anything-might-happen feeling. Walking back from the Rondo only this morning, Manly had felt exactly the way he had felt years before in Mexico, when he had strolled through a village square the day before a fiesta was to begin. There was a sense of exhilaration, not altogether healthy.

But of course he was exaggerating. A lot of petty things will build up like this, to bug you. Manly looked out the window again. The square was empty now except for an occasional car and the old men who stood on the corner until total darkness fell. Soon the sidewalks would fill again with people bound for the Bijou's seven o'clock show. Manly was damned if he could smell the paper mill.

That was another thing that bugged him. The biology department at the junior college was raising hell about the paper mill, calling Manly, sending him copies of particulate studies, inundating him with percentages and frightening projections. They frequently sent him booklets and graphs. Manly liked to give everybody equal space, but those biologists would not leave him alone. Manly was of the opinion that Speed was still in no position to be picky; they ought to be thankful for all the jobs they could get. There would be plenty of time for particulate studies later. It was all so simple. Yet Manly's own opinion left him slightly uneasy, the same way he felt when he condemned the student revolutionaries elsewhere in the country. He was not so much older than they; and actually he wished all young people well. Manly could not see what all the fuss was about.

He felt the same way about Lloyd Warner's housing suit. Manly was running the smallest story possible on it, three inches of type on page three, stating the minimum facts.

"I don't see any sense in getting everybody all worked up, Lloyd," he had told Warner on the phone, when Warner had volunteered more information.

"I don't either, I'm telling you. But they've got all kinds of stories going around. One guy told me seriously today that outside Communist agitators were behind the whole thing. So I figure you'd better put it all down, explaining what this Afro-American Society is and everything, to relieve everybody's mind. I mean it's just a standard suit, you know that. I can come on over there any time after three."

"Thank you, Lloyd," Manly had said, "but I guess we'll just go with what we've got. I hate to get in a big thing."

Then Lloyd had called him several names, to Manly's great surprise. One of the names was "selfish bastard," which didn't even make sense. Anybody who knew Manly knew he wasn't selfish. Manly sighed. It was all the *demands* that everyone was making, which really got him down. You were either for them or you were against them. Everyone kept forcing you to take a stand. Manly wanted to avoid this polarization altogether, wanted to be left alone to enjoy his life. That was why he had returned to Speed in the first place. And now people were turning unreasonable on him, and the old familiar certainty eluded him. He felt as he had felt once in college when he had attended a Jewish wedding with one of his friends: a little itchy, fighting the urge to look at his watch. At the reception, or whatever it was, he had smiled and smiled. Yet he had been out of his element and he had known it and had been glad when it was time to go. Now he felt much the same way.

He gulped air, stretched, and held his breath. For several years he had been doing isometrics. Then he put back on his shoes and socks, locked the crank letter in the safe, stuck his tie in his jacket pocket and picked up his jacket and went home. His steps echoed solemnly, one by one, on the wooden stairs, making him feel whole and important again.

Peeping through the draperies. Monica watched him walk across the lawn from the garage. She was filled with a mixture of disgust and elation and some sort of wild hope—she felt that she would literally burst. She had fixed a bourbon and water for herself and one for Manly. The ideal wife. The drinks were sparkling on napkins on the glass table; she sipped hers; it was too full; she spilled it, soaking the napkin. She wadded the napkin up into a wet, solid ball and threw it behind the couch. Then she leaned back with her hand to her mouth, giggling. I am completely mad, she thought. Tomorrow I'll tell Suetta she missed some trash behind the couch. She peeped again at Manly, who had paused to examine a bush. Goddamn him anyway; he acts like he invented the goddamn bush. The country squire. Well, squire, you're getting a little paunchy there. She watched him come over the grass, swinging his jacket. You could not deny he was attractive. He had this appeal, all right.

When they were dating, Monica had called him her Teddy bear. Unfortunately, it still fit. Manly looked like a big, good child of twelve who plays at being adult. Something about him made Monica want to run to the door and fling herself upon him and tell him that it (what?) was going to be all right, and then give him about eight hundred goddamn homemade cookies and milk. The real trouble was that Manly never needed to be told that it was all right. He was always the same. But that's good, isn't it?

Isn't that the way adults are supposed to be? She must remember not to make judgments, since she seemed to be insane. She was fingering the stiff, raised pattern of the brocade draperies. Oh, God, she didn't *want* to meet Buck Fire.

What she wanted was for Manly to burst through that door—that gorgeous handmade front door with its carefully distressed wood—and rip off her Tanner dress so violently that the buttons would sound like bullets as they hit the wall, and throw her down upon the floor. Once she had read this really sexy scene in a book about some perversion that involved glass coffee tables, but she couldn't remember what it was. The woman got on top and did something while the man lay underneath, or vice versa, or something, but Monica couldn't remember what had happened after that. Not that it mattered. It had surely been spectacular, whatever it was. I wish to hell Manly would do something like that, she thought, because things are getting tight. Part of Monica's exhilaration came from the growing sense she had had lately of being in a race. It was an odd sensation actually, because she was never sure who was running and whether she was the prize or whether she was running too. She had the sense of running too. Obviously the dream lover had been killed off and now it was Manly versus Buck Fire. But Manly didn't even know about the race, and even if he had, Monica was not at all sure that he would run. She wished he would, though—she wished he would strip her and set her up on the coffee table and make her do terrible things. Or something. *Anything.* Then things would be so much easier and there wouldn't have to be a race at all because Manly would automatically win.

"Hello, darling," Monica said. Her dress was a blue-and white-flowered print, she wore her hair down, and Manly thought she looked just like spring. The way she sat there on the golden couch in that dress, with the drinks before her, satisfied his sense of the way things ought to be, and he felt firmly anchored again in the world.

"Hi, sweetheart, how was practice?"

How was it? Absolutely exquisite, Buck Fire with a megaphone and a yellow shirt. "Oh, it was all right," Monica said. "We have to do this little dance. You ought to see us, all these fat old matrons. It's a scream."

"You aren't a fat old matron." Manly grinned at her, then threw himself down in the wing chair across from the couch. "What a day," he said. "I'm glad to be home."

"I'm glad to *have* you home," Monica said. The sentence rang blatantly false in her ears, like the unexpected sound of a Chinese gong right there in her living room. Inadvertently she glanced about the room, but all was as usual. Monica's ears were still ringing, and she missed his next remark.

"What?" she said, shaking her head as if to clear it.

"I said I like that dress. Is it new?"

"Oh, sort of," Monica said vaguely, waving her drink.

"What's the matter, Manly?" Monica asked then, as the pause lengthened, because he was almost never silent. He always came home and watched the news and discussed what had happened to him during the day. Not that I ever have anything to discuss, Monica thought grimly. Not that anything ever happens to me. Manly came home and talked about events but never, never about thoughts. This was something new. Now he was fixing a drink at the dining-room sideboard. He walked back slowly to her in his sock feet, rattling the ice. It made her extremely nervous to hear him rattle the ice. I could become an alcoholic, she thought suddenly. That's something I could do at home in my spare time.

"I don't know exactly what's the matter," Manly said.

"A lot of little things, I guess, and nothing serious. I have this feeling, all of a sudden, that having such a big Sesquicentennial isn't such a good idea. Things about it don't set right, that's all. I can't put my finger on it." Manly reached over and pressed her hand. To Monica's horror, the hand simply lay there, limp and white, without returning the pressure. She stared at it there in her lap, ornamented with rings. Could it be hers? Oh, shit, she thought, oh, fuck you, hand.

Rallying, then, she said, "You're just tired, darling, that's all. I'll get dinner on the table; it's all fixed, and you'll feel better after you've had something to eat."

"I guess so," Manly said heartily, and Monica saw that he had already bounced back, the same old Manly. Oh, no, Monica thought, don't pay any attention to my hand (but she knew that he had not), don't go all cheerful, tell me what was the matter, please need me just one time. She tried again.

"Is it about Miss Iona?" she asked. "Have you been getting complaints about her again?"

"Oh well, I get those all the time. One of the hazards of the job."

"Manly, why don't you get rid of her, really? People talk about her all the time. She's just a disgrace."

"But she's *enjoyable*." The whimsical, little-boy grin.

"Well, you might enjoy her, but nobody else does. What if you spent two hundred dollars on a dinner party and she wrote up the whole thing wrong? What would you think then? I think it's very sweet, Manly, you saying we need to take care of Miss Iona and all that. But it's just not practical."

"As a matter of fact, honey, I've decided to let her go right after all this is over with. She's way past retirement age, so there won't be any problem. But let me tell you what else happened today." He told her about the crank letter.

Fighting back that wild giggle, which kept popping up now at all the most inappropriate times, Monica went off into a protracted coughing fit. Manly pounded her on the back until, practically weeping, she motioned him away. "You don't know your own strength," she said. "I'll be back and blue." Instantly he was contrite, apologizing. Oh, hell, she thought. I'm not hurt.

"Don't be silly, Manly," she said, the patrician wife. "That's a shame about the letter, I can understand why you were upset. But I'd just forget about it if I were you. Now let's have dinner."

She stood, then leaned down to kiss his forehead, tanned from golf. Now was a good time for him to throw her down upon the coffee table into an outrageous position, but he only stood and looked at her.

"I love you, Monica," he said. "Is it all ready? Good, I'm starving."

"I love *you*," she murmured to his massive, disappearing back. Oddly enough, it was true.

The next morning Manly Neighbors arrived at work to find a small crowd gathering inside the business office, where Will was grinning and sweeping glass. Will pointed at the window and then at the floor, delighted. Then he raised both palms in a gesture of excited disbelief, and dropped his broom. He was having a wonderful time.

"What's going on?" Manly asked Susan, his secretary, who was talking to several women from the shop next door. "I don't know, Mr. Neighbors," she said. She was a big-boned girl from outside Demopolis, recently engaged. Her new diamond sparkled and she held her hand out too long when she pointed at the floor. "The window was broken when I got here and Will found this brick on the floor.'' She pointed at the floor and then at the brick itself, which now lay incongruously on the advertising desk. An envelope was fastened securely around the brick with two red rubber bands. ''Nobody opened that yet,'' she said unnecessarily. Her diamond gleamed.

Manly stared at the brick and then took the rubber bands off and smoothed the wrinkled envelope.

EIGHTEEN

AFTER supper, Bevo practiced the bugle without making any noise, a hard feat, but Ruthie was upstairs asleep in her room. He sat on the sofa in the den, imagining, the bugle at his lips. When he closed his eyes he could see himself smack in the middle of a football field on a sort of podium, carried along by a marching band. They carried him all over the field rapidly without missing a step as they played a zippy little march tune and formed themselves consecutively into all the letters of his name. One by one the letters formed and dissolved on the green field until Bevo's whole name had been spelled out: Bevo Earl Cartwright. When they had finished that, they deposited the podium squarely in the middle of the field, right on the fifty-yard line across from the President of the United States, LBJ, who had canceled a meeting of the Security Council to be a part of the capacity crowd. To thunderous applause, Bevo took his bugle out of its black leather case and played "Reveille," the only thing he knew how to play.

Bevo's Mamaw came through the den, carrying a Coke.

"Why don't you go on outside and toot your horn?" she said. "If I was going to fool with it at all I would leastways make some *noise*." She snorted and spurted Coke foam. Bevo stared at her; she was a smart old woman, all right. He hadn't thought of going outside. But if he did go outside, then Sharon DuBois might hear him and he wasn't ready for that yet. He didn't want her to hear him until he was perfect, until the pageant rehearsals began. Bevo was now the official bugler of the Speed Sesquicentennial Pageant, and he was to play when the Confederate soldiers charged. Of course he had been the only bugler who had auditioned for the part of Bugler, as J.T. kept pointing out, but J.T. was just jealous. Bevo didn't want Sharon DuBois to see him until the time was right, until she was leading the official parade and he was officially bugling. Then they would see each other across the crowded stage, their eyes would smolder, burn, and it would be like they had never seen each other before in all the world. He hoped.

J.T. came in without knocking, as usual, wearing a T-shirt and jeans. " 'Lo," he said to Bevo's Mamaw, but she spat foam in his direction, and left, banging the screen door shut. J.T. shot her a bird when he was sure she was out of the house.

Bevo wrapped his bugle up in a clean white dust cloth and put it back in its leather case. He could practice later, when he would be able to make noise.

J.T. was acting funny, jerking around the room, occasionally going spastic and making sounds of "ping," and "blip," and "dong."

"What are you doing?" Bevo said, entranced.

"I'm a secret weapon," J.T. said. "Yongo." He wove between the chairs.

"You feel all right?" said Bevo.

"If I told you how I felt you wouldn't believe it," said

J.T. He staggered and fell to his knees. "Yip, yip, ag." He pitched forward onto the floor, then raised his head and smiled. "Feedback," he added mysteriously.

Bevo began to feel that J.T. was making fun of him. "Now listen here," he began, but J.T. cut him off.

"Come on," he said. "Let's go on over to my house. Mama's gone over to Coreys' to a Tupperware party and Daddy's out bowling someplace." He looked out the window and said, "Zip, zip, blop," rather noncommittally, then recovered himself. "I mean there's not anybody there," he said, leading the way.

"I guess you mean nobody's home," Bevo said, trying to be sarcastic, but as usual it didn't work. None of his jokes worked. Bevo puzzled about the nature of sarcasm and followed J.T. across the yards. J.T. went right through two revolving lawn sprinklers. He seemed not to notice the water.

"Inhale," he said later to Bevo. "No, you dumb ass, suck it all down in your gut and *hold* it there. See how long you can hold it. Yeah, that's right. Yeah. Now do it again. Cut it out, dumb butt. If you cough you blow the whole thing. O.K. Here. Now. No, you're wasting it. You're wasting it. Oh, crap. O.K., one more time. You feel anything yet?"

"No," Bevo said, which was a lie. His throat was killing him because he had never smoked. They were sitting on the concrete floor in J.T.'s basement, next to the washer and dryer. He couldn't believe that he was smoking marijuana, that he was smoking at all! He leaned back against J.T.'s mother's clothes dryer and contemplated her clothes washer, not five full feet away. Bevo and J.T. were in what J.T.'s mother termed her "utility alcove," and J.T. assured Bevo that nobody ever came here except to wash clothes, which nobody, not even his mother, was going to do right now. Bevo drew it in and held it in his stomach and thought his throat would burn up. His eyes hurt too, and they were watering, but he didn't want to wipe them with his hand. He didn't want J.T. to think he was crying at the height of his high school career. All his life, Bevo had felt that other kids were sitting around in basements or on patios, a hundred million recreation rooms and patios all over America, making out and turning on and doing a thousand variations of those things, all of which for some mysterious reason had been withheld from him, and now he was doing it too. J.T. handed it back to him—J.T. called it a "J"—and Bevo sucked in the smoke and it almost burned his lips because it was almost gone. Carefully, J.T. put the last little bit in one of his mother's miniature Corning Ware casseroles, which he had borrowed discreetly from the kitchen on the way down-stairs. "That's the roach," he said to Bevo, a bit supercilious. "We get us three or four of them, see, and then we put them in a pipe and smoke them too. You don't want to waste any." The casserole had little blue flowers on its curved white sides.

Bevo leaned back against the slick clean dryer and marveled at J.T. and all his equipment. J.T. had always done a lot of talking, but Bevo had thought it was just talk. Roaches and Js and Darvon. J.T. had started another and Bevo took a drag and handed it back, his eyes smarting. Finally he decided he didn't care what J.T. thought of him, he had to wipe his eyes anyway, and he reached over into a plastic laundry basket and pulled out the first thing he touched: a clean Argyle sock belonging to J.T.'s father. It was the weirdest thing. Instead of bringing the sock up to his face, Bevo's hand remained suspended in mid-air, dangling the sock. It was the most beautiful sock Bevo had ever seen. It was turquoise and gold and brown, patterned in diamond shapes.

"Snake," J.T. screeched suddenly, and grabbed the sock and threw it into the empty washer.

Bevo laughed hysterically. "That's not anything but a little old sock," he said, waving his hands. "Nothing but a sock." But his hands would not keep still. They kept waving back and forth.

"You're stoned," J.T. observed, with a great deal of satisfaction.

"Nin," Bevo said. He had intended a longer sentence.

J.T. whooped. "Stoned out of his gourd," he announced to the washer and dryer.

By the time they had put the third roach into the Corning Ware casserole, Bevo couldn't talk at all. Which was a shame, because for once he felt like he might have something to say. To begin with there was the incredible beauty of the small blue flowers on the Corning Ware, so delicate, so perfectly proportioned, as if they had been handpainted by a Japanese. And the glistening white sides of the washer and dryer, looming above him, began to take on a wondrous aura. Bevo plunged both hands into the plastic basket and pulled out a bra and two pairs of underpants. He rolled over on the cool concrete, pressing them into his face and breathing deep, choking on their freshness. Like a *flower*, he thought, and dreamed of deflowering Sharon in a rustic glade like those seen in the Salem cigarette commercials, after which he would stand to blow "Reveille" and then take a sauna bath, which previously he had only read about in books. Then his head was back in the basket and he was saying "plastic" and "basket" over and over to himself and trying to figure out if they rhymed. Then J.T. seemed to be handing him another J and J.T.'s face was going in and out, convex to concave and back, as if Bevo were looking at him through a crazy mirror at a fair. After that, Bevo couldn't remember what happened. He had one vague memory of J.T. turning on the washer, and of the two of them grooving to the slush, ears against the washer's warm sides. Beyond that, nothing. A blank extending for an indefinite period of time. Bevo could not remember anything at all which happened in J.T.'s basement after the slushing began. He didn't know whether they had smoked the roaches in a pipe. He didn't know what had happened to J.T., or how he himself had travelled the dark lawns and made it home alone.

Sitting on the couch again, Bevo came back to life. He couldn't tell how much time had passed. He was very hungry.

"Mother," he called, but nobody answered. Nobody was in the kitchen and obviously he was alone in the den. Bevo guessed his Mamaw had gone to bed; maybe Anne and Lomas were in bed too. Maybe it was late, who knew? Ruthie was undoubtedly out and he was alone in what seemed to be a sleeping or empty house. Bevo felt himself swelling within his own strange and imperfect skin: he had to do something.

He pulled out the last scrapbook, the one that was not yet filled. He looked at the pictures one by one. His own face in the pictures looked as blank as his mother's. Bevo turned the pages one by one. Where were Ruthie and his Mamaw and Lomas? Where were they? There was only Bevo himself, the pleasing and unfamiliar face.

Bevo picked up the great green porcelain fish from the coffee table, held it up to his face, and stared long into its iridescent eye. His head felt heavy and it wanted to roll to one side but his arms and legs were light as air, felt in fact as if they were rising up into the air, floating through water, even though when Bevo looked at them they were right where he had left them a moment before. It was crazy. Even the den in his own house looked funny to him: the fish, the café curtains, the vibrator chair. Everything was ugly.

He got up and started to look for Anne's Instamatic. He knew she kept it downstairs someplace, always ready to catch those candid shots so dear to everyone's heart. Those candids of him. Slowly, Bevo went through the kitchen cabinets, one by one. It was astonishing. He had never before comprehended the extent of his mother's order. Everything was canistered, boxed, Tupperwared or Baggied. Nothing was allowed to sit by itself in its natural state on Anne's shelves. Even the stacks of dishes and plates had little cloth covers. Even the glasses were turned upside down, most unnaturally. Bevo became depressed and angry and frightened. Who could deal with such a woman? When Bevo closed his eyes he heard the blood sloshing around inside his body there, inside his veins, and heard the gurgle of other bodily processes. He could hear his heart. He was getting very tired. From time to time he let his mind go and the little blue flame ran through it.

Finally he found the Instamatic. Anne had had a system of divided steel shelves installed at the rear of the coat closet. If you weren't careful you would miss the whole setup since you couldn't see it for the coats. Various things were stored on these shelves: masking tape, twine, a flashlight, etc., and there was the Instamatic, encased within its leather shell. Bevo got it and got the flashlight and turned it on and went outside in the dark to his Mamaw's leanto.

He flashed his light around the leanto, saw the flowerpots and the grasping tentacles of the green hanging plants. He put the Instamatic in a clay pot on a small iron table and looked at it for a while. He was tempted to burn it but it probably wouldn't make much of a fire there in the pot, all those little metal parts. Anne might even be able to have it fixed. Bevo poked around in the corners of the leanto and shone his flashlight around until he found a lethal-looking thing with long handles and thick round blades, used to dig holes for rosebushes. With this Bevo beat the hell out of the camera, working methodically. Finally the Instamatic was reduced to little pieces and the table was all bent up.

"O.K.," Bevo said aloud. He was tired, like a man who has come home after a long day's work. He put the rosebush planting tool back where it belonged, but left the little table and the camera where they were. Let them find it, so what? He *wanted* them to find it.

Bevo washed his hands at the spigot sticking up from a pipe in the ground, and went slowly back into the house. What had he forgotten? Nothing. He put on clean pajamas and got into bed, doing it all by the hall light. He heard Lomas snoring. He had no idea what time it was or whether he had eaten supper or not. He lay still and content in his bed and let it drift up slowly from the darkness all around him, like air, like gas; he felt it the length of his body: a gathering craziness.

NINETEEN

SANDY DuBois sat in her Thunderbird beside the highway, fuming, and waited. What was the matter with him lately? She was a married woman with three kids; she had things to *do*. Like today she had to go to the beauty shop and then she had to pick up the cleaning if she wanted to wear her newest dress out to the show with Johnny B. Oh, yeah, and she had to pick up some barbecue or something for supper. Maybe Johnny B. would bring some chicken home from the chicken store if she got a hold of him in time. The thought of the chicken store made her laugh. Twenty-two secret spices, what a joke! People were all the time asking her what those spices were. And the Colonel—that old fart never cooked a chicken in his life, she would bet money on it. He just sat up there in Memphis or Louisville or wherever it was he lived—New York probably—and raked it in. Twenty-two secret spices, my ass! Advertising was the whole thing, like Johnny B. said. Everybody used to think that Johnny B. was dumb, but now they were catching on. He might not know much but he knew a thing or two. You had to hand it to Johnny B. Sandy laughed, remembering what Johnny B. said after he went up and got his picture taken with the Colonel for being in the Executive Sales Club. Johnny B. said the Colonel had little old wires sticking out of him all over, sticking out of his ears and his pockets and everywhere, and he had one whole pocketful of little dials he was always twisting and working on. Johnny B. said he didn't think the Colonel was real at all. Said he thought the Colonel was a little Fisher-Price windup toy that somebody had given a recipe to.

Sandy giggled, then sobered. OH, HELL. Where was that fool? She had a good mind to just up and leave and go on to the beauty shop. If she got there in time Rose could give her a manicure too, and Sandy loved to have people work on her hands. It felt so good. Sandy looked up and down the road and lit another cigarette. A sign about ten yards ahead on the shoulder of the road said KEEP ALABAMA BEAUTIFUL. Sandy snorted. Alabama was the asshole of the world. But at least it wasn't a *Communist* state, as Johnny B. always pointed out when she said she'd like to move someplace where they had some night life for a change.

"Well, finally!" she said to Bob Pitt sarcastically. He had parked across the road and now he was panting outside the car with his striped tie blowing every which way in the wind. "I was just fixing to leave," she said.

"To *leave*?" he repeated stupidly, and his face looked so gray and dumb that she said, "Well, I didn't, did I? What's the matter with you? Get in this car, I really have got to go in a minute."

Bob Pitt went around the car and got in and sat staring at the "America: Love It or Leave It" sticker on the windshield in front of him. It was a beautiful day; he suddenly doubted that Sandy noticed beautiful days. He rolled down the window on his side of the car to let out some of the smoke and stared at her across the console which separated the bucket seats. Her hair was loose around her face in a way which he found charming. Her complexion was not so good, seen like this in the bright spring glare of the sun: little red cross-hatching marbled her cheeks and there were other, deeper lines around her eyes and her mouth. Her nose looked more prominent than usual, jutting over the steering wheel with a birdlike thrust. She wore a pullover jersey of some shiny material and yellow slacks. Her thighs bulged out in little pouches where they touched the seat of the car. Looking at the pouches, Bob felt very tender. But she stared at him, tapping her foot. "Well, what is it?" she said. "I told you before, I haven't got all day."

Now that he was here with her, Bob Pitt himself could not remember what it was. Something he had wanted to tell her. Something so urgent that he had left his office and told his new secretary a really transparent lie that anybody in their right mind would see through. But what a nice day. Bob looked up and down the road. Some of the trees looked like summer already. He looked back at Sandy.

"Quit looking up and down the road," she said.. "You afraid somebody's going to see you?"

"I wasn't looking," he said, and wished for a Tum.

"Sure you were. You ashamed of me, is that it?" She was just deviling him now, and both of them knew she was doing it. She enjoyed it, and they knew that too.

"No, I'm not ashamed of you," Bob said wearily. "We must have been through all this a million times already. I don't see any sign that says you can't look up and down the road, though. But now that you've brought it up, I don't see why we have to meet right here on the side of the road in the middle of the day, when I want to talk to you. Anybody *could* go by and see."

"I like the highway," Sandy said. She smiled. "No guts, no glory." She lit another cigarette. "I like to look at the cars," she added. As a child, she had sat long hours on the front steps of the house they had lived in, right outside town, watching the cars go by. When she thought of her childhood now, that was practically all she could remember: watching the cars go by with Lester, her little brother, who had died of pneumonia when he was thirteen. They had a game they used to play about what color the next car would be, and another game about where all those people were going and what they were going to do when they got there. Sandy and Lester had had plenty of toys to play with, but Sandy would rather watch the cars than anything else. After she had watched them for a whole long afternoon, she would sometimes have to go upstairs and lie down or else out back and hit something; her stomach would be that full of butterflies. "Well, go on, I'm telling you the last time," she said to Bob Pitt. In front of her car and behind it the road stretched straight and shiny, wavering a little bit through the layer of exhaust fumes, like maybe it wasn't quite real after all, and the flashing cars were some kind of trick.

"I don't know how to tell you this exactly," he said. He didn't even know if he should tell her at all, now that he had remembered, but he had to tell somebody.

"I bet I know," she said.

"What?"

"I bet you're the one that's been writing all those letters to the paper, aren't you? That's why you've been acting so weird."

"*What?*"

Sandy had said it just to shock him. Now she giggled. "Oh, come on," she said. "I just bet that's it. You're the type they'd never guess, that mild-mannered type."

"Cut it out," he said.

"Well, I don't care, God knows," Sandy said. "I might have done it myself if I'd thought of it."

"That's not it," Bob said. His throat was tightening up, making it difficult to swallow.

"What made you think to do it anyway?" she asked. She was having a big time.

"I said cut it out!" Bob slammed his hand down on the console. His face had turned red and the watery eyes seemed to leap out from behind the glasses. "I've had just about enough out of you today!"

Sandy stared at him in astonishment. This was better than getting her nails done. She had never seen him so mad. "Well, I think it's exciting," she said.

He opened the car door. "I can't talk to you," he said.

"You wait a minute." Sandy leaned across the console and put a hand on his arm. All I have to do is touch him, she thought.

He slumped back into the bucket seat.

"Now tell me," she said, making her voice all soft and runny.

He reached for her hand but continued to look straight ahead at the passing cars. He felt her sharp, hard nails. "It's about Florida," he said. "Now wait a minute, let me finish, I don't want you to say a word. I've got to go on down there after this is over. I've got to go on down there and take you with me. I'm going crazy, the way things are now. I can't stand it any more. Let's go the day after the pageant. I can't hardly wait any longer." Sometimes when he was tired or bothered, Bob fell back into the grammar he had used as a child and of which he had so painfully rid himself. "We can start a whole new life, Sandy. We can get married, change our names. People do it all the time."

"You're just talking crazy now," Sandy said. "You know you are. You don't mean a word you say."

"Don't you fool around with me, Sandy," he warned. His voice cracked. "Are you going with me or not?"

"Well, just don't *rush* me so, honey," she said. "You act like we're on a quiz show or something."

They were silent, watching the cars.

"I can't see why you want to run away to Florida," Sandy finally said. "Now don't get mad. But I mean, why don't you just get a divorce and ask me to get a divorce? I mean, that's how most people do. Now I'm not saying I'd do that either, you understand, but that's how most people do."

"I know it."

"Well, if you want to leave Frances it looks like you could get a divorce first," Sandy said, "even if it is old bitchy Frances."

Bob squeezed her nails into his palm. "I can't stand it," he said.

"I think you're acting kind of crazy if you want to know what *I* think," Sandy said. "It looks to me like you've got it made. You're the head of the Bushy Brothers and everything. Your business is doing good. I don't see what you can't stand. I don't see why you have to pick up *right* now and decide you can't stand it." In September, the Colonel's Executive Sales Club would meet in Hawaii, and she sure would hate to miss that.

"I love you, Sandy," Bob said. From behind the glasses, his eyes drove into hers.

"Well, I love you too," she said briskly, getting worried. He *is* crazy, she thought. "But I mean, we get to see each other a lot and all, and you said your business has picked way up, and I don't see why you have to go getting all hot and bothered *right now*."

"That's why," he said hopelessly.

"What's why?"

"Nothing," he said. He paused. "Are you going with me or not?"

I wouldn't go to New York City with a lunatic, is what

203

she was thinking. I wouldn't go to Paris, France. But she said, "I guess so, honey. I mean, you have to let me think about it a little bit longer and I'll let you know. I sure do *want* to go, honey."

"I can't live without you," Bob Pitt said, knowing suddenly that it was no longer true. He had gone beyond that now. "I can't live in that house." This was true, although the thought of leaving his son Bobby Joe made Bob nearly weep. Bobby Joe was pimpled and unpleasant, true enough, but still he was his son.

"Why don't you think it all over for a while?" Sandy said, sliding over the console to press against him, caressing him, watching the cars.

TWENTY

CAROLINE Pettit sat down heavily at her desk in the Sesquicentennial headquarters and rested for a minute before she prepared for the rush of Queen Contestants. Her back hurt but the doctor said that was normal. Pressure on the kidneys, he said. Her legs hurt but the doctor said that was normal too. Increased circulation, he said. Everything was normal and she was in fine shape, and the baby was due three weeks from tomorrow. Thinking about it made her gulp.

Monica Neighbors came in the door with a rush of wind, her hair disarranged, swinging her shoulder bag. Her dark eyes looked feverish and her cheeks had small, bright blotches of color. "Hello, Caroline," she said in an unnatural voice, higher than her normal tone. "How are you?"

Caroline raised her dreamy blue eyes. "The baby's dropping," she said.

Monica stopped by the desk. "Is that good or bad?"

"Well, it's *good*," giggled Caroline. "That means I'm right on time. A lot of first babies are late but the doctor says this one probably won't be because it's already dropping. He says everything is just fine."

"That's good," Monica said absently, continuing to stare at Caroline with her dark bright eyes. The pause became too long and Monica pulled herself together and said, "Do you think you ought to be here? Maybe you ought to go lie down or something."

Caroline laughed merrily. "Oh, honestly! You sound just like my mother. She's always trying to make me lie down. They don't *have* babies like that any more! You're supposed to stay real active. Then you know what they make you do right after you have it?"

"I can't imagine," Monica said.

"They make you walk," Caroline said placidly. "Up and down. Just as soon as you wake up. Isn't that something?"

"It sure is," Monica said, and shuddered.

"When are you and Manly going to have a baby?" Caroline asked suddenly. "I mean I don't mean to get personal or anything, but you really ought to think it over. It's just wonderful, you have no idea. It's a real experience."

"I guess so," Monica said, still standing before Caroline's desk. "What was it you said when I came in here? When I asked you how you felt?"

"The baby's dropping?"

"Jesus Christ," Monica said. "Dropping." Swinging the shoulder bag in a wide arc, she turned abruptly and went into the next room without another word. Caroline stared after her, open-mouthed. Now what had gotten into Monica? She always was a funny one. Caroline sighed and gently belched.

Monica went into the side parlor, where she was to give out pageant costumes, and stared furiously out the window at the daffodils. "Bloom, you mothers!" she said aloud, then turned quickly to see if anyone had heard. But no one else had come in yet—she wasn't supposed to give out the costumes until four—and she was alone in the narrow, high room. I am absolutely furious, she thought, to her own amazement. I am livid with rage. Why is it that pregnant women have to pick on me? Why is it that they have to give you all this body gossip? Don't they know how terrible they look, all puffed out like frogs? If it's all so wonderful, why don't they just shut up about it and go off in a little room someplace and rub their stomachs by themselves? Monica could not count the number of friends she had—good friends, although she had never had any real intimates—who had gotten pregnant and gone away from the world into that other place from which they only seemed to emerge occasionally, at cocktail parties or the Country Club, to announce that the kid was teething. There was nothing much for Monica to talk to them about, after they had babies. Monica wasn't all that wild about talking to women anyway, so she hadn't particularly minded, but now she looked out the window and thought of Caroline's vacant moon face. Maybe all of them got so wrapped up in their babies because it was their only defense. After it happened to you, you really had only two choices: you liked it or acted like you liked it, or else you hated it, in which case your husband would hate you and you would hate yourself and probably go crazy. Monica thought she could understand that. She was beginning to think she knew a lot about going crazy.

Just now, as she pulled up a chair to the window and sat down, she felt as if she were sitting on a powder keg, like a cat in a cartoon. Or like she, too, was pregnant. Things were building up and preparing to explode—not only in her personal life but all over town. It was something you could sense. Of course those crank letters and the housing suit had some people worked up, but it was more than that. Monica had decided it was bad for the people of different classes—she still thought in terms of "classes"—to be thrown so much together. At first she had thought it was fine, but now she saw that people were becoming confused, forgetting their places. It was unsettling. I don't care if I'm a snob or not, Monica thought. At least I'm honest. If I change my mind I say so. I say what I think. I'm also not a snob in that other, secret sense.

"Yes?" she said as snobbishly as possible, purely to be perverse, as a crew-cut man angled shyly through the door. He looked like he might be a worker from the rubber plant. "This where the costumes is at?" He grinned, tripping over the word "costumes." Monica bet that his wife or his church had forced him into it.

"Well, give me one of them Confederate soldier suits, please ma'am," he said, grinning more broadly still. Monica sighed and went to work, as more people lined up behind him. Out the window she could see the Queen Contestants clustering about the front gate, coming in for their weekly tally, being overly vivacious and overly polite to everybody.

The Queen Contest had narrowed down and taken on a life of its own. Speed values its Queens highly, and there was almost as much interest in the Queen Contest as in the pageant itself. Everybody knew somebody who was running. The top ten contenders each had a group of other contest dropouts selling tickets for them now, and little informal staffs of their own. There was a great bitterness among the top contestants, carefully masked. The top ten, in no particular order, were these:

—Ruthie Cartwright, who wasn't the sort at all. Ruthie's name produced a number of winks whenever it was mentioned, and she was a mystery to the "nicer" women in town. "Who *is* she?" they said, meaning who are her people, and when they found out, they weren't at all pleased. It wouldn't do to have a red-headed junk dealer's daughter as the Queen. And yet no one had anything specific against her, but she seemed a little rough, they thought, or a little smart, or *something*.

—Sharon DuBois, who had a whole string of twirling and beauty contests under her belt and whose looks were much admired. You might not like her mother but you had to admit that she was a pretty thing, and the high school football team was selling tickets on her behalf. It would be all right if she won, they felt: she was the type.

—Jennifer Treadwell, another high school student, known for her long horse face, whose father owned the paper mill. Jennifer was extremely shy, speaking seldom if at all, and she rode in horse shows around the South, where she won occasional white ribbons. A lot of people bought tickets from her because of who her daddy was, calling her up to get them since she didn't go out soliciting like the others did. The general consensus was that her mother had made her run, and that she wouldn't go far in the contest once all the people who owed money to her daddy had bought their tickets.

—Mrs. Lu-Ann Brady, whose husband, a Vietnam war veteran, was paralyzed from the waist down and who was actively supported by the VFW, the Shriners, and several other town groups. Although she was nearing forty, she was a hard woman to say no to because of her husband's condition. Lu-Ann would cry at the drop of a hat. If she won the contest, she told everybody, she was going to pack Grover up in the back of the station wagon and take him down to Gulf Shores to get him a little sun.

—Judith Sardis, a home extension agent, who had surprised everyone by entering the race. Miss Sardis was tall and buxom, a fine figure of a girl, although not the sort that would naturally come to mind if you said "Sesquicentennial Queen" to yourself. Miss Sardis looked more like your cousin. Two years ago she had graduated with honors from Auburn University with a major in home economics. All the 4-H'ers were selling tickets for her, and her support was particularly strong out in the county. Miss Sardis had tight blond curls, and made all her own clothes.

—Mrs. Ginger Grimes, cashier at the drive-in branch of the First National Bank, who was as bouncy and pert as her name. The bank president—Cecil Burns—had given her two weeks' paid leave of absence in order to "campaign," as he put it, evidently feeling that her victory would shed great glory on the bank. The other contestants strongly protested Mr. Burns' attitude, and signed petitions to that effect. They had to campaign after work and on weekends and at night, they said, so Ginger shouldn't get any special breaks. The White Company ignored the petition, and Ginger stayed in the race. She got up each morning at seven o'clock and dressed and went out to sell tickets, as if she were still at work in the bank.

—Anne deColigny, whose grandmother had been the Centennial Queen at the celebration fifty years ago. Anne was distantly related to Miss Iona and more directly related to the Victors, one of the town's oldest and best families. Anne was a languid, willowy blonde without much energy. She did not seem to care whether she won or not. In her second year at the Junior College, she was a member of the prestigious Tri Delts. Anne was supported by the "nice" people in town, who felt that it would be most appropriate for her to win because of her grandmother and also because her winning would be a sort of victory of the nice people over the White Company, which had emerged as something of a villain in the Queen Contest because of its policy of letting "just anybody" into the race. A few people criticized Anne's posture, but they were generally ignored.

—Lucille Spaulding, of Mobile, who was Speed Junior College's Homecoming Queen. A lot of people thought it was unfair for her to be a contestant, but the White Company had ruled in her favor since she went to school in Speed. She was a pretty girl of Creole descent whose only flaw was Catholicism.

—Mrs. Grace Henley, a blond beautician in her middle thirties. As the contest progressed it became more and more evident that she was p.r.e.g., a crying shame since her husband (who wasn't much anyway) had gone off to work on a pipeline and hadn't been heard of since, except for a single postcard from Washington, D.C., with a picture of the Washington Monument on it. Grace Henley had showed that postcard all over town like it was made of solid gold, but you could tell that she was worried and everyone knew she needed the money, what with two kids already in school. Grace was "tough" and she could "take care of herself," it was unanimously agreed—traits which served, paradoxically, to produce a large sympathy vote in her favor among the working people of Speed.

—Johnnie Sue Billings, the youngest girl in the contest. Only fifteen, Johnnie Sue had already won everything there was to win on the junior high level. Her titles included second runner-up in the Little Miss Alabama Contest, which she had won when she was only five! Johnnie Sue had started early and now had a mechanical poise which was much envied—though openly ignored—by the older girls.

The Queen Contest generated a lot of talk, and everyone had an opinion. You heard things everywhere you went: Lucille Spaulding had to do anything the priest said, Grace Henley was four months pregnant and hadn't her husband been gone five?, Ginger Grimes and Mr. Burns at the bank were having an affair; Johnnie Sue was uppity, Jennifer Treadwell did it with her horse. (The last was contributed by union foes of her father.)

The girls clustered on the walk and the steps of the

headquarters like so many bright spring flowers, and to look at them you could never tell that they were aware of the rumors about themselves or about each other, or that any enmity existed among them at all. Something was unnatural about the way they stood waiting for Caroline to tally up the week's results, however: they fingered their hair, and they stood long moments in careful positions as if an invisible photographer were at work.

Monica, glancing out the window as she got an Indian suit for a high school boy, wondered how they could stand to parade themselves that way. Their high voices came through the open door, making it hard for Monica to concentrate on the sizes. *Fools*, Monica thought. Don't they know? But then she thought, know what? and couldn't answer the question. "You'll have to speak up," she said acidly to a timid woman mumbling down at her feet.

Caroline smiled placidly to herself as she totaled the week's votes. Who would have dreamed that she was perfectly capable of handling all this by herself? She wished it could go on and on, the Sesquicentennial and her pregnancy, with no end ever in sight. People were so nice to you when you were pregnant. She would be sorry when the baby and the pageant were produced, although she was excited about seeing them both. She could not conceive of either one—only of individual components: the baby's navel, the Indian costumes. Caroline dreaded the end of things. She wished that this particular afternoon could extend indefinitely into a future full of dreamy, unfulfilled expectations.

TWENTY-ONE

BUCK lay flat on his back on the king-size bed, flexing his bare stomach muscles. His one-bedroom efficiency apartment was the best Speed had to offer in apartments of its type. It was bare, beige, and institutional, its pseudo-Spanish décor shot through with cheap plastics. Luckily Buck was not a man who noticed his surroundings. Besides, he had stayed in a million places like this. And he had stayed in some real dumps. As long as you had your own color TV and didn't have to go out for ice cubes and didn't have a bunch of goons puking on your head you were all right, he figured. This place was a goddamn palace compared to a lot of places he had stayed in. Buck rubbed his stomach and looked down the compact length of his body to his feet. "He has the cutest little feet!" his mother used to shrill at relatives and anyone else who would listen. "Just look at his little feet! You'd think he was a Chinaman from the size of them." Buck hated his feet: small and delicate as shells, no matter what sort of exercises he took. His ex-wife used to call him "Goody Two Shoes." Apparently that referred to some song she had heard as a kid. Whatever it was, Buck hadn't heard it. He thought the name referred to things he wouldn't do or let her do—she had been crazy, that one. A bat straight out of hell. Just the other day Buck had read that she had a part in some film, and a bitter taste like the aftertaste of a wine drunk had come into his mouth. Women were all alike or else they were crazy, in which case you had better get out. Unbidden, a picture of her the way she had been when Buck first knew her flashed across his mind: very young, a runaway from Cleveland, standing alone in the park in her jeans while the wind blew her black hair wildly about her long, thin face. Cold. She had been cold that day in the park. Shit. Now he made it a practice to leave the crazies strictly alone and not to get involved, really involved, with anyone. He preferred rooms like this, which made no demands, and women who made no demands.

Buck had done nothing to make this room his own, in spite of his lengthy occupancy. It was as fiercely impersonal as it had been the day he had come to Speed, as impersonal as all the rooms which he had moved into in all the towns. Women were always trying to bring him things for his rooms: potted plants that he had to water, things to eat in dishes that he had to return, and little things like colored glass eggs that he had to look at. He had no use for any of them or for the women who brought them. They stayed around for exactly as long as the women did and then out they went. Sometimes Buck sent them to one of his sisters for Christmas, if it was something appropriate. Most things finally went out with the trash.

Buck rubbed his flat stomach back and forth. He wondered if she would come. Was it time yet? Yes, it was time. A white plastic alarm clock—his own, although you would never know it—ticked loudly on an appendage of Spanish décor. A large picture of Buck himself adorned the heavy dresser, and a bunch of ties and socks were thrown across the rocking chair in the corner of the room. Buck smiled at the smiling picture of himself. You devil you. Sure she would come. No one had failed to show up yet, and Mrs. Mousy had all the characteristics of her kind. Buck heard hesitant steps on the stairs and grinned more broadly. What do you know. He reached up and took a drink of gin from the sweaty glass and set it carefully back on the bedside table.

Monica paused before the plain white door. Here she was. All the way over in the car she had wondered whether she would actually come. What was beyond that white door? It could be anything, the most astounding thing in the world, she felt, although logically she knew it was only Buck Fire. Only Buck! But for her it could be another country, full of wild beasts and rich fruit, or the bottom of the sea, lit by swollen, phosphorescent fish. Monica knocked on the door, fighting down that urge to giggle.

"Hi, there." Buck's voice, deep and different.

"Hi." Monica stood where she was. It was not too late to leave. She could still do it, if she wanted to. She could turn now and run down those stairs and she would never have to face him at all.

"Come on in." Buck sounded almost bored, as if her coming to see him were a routine thing. Like ordering the milk, Monica thought, annoyed. Like making the beds. That stopped her. "Come on," Buck said. "Shut the door." He sounded too bored for words. Monica slammed the door.

She held her purse against her body and looked around the room. It was ugly and ordinary, with a gray linoleum floor. It was difficult for Monica to believe that a creature as flashy as Buck Fire could issue forth each day from a place as drab as this. A loose stack of papers—pageant stuff—and a half-full ashtray sat forlornly on the coffee table. Monica thought of her careful eclecticism, the dried flowers and small carved boxes. She would have to bring him something for his room. Nobody could live like this. She was shocked as she realized that she had automatically supposed she would come again. Oh, Christ.

"Come on in if you're coming."

"Well, where *are* you?" Monica was annoyed by the high, adolescent tone of her own voice. She had meant to be ripe and mysterious: velvet.

"I'm back here in the bedroom. Come on back."

The nerve of him. But at least he was laying it on the line, so to speak. On the bed. She could go back there, or she could not go. The image of her ancient humanities professor rose before her, beetle-browed. "Man is not free until he is cognizant of his own free will," the professor said. Buck ought to come and kiss her, though. He ought to try to make her feel at home. If she did go back there, supposing she did, what should she do with her sweater and purse? To leave them in here would be an immediate victory for him. But to take them into to the bedroom would be gauche. Not velvet at all. Monica dropped her sweater on the couch, kept the purse, and walked like a sleepwalker in the direction of his voice.

Buck lay flat on his back and waiting, making bets with himself. It might not be what Mrs. Mousy had in mind, this approach. But he had found that in the long run it worked best. Don't give them any romance or you'll get in way over your head. Particularly with the married ones. Then he heard her coming and smiled. "Hi, honey," he said, sitting up.

Monica blinked and sat down abruptly in a green chair just inside the sliding bedroom door. His chest was covered with red-gold hair and his teeth were as white and straight as bathroom tiles. He sat cross-legged on the bed, wearing only khaki pants. He looked wonderful.

"You certainly are in good shape," Monica said brightly,

then collapsed in a fit of giggles. "I can't believe I said that," she gasped. Think velvet. Oh, Christ. She laughed until the cheap chair shook.

Buck sat on the bed and looked puzzled.

"I blew it, didn't I?" she said when she had recovered. "I had this way I was going to act."

"You didn't have to come here," Buck said, mad. Nothing was going according to plan. She was supposed to become tremulous and shy at the sight of him; he would go to her; bingo. He had a rehearsal at five. There wasn't time for a lot of talk.

"Oh, yes I did," Monica said. "You wanted me to. You asked me to. Remember? You've wanted me to for a long time." She felt completely free now to say anything she liked. Nothing mattered; they weren't going to do it after all, and she was back on safe, familiar ground.

This was so outrageous that Buck stood up. "Listen, bitch," he said, "I asked you because I thought it might do you some good to get it out of your system. You obviously want it. So here's your chance, baby."

"The great humanitarian," Monica sneered. She hadn't realized that she could actually sneer.

"That's right, sugar," Buck said, walking back and forth now beside the bed. "If you want it you know where to get it."

Monica couldn't breathe. "I'm leaving," she said. "So long, Albert Schweitzer." She went back into the living room, picked up her sweater from the back of the chair, and then sat down suddenly in the chair and buttoned up all the buttons on the sweater and then unbuttoned them again. Goddamn little nobody, she thought. Nobody at all. *If you want it you know where to get it.* That was the rudest thing she had ever heard of. It was the least gentle-manly thing in the world. Then Monica laughed. Well, what did she want after all? A gentleman? *Manly?* Somebody with a goddamn monocle of something? She began unbuttoning the buttons again. If she didn't do this now, there might never be another chance, never in all her life. She would go crazy and they would send her off to Bryce's, a raving fool in a wig. Why did I say wig? she thought.

"You still here?" Buck strutted into the room.

"I changed my mind," Monica said. "I want it." She sat completely still with her feet crossed at the ankles.

Buck stared at her. Women. You couldn't figure them. He had been all ready to apologize, to say he had made a mistake and that she wasn't that kind of girl after all. You couldn't afford to antagonize the headquarters staff. She sat now perfectly demure, looking up at him expectantly with her dark hollow eyes. Right now she wasn't mousy at all. She was kind of beautiful in a funny way, like that Mexican girl in *One-Eyed Jacks*. Buck moistened his lips and held out his hand. "Come on," he said. Monica carefully folded her sweater and laid it on the coffee table and put her purse on top of it. She took his hand—ringless, hairless, and almost exactly the same size as her own—and kicked off her shoes and walked back to the bedroom with him. She had kicked her shoes high into the air—frivolously, extravagantly—and behind her she heard them clunking back onto the floor. He placed her inside the bedroom as if she were a doll, and gravely slid the door together and turned her to face him, looking deep into her eyes. "Monica," he said.

"You don't have to say any of that shit," Monica said, surprising him. Her eyes were enormous. The late afternoon sun came through the Venetian blinds and lay in long stripes across the bed. Buck pulled her to him and kissed her and she kissed him back the way they did in paperback novels. He unzipped her zipper and her dress fell to the floor soundlessly, exactly as Monica had thought it would when she had picked it out of her closet. Velvet, what a farce. Think velvet. Think of this man's hands on you, think of all the women he must have had. You are nothing to him. This means nothing. Then she didn't know what she was doing. She was off in a new place where she didn't think at all and everything was touch. Sometimes, with Manly, she had planned the next day's menus while they made love. All Monica could remember later, about this first time, was the sun coming down in stripes and looking down at her own white legs flashing in and out of the stripes and Buck's glowing, rough red hair.

They lay on their backs and Buck said, "Well, if you get tired of marriage, baby, you can always get a job."

Monica smiled up at the ceiling and stretched and felt as if her skin were a skein of nerve ends. "Do you think I'm good at it then," she said. She had always known the answer.

"You're O.K.," said Buck. He looked over at her, white and black on the bed. You can't tell a book by looking at the cover, he thought.

"How good?" Monica said, tickling him. "A little good? or super?"

"Hey, cut that out."

"How good?"

"Now look. See what you did."

"I did that?"

Then Buck was doing several things she had thought about for a long time. "That's great," she said after a while, "but it's against the law."

"What?"

"I said it's against the law. In Alabama. I swear it is. Oh."

Buck was lying on his back laughing. "You crack me up," he said. "Oh, hell." Monica had never known anybody who would say, "You crack me up." She laughed and he said, "You haven't ever done that before? How many years have you been married?"

"Four," Monica said. "No, I haven't," she said. "What I usually do is this."

"You broke the law," she told him later. "I'm going to make a citizen's arrest."

"I'm going to get a beer." Buck got up and walked naked into the kitchen while Monica lay in bed, not even bothering to cover up, and watched him priss out the door.

Buck came back with the beers and then he disappeared again and came back with some potato chips and they ate them in the wide bed and drank the beers.

"Uh-oh," Buck said suddenly, looking at the small white clock. "I've got a rehearsal at five."

"But that's only ten minutes away," Monica said.

"Yeah. See you." Buck was out of bed and into his pants in a single motion.

"Are you just going to *leave* like that?" she asked. Now he was in the closet.

"Yep." He emerged, pulling on a green velour jersey which almost made her laugh, it was so outlandish. He was abstracted, rushing, pulling on his boots, and then spending what seemed to Monica an abnormally long time combing his hair before the mirror. He went into the bathroom and Monica heard the whoosh of an atomizer of some sort, and then without even kissing her goodbye he was saying "So long" from the door.

"When am I going to see you again?" Monica said. She didn't mind saying it at all.

"Whenever you can make it, doll. Just give me a ring. The number's on the phone. Bye now."

"Where's the phone?" Monica said, but he was gone.

She got up, still naked, and prowled through the small apartment. The telephone was in the living room, 752–2002. She started to write it down but she thought no, better not, and memorized it, feeling like a detective. She looked into the bathroom, and saw a large container of hair spray, uncapped, on the sink before the mirror. She went back into the bedroom and lay back on the salty sheets. She loved their messiness. I bet I look like hell, she thought, smiling into the stillness. I have had an affair with a man. I have had a purely physical affair with a man who uses *hair spray*. She wriggled further down in the bed and propped pillows beneath her head. She found that she was staring straight at a garish print which the apartment owner had hung on the wall at the foot of the bed. Funny she hadn't noticed it before. It was a plump, long-throated, pinkish bird surrounded by little blue streaks which apparently indicated rapid flight. "The Elusive Hummingbird by Rosa Gray," the caption read. Monica smiled into the elusive hummingbird's bright blue eye. Surely that was wrong. No bird like that had ever existed in nature, ever would. Who was Rosa Gray? Suddenly Monica realized that it was past time to go home. She stretched and dressed, feeling wonderfully sinful. I will go straight to hell, she thought with satisfaction, since she didn't believe in it anyway. Dressed, she felt clean and light and new. 752–2002. She stalked the living room, seeking her shoes.

It was funny. For so long she had wondered if this was all there was to life, what she had. She had been reasonably happy. Someone had always been there to take care of her. First her parents, then her friends at school, then Manly. Except for that brief time in Europe. But all that time she had wondered, Is this all?, and had been half-consumed with daydreams. She felt fully shed of daydreams. It wasn't all; she had been right to wonder. Monica remembered walking down a long street in some city, possibly Atlanta, and wondering what went on behind the tiny panes of glass. Somewhere somebody was murdering his wife, somewhere somebody was beating a child; right there on the corner, perhaps, someone was carrying a gun. But she never knew any people like that. It wasn't the criminal aspect that drew her, she thought, it was the unusual. And now she had done it herself, committed the unusual, the illicit, the extraordinary act. Think velvet, my God. The Elusive Hummingbird by Rosa Gray. 752–2002. Monica put on her sweater and walked out, carefully shutting the door.

TWENTY-TWO

V ISUALIZE an isosceles triangle, superimposed on the town. The town itself is throbbing with spring. Forsythia is everywhere, bright yellow. Daffodils sprout in even the unlikeliest places. The wind chases Coke and Icee cups over the sidewalks and makes small children difficult to control. Old ladies emerge from shuttered and columned houses armed with pruning shears, and go at their camellias. Ancient Lurch Lamb returns to the square, where he sleeps on the bench in the sun, a snowdrop in his lapel. The town is vibrant, pastel, humming with spring and another excitement. The lines of the isosceles triangle are straight and black, outlining the other excitement.

At one point of the triangle, Manly sits at his desk, feeling paranoid. It is difficult to know what to do. Before him on his desk are three more letters similar to the first ones he received. He ignored those, but was finally forced into action when other people in town—Mayor Higgins, John Cloud (head of the Chamber of Commerce), some of the pastors, Miss Iona, etc.—began receiving them too. What he had done was, he felt, wise: he had published two representative letters on the editorial page, followed by a heartening, civic-minded editorial. The response was out of all proportion to the letters themselves or any possible threat they represented. Letters poured in, the next issue of the Speed *Messenger* was sold out as soon as it was on the street, advertising rolled in. Business boomed. Manly will probably go biweekly after the Sesquicentennial and add several new members to his staff. But, while once he would have felt unconditionally proud about the planned expansion, now he feels ambivalent. He wants to be successful because he is good, not because he has inherited some nut. Well. The latest letter says:

Dear Sir,

I have seen yr. story in the paper and read yr. words between the lines too. If you are trying to scare me I don't scare. You say I am trying to cause trouble and divide the town. Well that is not true. The town has been divided already and we dont want to sellabrate this. All you think of sir is dollar bills. You will be counting money when it is too late. The water will rise, the time will come, the wood will burn again. You can tell the people to look right and left.

The Avenger

It was written with a ballpoint pen and had arrived in a smudged, plain white envelope along with the regular mail.

Almost automatically, Manly edits it and sends it down for inclusion in the Letters to the Editor section of the paper. He cannot decide whether he is being weak or strong in doing this. Perhaps, as Lloyd Warner implied in another connection, he has not the right to suppress any sort of news. On the other hand, as Higgins has recently pointed out in an unnecessarily irate telephone conversation. Manly does not want to wreck the celebration. A lot of money has been invested. To this extent, the crank is right. This is upsetting to Manly.

Manly has become obsessed with the crank. He views this crank as his particular persecutor, feeling that he has been forced into all sorts of moral and practical considerations which in the normal course of his life would never have come up. He hadn't bought the Speed paper with the idea of doing any heavy thinking, but his crank has thrust it upon him. Now all Manly's imaginative powers are focused upon the crank: through wooden walls and brick walls, Manly seeks him out with his mind's eye. He thinks the crank is probably a middle-aged or older man, living in gray seclusion. The crank has sunken features and yellow eyes beneath his sparse hair. He emerges now and then only to buy a loaf of bread—always at different stores. He will never be caught, though Bill Higgins and the whole police force look for him. He is a migrant, living on God knows what, going from town to town to wreck civic celebrations. He has wrecked county fairs, centennials, fiestas, and fish rodeos. Nothing is sacred to him. He will try anything short of a state fair. The Avenger. Manly laughs at himself. He is letting his imagination run away with him. It frightens him to find that he has such an imagination after all.

But of course this is not as important as it seems to him. It is his own jaundiced viewpoint which is at fault, and there is nothing to worry about at all. Monica seems unconcerned, and he has worried that she will be frightened. He has cautioned her to lock the doors. But he hears her singing in her bath. Maybe he shouldn't have sent that letter down. Hell, too late now. Manly decides to take advantage of the weather and play golf after lunch.

The next point of the isosceles triangle falls upon the football field and and the adjacent junior high school gymnasium. Here, rehearsals are in full swing. Luther, Buck Fire, and several high school speech teachers appear to be somewhat in charge, yet there is an air of frivolity and confusion. A visitor receives the impression that no one knows what is happening, and this is largely true. There is a master script, kept by Luther and Buck. It is never opened or referred to. All the rehearsing is done in small snatches, according to the White Company's tried and true technique. Each actor knows only which scene his group of actors is to do. He does not know when he will do it or what his scene signifies in the pageant as a whole. None of the actors have speaking parts. All the speaking will be done by five narrators, three men and two women. In addition to the actors, narrators, and directors, the junior high school gym is overrun with technicians of various sorts: persons who have to do with the costumes and properties, with construction, with lighting and sound. It has been rumored that an expert in trick lighting will fly here soon in a private plane, but this rumor has not been officially confirmed or denied. People mill about. There are no black faces.

The junior high school gym itself is large and drafty, resembling an airplane hangar. Its steel beams are exposed and light pours in through large glass spaces near the roof. The walls are made of gruesome yellow tiles. Fiberglass boards and basketball goals hang at either end of the long room. Above one of the baskets, a Pepsi clock keeps time, and the Lions Club scoreboard hangs idly above the other. The bleachers have been removed in order to make more room for the pageant rehearsals.

In a corner, a phys. ed. instructor from the county school system blows a whistle hung around her neck. Her thighs flare beneath her short black shorts, the muscles bulging. Her white legs terminate abruptly in rolled blue socks and high-topped P.F. Flyers. "One-two," she screams. "Swing your partner and dosey-do. Back and forth. Okay, *curtsy*, like *this*. One-two, don't lose step."

She is teaching the Virginia Reel to twelve panting middle-aged square dancers.

"It's a wedding, you're in love with him, *look* at him, please. Just look him in the eye, there now. Take his arm, that's right. Lift your train. What do you mean, what train? Sure you're going to have a train on your dress; it's a *wedding* dress." Buck Fire is coaching two brides and two grooms, who stare awkwardly at one another.

"Oh Lord my God, when I in *awe*-some *won*-der, con-sider awwwwl—" Here are the Community Singers, fea-turing Warren Burton on the portable organ. His name is engraved in glitter on his organ.

"O.K. now, you're going to amputate that leg and when you chop, you *chop*, you hear me, so they can see you in the last row. You're not going to be any bigger than a bird, partner, from way up there. And you, what's your name? You yell like crazy. He's chopping off your leg, remem-ber. This is *war*. All right, let's see it. Not the knee, I said. The whole leg. Well, chop it three or four times then, I don't care." Luther directs a battlefield amputation.

Snakelike, a string of high school boys and girls creeps around the gymnasium, in and out of other groups, led by a YMCA director named Mrs. Almond. They are prepar-ing to ambush a settlement. Each of them will carry a torch, she explains, and the stage will be dark. "You'll look like a living firework," Mrs. Almond tells them with satisfaction, echoing Luther. They giggle. Perhaps because their rehearsal seems no more serious than a child's game, dissension runs through them like fire traveling a fuse. "Mrs. Pecan," they begin to call her. "*Mrs. Peanut,*" they scream.

Some of the groups leave, others form. The tumult grows louder and is echoed, reverberates from the tiled walls, rebounds. Patterns form and then dissolve on the wooden floor as if the occupants are pieces of glass in a kaleidoscope. Occasionally one group alone is in action. Dissolves. Occasionally a single voice is heard, but most remarks are swept away into the din.

"You don't reckon anybody would notice, do you, if I slipped right off there in the little girls' room and took off my panty girdle? It's about to kill me."

"I don't care if he *is* little, he knows them all. I heard he knows Troy Donohue."

"So I just told her, 'If you haven't got time to go to church, well what *have* you got time for?' It might not have been my place but I just spoke right on up."

"I'm not prejudiced one bit, but the way I feel is, I don't see what they want to go living in a brand-new apartment for. They've got houses all over town they can live in if they've got a mind to. They can live nice places. I just never heard of one in an apartment like that. What they going to do in an *apartment*, you reckon? I mean that they can't do in a house?"

"You like peanut-butter sandwiches, Mrs. Almond? You like cashew nuts?"

"And then right after Georgie got his cast took off, the rest of us got that bug where you vomit for twenty-four hours. It was just awful. I kept my washer running night and day. Sue Ellen had it the worst. She had it so bad we took her over to the hospital and they shot a glucose right in her little old vein."

"Let's you and me go over to Pete's and get us a Blue after this is over, Henry. I don't mind telling you I feel like a fool. I wouldn't be here at all if Mr. Dinsmore didn't call a sales meeting and tell everybody it would behoove us to get our asses over here and volunteer for something. *Behoove* us, he said. I said I'm a real-estate salesman not an actor and he said you're a real-estate salesman *right now*, get it?"

"Now I am certain that you know your business, Mr.

Luther, but I feel that you are not allowing those of us who know choreography to become creatively involved, if I may say so. And if I might be so bold as to suggest—"

"Well, I came in on Wednesday and you said we were supposed to meet on Thursday at ten and I came then too and you said no, come today at noon which I did and have to get a sitter and everything, and now you tell me you've got all the can-can girls you need. That's not a very nice way to treat somebody who is paying good money to come over here in the first place and the more I think about it, the whole thing just burns me up. I don't have to beg anybody to look at my legs."

People go in and out. There are 750 students in the high school who find it difficult to concentrate craning out the windows at the junior high gym. In the junior high, the students are beside themselves. From outside, the cinderblock gym looks old and almost sleepy in the steady sun. You would never guess what's going on in there. In the nearby athletic field, men are taking off their shirts for the first time this year as they work on the pageant stage. The work is being done by Oman T. Bird, a local contractor. He is talking on a telephone inside a pickup truck. The men who work for Oman call him "birdbrain." He is good on paper, they say, but he doesn't know shit about construction. The men are getting sunburned as they build a bunch of platforms. Later these will be raised to different levels, three levels in all. Later the men will put together the large, prefabricated sheds to be located behind the stage. Already the stage looks like nothing that anybody has ever seen before. It doesn't fit anybody's idea of a stage. Oman apologizes for it, and says he has to go by the plans. A line of spectators have driven up to park along the edge of the field. It is better than a Little League game, they say, taking Cokes from their Styrofoam coolers. Oman hangs up, whistling.

Across town, in the air-conditioned Rondo coffee shop, Lomas Cartwright holds forth beneath the third point of the triangle. "What I'm saying is that you can't ever tell what a man like that is going to do," Lomas says earnestly. "Now it might be some poor crazy son of a bitch with a polio or a crippled leg or something, just lying up in the bed writing all those letters for the hell of it and not really meaning anybody any harm. But you can't never tell. I had a first cousin, a real pretty girl from Marks, Mississippi, who got these anonymous phone calls all the time from somebody who never said a word, just breathed real hard into the phone whenever she picked it up. Well, this cousin of mine was a schoolteacher so she figures it's one of the kids playing a joke and doesn't think any more about it until one night she wakes up and bingo, there he is standing there breathing right over her bed."

"Then what happened?" asks Gene Bigelow. His mustache twitches.

"What do you think happened? This breather tried to have his way with her but she hopped right up and kicked him you know where and he ran all doubled up out the door. There never was anybody could keep up with her, anyway. The thing is, gentlemen, we've got to protect our women."

"Amen," says Bigelow, a bachelor.

"You don't know what somebody like that is going to do," Lomas goes on, "even supposing that it's not any kind of an organized group trying to harass us like some of us think it is." He gives a dark, meaningful look around the room and some of the men at the plastic tables nod seriously.

"What you going to do about it, Lomas?" someone calls out derisively.

"I say we can't let them get away with it." Lomas nods wisely, as if he has given the matter a lot of thought. He is just talking. "I say we can't let them get away with it. I say if Higgins or the White Company aren't going to do anything about it, which they aren't, then it's up to you and me, as Americans, to do something. We got to protect our women."

Manny Goldman, who has been silent, now speaks up: "Those letters never said a word about women."

But Lomas is talking a blue streak now, and doesn't hear. He thinks the letters are Communist. He advances the two-crank theory and the conspiracy theory. "I tell you what we ought to do, boys," cries Lomas, slapping the table with the flat of his hand. "We ought to form ourselves into a group for our own protection. We ought to track down where these things are coming from before they mess up the whole show. I've got a daughter and a boy in that pageant myself, and I don't want them getting hurt." Lomas' eyes are shining. "Why, he might throw a bomb in there!" Lomas pronounces it "bum."

"Yeah, you're right," says Gene Bigelow.

Manny silently rises and leaves the Rondo and nobody misses him. They are full of plans. Manny shakes his head and mutters to himself as he walks back up the sidewalk to his drugstore. He will never leave Speed; it has made him rich.

Inside the Rondo, Lomas goes on talking. He can go on for hours, give him a subject and a bunch of men. He has rarely had such an interested audience. It is satisfying and inspiring and Lomas is inspired to go on and on, embroidering. He loves mass actions of any sort; he won two medals in Korea. Occasionally someone will object to something he is saying, but most are in agreement. These men have heard on Walter Cronkite, night after night, reports of disturbances throughout the country. They don't want it to happen here, they say vigorously. Yet the idea of it brings a heady excitement and a new glint to their eyes.

Outside, the day turns even warmer, and over at the Junior College the coeds take blankets up to the rooftops and spread the blankets themselves out in the sun. They do not know, or care, about the isosceles triangle superimposed on the town. Most of them are liberal arts and education majors, anyway, with little knowledge of geometry.

TWENTY-THREE

LLOYD Warner stood at the wrought-iron gate, looking up the long hill at his mother's house. Actually it was his house, but he would never live in it. He swore under his breath and pulled at his tie. He hated to come over here, yet he came here every day. Lloyd sat down on the broad stone steps, the first of many small flights of such steps in the long walk up to the house. It had been different when his father was alive. Lloyd Sr. had had arteriosclerosis, a heart condition, and too many other ills to name, including some stomach thing—Lloyd had forgotten the exact name— which was supposed to have kept him on a rigorous diet. By the end of his life he had been a walking land mine, a collection of enough mortal illnesses to have killed any-body else years before. But Lloyd Sr. had been a stubborn old man, refusing to die, refusing to be beat out of his last and most contemptuous act: his suicide.

Lloyd grinned, thinking of his mother's reaction. She had played the grande dame all her life; nothing so prepos-terous as her husband's suicide was going to strip her of her role. "When Mr. Warner bravely met his end" was the way she referred to it, exactly as if he had died in a war. All events came to be dated by old Lloyd's suicide. "When we went vacationing at Gulf Shores several years before Mr. Warner bravely met his end," she would begin. Or "Since Mr. Warner bravely met his end, I have had to struggle for my livelihood." Which was a lie. His mother liked to poor-mouth, that being naturally more genteel than talking rich. Old Lloyd would have snorted, dilating his hairy red nostrils, the way he had snorted all his life at pretension and cant. When his father was alive, Lloyd could not see why he didn't leave her. Now that his father was dead, Lloyd could see it, but he couldn't understand it. It was the same thing, obviously, that kept him walking over here every day of his life and hating every minute of it. His mother was not the kind of woman you could leave.

"Natural man is an asshole," old Lloyd had shouted once, drunk, "and civilized man is a damn sight worse." Old Lloyd was a huge man in his prime; at the end his clothes hung on him like a rack, but he obstinately refused to have them taken in. He had a long, hooked nose; bushy eyebrows that ran in a straight line over fierce, squinting eyes; sparse, erratic white hair; and a veiny, mottled complexion. Lloyd remembered seeing the red network of small veins visible through the nearly translucent skin of his father's face right before he killed himself. He particularly remembered his father's hands, long and elegant and incongruous. He remembered all the gestures—that characteristic jab into the air, meaning disagreement; the eloquent wringing of the hands; the hands thrown up in mock astonishment; the incredibly long, pointing finger. Lloyd Sr. had been one of the best courtroom lawyers in Alabama. He had lost only two jury trials. He had been widely respected, feared, and—occasionally—loved. He had used the law like a toy, Lloyd reflected, playing with it, shaping it to suit himself to his own devices, twirling it like a magician, to dazzle and confuse. He had been cynical and contemptuous of it, of those around him, of himself as well. Not an illusion to his name, Lloyd reflected, except maybe the final one. Or. He could not decide.

Lloyd got up from the warm step, squared his shoulders, and started up the long hill. The huge yard reminded him of the grounds of certain country houses in France. It had the air of an unkempt park, as though the owner had plenty of money to turn it into a garden if he chose to, but he had better things to do. Huge, century-old magnolias were planted at regular intervals, throwing the entire yard into shade. Little stone benches and angels, half-hidden by leaves, crouched here and there among the overgrown bushes and vines.

The long slope rounded off into a smooth plateau known as the bluff; here Lloyd's grandfather had built the house. It was a strange, asymmetrical house. Soft pink brick, it rose in three tiers like a Gothic-Greek Revival wedding cake. Each floor had a porch running the length of the front of the house, small white columns and gingerbread railings. The design of the gingerbread and the number of columns varied from floor to floor. A sort of cupola was perched on top of the house like a party hat. It was here that old Lloyd had shot himself. God knows how he had gotten up there, the shape he was in. But the house was at its peak now, in full spring. With all the cherry and peach trees blooming at the side, it had a festive air to go with its party hat. Lloyd squinted at it appreciatively against the hot sun. Very nice. But it was bad at night, when all those white railings gave it an unsteady, ethereal look, so that it seemed to sway and sigh above the bluff. No, he would not live in it. He hadn't spent a night there since finding his father.

Lloyd climbed the steps to the porch. He opened the screen door and then the front door with its round pane of cranberry glass, shaking his head to find it unlocked. He had told her repeatedly to lock the door, but she always threw up her hands dramatically and said, "But, my dear, anyone so unfortunate as to have recourse to robbery is welcome to anything I have." Lloyd heard her now, the airy tones of her voice floating through the stiff, over-furnished room. He could not distinguish the words but the voice had a nearly hypnotic lilt. Lloyd moved through the stuffed Victorian pieces—as a child he had imagined the furniture to be a herd of unimaginable animals, roaming the house at night—to the sun porch, where his mother sat with his sister Florence in the padded wicker chairs. He stopped out of sight behind the huge rubber plant.

"What do you suppose she meant by that!" his mother cried.

"Well, don't ask *me*, Mama! All I know is she locked him out of the house and threw the key down the toilet and he had to spend the night at the Holiday Inn without so much as his toothpaste. All out of spite."

"All the Merrits are spiteful."

"And you'll never guess who I saw downtown today," remarked Florence, a teasing note in her voice. The local librarian, Florence had never married, and had a great psychological advantage over her mother because she got a great deal of first-hand information every day, while Mrs. Warner was restricted to the telephone.

"Hello, ladies," Lloyd said, stepping down onto the sun porch.

"Why, Lloyd," his mother said. "How *are* you?"

"About the same as I was yesterday," Lloyd said, easing into the swing.

"Hello, Lloyd," said Florence. Florence thoroughly detested him, affording Lloyd much amusement. She was forty-two years old, thin and colorless, with a total lack of humor. She spent her days returning *Misty of Chincoteague* from the Return Books pile to the shelves. She lived downtown over the library in an apartment with another thin spinster who had been her friend since childhood. Lloyd had an idea that his mother despised Florence as much as he did, yet she could not do without her. Florence was necessary as a bringer of news.

"Any news?" inquired his mother now as he always did, as if there were a vast emergency in the town. She leaned forward in the chair. Her thin blue hair curled girlishly about her face, which was thickly plastered with orange-tone makeup. A tall, thin woman, she wore a blue voile dress with powder stains about the neck. She would have died if she had known about the powder stains, but her eyes were failing her now, and despite her immaculate daily turnout, there were certain things she missed.

Lloyd thought awhile. "Bill Higgins was shot," he said.

"Shot!" cried his mother in a rapture.

"Killed on the courthouse steps by a man with a bow and arrow. They said his last name was Hood."

"Oh, Lloyd," said Florence, disgusted. "Why don't you grow up? He's kidding," she said emphatically to her mother.

"Ah, well," Mrs. Warner said philosophically, as if you couldn't expect much from Lloyd.

"How are you, Mother?" asked Lloyd.

"I didn't sleep a wink," she said with an air of martyrdom. "I just tossed and turned all night long. I'm very tired, Lloyd, and I think my sciatica is acting up again. It is such grievous pain. And the sink in the downstairs bathroom is stopped up, such a nuisance."

"I certainly am sorry to hear all that, Mother," Lloyd said. "I'll get somebody over here to fix it this afternoon."

"Well," Mrs. Warner said, pursing her lips, "that sink has been stopped up no less than four times since Mr. Warner bravely met his end."

"No kidding." Lloyd whistled appreciatively. Florence eyed him with suspicion.

"Have a drink," his mother said. "I'll call Millie."

"No," Lloyd said, suddenly edgy. "I've got some work to do."

"Well, yes," his mother said vaguely, waving her hand. She never referred to Lloyd's profession, as she had never referred to his father's. To her, men went to work and came back home and that was that. That whole long summer when Lloyd had worked in Mississippi, she had always greeted his reappearances brightly: "Having a nice time, dear?" she used to ask, as if he were on an extended vacation.

Florence sat primly with her feet together. Mrs. Warner leaned forward in her chair, holding the smile.

"I'll send somebody right on over here to fix that sink," he said, then stood for a second as if about to say something more. But there was nothing to say. "See you," he said, and left.

He threaded his way through the monstrous furniture and closed the heavy door behind him. He took each small flight of steps in one leap as he went down the slanting walk. He knew exactly what was going on behind him on the sun porch, not so much through speculation as from a sound basis of eavesdropping, carried on over the years. He imagined the two of them immediately regaining their vitality, picking up the phone, chattering on and on in their incomprehensible language.

They reminded him of the CIA. Each bit of information was picked over, mused upon, interpreted until it often bore no relation to its context—if, indeed, it had ever had one. Lloyd could not see the point in it. Yet his mother was linked, through the white telephone, with a score of other old ladies in town who spent their days at virtually the same occupation. Perhaps the other ladies were not quite as obsessed as his mother, though. The contrast between her careful gentility and her rapacious curiosity never failed to astound Lloyd. Whenever she was told of a pregnancy, she moved her fingers surreptitiously, counting. Nobody was beyond her curiosity; nobody was above suspicion. Yet you would never guess her vice, to see her.

Lloyd felt that she disliked him as much as she disliked Florence, yet she needed him to transact her business. Odd that he should be the one to do it, but there was nobody else. His sister Diane had run off and married at the age of eighteen, and had been seen only intermittently since. She lived in California with her second husband and a confused batch of five children, some hers and some his, and couldn't come back to Speed because of her great responsibilities. Not that it was any great loss. Lloyd had never known Diane, anyway; she had been a child when he went away to school and then she was married and gone. Hugh, two years older than Diane, had disappeared by degrees, after a series of mental breakdowns which began when he was sixteen. Hugh was in London now, where he had been for years. Lloyd thought of Hugh and Diane without much emotion. They were smart to get out when they did. He could not, however, figure out how they had been able to leave and he had not. In his checkbook, Lloyd wrote himself a note to call a plumber.

TWENTY-FOUR

IT had all happened so fast that even now Bevo was not sure that any of it was true. That it had happened to him and not to somebody else. It had begun when Bevo and J.T., out in Bevo's back yard, had heard music coming from somewhere and followed it and found Sharon DuBois just over the wall, sunbathing. They were on their way to an afternoon show, but Bevo had stopped cold and refused to go any further.

"Oh, come on," J.T. had said. "You've seen girls before. What do you want to stand out in the hot sun and look at old Sharon for? I got better things to do, myself."

"Shut up, shut up," Bevo said through grinding teeth. "She'll hear you."

"So what?" J.T. said. "It isn't anybody but old Sharon DuBois." J.T. hopped from one tennis shoe to the other. His glasses sparkled. "Let's get a move on," he said.

"I said, you go on," Bevo whispered. He found himself incapable of moving his feet. They were stuck in the soft rich soil of the flower bed nearest the wall. He could see right over into the DuBoises' yard, where, not twenty feet away, Sharon lay supine, spread-eagled, in the posture he had dreamed about for years. The plastic lawn chair, a yellow and green tubed thing, had been pulled flat, and there she lay, small white pads of some sort covering her eyes. She wore the same bathing suit that she had worn when she placed second in the Miss Speed High Contest and first in the Miss Guntersville Lake Contest. It was black-knit, two-piece, with rhinestone spaghetti straps. Her bare, flat midriff glistened with a sheen of oil. All her limbs shone too, and one bare foot (she had rather large feet) jiggled up and down to "Lucy in the Sky with Diamonds" coming from the tiny transistor radio in the grass.

Suddenly, with absolutely no warning at all, she sat up. Bevo was stunned. He had never expected such a thing. Her midriff folded into three symmetrical creases, from which he could not raise his eyes.

"I didn't even know you were there," she said, turning down the transistor and stretching her arms. "What you up to?" She was speaking languidly to J.T. It was a Saturday afternoon, one week before the pageant.

"Nothing," J.T. said.

"Yeah," said Sharon. Bevo was dazzled by their sophisticated style of conversation.

"How you doing in the contest?" J.T. said after a while.

"All right, I guess," Sharon said. "I got a lot of people selling tickets for me. Of course nobody knows until the very end, but I think I'm doing pretty good." She smiled brilliantly, trying out a new lowering of the eyes on J.T. and Bevo.

"I'm in the pageant," Bevo blurted. "I blow the bugle," he continued, appalled. "I'm the only one in the whole thing that blows the bugle."

"I didn't know you blew the bugle," Sharon said, adjusting her straps. She looked bored.

"Oh, yeah," Bevo said. "I have to practice all the time; it's this real important part. I have to go to practice right after supper, in fact."

"Do you know Mr. Fire?" Sharon asked, suddenly interested. She had seen him from a distance, but he didn't have much to do with the contestants. All that was handled by Mr. Fletcher, fat slob. Mr. Fletcher was not the kind who would discover you and make you into a star. But Mr. Fire! He could take you places.

"Oh, sure," Bevo said.

"Well, I might just ride over there with you and see what you all do."

Bevo was dumbfounded.

"I won't be able to make it," J.T. said, exactly as if he had been asked. "I've got something going."

"Well, is that all right?" Sharon said, shading her eyes.

"What all right?" said Bevo.

"If I ride over there to practice with you."

"Sure," Bevo said, trying to be cool.

He was so cool that Sharon seemed to take offense. "If you don't want me to go, just say so," she snapped. Bevo was terrified that he had lost her.

"I'd love to have you go," Bevo said sincerely, which seemed to disgust her. J.T. was grinning. Had Bevo sounded sarcastic? The intricacies of sarcasm were beyond him.

"Well, what time are you going?" Sharon said.

"What?"

"I said what time are you going, that is if you want me to go." Now she was snooty.

"I'll pick you up at six-thirty," Bevo said. It was the line he had dreamed of saying for years.

"Pick me up!" she said. "I can just walk over. It's not but about ten feet."

"Well," said Bevo.

"I'll come on over after supper," Sharon announced.

She put the little pads back on her eyes and lay down again, dismissing J.T. and Bevo.

But now Bevo's Mamaw was coming at them across the driveway, waving a hoe. "You all get out of my phlox," she screamed. "Get out! You, Bevo! You, J.T.! Hiyah!" She yelled as if she were driving a team of horses in a race. Her long, shapeless dress flapped about her thin legs. "Move," she screamed, working her beaklike jaw. They stood for a second as if paralyzed, then ran down the driveway, J.T. was hooting with laughter. Mamaw waved her hoe. Bevo thought that personally he would die.

Bevo sat through a cartoon, a Western, and a whole spate of previews without seeing a thing. Methodically, he ate two Hershey bars and a bag of popcorn, tasting nothing. It was not that he was thinking of Sharon. He thought of nothing, simply nothing at all, and it was with an effort that he pulled his mind back from some limbo behind the screen and left the Bijou. Later, he could not remember parting from J.T. He went home and sat in the orange armchair in his room, thinking that he should begin to get ready. It was time to get ready. Yet the occasion was so important that it paralyzed him. He thought of the things he should do but he could not figure out in what order he wanted to do them. His bugle was under the bed. How had this all come about? His new shirt was in a drawer. He ought to take a shower. A series of frames formed in his mind, each of them enclosing an action shot of him doing one of the things he should do. Finally he got up and went downstairs to supper, simply because he felt incapable of standing the fuss they would make if he didn't show up.

His Mamaw bit a corn stick with quick, successive nips until the whole of it was in her mouth. Then she pointed at Bevo and began to make unintelligible birdlike cries, spewing crumbs. Bevo assumed that she was talking about the way he had stood in her flowers.

"Oh, for God's sake!" Ruthie burst out. "Can't a person eat in peace?" She glared at her Mamaw.

Anne looked out at them all from the depths of her profound calm, gently smiling, while Lomas bent low to his plate and got on with it.

Bevo pushed some pieces of ham around and spent a long time examining a forkful of black-eyed peas. "I'll need the car tonight," he said abruptly, unnecessarily loud.

"Oh?" said Anne, soft and surprised. "What for? I'm supposed to go to the Eastern Star initiation." Anne was a Worthy Matron.

"I've got to go to practice," Bevo said. He thought he was going to throw up.

"But you always walk to practice," Anne said. A slow, puzzled smile. "It's just a ten-minute walk."

"Mama, I've got to have the car!" Bevo said. "You don't understand. I've got to have it."

"Take the truck," Lomas said with his mouth full.

Anne opened her wide eyes still wider and progressed another degree into the reaches of calm. "Well, if it's so important, I suppose your father could drive me to—?"

"I'm not driving nobody no place," Lomas bellowed. "If he's too damn good to take the truck then he can scoot over there on his ass for all I care."

"Now, now," Anne said mechanically.

"Oh, Jesus, take my car," Ruthie said. "Just everybody shut up." She disappeared from the table, came back with a lighted cigarette and the convertible keys, which she threw at Bevo. The key chain had a charm on it, a new penny pressed in plastic. "Don't wreck it," Ruthie said nastily, and was gone. She was awful lately. She was a real bitch. Bevo's Mamaw cackled because she liked to see a show of spirit now and then.

Bevo got right up, the Robot Man, and left the table.

"But you haven't finished your supper," Anne protested mildly.

"Too good to drive a truck," Lomas said.

When Bevo came back downstairs twenty minutes later, cleaned and smoothed, wet-haired and pale, Anne said, "Oh!" very significantly, with a certain small pursing of the lips and an air of comprehension. He hated the look of profound sympathy which she next proceeded to turn upon him. If this had happened last week, she probably would have taken his picture. Now she couldn't do that, at least. Funny the way she had never mentioned the camera.

"Anyone we know, dear?" Anne said brightly.

"No," Bevo said, surprised that the lie came out so easily. Lomas was involved in Andy Williams on TV, but Anne's tone was unnecessarily confidential.

"See you," Bevo said. He walked out the front door and across the green grass to the DuBoises' front door, where he rang the bell. A very fancy chime sang through the house and then Sharon opened the door herself. "Bye," she called, and stepped out while Bevo held the screen door, as if she were a princess.

"I would have come on over," she said, but Bevo could think of nothing to say in reply. "I know it," "That's all right," etc., passed through his mind, but he said none of these aloud. He walked slightly behind her down the walk and collided with her when she suddenly stopped and said, "What are we going in?"

"Oh, I'm sorry!" Bevo exclaimed.

"It's all right," she answered, a little nasty, since he could have made her hair come down. She felt it, but luckily it was still in place. Sharon had gone to no little pains with her looks tonight. After all, she planned to be discovered! She wore very tight white pants, through which the ridge of lace on her panties was visible and she knew it was visible, so what; a striped jersey pullover and a pushup bra; little red stacked heels; and it had taken her twenty minutes to wind her blond hair into fat sausage curls and fix them securely (she hoped) on top of her head. The result didn't look exactly like it had in the magazine, but it was plenty good enough. Little wings of blond hair swooped down over her ears and then went back and up into the frantic area of the greatest height, which resembled nothing so much as a pile of lumber shavings. Sharon sat very stiffly, not leaning all the way back in Ruthie's car. She wasn't going to mess everything up now!

Bevo planned to say it was his car, if it came up. He had several answers planned, in fact, to questions he thought she might ask in making conversation on the way to practice, but now it appeared that she would not speak at all. She had twisted the rear-view mirror so that she could see her face in it, and she was working on her lips.

"You look real pretty," he said involuntarily.

"Why, thank you, Bevo," Sharon said, and practiced her shy smile on him. This particular smile involved a look in the eyes, a hesitant glance away, a little smile, and then another look in the eyes. It was such an involved smile that Bevo almost wrecked the car.

"Oh!" she cried as Bevo swerved. "Where are you going, anyway?" They could have been at the junior high by now. It was only four blocks away from their neighborhood.

"I thought you might like to go by Fast Eddie's for a Coke first," Bevo said. He knew that everybody went to Fast Eddie's. "They're always late getting started at practice anyway."

"Oh, I don't think so," Sharon said sweetly. "We'd better go on back to the junior high. I think your watch is slow." She knew he didn't have a watch, and she also knew that he wouldn't dream of disobeying her wishes. And, as the (probable) future Sesquicentennial Queen, she didn't want to be seen at Fast Eddie's with Bevo Cartwright. He was just a kid, she felt, compared to her—even though they were the same age. And besides, everyone thought he was weird. She might consider being seen at Fast Eddie's with somebody else, just to make Red jealous and keep him on his toes. But not Bevo. Red would never be jealous of Bevo in a million years. All he would do was laugh.

Bevo obediently left at the next light. He drove very slowly because he had read in a teenage column that girls only *pretended* to like restless boys. In the long run, all of them were searching for "stability and maturity" in a man.

"You better hurry up," Sharon said, shattering him. She would like to meet Mr. Fire, she thought, in a free moment. Nobody had time to discover anybody if they were in the middle of directing a pageant!

Bevo had to drive up and down in the junior high parking lot, looking for a space. He *was* late, he guessed. It seemed a lot more crowded than usual. Finally he found a spot, pulled in, and turned off the ignition. Sharon was occupied with the mirror. She wondered if her personality would change after she got famous. Before getting out (remember to go around and open the door!), Bevo leaned across the blue vinyl toward her and asked brightly, "Having a good time so far tonight?" It was something suave he had planned to say. But Sharon was collapsing with laughter—at his very question, it seemed!

"You're a riot," she said.

Bevo opened her door blindly and took her, still giggling, into the gym.

It was as if he had entered on cue. "Where's the bugler?" Buck Fire was demanding through a megaphone. The Confederate soldiers crouched in a corner, ready to charge. In another corner, a small squadron of the National Guard drilled diligently.

"Right here, sir," Bevo said, out of breath. He hurried across the wooden gymnasium floor with Sharon right behind him.

"O.K., soldiers," Buck shouted. "Ready?" The soldiers nodded. Sharon stared at Buck, who was wearing his yellow jumpsuit. Oh, yes, she thought, this is the one. If he wanted her body, she decided, he could have most of it. She sucked in her stomach and stuck out her rump as she stood alone—conspicuously alone, she hoped. Bevo had joined the soldiers.

"Bugle!" Buck shouted.

Silence.

"Ready for the bugle," Buck shouted again, and again there was silence.

"O.K., where's the bugler?" Buck said in an irritated yet resigned voice.

"Here, sir," Bevo said, waving his hand.

"So blow your bugle," Buck said, pacing back and forth. "I haven't got all night."

"I can't," Bevo said.

"Well, why the hell not? You're the bugler, aren't you?"

"I forgot my bugle, sir." It was still at home, under the bed. The other Confederate soldiers laughed and gave Rebel yells.

"Oh, come on." Buck snorted. He had had a long, hard day, without a break since early that afternoon. "Well, we've got to practice this scene anyway. Sound like a bugle and we'll go ahead."

"What, sir?"

"I said, sound like a bugle," Buck replied, very short. "Make like you're a bugle and we'll go ahead."

Exactly at that moment, the National Guard ceased drilling, and a deathly, unexpected silence—the first all day—descended suddenly upon the cavernous gym. Into that silence piped Bevo's trembling voice: "Ta-ra-ta-ra-ta-ta!" Even the rafters shook with laughter. Even Buck Fire laughed. "O.K., O.K.," he said through his megaphone when he had re-established order and put the Confederates back in their corner. "Try it again, without the bugle!"

They raised the Rebel yell. They charged.

"Time for the amputation," Buck blared, and the doctor and the amputee went to work on the shiny wood floor. In the background, the familiar voice of Ron-the-Mouth, intoned, "Battleground conditions were often primitive. The brave men in gray underwent terrible deprivations, walking miles with only rags on their feet as they died bravely for a losing cause." The amputee started screaming.

When it was over, Sharon clicked across the floor and grabbed Bevo's arm so tightly that she stopped the circulation.

"Introduce me," she whispered.

"What?" Bevo said, still dazed.

"You said you'd introduce me to Mr. Fire." Sharon's lovely nostrils flared. "Come on." She began to drag him across the gym in the direction of the yellow jumpsuit; he slid meekly in her wake. Then they were there, amid the hubbub of incoming frontiersmen and legislators, at Buck's slight yellow back.

"Well, go *on*." Sharon squeezed his elbow so tightly that tears came to his eyes.

"Mr. Fire!" Bevo said, not believing the sound of his own voice. Buck turned abruptly.

"Mr. Fire, I'd-like-you-to-meet-Sharon-DuBois," Bevo said at the same time a burly businessman bellowed, "I've got to be at Kiwanis at eight-thirty."

"Hello." Buck nodded briskly. It was clear that he had no idea who Bevo was. He immediately turned his back and raised the megaphone.

Bevo turned to Sharon but she was gone, running, or

rather strutting (so deeply ingrained was her training), across the floor and out the open door. Bevo followed, feverish, but it had grown dark and he couldn't see her among the humps of cars. Finally he went back to Ruthie's car and there she was inside, huddled against the window.

"Sharon?" he said.

"Let's go," said Sharon. On the way back she made many small retching noises and Bevo thought she was sick until they stopped for the light and he saw the black marks that running mascara had made on her cheeks. Sharon was crying! Sharon, who had less reason—as far as he could see—to cry than any other person in the world!

"Do you want to go to a show?" he said, without much hope. The Western at the Bijou which he had seen that afternoon was the only film in town, but he was prepared to see it eighty-five more times if Sharon wanted to go.

"I want to go home," she sniffed.

Bevo pulled up before her house and suddenly she flung herself on him, sobbing. He held her stiffly. He was terrified; what should he do? He had no handkerchief. He had no Kleenex. Her hair was at his nose, sprayed hard as porcelain, sweet-smelling. Bevo shifted. His arm, beneath her weight, was going to sleep. For such a buoyant majorette, she was surprisingly heavy. "You sure you can't go to the show?" he said.

"I've got a date." Sharon pushed him away as abruptly as she had grabbed him, picked up her purse, and was gone, slamming the car door, a flash of gold hair beneath the gaslight at the end of her walk, a slamming door.

Bevo carefully backed the convertible into his own driveway and into the carport and sat in it awhile in the dark, overcome by a profound inertia. He could not complete a thought, any thought at all. He was mystified and strangely cold, although the night was warm.

Before long Red pulled up next door, gunning the motor. He blew the horn and out she came like the lady in the cuckoo clock which the decorator had placed in Bevo's den. She bounced again in her old accustomed way, as if she were walking on foam rubber. Bevo could see the glow of Red's cigarette in the dark. He saw Red's mag wheels in the gaslight, the gleam again of her hair when the light flashed on as she opened the door. Bevo leaned forward and banged his head gently, a number of times, on the cool plastic wheel, molded to fit his hands. *Grooved* to fit his hands. *Groovy.* Everybody said that now, yet he had never said it. "Slang is a lack of vocabulary," Anne used to say. He could get her Bank Americard out of her pocketbook and take off right now in Ruthie's car and never be heard of again. he wouldn't, though. He would stay right here and somehow show them all. The echoing laughter of the Rebel soldiers filled his head, filled the gym, filled this carport. What had been wrong with Sharon? He couldn't understand any of it. Fire filled his mind and he had a terrible headache. With his hand, he felt the shoulder where her head had lain. Now she was out with Red. He heard the Confederates' laughter, and laughed himself as flames consumed them. Bevo thought he had been miserable before, but it was nothing like this. A bugler without his bugle! Forced to shout, "Ta-ra-ta-ra!"

TWENTY-FIVE

THESE days it's hard to find a carpenter like old John Mills. John is almost seventy, but he won't retire. The thought has never seriously entered his head, although he would like to be able to make more golf clubs in his spare time. John doesn't play golf. But he has made the clubs for thirty years, at night, working slowly. He specializes in No. 2 woods and it takes him a long time to make a single club. Every really prominent man in Speed has a club which has been handcrafted by John Mills. When he is working on sunny days, John occasionally thinks about these men out playing golf, using his clubs, crossing wide water hazards. But he doesn't envy them. He merely hopes that they are using his clubs well, and in some way this thought comforts him, because he has raised and educated three sons, none of whom cared enough about his business to take it up themselves. When they were in high school, he never could make them properly clean their tools. The young boys who work with him now are the same way: always listening to transistor radios, always trying to find a faster way to get the job done. They don't have any pride in their work or any understanding of wood. So John is still a one-man operation, working small jobs himself and sometimes working for the large contractors.

Today he is at work on the type of job he most despises. But his insurance payment is due, and lately most cabinet-work in the new houses around Speed seems to be of the prefabricated variety, so times are not good and he has had no choice. Oman Bird is hiring anybody who can use a hammer. He doesn't want craftsmen, just bodies on the job. This stage will be torn down after it is used anyway, he explained to the workers, so he doesn't much care how they do it as long as it looks O.K. Just get it together by Thursday. It's a jerry-built, ungainly thing, cheap pine on oil drums at one level, on steel higher up. John Mills shakes his head and mutters to himself, not missing a lick with his hammer. He's on the top level, in the wind. The younger men around him have taken off their shirts, but he disapproves of this. His own blue work shirts sticks to his back, wet with sweat. Below him he sees men on all the different levels, carrying wood, mixing paint. John, who is a lay preacher, thanks God for the beautiful day. From his perch, the men on the ground look like large ants. Oman Bird looks like an ant. This is some consolation to John for working on such a thing.

Inside the gym, Buck O.K.s the scene featuring the Devil and the History Book. Now what? Rehearse the WPA, then back to Monica. Buck doodles on the old wooden card table. Monica will probably be in his bed by now, frowsy-headed and wild. She can wear him out. Sometimes in the middle she hums little tuneless songs over and over, her breath in his ear. Buck can never tell what she's thinking, though. Sometimes her eyes go blank and distant on him, and whatever he says, she only nods in reply. Like she isn't really listening to him. Sometimes she laughs and laughs when there isn't any joke. Other times, when he makes a joke, she doesn't laugh at all. They scare him when they're like that, but this time he can't stay away. Already he is figuring out ways to meet Monica later, after this pageant is through. After Speed has shot its wad on the White Company. It shouldn't be too difficult. Monica has plenty of money and seems to do whatever she wants. If she's not in bed in his apartment right now, she's straightening it up. Says she never does housework at home. Maybe it gives her a kick. Whatever does it for you, Buck thinks. As many times as she has been there now, Buck can't figure her out. Maybe he'll let the WPA go a little early today.

A farm man collars Buck, saying he never even voted for the crippled bastard and now here he is in the goddamn WPA, what about it! He wouldn't even be here if the Grange hadn't put him up to it. He is apologizing wildly in all directions, grinning like mad. The mud is caked on his boots, dried on his bootlaces.

Buck gets the megaphone and puts it to his lips, ready to organize the WPA into a group in center court on the gym floor, but he is suddenly stopped by a noise from the football field. He has never heard anything quite like it. It is a long slow rumble, followed by a crash and the scream of a crowd. This is a single loud yell, nearly simultaneous with the crash, and it sounds like the crowd at a football game where someone intercepts the ball and goes all the way for a touchdown. After the yell and the crash, a loud hubbub continues.

The people in the gymnasium stand for a second in silence, listening, and then begin moving steadily toward the open door, picking up momentum, and the kids and the younger men break into a run.

"Stay here," Buck directs belatedly through the megaphone; "close that door," but everyone ignores him, if they hear him at all. His authority extends only to the pageant itself, in any case. He can't tell them not to go see what's going on outside their own high school. The roles are suddenly reversed. No longer the initiate, familiar of all the wonders of the stage, Buck becomes merely another body in the crowd which pours out onto the field.

It is bright outside and it takes a second for the eyes of the gymnasium crowd to adjust to the sun. It's like coming out of a movie. Then vision clears, and the gym crowd gasps all at once. Buck stops where he is. "Son of a bitch," he says, and someone runs into him from behind.

An old man stands under the goal posts, plucking at the steaming crowd, retelling it to anybody who will listen. "I tell you it was like a bum was stuck in the middle of it, all of a sudden it started shaking and everybody went to hollering and running and then the middle of it fell right out and the rest of it went down that way. I was standing right over here—"

But nobody pays him much mind. They want to see for themselves. The field is full of people now, running, climbing around on the fallen timber, clustered in groups to watch. Nobody knows if anybody is hurt. Then an ambulance is coming (you can hear its siren long before it comes into view, going absurdly slow), and two police cars pull up with *their* sirens going too, and a bunch of cars come in from downtown (you know how you follow police cars). This is really something; somebody must be hurt. But there are so many people that no one can see who it is.

Right before the stage collapsed, old John Mills was wiping his face, thinking—as he always did on a bad job—of his finest hour: several years ago, one of his golf clubs had played golf with President Eisenhower. The President of the United States. The man who had used it was the brother of a woman in Speed. His golf club had played nine holes with Eisenhower himself, at The Green-

Lee Smith

brier in West Virginia. Old John felt the stage shake and then shake again, like what he had heard about earthquakes. Only he knew it wasn't an earthquake. It was wood giving. He had turned to start down when the whole thing went.

A swelling murmur, almost like a cheer, goes up as two white-uniformed hospital orderlies hop from the ambulance with a stretcher, ascend the wreckage of the stage, are lost to sight, then reappear, carrying someone on their stretcher. Who is it? Is he dead? Then the information passes back through them like a wind: it's only John Mills. O.K. except he broke his arm. He'll be all right, and everyone else is fine.

TWENTY-SIX

"SHE don't have all that red hair for nothing," Bevo's Mamaw cackled as Ruthie marched out of the house.

"My, my," Anne said, looking after her daughter and shaking her head. "For heaven's sake."

Lomas was still raving. "Either she can act like a lady and watch her goddamn language or else she can get out!" he yelled as he went into the den. He flung himself into the vibrator chair with a loud grunt and turned himself to HIGH.

Mamaw bit a toothpick in two. "It ain't no skin off my back," she said, leaving the kitchen by the back door.

Bevo stared out the side window in the den, watched Ruthie getting into Ron-the-Mouth's car. Ruthie was jerking and slamming; she never opened a car door like anybody else. What had gotten into her lately?

But Ruthie's fury seemed to disappear as soon as she got into the car. "Hello, lover," she said sweetly, and leaned over to give Ron a kiss on his famous mouth and pinch his cheek.

"That's a laugh," Ron said.

Ruthie was playing demure. "What have *you* been up to today?" she asked.

"Oh, the usual." Ron said. He wore wrap-around sunglasses and looked over at her through the wrap-around part. "Screwing the secretaries, refusing offers of dates, turning down money to pay lovely girls a simple visit."

"I bet," Ruthie said. She crossed her legs so he could see them better. "Where are we going anyway?" she asked with her nose in the air.

"Meridian," Ron said.

She stared at him, noticing for the millionth time that his face was too fat. Like a little old pudgy doll face. Oh, if it was a doll face, she would stomp it right in! But she couldn't keep from laughing. Meridian!

"That's me, the one and only laugh-a-minute Wonder Mouth," Ron said.

He was turning onto the Interstate. He really was.

"We can't go to Meridian!" she cried, delighted. "That's two whole hours away. I've got to go to work."

"You can't make it tonight, baby. You've got this migraine."

"Oh, yeah?"

"It's a pity." Ron clucked his tongue. "You were halfway out of the house on your way to work when you felt this headache coming on and you fell right down on the sidewalk blinded with pain and didn't even know what was happening until the next day."

"What day?" Ruthie asked, suspicious.

"The day after this one. It's usually called tomorrow. *Mañana* in Spanish. I remember one time down in Mexico. . . ."

"You can just turn this car right around if you think I'm going to spend the night down there with you," Ruthie said, lighting a cigarette.

"Did I say that?" Ron threw up his hands in great

alarm. "Baby, would I even suggest such a thing to a girl like you? You've got me all wrong, sweetheart. I just meant we'd be too late getting back for you to go to work, is all in the world I meant, sugar. Do you think I'd try something like that with you? Why, I couldn't sleep nights if I did a thing like that."

Ruthie piled her hair up on top of her head, then let it fall over the back of her seat. She glared at him. "You bastard," she said. She turned on the radio, turned up the volume, and began to sing along. Abruptly she turned it down. "Let's get us some road beer," she said, "as long as we're going on this trip."

"Reach behind your seat there," Ron said. "And there's a church key in the glove compartment." Ruthie pulled two Buds out of the ice in the Styrofoam cooler and opened them, handing one to him. He thought of everything. It was maddening. She looked at his suède shoes and got even madder. Oh, nobody wore shoes like those! Look at those pointed toes.

It was six o'clock and they were driving southwest into the sun and she got a headache from the glare in her eyes and then she had another beer and the headache went away and she decided it was fun after all. They went through small gray towns past people sitting out on their porches, and occasionally Ruthie shot them a bird from the car. She would never, never live in a place like any of these. As soon as she won the Queen Contest, she was cutting out. The sun went down and she fought with Ron, in the pattern they had fallen into, all the way to Meridian. If Ruthie ever got the best of him, she was going to quit going out with him altogether. And it couldn't be too soon, she told herself, as far as she was concerned.

Ron thought that it was a shame he had to take this shit off somebody like Ruthie. He ought to save himself for the high life. But until he actually made it over to the new job in Atlanta next month, he had to do *something*, didn't he? A man can't twiddle his thumbs. But he had to admit that the first time he saw her he had never expected to get into anything like this. He would hate to count up the money he had already spent on Ruthie, without even a good feel in return. And it wasn't like she was a virgin, either. Oh, Christ, it wasn't anything like that! Now, when he mentioned her name at the radio station, the other guys grinned and whistled and stomped. What would they say if they knew he wasn't getting any at all? The downfall of Ron-the-Mouth.

He grinned.

"What's so damn funny?" Ruthie asked sourly.

"Private joke," he said.

Ron had tried everything. He had tried flattery, spent money on her, bought flowers—stuff which he had never needed to do before. No good. Way back in the beginning he must have done something wrong, but he was damned if he knew what it was. She was a bitch, anyway.

Ruthie didn't know why she was so bitchy to Ron. Why she was putting on the virgin act, for instance, when she didn't give a damn who she did it with, it was fun, and he knew it. It was so stupid. Why, she was practically sex-starved this minute, like the girls you read about in the love magazines. SEX-STARVED GIRL RAPES 80-YEAR-OLD PLUMBER. It was just that everybody else had acted like they wanted it real bad, and in spite of all the kidding around, Ron acted like he didn't care if they ever did it or not. Well, Ruthie Cartwright wasn't giving out welfare! She might give in sometime, maybe, but he would have to come crawling. He'd have to change his attitude all right. On his hands and knees.

So she kept on bugging him, and in the restaurant, in the middle of eating the steaks, she went too far. She was baiting him, making fun of his family in Panama City even though she knew he liked them pretty well. "I bet your sister is real pretty, isn't she?" Ruthie said viciously, not sure why she was into this in the first place. "I bet she's got boy friends all over the yard."

"Get off my sister, lady," Ron said quietly. He wiped his mouth with his napkin and something about his gesture really got Ruthie, like he thought he was so good.

"You just get out of my life," she shouted, and a group of men in a neighboring booth turned around to stare.

"Whew," one of them said, "I wouldn't want to get messed up with that one." The other men, in their shirt sleeves, grinned at Ruthie.

Ruthie felt herself going as red as her hair, something she thought she had gotten over. She hadn't blushed for years! Perversely, she couldn't think of anything to say. Ron was such a fast talker, he'd say something smarter back. The men continued to stare and comment, and one of the white-clad waitresses was pointing at their booth.

"Just go on," she yelled again. "Just go on and get your ass out of my life." She gripped her spoon until the knuckles on her hand went white.

Ron ate like a machine, methodically putting small square pieces of steak into his mouth. He whipped his hands on the white napkin, slowly, and waved for the waitress before he answered Ruthie. "I'll be glad to, baby," he said. "Just as soon as I have my coffee."

The men hollered and slapped their knees. "Way to go," they said.

Ruthie knew when she was beat. She stood and hiked at her skirt and flounced off to the ladies' room without another word. She pushed the ladies' room door so hard that it flapped back and forth on its hinges long after she was inside the little cubicle, seated on the yellow plastic seat, cursing the orderly pattern of the yellow and black tiles on the floor. She sat there for a long time, hugging herself and rocking slightly from the waist up. She was so upset she thought she would pass out. The goddamn tiles danced all over the floor. Then suddenly, without any warning, all the fire went out of her and some sort of momentous mood descended from the ladies' room ceiling. Ruthie stood and checked her hose for runs. She had made some kind of big decision, but she didn't know what it was yet. She wouldn't know until she did it. That's the way all of her decisions were made; all of a sudden they dropped down on her and that was that, that's the way her life would go from then on. Ruthie went out in front of the mirror and brushed her long hair and put Burnt Sienna lipstick carefully on her mouth. She lit a cigarette, inhaled, exhaled, watching herself in the mirror. What was she going to do next? She put her makeup back in her purse and walked out, back through the tables, enjoying the stares. She liked how she looked.

Ron stood in the little hallway at the restaurant's entrance, between two racks of postcards, staring at a revolving display of cheap jewelry.

"Buy me that bracelet," Ruthie said, pointing at something made of large pink daisies linked by a plastic chain.

"But it's awful," Ron said, not seeming surprised to see her. They both watched the bracelets revolve.

"I said I want it," Ruthie told him flatly, and this time he looked at her.

"All right," he said, and bought it: it cost $5.47 with tax. But it was going to be worth it.

When they were back on the Interstate, pointed through the dark toward Speed, Ruthie threw it out the window. Then she slid across the seat to Ron and the air from the open window blew her hair like a net across his face.

"Hey, I can't see," he said.

"So wreck the car." She pushed closer and closer. She knew she could drive anybody crazy when she wanted to.

Even old Ron-the-Mouth. After a while, Ron pulled off the side of the road. "O.K.," he said thickly, pushing her back.

"Oh, no you don't," Ruthie said with sudden violence, slamming his head into the radio. "You take me back to Speed."

"What?" Ron said, groggy. He couldn't believe it.

"I said, you take me on back," Ruthie said with satisfaction. She pulled her bra straps back up and buttoned her dress again and they both knew she was calling the shots.

Ron swore.

"You drive careful now," she said.

"Bitch," said Ron. But she still sat close to him on the way home, with her hand on his leg, and it was the longest one-hour drive he thought he'd ever had. Then he started getting mad, sneaking looks at her smug face. Instead of taking her straight to his apartment, he thought he'd take her by this late party he knew of, that some boys from the station were having. It ought to be just her style. Besides, he might as well show off what he was getting. He might as well make her work a little.

It was a motel that Ruthie knew, but she gave no sign. She stood on the cracked cement walk with her hand on her hip while he knocked three times on the thin door. "Who is it?" somebody said.

"Ron."

The door swung open to the inside and in they went, Ron first. There was not much light and a lot of giggling. Two big, barefooted men, wearing only their pants, sat like twins on one of the chenille-covered double beds with a girl between them, lying face down. They were tickling her. She rolled over in her underwear and grinned at them. She was fat. The room was smoky and the only light came from the soundless flickering television. Sounds of splashing water and more giggling came from the bathroom. The bathroom door was closed, outlined by a slit of light.

"I said cut that out, Jim Mac! I said don't get my hair wet."

Then the bathroom door burst open and a blond girl in a towel rushed out, followed by an older man. "I want a drink," she said, then broke into fresh giggles at the sight of Ruthie and Ron. She leaned against the cinderblock wall, still giggling. She was drunk and very young.

"You all get a drink and join the party," said the man who had opened the door, the one who knew Ron. Ruthie took off her sweater and all the men were staring at her. She tossed her head, thinking vaguely, I'm not afraid of anything. She still didn't know what she would do.

Then they turned on the radio and the men were dancing with the girls and one of the men on the bed got up and asked Ruthie to dance. "I'd love to," she said.

"I didn't even know where we was going," the young girl was suddenly confiding to Ron. She had disappeared and reappeared in a man's shirt, unbuttoned. "He asked me out for a date and said he was going to take me over to his apartment but we wasn't here long before I caught on and said, 'This ain't your *apartment*, Jim Mac! I can tell an apartment.'" Suddenly she slid down the wall and sat propped against it. Ron sat in the chair.

"How'd you know it wasn't his apartment?" Ron asked, his eyes on Ruthie.

"Oh, I knew it real fast," she bragged. "I said, 'If this here is your apartment, smarty pants, how come you don't have no *stove*?' And he just didn't have anything to say to that. I knew I'd never seen a place without a stove."

"That's real smart, honey," Ron said. His friend was holding Ruthie tight against him now, and they were barely moving, not in time to the music. When they turned slightly, Ron saw Ruthie's face: white, set, eyes staring at nothing. Then the man said something and she laughed a coarse, mechanical laugh.

The girl on the floor said something.

"What, honey?" Ron leaned toward her but he couldn't make out the words. He stared down in her white face. The features were small and flat, and when she grew up, she would be ugly. Her hair, frizzed into a permanent, drying now from the shower in tight, unstylish wisps all over her head, was a light sandy red.

"How old are you?" Ron said suddenly, shaking his shoulder to keep her from going to sleep.

"Almost seventeen," she mumbled, then held up her head for a minute. "Only don't you tell Jim Mac," she said. "He'd have a fit. Hey, is he married?" she said suddenly.

"I don't know him." Ron said. The girl's head rolled over on her other shoulder and stayed there.

Ron got up and tapped the man Ruthie was dancing with on the back.

"Cut it out," the man said. He had hair on his shoulders and on his back. He was about twice as big as Ron.

"Why don't you all just relax and get comfortable?" Jim Mac said from the floor.

"We're going," Ron said, and even here his voice had authority, an official voice, so that the man let go of Ruthie suddenly and she swayed all by herself to the music.

"What's going on?" she said, dancing around.

"Where's your sweater?" said Ron.

"Honey, if you want to stick around . . ." the man said.

"She doesn't," Ron said, finding the sweater.

"You listen here," the man said. Ruthie was still dancing.

"Shut up," Ron said. He pushed Ruthie roughly out the door and into the car.

Ruthie, still outside herself and waiting to see what could happen, suddenly snapped to life. Why, she had made him jealous, that's what had happened! That's what she had done. Look at him, all tight-lipped and mean, running a red light. Now she had him. "Where are we going now?" she said, noticing that he didn't turn down the street his apartment was on.

The streets, all of them, were completely still and deserted. It looked like a ghost town.

"I'm taking you home," Ron said.

"But we can't do anything there, I mean—"

"That's all right," Ron announced in his authoritative radio voice.

Ruthie sat straight up and stared at him. She had been wrong. Whatever was going to happen was going to happen now. She started crying, something she thought she had given up long ago along with blushing. He parked in front of the Cartwrights' house, big and dark on the quiet street, and began announcing formally, exactly as if she had turned on the radio, "Ruthie, I—"

"Shut up, shut up," she wailed. "Just shut your goddamn mouth for once."

He leaned forward and kissed her forehead. "Good night," he said, and stayed where he was until she had walked up the walk and gone in the house and shut the door behind her.

TWENTY-SEVEN

"GOOD chicken," Manly exclaimed at the picnic, between bites.

You idiot commercial, Monica thought—but idly, very idly. He didn't bother her any more. She toyed with a slick deviled egg, sliding it around on her plate, perilously close to the colorful mounds of potato salad, green beans, fried chicken, and quivering red Jell-O. Five, four, three, two one, CONTACT. Monica slammed the egg into the slaw. She nibbled at a roll.

"What are you humming?" Manly asked.

"Humming? I'm not humming." Monica looked up at him.

"Sure you are," Manly said affably. "Ha ha. Don't even know you're humming."

Monica ate the yellow part of the egg, which left a little white boat. She hummed "Anchors Aweigh," and sailed it into the beans.

Manly watched her out of the corner of his eye, noticing the fine line of her cheekbone beneath her pale white skin.

"Eat up, honey," he said. "What a picnic." Often, he

felt almost fatherly toward Monica. She looked like such a child today, for instance, her hair held back by a wide pink band, wearing a pink sleeveless pantsuit. Her elbows were knobby, he thought. And she *was* humming, definitely humming. Didn't even know it! Manly shook his head fondly and complacently thought: Women are beyond me. He figured it was just as well.

Manly was very happy. He ate four pieces of fried chicken, interspersing the bites with shouted greetings to his friends. His elbows were propped firmly on the checked oilcloth covering the table and his bare head felt good in the sun. He looked contentedly around the Jaycee Ball Park. Long strings of tables commandeered from the American Legion had been placed in rows on the grass up and down the baseball field, and the citizens of Speed sat at them on precarious folding chairs. Occasionally one of the chairs collapsed, causing great merriment. A continuous tide of picnickers flowed to and from the food table—which had been set up along the first base line—filling their paper plates again and again. The food table was manned by ten large black women wielding big spoons, which they dipped again and again into the rectangular containers. Children played between the rows of tables, and here and there a baby had been set out on a quilt on the grass. Older kids sprawled about in the shade of a large willow tree at the edge of the park.

This was the official Sesquicentennial Picnic, and this was the second day of the official Sesquicentennial Week. Yesterday, Saturday, had been the Sesqui-Sidewalk Sale in downtown Speed—a roaring success! Merchandise had been rolled and hauled out onto the sidewalk, and business had never been better. Everyone had come to town for the fun, and if you came you had to buy. You couldn't avoid the merchandise. Thirty American flags had been placed at intervals around the square and everyone had taken pictures.

Today, red-white-and-blue bunting was draped gaily over the chain fence which separated the Jaycee Ball Park from the Negro housing project. (There had been a controversy over exactly who was entitled to use the ball park back when it was built, but, as Higgins had pointed out at the time, you couldn't let everybody in it. Why, it would get worn out, and then *nobody* would have a park. Better build that chain-link fence.)

Higgins himself strolled among the people, shaking hands, and Jimmy Ted walked behind him carrying two beaded Cokes. Higgins was wearing his costume, like most of the people there. The men wore dark frock coats, with vests and funny ties and stovepipe hats. Most of the clothes had been rented from the White Company. Many of the coats and hats had been removed now because of the heat and for the increased mobility needed in serious eating. The women fluttered like butterflies in their long dresses and bonnets. Some wore bustles and some wore crinolines and some wore straw hats with streamers. A lot of the women had scorned the White Company costumes, preferring to make their own or resurrect things found in attic trunks. They strolled about now in the sunshine, gently showing off. How pretty the womenfolk look, Manly thought. He had been thinking in terms of womenfolk ever since Sesquicentennial Week began. Funny that Monica wouldn't wear a long dress like all her friends. She would have looked real cute in one. He turned to smile at her again but she had gone, slipped silently away, and after a few seconds he saw her talking to Caroline Pettit and the pageant director, laughing. Manly, too full to walk over there, was content to sit where he was for a minute and let it all digest—the chicken and the picnic. It was the kind of scene he needed to see in order to keep on thinking what he thought. This is what it's all about, thought Manly.

He got up, threw his paper cup and plate into a garbage

can, and nodded to the women at the serving table as he went by. "Hello, there," he said affably to one of them. "Fine," she said, bobbing her head.

Smiling, Manly moved among the crowd. He headed, vaguely, for a group that stood near the fence. For some reason, this group bothered him. They stood still, in a tight circle, while the other picnickers milled about. Maybe they were organizing a softball game? Manly joined the group.

"I came to bring my mother and sister to the picnic," Lloyd Warner was saying mildly. "What the hell, Bill." Lloyd was grinning, pushing the hair on his forehead back in place. He wore a wrinkled khaki suit, no tie, and nothing about his appearance suggested that he had made any effort to dress for the Sesquicentennial. He made Manly feel a little silly in his mustache and figured silk vest. "I don't need your permission to come to a picnic, now do I?" Lloyd stood easily, feet apart, smiling at the mayor. The more he smiled, the angrier Higgins became. The Sesquicentennial Committee had carefully set the price of the picnic well above the heads of all but the affluent, what they saw as the upper class of Speed. Of course there hadn't been any way to exclude Warner, but nobody had thought he would come. Why should he, when he had steadfastly refused to have anything at all to do with anything civic for years? But here he was, without even the decency to wear a costume. You might have known.

Higgins was smiling too, but the smile never made it up to his eyes.

"I was just wondering if you was having a good time. I like to see everybody enjoy themselves, isn't that right?" He turned to Jimmy Ted for confirmation, but Jimmy Ted was unprepared and only grinned, stupidly, clinking the cold Cokes together.

Lloyd winked at Jimmy Ted, who turned bright red and stared fixedly at the ground. Manly watched. Lloyd leaned against the bunting-covered fence, nonchalant, and the wind lifted his hair. Higgins faced him, flanked by a half circle of admirers. Probably Higgins wouldn't have come up to bug him at all, Lloyd thought, if there hadn't been a ready-made audience. Lloyd wondered what Higgins would do in a room alone. It was impossible to imagine the man without an audience, without that pukey Jimmy Ted in particular. Higgins rolled gently upon the balls of his feet, swaying with the wind.

"Where's your costume?" he asked, squinting at Lloyd.

Lloyd snapped his fingers.

"Damn. I must have left it at home," he said easily, and the men behind Higgins began to lose interest.

"I don't think you left it at home," Higgins said. "No, sir. I reckon you never did bother to get you one because you figure you're too good for us, isn't that right? You're not about to get dressed up, I know you. You want to wear your New York clothes around, and I can tell you why."

"Why?" asked Lloyd.

"Because you'd like to mess up this whole show if you could," Higgins said, still smiling. "Here you've got to go stirring up the colored people right before the most important day in the history of Speed, just about. You got to go riling *them* all up. Now ain't it a sight, that a grown man would act that way?" Higgins shook his head.

Lloyd, who had determined not to display any emotion at all, since that was the one way to get Higgins down, felt himself growing angry. But this words came easily; he knew how to talk to these people. He had been talking to them for years although none of it, as far as he could see, had done any good.

"I tell you what, Bill," Lloyd said, shifting feet, "why don't you forget all about this so-called housing suit until after the Sesquicentennial? You've got your hands full anyway. This suit hasn't got a thing to do with you, you know that, or with the Sesquicentennial either. It just happens that court meets a week earlier this year so it's all happening at once. But, hell, man, it doesn't have a thing to do with it and I can't see why a man in your position would go on about it. I wouldn't if I was the mayor."

"Well, you *ain't* the goddamn mayor!" said Higgins. "And you're lying through your teeth if you tell me that suit hasn't got anything to do with the Sesquicentennial. You filed that suit right now just so you could spoil it and you're doing a pretty good job of it too. If I was that old man in the hospital, I tell you what I'd do: I'd send you a bill."

"What old man?" Lloyd asked evenly.

"Old John Mills, the one that got hurt when the stage was sabotaged."

"Sabotaged?" Lloyd broke out laughing, honestly amused. "You must have been taking a course in how to improve your vocabulary, Bill." This made Higgins' men laugh.

"You can go on and deny it," Higgins said, "but I'm going to prove it. It was that bunch of coloreds from the college that did it."

"Listen here." Lloyd felt suddenly bored, suddenly tired of shit. "I'll give you another word to look up the next time you've got your dictionary out. It's paranoid, p-a-r-a-n-o-i-d. That's you, Higgins. In a way I can't blame you, given your whole setup. But that has got nothing to do with this lousy little two-bit suit. The only reason we're going to court is because we've got a rich black boy on our hands who wants a private pot, and a poor black boy who wants his name in the paper for once. That's all. This rich boy doesn't want to walk down the hall with everybody else. That's all there is to it. All he wants is a place to piss in peace. Which he deserves, if he can pay for it. And he can. So all you're doing, Bill, is trying to make something out of nothing. There is no connection between this suit and your little puppet show or whatever it is."

Behind Higgins, his fans looked at each other. What was Bill going to say now? Their jaws hung slack, waiting.

"I see what you're trying to pull on me now, Lloyd." Higgins looked smart and sly. "But it won't work, not with this old fox."

"Hyeh, hyeh," Jimmy Ted threw into the pause, but Higgins' fans were discomfited now, not satisfied with their man's performance. They began to look around.

Higgins swung his right arm through the air in a short, chopping motion. "I've done more for the colored people than any mayor in the history of Speed," he said. "Can't nobody say I'm against colored people. Didn't I get them a bus line down there? Didn't I? Didn't I get them some paved road?"

Lloyd interrupted him. "You and Wallace. You and your roads. I could listen to you all day, sweetheart, but I've got to be moving on. Enjoyed it." He smiled and walked off unhurriedly between two of Higgins' men, nodding to Manly. He walked away from them without turning back, slightly bowlegged, and they watched him go in silence before they all started talking at once.

"That's just a born fool, Bill," Manly heard somebody say as he walked rapidly after Lloyd; then he changed his mind and started in the other direction, to look for Monica. The picnic had soured for him and he wanted to go home. Something was going on there, between those two men, that was brutal and personal and had nothing to do with the suit or the Sesquicentennial at all. Manly did not understand a thing like that. Manly had never really approved of Lloyd Warner—never liked the man, had thought him a wastrel—yet now he was inclined to change his mind. Maybe it was pure physical grace, but Lloyd had leaned against that fence like a man who knew what he was doing, who was at peace with himself. Manly was a great admirer of men who had it, whatever it was that constituted Inner Peace.

In contrast, Higgins had come off a very poor second. Higgins had been childish, stupid, and rude. He had reminded Manly of a boy named Ray, back in the sixth grade, who had instigated countless fights but never took part in them himself. Ray was an expert at making something of nothing, at finding insult in the most innocent remark. Manly wondered what had become of Ray, where he was now. Probably he was the Bill Higgins of another town like this one.

Three perspiring men in their shirt sleeves now began to saw diligently away upon their instruments, doggedly stamping their feet to what Manly supposed was the tune. A circle of giggling womenfolk paraded, more or less in time to the music, while a ring of men and children watched them, shouting encouragement. "Smile, mama," one child kept yelling, about an octave higher than everyone else.

This was the Costume Contest, then. Manly smiled to himself, satisfied. That strange scene between Warner and Higgins had thrown him temporarily out of kilter so that, for a second, the Costume Contest had appeared ridiculous. Now he remembered. And the Beard Judging would be later. The final ceremony scheduled for this afternoon had been suggested by Manly himself. A time capsule was to be buried beneath a special marker at the edge of the park. Among other items, the time capsule contained: ten recent issues of the Speed *Messenger*; last year's Speed High School yearbook, the *Phoenix*; recent church bulletins from the four largest churches; three 45-rpm phonograph records selected by the ninth-grade class as the three top songs of the year; a personal message from Bill Higgins to the mayor a hundred years from now; and a signed eight-by-ten color photograph of George and Lurleen Wallace.

Children were in the circle now parading. Mrs. Grady Beauchamp, the dentist's wife, had won the ladies' division of the Costume Contest. (Everybody was glad, since she had just had a hysterectomy.) Manly stared at the costumed children, overwhelmed again by that sudden sense of amazement, of not being able to comprehend what was going on. Everyone was laughing at a two-year-old who stubbornly refused to walk in the same direction as everyone else. She turned her back to the crowd, flopped forward from the waist and lifted her petticoats for all to see "Daddy's Girl" emblazoned in red on her panties. She had to get a prize, no question. But where was Monica? Not at the contest. Manly moved away, feeling a little edgy. Maybe he had had too much to eat. And the glare, or something, was giving him a headache.

Two black vans were parked parallel and very close to each other, as unobtrusively as possible, just inside the park gates. Each van contained five chemical toilets and one small, compact washbasin, similar to the bathroom equipment found on trains. There were no windows in the chemical-toilet vans, so that Monica and Buck, wedged between them and obscured from the festivities by a thicket of bushes on one end and the bulldozed hill beyond the fence on the other, were absolutely safe. Yet it was an odd feeling. Monica thought, rather like being in an envelope which has not yet been sealed for mailing. At one end was a gay swatch of red, white, and blue, where the vans had been pulled up against the bunting-covered chain-link fence—above that, the rocks, the hill, the sky. At the other end of their envelope were the green leaves. The long walls of the envelope were smooth and black, with SANI-FLUSH lettered on them in delicate script with several flourishes. Monica lay on her back, dreamily chewing at a piece of grass, and stared at the blue, blue sky. She had protested, but Buck was right: "Who's going to look under a Sani-Flush van?" Buck was talking now, going on and on, something about meeting him in Memphis next month, but Monica didn't listen. She wriggled her bare backside in the grass and stretched, in a state of suspended animation, waiting for the envelope to be sealed. The toilets were flushed intermittently on either side of them; it was like lying near a waterfall. Monica giggled. In an envelope near a waterfall. From her worm's eye viewpoint, the white lettering of the Sani-Flush sign appeared strangely elongated and graceful. This was as wild as anything she had ever dreamed up. Wilder, even. Monica smiled a long, lazy smile which bore no relation to what Buck was saying; he frowned.

"Well, I've got to split anyway," he said. "Doesn't that husband of yours ever get curious? Doesn't he ever miss you?"

"He likes picnics." Monica stretched. She pulled on her pants and stood up to button them.

"You go on," Buck said. "I'll wait awhile and come out after you."

Monica pushed through the bushes, walked around to the front of the van, and nearly collided with Manly.

"My God!" she said.

Manly frowned. It was not like her to swear.

"I was just coming out of the bathroom," she said in a loud voice, walking ahead of him back toward the picnic.

"Me too," Manly said. "I guess I just missed you. What's that green stuff on your back?" he added.

"Green? Where? On my *back?*" Monica's voice rose.

"Looks like a grass stain," Manly said.

"Oh, well, I leaned back against the wall in that Sani-Flush thing," Monica said illogically.

"Hey, Mr. Neighbors. Wait up." It was Buck Fire,

hailing them from behind. Buck knew that some women got their kicks from a situation like this, seeing their lover and their husband together. Buck imagined that Monica might be this type. He also imagined that he would show up to great advantage beside Manly, and he was curious about Manly, anyway. Monica never mentioned him.

"Nice picnic," Buck remarked. He wore a brilliant blue Lacoste knit shirt and blue-checked pants which flared above the side-gored boots.

"How are you, Mrs. Neighbors?" Buck nearly sang.

"O.K.," Monica mumbled, and too late Buck saw that she wasn't pleased. She had had enough for one day, he guessed.

"Come on," Manly said, quickening the pace. "They're about to bury the time capsule."

"I think you're to be congratulated, Mr. Neighbors," Buck said, determined to impress her.

"Why is that?" Manly said, interested.

"Because you think there will actually be a year 2065. I think that's pretty optimistic."

Manly blinked at him. The idea that there might not be a 2065 had not really occurred to him, not as an actual possibility. He had thought—without thinking much about it—that the 2065 celebration would be a lot like this one, in fact, with the people driving futuristic cars and wearing some sort of functional clothes.

"Oh, come on," Monica suddenly cried, pulling Manly's hand. "Come on!" She pulled him into the crowd. "Interesting fellow," Manly remarked, but Monica didn't answer.

Later, in the car going home, she tried to analyze what had happened. Buck had lost her, of course—though he didn't know it yet—and Manly had won. Monica supposed it was inevitable that Manly would win, but she hadn't realized it. When Buck had made the 2065 remark, suddenly it was clear: his cynicism, his negativity. Of course it was the cynicism that had attracted her to him in the first place, but now she saw that her revulsion had been, all along, nearly as strong as the attraction. In fact it had been part of the attraction. Buck is a transient, she thought. That's what makes him beautiful. But finally she needed more. That's why she had married Manly in the first place, for permanence. A place. Now maybe she had stored up enough guilt to keep her happy for another twenty years or so. She leaned back against the seat and closed her eyes and smiled. The Waterfall Envelope was the perfect, the ultimate perversion, and she, Monica, had done it. It was hard to believe. She didn't need to do anything else for a long, long time. She would go back to Buck's time or two, just to play it out, but it was over.

Manly, who had stopped for a red light in front of the junior high school, said, "I wonder what's going on over there."

"Where?" Monica said.

"Over there on the field. Look at all those cars. If it's some kind of game, we haven't got anybody covering it."

"They're just building the pageant stage, stupid," said Monica. "They have to work today because it all fell down, remember?"

"But look at all those people," Manly said. "That's practically as many people as there were at the picnic."

"Green light," Monica said.

But Manly turned into the junior high parking lot and pulled in beside a pickup truck full of kids. The man in the truck nodded to him. "Evening."

"Hello," Manly said. "What's going on over there?"

"Daddy said it was going to fall in again," squealed one of the kids, a girl about ten years old. "But there hasn't a thing happened yet."

The man in the cab of the pickup stared straight ahead at

the field, covered with a swarm of men. Gradually, the stage was rising again.

Manly backed out of the lot. "I still can't see why so many people are over there watching," he said. Except for the workmen, they had been a strangely quiet crowd.

"Don't you know?" Monica asked impatiently. "They think something awful is going to happen. They think it's going to fall in again and somebody's going to get hurt. At least they hope so. That's why they're all over there watching. It's the thing to do on Sunday afternoons, didn't you know?"

Manly glanced over at her. "Is that *right?*"

"Sure," Monica said. "That's where all the kids go now to make out." She reached for his hand on the wheel and scooted closer to him. Their hands rested, locked, on the seat between them. But Manly could not get it out of his head all the way home: that vision of the parked cars, jewel-like, the metal and polished chrome, hushed and waiting for catastrophe.

TWENTY-EIGHT

*I*N spite of the weatherman's promise, Wednesday dawned gray and cloudy. Low, puffy clouds slid across a neutral sky and wind gusted suddenly in short spurts, whipping the ladies' long skirts about them and occasionally displaying the Rockettes' new red satin panties.

But earlier, beginning at 6 A.M., the telephone had rung and rung in Bob Pitt's home as possible paraders asked if the parade would proceed as planned. "Yes," Frances told each of the callers officiously, "unless it actually rains." Frances had never felt so important; some of the callers were very prominent. "That was *Manly Neighbors*," she bustled in to tell Theresa, who was working on her hair. "That was *Dean Blackburn's* wife." She had pursed her lips and then added, "He's the dean at the college!" when Theresa hadn't seemed properly impressed. Theresa took a clip out of her mouth. "So what?" she had said.

It had not rained, so now the parade was forming as scheduled—behind schedule, actually, but Bob Pitt had allowed for that. Everyone looked up at the sky, which seemed to change every minute or so. The paraders were nervous, and talked of tornadoes.

"What you do is get down in a ditch and cover up your head," Lomas Cartwright bawled, splendid in his Kop uniform.

"Yeah, but there aren't any ditches downtown," somebody pointed out.

"I liked to got carried away by this tornado in Arkansas one time," Lomas went on, oblivious. "It killed twenty-two people but I got down in a culvert just in the nick of time."

The band members tuned their instruments, producing discordant, oddly unsettling scraps of sound. The Air Force Band from Montgomery stood in formation with its feet smartly spread apart, supposedly at ease. Bob Pitt walked up and down the length of the parade, helping the contestants onto the float, hurrying last minute crepe-paper adjustments, getting things ready to go. The horns on the giant Beef for Bama bull were drooping, and finally Bob resolved that crisis by designating two of the milkmaids to stand on either side of the head and hold the horns in place during the ceremonies. Everyone came to him with questions: where was the police escort, should the firemen ring their bell, shouldn't the bands be farther apart if they were going to play at the same time, what if the pioneer children have to go to the potty? Some of the ladies felt that the drunkards and the giant hypodermic needle on the inter-religious float were in poor taste and was it too late to do anything now?

Bob answered all the questions efficiently, impressed with his own efficiency, since he couldn't seem to get his mind on the thing at all. Instead, a childhood memory kept occurring and recurring to him: he was small, he was helping out at the truck stop, and he spilled coffee into the lap of a fancy lady tourist. Instead of being angry, she had given him a dollar and patted him on the head. He remembered the new green dollar bill, signed by Henry Morgenthau, Jr.

Finally the parade was organized and—just at the last minute—the clouds parted and the sun came out, causing the paraders to whistle and shout. The Air Force bandleader raised his white-gloved hands. The parade was on! The units in front moved out smartly as argument rocked the Queen Contestants' float and the girls juggled about for prominence. Bob Pitt stood in his stovepipe hat and checked off each unit on the official list in his notebook. Here came the pageant cast, a huge and motley crew, and here came Sandy DuBois in her scant Indian costume. She wore some sort of fuzzy cloth jerkin intended to resemble animal hide, strings of bright glass beads, and a green headband around her forehead which dented the French twist in back. Her feet were shod in Hugh Puppies embellished with fake fringe, and purposeless leather thongs wound up her long white legs. There was a holdup in the parade about then, and the pageant cast was stopped across from Bob. He kept trying not to look at her, kept toying with the official list in his hand, but now he was getting a headache and the notations which he had made in the notebook in his tiny, methodical hand seemed to him meaningless, some sort of mockery upon the red-ruled page. Everyone spoke to Bob and nodded. He stood with the notebook and realized that he was the most important person at the parade.

In fact, at this moment, he was the most important man in Speed. He dropped the notebook onto the sidewalk, as carelessly as if he were tossing an empty Coke cup into the trash, and elbowed his way into the pageant cast.

"Sandy!" he yelled in a hoarse voice.

"What do you think you're doing?" she spat at him, for once the prudent one. "Go on, you must be crazy."

Up close, her full lips were reddened by stage makeup

and green eye shadow was striped above her eyes. What a blond, fantastic Indian!

"You look great," Bob Pitt said. "Just great."

"Get out of here," she said between her teeth. They were surrounded by Speed's First Football Team, young men that both of them knew.

"I'm going to Florida day after tomorrow," he said. "The morning after the first performance. Are you coming with me?"

Sandy ignored him, smiling fixedly at some imaginary point far away. Her nostrils were dilated—a sure sign of anger—beneath her long nose.

Bob Pitt squeezed her elbow as hard as he could, feeling the bones shift beneath the loose skin. He wondered if he could break them, just like that.

"Ow, let go," she muttered. "That *hurts*. Jesus, Bob."

"Are you coming with me or not?"

"Yeah, sure, I'll be there," Sandy hissed, not looking at him, wanting only to be rid of him. What a way to act!

The parade was moving again; both bands played march tunes. Bob backed out of the pageant cast and ran to jump onto the Bushy Brothers float. "Great job," a Bushy Brother said, clapping him on the back. The Bushy Brothers' float was nothing much, merely a truck bed decked out in the omnipresent bunting, but the Brothers themselves wore their White Company costumes. Bob Pitt wove through them on the moving truck bed, accepting congratulations. He finally found a place at the very back of the float, but he could not spot Sandy. She had been temporarily lost, swallowed up by the seething pageant cast.

Waiting anxiously on the corner, Frances Pitt let out a yelp of dismay as the parade approached and she saw that Theresa was not leading it, after all! A bunch of soldiers came first. Mrs. Pitt became more and more agitated as one by one the floats passed and finally, way back in the middle, here came the Speed High Band and the jaunty Rockettes. Theresa led the Rockettes, all right, but it was not the same. What could have happened? It was not what had been promised, after all! Mrs. Pitt stepped out into the street, cupped her mouth with her hands, and shouted at Theresa. "What are you doing, honey, way back here? You was supposed to be at the front. Where's-your-father-I'm-going-to-give-him-a-piece-of-my-mind!" Frances' fellow onlookers stared at her curiously.

Theresa left her place and ran, jeweled boots twinkling, over to her mother. "Get back up on the sidewalk, Mama, and hush up," she said. "I'm so embarrassed I could die."

"My own daughter," Mrs. Pitt began. "I can't believe that my own daughter is treating me this way when all I'm trying to do is have you get what's coming to you, what you won in the Susan Arch Finlay—"

"Mama," Theresa said evenly. "The Air Force Band is from out of town and they said they wouldn't play if they didn't get to go first. Nobody cares anyway. It doesn't *matter*, Mama. Now if you don't shut up and get back up on that sidewalk I'm going to take off all my clothes right now."

Frances' eyes bugged right out of her head. "Why, Rose Theresa," she said.

"Oh, yes, I am too," said Theresa. "I'm going to embarrass *you*, for a change." She reached around her back and pulled at her zipper, the zipper which Frances had sewed there herself! Frances began backing up.

"Every stitch," Theresa said.

Frances ascended the curb. Theresa tossed her baton in the air, caught it, and scampered back to her place. The Speed Rockettes held their silver batons out parallel to the street and kicked high, touching the batons with their jeweled tassels.

On their truck bed, the Bushy Brothers broke into song. They sang "Dixie" in an exaggerated manner, swaying, their arms around each other's shoulders. The sun was now so bright it made everyone squint. Bob Pitt, swaying with the others and singing tenor, was near tears, filled with the excitement of the moment and the knowledge of his own disaster. The Keystone Kops dashed in and out of the crowd—now clowning atop a float, now whacking everyone over the head with their giant, weightless billy sticks.

TWENTY-NINE

M iss Iona sat alone at her desk in the late afternoon, staring at the front page of the Speed *Messenger*. Ah, that familiar Gothic script, with the ornate capital letters S and M. Her father had designed it himself, and had had the original masthead engraved in Memphis. That proud title, that elegant masthead—now defamed by the bare majorettes who marched beneath it. How could such a thing be? She, Miss Iona, had not even been consulted this time, although by rights the majorettes should fall within her jurisdiction. She had not even known about it until the paper was on her desk. There they were, all five Rockettes, unbelievably vulgar. They were marching down the street in the Sesquicentennial parade, booted feet outstretched in a manner reminiscent of the German goose-step. This little touch seemed particularly offensive to Miss Iona, who had long been an aficionado of certain other Germanic traditions such as Goethe. It was the last straw. Miss Iona stared at the ten white thighs and felt herself as weightless and frail as straw in a new, high wind.

Scarcely realizing what she was doing, Miss Iona took

her sharp silver scissors from their sheath and began to snip away. First she cut the whole picture neatly out of the paper. It ran across four whole columns—imagine! Then she folded the paper and placed it to the side. She stared at the Rockettes a little while longer before she began cutting again. Carefully she severed all the majorettes' heads from their bodies, then clipped them in two at their trim waists. Cut apart in this way, the pieces of majorettes were really quite small. She had to be very, very careful not to tear the paper as she arranged all the pieces in different ways on her desk like a jigsaw puzzle, placing Brenda Pool's bust under Sharon's head, giving Theresa four legs, making grotesque composite majorettes by overlapping the small squares. Once she made an especially outstanding one by putting Sharon's head over Martha Lou Renfro's bust and overlapping Wendy Watkins' body in, twisted strangely to the side, and adding three anonymous legs at the bottom and two batons for good measure.

Suddenly she giggled like a girl again—more girlishly than she had ever giggled as a girl, in fact. She straightened up and sat ramrod straight in her chair the way that she had been taught, and picked up all the pieces of majorette and compressed them into a wad. Miss Iona then read the poems of Matthew Arnold aloud and thought for a short while of a darkling plain. Manly Neighbors is young and foolish, she said to herself; if he would put these majorettes into the paper, God knows what else he would put into it! Miss Iona typed Manly Neighbors' obituary and headed it up "Editor Succumbs," with a ten-point kicker which read "Sudden Tragedy." She removed it from her typewriter, set it aside, and inserted a clean sheet of typing paper. Miss Iona never used copy paper as a rule, since it was made from inexpensive materials which might have been used for any purpose whatsoever. Then she typed a mass obituary for the majorettes entitled "Wreck

Claims Rockettes'' and a kicker reading "Prime of Youth."
Next she wrote obituaries for Frances Pitt and the yellow-
haired Mrs. DuBois.

"I've seen the last of them," she said and again she
giggled, still more girlishly, aloud. She swept the tiny,
maimed majorette portions from her desk into her trash
basket, then emptied her trash basket into the larger one in
the hall, freeing her office of the hateful high school girls.

Miss Iona took three volumes of poetry, including the
Victorian anthology, from her desk and put them and her
fountain pen and several other things which belonged to
her in a paper bag and put on her blue coat and looked
around once more. "I may not pass this way again," she
said. She was very pleased with herself. "Of course I
might pass this way again," she added as an afterthought,
and giggled. She could not have said exactly what she had
in mind, but as she remembered to herself (somewhat
haphazardly), it had not only to do with the silly majorettes and the Sesquicentennial, but with the quality of life
itself. It had been coming on.

After reading through the obituaries a final time to
check for errors (there were of course no errors), she
placed them neatly in a stack, with Manly Neighbors'
reposing on top, and put them all into a manila envelope.
This she sealed and wrote "To Be Opened in Case of
Emergency" across the front in red Magic Marker with her
spidery hand. She placed the envelope squarely in the
center of her father's desk. It was the only thing on the
desk. In case of emergency, they would find it. In case of
no emergency, she would find it. She smiled her small
smile to think of Manly Neighbors' obituary appearing in
the paper. People would start sending flowers and taking
food to Manly's snippy wife, Miss Iona thought. Silly
little wife. And big, silly Manly. She imagined the faces
of Mrs. DuBois and Mrs. Pitt as they read their own

obituaries. Serves them right. But what was she thinking of? Surely the obituaries would not be published; it was her own private joke. In any case, perhaps all these people would really die. No, these obituaries would be published in case of emergency. That's what the envelope said. No, they would not be published then. It was confusing. It was a joke. They would simply be found or not be found. But what emergency did she have in mind? Surely the pageant would be a success, as lovely as she had dreamed, and her mission a success. Why then was she making this joke? She could think clearly no longer; she felt as she had not felt for years, not since she had drunk champagne and eaten spiced peaches at her cousin Eugenia's wedding.

A vision appeared then to Miss Iona so vivid that she was not conscious any longer of being in the *Messenger* office or even of her father's desk before her. These things disappeared from view, replaced by Eugenia on a bed of flowers, in the manner of Madame Récamier, ruling as the Queen of Beauty, Truth, and Goodness in the World. Flowers were everywhere; everywhere was light. Little Iona appeared clothed in diaphanous robes, the Arbiter of Beauty, Truth, an Goodness in the World. Someond, a stately man (Alexander Pope?), appeared from the wings to announce, "Whatever is, is right," but the lovely little Arbiter arbitrarily cast him down to hell. "Whatever is, is not *necessarily* right," she chimed in sweet bell-like tones, as thousands of peons hung on every word, taking notes. "Art has the power to transform what is into what is right." A thousand quills scratched on parchment paper. "We must therefore create beauty in the world." Free-floating in her soft veils, Miss Iona set forth her aesthetic. Then suddenly she was seated on an incredibly soft throne, while before her a plum-colored velvet curtain rose sound-lessly upon a scene of indescribable beauty. This then was the Pageant—not the specific pageant, but the idea of

Pageant, the quintessence of all possible pageants ever. It began; it continued; the final curtain fell. Through it all, Miss Iona sat still as stone on her regal throne. It was more than even she had dared to dream. Nothing about the Pageant could be articulated through normal language. It had no recognizable form: all was color and light, and the meaning was assimilated directly into the senses without being translated into blocks of language and forced through the mill of the mind. At the close of this Pageant of Perfection, as she immediately christened it, Miss Iona found herself standing quite still near her office door. Surely her mission was successful! Surely her vision was a sign! Absentmindedly, she left the manila envelope where it lay. (Later, when it was opened and its contents made more or less public, a great furor was aroused. She had been crazy all along, they said, even before they found her over there locked in her house and had to send her away; see how crazy she had been: she must have written those crank letters as well. But this idea was, of course, erroneous.) Miss Iona, her mind filled with the fine white light of the Pageant of Perfection, moved in the darkness through the office and hall she knew so well, went down the stairs and out into the warm night air.

THIRTY

*B*EVO, very tense, sat on the edge of Lomas' vibrator chair, holding his bugle up to his lips. His cheeks moved in and out; he tapped his foot. The notes sounded singly in his head.

"Haw," snorted Mamaw, on her way through the den from outdoors. "That ain't much of a tune." She doubled over, laughing, at her joke.

Bevo could not work up the energy necessary to say anything back to her, or even to give her a dirty look over the shiny bugle. He had never, he suddenly realized, said a cross word aloud to anyone in his life. Wasn't it about time? He took the bugle out of his mouth, carefully wiped the mouthpiece, and opened his mouth into a round O. But no words came. The words were stuck in his head. Meanwhile his Mamaw was cackling aloud like the Wicked Witch of the West, wheezing, wiping her red-rimmed eyes with both hands. She moved again toward the stairs, but bumped into a coffee table—probably, Bevo thought, because she had her hands to her eyes and couldn't see where she was going. But why couldn't he just be GLAD that she had bumped into the coffee table? Without thinking about why she did it? "Damnit," she screeched, rubbing her bony rump. Bevo was filled with admiration.

"What time is this here thing?" Mamaw hollered from the bottom step.

"I'm sorry, I didn't hear you." Anne appeared as if by magic in the kitchen door, wiping her hands on a spotless dish towel. Bevo hadn't even known she was in there washing the dishes. Anne could do things more quietly than anyone else in the world. "I didn't hear what you said, Mother," she repeated.

"I said what time is this *play* we're going to? What are you, deaf?"

"It starts at seven-thirty," Anne replied, her face as smooth as wax. Suddenly that's what she reminded Bevo of: the slick-faced monsters in that old horror film *House of Wax*. He had seen it again on TV not long ago. And the way she was always sneaking around the house in her silent, wedge-heeled house slippers. For the first time she seemed strange to him, and he actually felt more like his father, Lomas.

"Are you going?" he asked Mamaw.

"Sure I am," she said. "I'm coming to hear you toot that damn horn." She raced up the steps as quickly as a young girl.

But what if Sharon saw her? Bevo thought. What if Mamaw said something awful?

Anne smiled at him. "Isn't it about time for you to put on your costume, dear?" she asked.

Bevo just sat on the vibrator chair, rubbing his bugle.

A tiny perpendicular line appeared between Anne's brown eyebrows. "Of course if you'd like to practice your piece aloud, I'm sure nobody will mind. I'd like to hear it."

"But Ruthie," Bevo began, when Ruthie herself glided into the room in a long bathrobe of yellow silk.

"Ruthie what?" she asked. "Mother, can I wear your pearls?"

"They're in my jewelry box," Anne said. "Bevo seems to think he'll bother you if he practices his part."

"Oh, don't be stupid," Ruthie trilled sweetly, a brand-new Ruthie altogether. "Go right ahead and blow your horn all you want."

"Really?" Bevo blinked.

"Ron says that music in the home is very important to children," Ruthie said to Anne.

Anne nodded complacently. "I've always regretted the fact that we couldn't afford piano lessons for you when you were growing up," she said.

Bevo stared at them. They must be crazy. Music in the home! Pianos! Ruthie must be sick. He had expected Ruthie to be even madder than usual tonight, since Anne had told him at supper that she had not won the Queen Contest after all. She hadn't even placed, and the Queen was still a mystery which would be announced at the pageant that night. But Ruthie didn't seem to care about it at all.

"Do you feel O.K.?" Bevo asked her.

"I never felt better in my life," Ruthie declared. Turning to Anne, she said mysteriously, "Oh, he doesn't know." Turning back to Bevo, her robe swishing with each turn, she said, "Bevo, I'm engaged."

"Oh yeah," Bevo said, looking at her.

"Well, don't look at me like that, silly, of course I am and we're going to be married next week."

"Who?" Bevo said.

"*Me*," Ruthie laughed, shaking her head in apparent wonder at the denseness of children. Bevo saw that he had ceased to be her enemy; in fact, he had ceased to exist. "Ron and I are getting married and then we're going to move to Atlanta, where he has this new job as program director of WBIC."

"Ron-the-*Mouth*?" Bevo said.

"Oh, honestly." Ruthie gave up. She turned back to Anne and they plunged into a long discussion about some French Provincial furniture that Ruthie had seen somewhere on sale. They might as well be speaking French as far as Bevo was concerned. They might as well be speaking Outer Mongolian. They even looked strange to him. His mother wore a dark green knit suit, heels, and her apron. Except for the apron, she was ready for the pageant. Above her soft green collar, her face still seemed as waxy and bright as the moon. Through some mad transformation, Ruthie's hair had, for tonight at least, ceased to be wild and curly. Part of it was done up on her head in big smooth loops; the rest hung limply down her back. Her face looked different, too. Before, all her features had been at war about something or other. Now her face, like Anne's, seemed whole and placid. Where had the old, hateful Ruthie gone off to? Then the really peculiar thing happened. Bevo's eyes went out of focus, and he couldn't tell them apart. It was like looking through a telescope that had been especially adjusted to fit somebody else. Before his own eyes they were merging: Ruthie was merging into Anne.

"Well, go ahead and practice," one of them—he sort of thought it was Ruthie—said.

"I guess I'll go and get dressed," Bevo said. As he watched them, Anne and Ruthie flashed in and out of each other in the manner of a man and a gorilla on the joke button which Lomas had once worn home on his hat from a fishing trip. Seen in a certain light, the figure was a smiling man; turned slightly, it became a gorilla saying "Hi." Ruthie and Anne were doing the same thing now, switching back and forth, but slowly, with each flash, Ruthie was becoming Anne too.

Bevo went to the window of his room and stood there

for a while before switching on the light. It was not yet dark outside, so the window was a mysterious light gray square in the corner of his room. He stood there, looking out and smelling the spring, and while he watched a car pulled up in front of the DuBoises' house and its horn sounded sadly through the twilight. Then the DuBoises' door popped open, spewing yellow light, and out popped Sharon like a shot. She ran across the lawn without bothering to touch the ground, glittering in a new white majorette costume and white, knee-high boots. She ran through the dusk like a falling star. Bevo held his breath. Then the car door slammed and somebody laughed and the car pulled out, tires squealing. Bevo knew that Red was in the car. Bevo looked at the empty yard for some time and thought of her running across. He knew he would never forget it.

"Get a move on in there," Lomas yelled from the hall, and Bevo switched on the light and undressed mechanically and put on his gray Confederate suit. It smelled funny and did not fit. As he dressed he smoked one of Lomas' cigarettes, coughing only occasionally. He put the ashes into an ornamental, boat-shaped blue dish which the decorator had put in his room, and put the cigarette butt out there too. Then he took three boxes of safety matches from his bureau drawer and placed them carefully in the pocket of his Confederate suit. The matches said "Peabody Room—Dine & Dance" on them. He got his bugle. *I'm not nervous a bit*, Bevo thought, surprised. He knew exactly what he was going to do.

Downstairs, Anne was taking a picture of Ron-the-Mouth, apparently dressed as an antebellum disc jockey, and Ruthie in an amazingly demure flowered dress. Lomas stood behind them in his Kop suit, billy club raised as if to strike Ron-the-Mouth. "Get in the picture, get in the picture," everyone screamed. Dazed, Bevo joined them and blinked in the blinding flash. "Now you have to wait thirty seconds," Anne directed. Bevo saw that it was a new camera. Mamaw came into the room and began to carry on about something. Ron and Ruthie (was it Ruthie?) held hands and began to chant, "One-two-three-four—"

"I ain't got time for all this," Lomas yelled. "Anybody that's going with me, come on." Bevo followed him out to the pickup.

THIRTY-ONE

T HE afternoon of the pageant, Monica had done two decisive things. She had slept with Buck for the last time, that was number one. Riding to the junior high with Manly, dressed as a squaw, she wondered if Buck believed it. Probably not. Behind that nice body lurks a brain the size of a pea. But anyway it was over; they had done it for the last time. Fucking Buck, was how she had thought of it, loving the purely physical terms they were on. I fucked Buck plenty, she thought. What a fine, sordid affair it had been. The potato chips on the soiled sheets. To remember it, Monica had taken the hummingbird print from his wall as she had left his apartment for the very last time this afternoon. It hung now in her living room, "The Elusive Hummingbird," probably the world's worst print in one of the world's worst frames. Monica had replaced a Thai rubbing with it, and it hung next to a Leonard Baskin. Manly had looked at her strangely tonight when he noticed the change. But he hadn't said a word. Manly never questioned her taste. Monica smiled to herself. She wanted that hummingbird right out where she could see it, all the time. Right out in full view.

The second decisive thing which she had done that day was to fire Suetta. Manly didn't know about that, yet. Suetta had taken three hours to wash two windows that afternoon, doing them, to Monica's astonishment, with vinegar and newspaper. "Why don't you use Windex?" Monica had suggested half-heartedly, before going over to Buck's, but Suetta had tossed her head. "I does them like I does them," she had said. Her tone implied that anyone who *didn't* use vinegar and newspaper was crazy. She was still at it when Monica came home in her brave new mood.

"Suetta," Monica had said, "I'm sorry but I've decided to do my own housework from now on. I'll pay you for two weeks, of course, until you find another job."

"Huh!" Suetta stood firmly in a sea of wadded newspaper, not believing a word. "You going to do your own work? I'll believe it when I see it, yes I will."

"You can go on now," Monica had said.

But Suetta didn't move. "Mr. Manly know about this?" she asked darkly.

"Manly has got nothing to do with this at all," Monica had said. "You go on home."

"What you going to have for supper, then?" Suetta asked scornfully.

"Boeuf bourguignon avec des pommes de terre frites et des petits pois et de la glace chocolat," Monica had said airily.

"Sure you are," Suetta said.

"Au revoir," said Monica.

"You a sight," Suetta stated flatly, getting her bag. "You just a sight. I'll be talking to Mr. Manly," she had hollered from the walk.

Oh, Monica might find somebody to come in once a week, but it would never be Suetta. Now Monica felt as empty as a balloon, and as inflated. What I need now is something totally new, she thought. Now I'm a little tired of myself.

She punched Manly. "Let's have a baby," she said.

He turned to look at her. "What did you say?" he asked.

"I said I've been thinking we ought to have a baby."

A slow grin broke out all over Manly's face. "No kidding," he said.

Monica smiled too. "Would you like that?"

Manly pulled over to the side of the road.

"What are you doing?" she said. "We'll be late."

"Let's go have a baby," Manly said.

"Oh, come on," Monica said primly. "We don't have to do it right now." But she was astonished. Never, never would she have believed Manly capable of such a thing. To think that he would actually forgo a civic pageant in order to screw his own wife! Perhaps she had misjudged him. Perhaps he had changed. Whatever it was, it really didn't matter. Manly reached over and held her hand. Monica scratched his palm slowly with her fingernail, something erotic that secret lovers did in those books she had stopped reading. Maybe she had underrated Manly after all. Monica looked through the windshield into the sky and thought of infinite possibilities.

THIRTY-TWO

FRANCES Pitt surveyed her nails. Usually she did them herself but today she had them done by Ruth at the Gateway to Beauty Salon. Ruth had done them while Frances' hair was drying into small, tight curls. It was an unaccustomed extravagance, but Frances felt that she was entitled to it as the wife of one of the most important men in Speed. Frances considered herself an expert judge of who was entitled to what.

She went down the hall and stood in front of Theresa's door and yelled, "Honey, you need any help?"

"I'm right here, Mama. I'm just about five feet away from you so you don't have to yell like that," said Theresa.

"You keep a decent tongue in your head," Frances began, but Theresa cut her off.

"I don't need any help, Mama," she said. "Thanks anyway."

Frances opened and closed her mouth several times. Her son, in his Scout uniform, had already left. Frances remembered the days when she had laid out their clothes and polished their little white shoes with Griffin's All-White.

Frances puffed back into the bedroom where Bob was tying his old-fashioned bow tie.

"You look kind of pale," she observed. "Don't you want an Empirin?" Frances was a staunch believer in Empirins and took several every day.

Bob mumbled something into the mirror.

"I'll go get you an Empirin." Frances headed for the bathroom.

"Frances, I don't want an Empirin."

"Your voice sounds funny, too," she said. "I bet you're getting that bug that Lucy's children brought over here. She said it was awful, said it was some Florida bug and kept them trotting all the time. I said, well, if it's so awful, how come you're bringing it over here then? I sprayed all over with Lysol right after she left."

"Frances, please," Bob Pitt said in a strained voice.

"Please *what?*" Frances asked, astonished. She sat down on the little gold chair before her dressing table.

"Just be quiet for a minute," he said.

"Well!" Frances huffed, and busied herself with applying a little more lipstick to her lips. But she couldn't hold her tongue.

"Have you got your speech all ready? You know what you're going to say?"

"Frances, I've told you a million times, it isn't a speech. All they're going to do is introduce me." Bob was adjusting his hat.

"Well, they're going to introduce you right after the Lieutenant Governor and the mayor make their speeches, now isn't that right? Isn't it?" she persisted.

"Hold still a minute," she directed, and stood up, and began picking invisible pieces of lint, or something, off the back of his black frock coat. Bob Pitt stared gloomily into the mirror. It was true, it was all true, what she said. In almost exactly one hour the spotlight would be turned upon him, a real spotlight, and thousands of people would applaud politely, and what's more, he deserved it. I can't stand it, he thought.

"Frances, quit that," he said.

"Now you just hold still. Everybody's going to be looking at you. Do you want to look nice or what?" She picked at him with her short red nails.

Bob saw her in the mirror as if for the first time: short and puffy, garishly dressed, striped and belted, picking. What did he have to do with her or vice versa? Bob felt that he had become involved with her through some sort of freak accident, such as a wreck, which must now be set right.

"Frances, I'm leaving tomorrow," he said. There it was. The words hung between them in the mirrored air. It was not too soon to retract them; Frances never was too bright. She would believe anything he told her. He could say, "I have to go to Livingston to see a man about some tax forms," and everything would be all right. But he continued, "I'm going to Florida with your cousin Sandy DuBois. We are in love. But you don't need to worry, Frances, because I'll take good care of you and the children."

Frances sat back down on the little gold chair. Her mouth hung slack for once, giving her a bovine appearance. Bob watched her carefully in the mirror. He didn't dare to turn around. She might come at him with her red nails, for all he knew. She might hit him across the face. He didn't have any idea what she would do, but he thought women usually cried at a time like this. He looked for tears but saw none.

"Sandy DuBois," Frances hissed. "I might have known."

"Yes," said Bob. "I'm sorry, Frances."

"Oh, *that's all right*," Frances puffed with great, elaborate scorn. "Don't mind me, I'm just your wife. Anybody that takes up with Sandy DuBois is asking for it, though, I'm telling you. And you! Everybody said I was marrying beneath me, all along, and they was all right. I guess blood will tell in the end. Having affairs," she hissed. "Sneaking around. Doing *adultery*." With each phrase, Frances was puffing up like an adder. "That's just like trash," she said.

Bob drew back, turned to face her. He was really alarmed. He had never seen her quite like this. What if she had a heart attack? Why couldn't she just cry and carry on? He could not figure it out. It was as though she didn't care personally, at all. He knew she had not liked sex—she undressed in the closet, and wore long-legged pajamas to bed—but didn't she feel anything at the prospect of losing her husband? Or did she realize that he meant to leave her for good? Hell, he might as well have left long ago. Bob stared at her curiously. She was literally exploding in his ears, and her small eyes had narrowed to slits. Yet, through it all, she seemed somehow *satisfied*. There was a great, overriding satisfaction in all she said. Her slack jaw had turned righteous and grim.

"I did everything I could," she finished. "I worked my fingers to the bone. I've been a good mother and a good wife—oh, nobody's been better than me. I've done my duty every day of my life, so help me God. And what do I get? *Adultery*. I should of known."

Bob stared at her. What did she mean, she "should of known"? She was incomprehensible to him.

She stood. "Well, come on," she said.

"What?"

"I said, come on, you're fixing to be late."

"You still expect me to go to this thing?" Bob wiped his glasses nervously.

"You'll go," she said grimly. "You'll stand up and do

your part. It's the *least* you can do," she added mysteriously.

Bob put his glasses back on and unfortunately she swam into focus again.

"Just a minute," he said, and went into the bathroom. After doing what he always referred to as his "business," he looked around nervously for an escape. But the only window was too small to accommodate him, even if—he thought—he had really meant it. The window gave onto a section of roof where the TV antenna stood. The roof, of which he had once been so proud, meant nothing to him now. Neither did the many-pronged TV antenna. He also found the bathroom meaningless: it was done in yellow, with a fluffy violet cover on the toilet seat. He opened the mirrored medicine cabinet to see if there was any suntan lotion. Back in a corner, he found half a tube of Sea and Ski, left over from the past summer. He closed the door and looked at himself and fiddled some more with his tie. Oh well. Time to face the music. Bob left the bathroom, suntan lotion in hand, whistling the theme from *Dr. Zhivago.*

Meanwhile, Frances was at the hall telephone downstairs, calling the DuBoises' home. With any luck at all, they would still be there. They were always late. Because Sandy has to primp so much all the time, Frances thought. And that daughter of hers just like her. Frances remembered waiting and waiting for Sandy on countless occasions throughout their youth, when their mothers had made them do things together. Waiting while Sandy primped. Well, Sandy really primped herself into one this time! Frances thought as she dialed. I'd just like to see how she's going to get out of *this* one.

The phone rang five times and then Johnny B. himself answered in his professional, fried-chicken voice. He was trash, too.

"Hello," he said.

"This is Frances Pitt," Frances said.

"Can I have Sandy call you back tomorrow, Frances?" Johnny B. said. "We're late as hell already for this thing."

"No," Frances said, clipping her words. "You're the very one I wanted to speak to, Johnny B."

"Oh yeah?" Johnny B. said, suddenly wary. He and Frances had never had anything much to say to each other before.

"Yes," she hissed into the phone. "I just wanted you to know, Johnny B, that my husband and your wife—*Sandy*—" she added for emphasis, "are having a sex affair. And not only that but they're going to run off to Florida tomorrow. I just felt it was my duty to tell you, Johnny B."

"Hoo ha!"

To her amazement, Johnny B. seemed to be laughing. Of course he could have been crying. But then great whoops of unmistakable laughter crackled through the phone.

"Is that a fact?" he asked finally. "Sandy and Bob?"

"I'm sorry to be the one to tell you," began Frances, feeling somewhat confused.

"Well, I be dog!" roared Johnny B.

While Frances held the receiver, the line went dead. She was furious. What a stupid, no-account fried-chicken fryer! He never was any count. Even at his age, he had a Honda.

When Bob Pitt finally came out of the bathroom with his Sea and Ski, his wife and daughter were sitting in the front seat of the car.

"It's about time," Frances snapped. In the dashboard lights, she seemed cast in Styrofoam. The straight red line of her mouth was ended abruptly by a prim vertical wrinkle at each corner, and her whole face was grainy with Merle Norman powder. She smelled so strongly of perfume that Bob rolled down the window. "Who do you think won the contest?" he asked Theresa, his enigmatic Theresa, sitting as still as an iceberg in her white majorette uniform. Bob was surprised that he could make such conversation. He wished Frances would say something, anything. She had never been so quiet in her life.

"Oh, I don't know, Daddy," Theresa said. She paused and then added, "You all want to know what I decided today? I decided I want to be a teacher when I get out of school."

"What kind of teacher?" Bob asked, just to keep her talking.

"Biology, probably," Theresa said.

That did it. "A teacher!" Frances squawked. Theresa might as well have said "a murderer" as far as Frances was concerned. Who ever thought that her Theresa would turn into a little old schoolteacher after all? Frances remembered the day of the Susan Arch Finlay in Tuscaloosa, the way Theresa had looked in her derby hat.

Bob couldn't find a parking place near the junior high; even the football parking lot was full. He stopped to let Theresa out and off she ran to join the rest of the band, forming near the goal posts. "I'll get a ride home with somebody," she yelled back at them. "Don't worry."

"You be home by—" Frances began, but Theresa was gone.

"Frances," Bob said and stopped.

"What?" she said. "You're not good enough to say a word to me; I'm surprised you've got the nerve."

"What I was going to say was, just shut up."

"Ha!" Frances snorted.

Now he could barely drive. Traffic was blocked for minutes at a time by streams of pedestrians pouring into the street, heading for the football field. Everyone seemed to be shouting. It was like the atmosphere before a football game played by traditionally rival schools. Finally Bob parked and locked the car.

"Not so fast," she panted, but he pulled her along in her white spike heels. In a very few minutes, he would see Sandy.

Frances stumbled along, filled with a curious exaltation. Her only daughter was going to be an old maid school-teacher. Her own husband was going to run off with another woman, her very own cousin that she had hated all her life. But she was going to sit in a special box with the mayor's wife and the Lieutenant Governor of Alabama and all the other dignitaries and hold her head up high. Just see if she didn't, in spite of all the awful things everybody was doing to her.

THIRTY-THREE

*L*LOYD Warner looked down at his uniform and laughed. He had decided, at the last minute, to join the Confederate Army. So here he was in smelly pants about three sizes too big and a hat like no Confederate had ever seen. The only reason he was here was that some of his old hunting buddies had talked him into it early this morning. He couldn't remember this morning. Right now he was blinded by the stadium lights—he did not see how anyone ever played football under lights like these. Lloyd blinked his eyes and swayed and Dave Bird held his elbow. Lloyd was drunk.

"Hey, man," Lloyd said to Dave Bird, with whom he had grown up.

"Hey what?"

"Bang, bang," Lloyd said softly, and the two men laughed.

The soldiers had furnished their own firearms, some of which were authentic Civil War weapons. A lot of the men in Speed collected guns, and Lloyd himself had had several to choose from. His did not date back to the war, but it was an old shotgun. The only difference between it and everybody else's guns was that Lloyd's was loaded. This was a private joke of Lloyd's, a spinoff of whatever had been happening to him all day, ever since Dave Bird had convinced him this morning in the Rondo that he really should appear in this goddamn pageant after all. Lloyd kept forgetting the joke but it was private and elaborate and harmed, he felt, no one.

The way he had arrived at the joke was by sitting all afternoon on the glider behind the garage apartment he rented from the much-divorced Mrs. Ida Duveen, drinking Jack Daniel's and chasing it with beer. When Mrs. Duveen had drifted through his field of vision for the third time with an obviously circumstantial hoe, having no intention of hoeing anything, and had remarked, "My, Lloyd, you certainly are in fine shape," he had taken her into her house and made a kind of love to her on the couch. He didn't much want to, but he had done it before so he figured he might as well do it again. Then he had stood by the window, fingering the slats of the Venetian blinds, watching her sleep on the tufted, uncomfortable couch for a while before he left.

So Lloyd had returned to the glider and resumed what he began to consider his vigil. He was watching out for night. As the vigil stretched on toward twilight, the vigil assumed great intensity. Mrs. Duveen left the house in her Buick convertible, wearing a little sheer blue scarf. She gave him a friendly wave, which he returned lustily, following the wave with several semaphore signals. Mrs. Duveen, obviously unimpressed by the expertise of the semaphore signals, giggled and drove away. "The coast is clear." Lloyd remembered saying that aloud, but he wasn't too sure why he had said it. He couldn't remember much about the rest of the afternoon. He seemed to remember telephoning his mother and telling her some outrageous lie. Then he had lain on his back for a while in the grass, imagining the rounds that lie was traveling now, over the telephone wires of Speed, and imagining the mutations and permutations it had probably undergone.

Ever-vigilant, Lloyd watched for signs of night. The foundry whistle blew, an omen. There was something involving a neighbor's dog and a child. He thought he had placed a call to New York. The one sure thing was the sun going down and the night coming. Lloyd had gone to the Zippy Mart for more beer with which to fortify himself against the night, and had engaged in a ridiculously flirtatious conversation with the counter girl. What had he said to her? What had she said? It was a wonderful conversation. Then twilight had come, shading first the little peaked dormer windows of Mrs. Duveen's house, and it was as he knew it would be.

A lapse occurred in Lloyd's memory between the time when the windows of Mrs. Duveen's house turned red in the sunset and the time he stood in the gravel beside the junior high school with Dave Bird, waiting for the pageant to start. Many things may or may not have happened during this time lapse, Lloyd figured. May not or may. The thing that kept coming back to him now, oddly enough, was Mrs. Duveen's round white face, which hung in the sky, disembodied, over the stadium lights. He checked his gun.

THIRTY-FOUR

*B*UCK was all business and dash. He sat at the control panel with his five narrators, with his electrician, with the virginal speech teacher from the high school who was in charge of the sound tapes, with a number of lesser flunkies. Back in the gym, Luther was supposedly heaving the whole show into place. Getting the show on the road. It was five minutes before the pre-pageant activities were scheduled to begin. Twenty minutes before the pageant itself would start. Generally, this was the highlight of any pageant for Buck: giving the final directions, basking in the final glory. He liked to be able to tell bankers and lawyers and people with college degrees what to do. He liked to give society wives reassuring pats on their lovely plump butts and whisper, "Smile, gorgeous," into their perfumed ears. But this time, although Buck paced busily before his control booth—the ideal harried director, playing it like he always played it, running his hands through his hair—his heart just wasn't in it. Something about this pageant could not be controlled from the booth. Something had happened which defied his giant screen and his aerial slides and the blinking lights and intricate electrical wiring; although, Buck thought, nobody knows it but me. He thought he knew what it was. Fuck Monica, he thought. Fuck Speed, the whole town. The truth was that Buck (although he would never even say the word aloud himself) had fallen in love. He was conscious only of a spreading dissatisfaction, general and corrosive, which even included himself. This was certainly new to him. He felt like he had been robbed. He felt even more like beating the shit out of Manly Neighbors, although that was, of course, impossible. In every other town, he had been keeping somebody off his own back at this stage of the game.

Monica, that very afternoon, had turned the tables on him. Sitting cross-legged in his bed, she had said, "Well, it's been fun, Buck," as chipper as a bird. His standard line. Just when he was about to say something about meeting her in Mobile, what the hell. He had looked at her good then, realizing that she was not his to do what he felt like with, and this was the one time he felt like it.

"Don't look so surprised," Monica had continued. "You said yourself there was nothing to it. You said so all along."

"Well, hell," Buck had said. None of his lines fit what was happening.

"Well, hell, yourself," Monica had said contentedly, lying back. She had seemed withdrawn and happy, inside herself, even though she was lying naked on his bed in his room. She was humming. Buck had not known what to make of her.

"You mean you can't come to Mobile?" he had asked, stalling.

"Afraid not," she had said, almost gaily. "But it was nice." Then she had giggled irrationally, turning on her side.

"What's the matter?" Buck said, surly, but she kept on giggling.

"I can't believe I said it was nice," she said. "I mean it *was* nice, Buck, it was terrific, but I can't believe I said it just like that. It's such a Hemingway thing to say."

Buck, who always got mad when he didn't understand something, had gotten mad then and had gone to stand under the hot shower for a long time, and when he had come out she was gone. Buck had dried himself, methodically, cursing.

Of course she isn't worth it, he told himself now as he paced before the booth. A good lay. A good *married* lay, the best kind, no responsibilities. But now he wouldn't mind the responsibility all of a sudden and it was too late. A comeback, Buck thought angrily, I've got to make a comeback. "O.K., dim those lights," he bawled authoritatively.

"They don't dim, sir, not those stadium lights," the electrician said timidly. "I can turn them off if you want."

"No, no," Buck said. "Turn them off for a minute and then turn them back on and then cut them off for good. Got it?"

"Yep," said the electrician, very excited. Installing GE dryers was never like this.

"O.K.," Buck directed, some of his old swagger coming back, "hit it."

"What, sir?"

"I mean, turn off the goddamn lights!"

Slowly the mercury-vapor lights went out, the rods continuing to glow for a few seconds after the light was gone. The crowd hushed suddenly and completely, then broke into spontaneous applause when the lights came back on again.

"Oh, shit," said Buck. "Take two."

"What, sir?"

"Will you just turn off the lights?"

"Sure, sir," the electrician said. He was not offended. It was just about what, he told his wife later, you could expect to get off an actor.

Swiftly, smoothly, the voice of Ron-the-Mouth vibrated through the warm air.

"We know you're all waiting," he said, "we're *all* waiting to find out who is the lovely Sesquicentennial Queen of Speed. So, without further ado, I ask you to turn your eyes to the center stage, ladies and gentlemen, and meet the top five constestants. As each gorgeous contestant is introduced, a close-up of her will be shown on the giant screen so that you ladies and gentlemen won't miss a single dimple. These girls have worked long and hard for weeks to make your Sesquicentennial a success, so let's give them all a big hand. There they are, ladies and gentlemen! Five of the loveliest women this side of heaven. Would you look at that! What a sight! A big hand for the lovely ladies, folks. That's right, let them hear it."

The crowd went wild as twin spotlights wobbled in to illuminate the five finalists on the lowest part of the center stage. They carried sprays of red roses and stood in a straight, proud line. To the people in the back rows of bleachers, they looked like a set of miniature dolls.

"Not to keep you in suspense, ladies and gentlemen, we will now introduce the fourth runner-up. Will Mrs. Grace Henley step forward, please?" Everybody clapped and Grace stepped up into the spotlight, moving carefully on the red carpet which had been borrowed from the funeral home. Grace looked big and blonde and slightly awkward in her white maternity dress. On the screen, a huge color slide of her face was flushed before the audience, stunning them.

"Carrying it high," somebody remarked as Grace turned to go back to her place and gave them all a profile view of herself. "I bet it's a boy. It's a boy every time if you can't tell they're pregnant from the back."

"Third runner-up is Miss Sharon DuBois, the daughter of Mr. and Mrs. Johnny B. DuBois of Speed," Ron announced, and this time there were whistles. Sharon was the only contestant not wearing an evening dress; she wore her bright white majorette suit instead, since she had to march right after the ceremony. She stood with her weight on one leg, the other leg thrust out in the timeless majorette position, holding her roses and accepting the whistles and applause as if she had been doing it all her life. She rotated her head carefully so that everyone could see her smile, as Ron-the-Mouth read a list of the prizes she had won. A large color slide of Sharon marching in her derby hat was thrown up on the screen. Bevo squirmed where Luther had placed him, near the gym, and held his head with both hands to keep it on his neck and to keep it from exploding into fireworks. Mrs. Frances Pitt averted her eyes.

Tension mounted as Ron announced the second runner-up, Johnnie Sue Billings. "Youngest contestant!" Ron shouted. The blowup of Johnnie Sue was pretty as could be—the child's face with the strangely older eyes—but Johnnie Sue bit her lip and stamped her little foot. It was the first contest she had ever entered which she had failed to win.

The audience rustled like a wind as they looked at the two remaining contestants, Anne deColigny and Judith Sardis. "Who will she be, folks?" asked Ron-the-Mouth, his voice full of doom and portent. "Who will own the diamond ring that's brighter than the sun? Who will go down in history as our chosen Queen? Our august mayor, Bill Higgins, will make the presentation." Bill Higgins stepped into the spotlight, rakishly doffed his hat, and bowed low, tickling his constituents. "Look at old Bill now," they said, "all duded up!"

Miss Speed Tot, a fat three-year-old, was prodded onto the stage, and at length was induced to give up her white envelope to Higgins. Then Higgins announced the winner, but nobody could hear what he said because the stage mike wasn't working.

"ANNE deCOLIGNY!" Ron shouted. "Miss deColigny is our new Queen. And nothing could be more appropriate, folks, since Anne's grandmother reigned over Speed's centennial festivities fifty years ago. How about that? What a coincidence! Let's hear it for Anne deColigny, the new Queen!"

Anne was a given a tiara and more roses and a fur cape which kept slipping from her shoulders. She stood smiling gently at the audience, loud and imaginary behind the blinding lights. She didn't know she had sold so many tickets. She never would have entered in the first place if it hadn't been for her mother and the girls in her sorority. Think of that!

Judith Sardis almost got lost in the to-do, in fact, but eventually Bob Pitt was introduced and he crowned her as Alternate Queen. She took her brief moment of glory modestly, head bowed, in a dress of her own design.

"She can really sew," a woman in the audience remarked. "She won't even *make* a seam without Frenching it, think of that. Her clothes is so neat, she could wear them inside out."

Ruthie sat happily by her mother, letting Ron's voice flow over and around her like a bath. She could have been up on the stage, of course; she knew damn well that at one time she had been ahead of everybody. Before she stopped working on it. Now she didn't even care. The warm wind blew through the crowd, lifting her hair, and she thought idly of patterns in stainless steel.

More dignitaries were presented, and then Harry Dulaney, in his Kop suit, gave the invocation and called upon God to bless this glorious undertaking, mentioning the names of the major Confederate generals and all the main natural resources and industries of Speed. Entranced by his own rhetoric, he went on and on, damning the Communists and the dissenters within, blessing even the little flowers, until his voice caught after each phrase with the old grunt and he was into chant, and some people in the audience cried "Amen." Buck fumed and looked at the luminous green face of his watch. But at last it was over and the Speed High Glee Club was singing "America," and then Mrs. Dodie Bidlow, a long-distance telephone operator, was announcing the gala entrance.

Frances looked around through lowered lids during the prayer, to see who was really praying and who was just looking around. Bob was twisting his hands nervously: he ought to, she thought. Him standing up there so proper to be introduced when all the time he was an adulterer of the first water. Ha. But the spotlight had fallen on her, too, and she had sat there like a lady, she was proud to say. She had held her head up high. Later on when it all came out, everybody would say wasn't it something how she she had sat there so you couldn't even tell. Frances compared herself to Jackie Kennedy and came out on top.

THIRTY-FIVE

*E*VERYONE in the pageant marched briskly onto the field, filling it with small American flags. Five hundred people, weaving in and out and waving those flags in a secret pattern known only to Luther, who sweated inside his white summer suit and dreamed of a tall, cold beer. A Sousa march blared out of the PA system, and ahead of them all were Sharon DuBois and Theresa Pitt, leading the march with giant steps—the fanciest fancy strut anyone had ever seen—and here came the Rockettes and the Boy Scouts and the ROTC and the Indians and Lord knows what all, everybody waving those little flags until it seemed the field was full of them. Sharon kicked higher than she had ever kicked before. She wondered who might be in the audience, even now, watching. You never knew. She hoped he might be dark and attractive and—what was the word? Satanic. She hoped he would be satanic. Theresa, on the other hand, wasn't enjoying it much. You couldn't have known it, to see her, but suddenly, for no good reason, she wished she was someplace else. Now they lit their fire batons and twirled them, and the cast waved their flags in a circle. You never saw anything like it. Several ladies in the audience were moved to tears, and clutched at their nearest neighbors.

Bevo stood by the microphone at the control booth, bugle raised. Now he was supposed to blow a fanfare, announcing the Devil's arrival. But Bevo watched Sharon marching. How could anybody be the way she was? "Go on, goddamnit," Luther said, punching him for the second time.

"What?" Bevo said, not looking around. The bugle dangled useless from his hand.

"Toot that thing!"

Bevo raised his bugle and loudly blew all the wrong notes. The audience, thinking it was supposed to be funny, part of the show, laughed and applauded. Then the Devil entered in a huge puff of green smoke, swinging his pitchfork, and the whole cast fell flat and silent on the field as the atomic bomb went off. The audience was astonished. It was the most people they had ever seen lying down at once.

Solemnly, Ron-the-Mouth began: "We are threatened by the Devil at every turn. People speak of nuclear holocaust, of world war, of death and destruction. What is the future of the world? Of this country? Of Speed? What will be the outcome of this never-ending battle between good and evil, between the Devil and the American way of life?" The Devil scampered about the football field, poking at the fallen cast with his pitchfork. "Will the Devil win?" The Devil jumped with glee. "Will God be victorious?" The Devil pointed at the sky and cowered, and there was scattered applause for God. "Slowly we are losing our convictions one by one," Ron went on, "America is in danger, besieged from without and within. Where is our patriotism? What will be our fate? If you don't believe me, just sing 'America' the next time you're at a party. Sing it out loud and clear, my friends, and see where it gets you. It will bring ridicule and averted eyes. What does this portend?'' The Devil sent up another puff of green smoke. ''Not so fast, Devil,'' Ron warned. ''If we would know the future of our country, let us look to the past.'' The giant History Book appeared on the stage. ''Let the youth of today, citizens of tomorrow, guide us in our search through the past,'' suggested Ron-the-Mouth.

Lewis Morris, a tenth grader who had won the Junior Toastmaster Award for two years running, spoke from the control booth while the History Book danced. ''I will speak for the youth of America,'' he enunciated. ''And I say that education is the greatest asset confronting us today. Through education we may avoid the mistakes of the past to build a rosier future for the betterment of man. We may make science serve us, instead of serving it. Now let us go back through the years, back through the *decades*'' (on his speech, Lewis had underlined the words he planned to emphasize) ''and see what our heritage is. For we must know the past in order to shape our future.''

The lights dimmed and solemn organ music filled the void as, on the field, the entire cast got up as quietly as possible and trooped out. Most of their muttered curses and whisperings were drowned out by the recorded organ strains, but here and there a squeal penetrated the music as some of the boys in the cast took advantage of darkness to get in a grope or two. The mass exit took a lot longer than it was supposed to, and the audience began to fidget and giggle on their hard wooden seats.

Bevo heard none of it. He stood under part of the giant stage with the audience's laughter still ringing in his ears. It was the worst moment of his life. He thought of all that practice—for what? To be scorned and laughed at. Sharon had probably laughed hardest of all, yet in his dreams he had imagined her strutting to him at that precise moment, strutting toward him as he stood revealed in the blinding light of his talent. And the worst part was that it wasn't over yet. He had to blow for the Confederates. Bevo sat in the gravel. He didn't see how he could possibly do it. Bevo took the box of safety matches from his pocket and began toying with them, lighting a few and then crushing the flame with gravel. The sulphur smelled sweet, sharp and strange. Above him, Bevo heard the Indian maidens beating on tambourines and doing their dance. The human sacrifice took place.

Bevo moodily lit matches and stamped them out. Restlessly, he went from section to section of his subterranean world, looking up occasionally at the feet and hips over his head. He thought he would stay under there forever. Moving catlike under Section E, he almost stumbled over Sharon and Red. It was so dark that he could barely make them out. They were sitting on a pile of old lumber—boards and trash were everywhere—so close to each other that at first Bevo took them for a single person there in the dark. Then Sharon said one word and Bevo knew.

The word was "because."

"Why not?" Red said, sounding mad.

"Be*cause*," Sharon said again.

Bevo moved behind a supporting post, his heart beating even faster than it had beat when he blew his bugle, and he stood still as a post himself and listened.

"That's not any kind of reason."

"It is too," Sharon said firmly.

"If you don't love me I guess I can always find me another girl."

"You just go ahead and try, then."

"Oh, Sharon, come on. "Who's going to know?"

"That's not the point."

"Well, what is the point then? Why not?"

"Be*cause*," Sharon said.

Red sounded like he was really getting mad and Bevo hoped he was. He imagined Red's face the way it had always looked at the pep rallies: squint-eyed and jut-jawed and mad. Ready to fight. Maybe Red would get real mad and go away, leaving Sharon there in the dark, and Bevo could go to her aid. He could comfort her and she would see him anew. Probably she wouldn't want him to go to her aid, though. Probably she hated his guts.

"Just be*cause*," Sharon said very emphatically.

"O.K., if that's the way you want it." Red sounded disgusted and the single seated figure seemed to separate momentarily in the gloom.

Quickly Sharon said, "Well, you might do it just a little," and the figures merged again.

Bevo moved from post to post. He could not listen to Sharon and Red any more. He thought he had finally gone mad. He couldn't stand the shuffling feet above his head. He couldn't stand the blue lights now on the field; they reminded him of the Blue Flame in Cleveland, Tennessee, and he couldn't stand to look. Not wanting to, he crept back toward Sharon and Red.

"I've got to go," Sharon said. They seemed to be struggling.

"Just a minute," Red panted.

"I said you couldn't do it but a little," Sharon said icily. "You quit that now."

Bevo couldn't imagine exactly what Red could be doing.

"You quit now, I'm telling you," Sharon said louder. "Quit!"

Red apparently continued to do whatever it was that he was doing.

"I've got to march in the grand finale and you're going to get me all messed up," she said. "I bet my hair is a sight right now."

Bevo heard them both breathing hard, and then the

shadow split and Sharon stood, her face a pastel blue in
the sliver of light from the field.

"Now see what you've done!" she said ambiguously,
and turned and ran away. Red stood up slowly, stretched,
and said, "Oh shit," out loud to himself before he left.
Bevo sat in the gravel and tried to puzzle it out. Was
Sharon upset or what? What would she do if he tried to
comfort her? Nothing, he decided sadly. Not a thing.

Bevo knew that they would be looking for him. Fat
Luther would be pacing up and down, looking. But he
couldn't leave his sanctuary yet. Someone threw a white
Kleenex down between the boards and it drifted slowly,
beautifully, through the shadows to land at his feet. Bevo
sat down again and waited for another sign, and in a few
minutes a nearly-empty Cracker Jack box fell his way.
They could just have the war without him then, Bevo
decided. They could get on the field the best way they
could find because he wasn't going to be there to blow
charge.

Beneath the lowest level of the stage, Bevo gathered
quite a pile of empty popcorn and Cracker Jack boxes,
Dixie cups, lipsticked Kleenex, and other trash. Over this
pile he erected several pieces of scrap woods in teepee
fashion, the way they had taught him in the Boy Scouts.
The wood caught right away, with no problem. Bevo had
been afraid it might be damp. "The good Scout needs only
one match," his Scoutmaster had been fond of saying.

"Red? Red?" It was Sharon, coming back. "Bevo!"
She stopped dead still and stared at him across the flickering
fire. Then, without a word, she put a hand across her
pretty mouth and turned and ran.

THIRTY-SIX

*I*N the dignitaries' box, with no emotion at all, Bob Pitt had watched his daughter marching. He did not even know her, he thought. Theresa seemed a part of that accident, too, whatever accident had paired him with Frances. He would not miss her, or Frances. But he could not stand to think of Bobby Joe, whom he would miss very much. Still, Bobby Joe was now so much like he had been that it pained him; so maybe it would be a relief not to see Bobby Joe either.

In a way, Bob felt that he had already left. He felt that everything happening now was happening in the past. He looked around him in the box: all the jockeying, all the vying for places here seemed pointless. Within the box sat Mr. and Mrs. Bill Higgins, the Lieutenant Governor and his wife, the police chief and his wife, Manly Neighbors, the superintendent of schools, the presidents of both banks and their wives, the members of the Town Council, the president of the Speed Junior College and his wife, the high school principal and his wife, all the members of the school board and their wives, and the presidents of all the major clubs in town (the presidents who were not actually in the pageant, that is). Miss Leola Bradshaw, still angry that she had failed to procure a seat in the box for herself, sat next to it, separated from it only by a rope, staring enviously at the chosen. Behind him, Bob could feel the press of people. The stadium held fifteen hundred people, and every seat was taken. Some people were standing in the back and by the sidelines. For a town of fourteen thousand, that was quite a turnout. He had done much of the real work involved here, and it was a great success. No one could deny that it was a success. Bob Pitt thought of fine white sand.

After the exit of the Indians, a group of happy pioneers frolicked onto the stage. The Senior Citizens performed the Virginia Reel, somewhat slowly. A group of pioneer children sang their ABC's, making a cute pun on the letter "P." A double wedding ceremony ensued, at which the minister pantomimed the "Double your pleasure, double your fun" ad for chewing gum while the chewing-gum jingle itself was played over the loudspeakers. Then came the important ceremony of the naming of the town. The first mayor, Ira Bell (played by Manny Goldman), asked for suggestions. One by one, buckskin-clad pioneer men stepped forward, pantomiming the suggestions which were read aloud over the PA in the melodious tones of the telephone operator. "Riverdale!" she cried. "Forest View!" "Maple Heights?" The pioneer men scratched their heads with large gestures, indicating perplexity, while their women huddled together as if for warmth. "Bellboro?" "Flower-dell?" The list went on. Then a small boy separated himself from his group of slate-carrying preschoolers, and shouted, "Speed!" At that instant, recorded thunder shook the stadium and on the stage an angel appeared all in white, carrying a gigantic sequined pasteboard trumpet. She raised it to her lips and a trumpet solo echoed through the air, causing the pioneers to cower in consternation. At length Ira Bell picked himself up and proclaimed that the town should be known to posterity as "Speed." The pioneers moved out under cover of darkness as Roman candles were released.

Spotlights went on to illuminate the Community Interreligious Choir in white choir robes on the second level of the stage. They broke into "How Great Thou Art," signaling the third act on everyone's program, the "History of Religion and Speed." As the chorus sang, blue spotlights played at random over the darkened field. Then all the lights went black, and a nearly invisible line of black-clad marchers moved out in single file from their waiting places near the gym. They lit candles as the chorus switched to "Just As I Am, Without One Plea." At last the marchers formed themselves into a big, straggling star; and in the center of the star, Martin Miller, who carried the cross with its rows of blue light bulbs, switched it on. From the bleachers it was quite effective: all you could see were the candles forming the star, and the electrified cross at its center. The chorus sang, "Let My Little Light Shine," followed by the "Lord's Prayer." An uneasy hush followed the much-reported and ornate amen. Nobody was sure if they ought to clap or not; can you clap for something *religious*? Somebody gave a derisive wolf whistle, quickly squelched by Christians. One by one, slides of the major churches of Speed were flashed upon the giant screen, each one greeted with applause by members of the particular denomination in the audience, and a recorded history of each church, given by the minister of that church, was played. This part of the pageant lasted for many minutes and brought about a general fidgeting in the stands. Children who had been clamoring to go to the bathroom were taken at this time.

Then the recorded roar of cannons, great puffs of acrid

smoke, and the VFW band playing "Dixie" brought the audience cheering to its feet and heralded the beginning of the Civil War, Act 4. A short and slanted history of the events leading to the necessity of secession was read by Ron-the-Mouth, as the History Book performed a tap solo on the third tier of the stage. There was some confusion when the bugler failed to bugle at his appointed time, but at length the brave Confederates, a hundred strong, rushed onto the field with wild Rebel yells. The Union men appeared with less dash, and the battle of Appomattox began. It was briefly interrupted by the pathetic battlefield amputation. The Confederate lad's last pitiful cry of "Mama," as the surgeon's oversized ax descended, brought tears to the eyes of some real mamas in the audience. Then, on with the war! This was truly the highlight of the show as far as many of the spectators were concerned: such yelling, such action, such gunfire! At times the field was so filled with smoke that it was difficult to see what was going on. The pageant viewers cheered as if they were at a football game. Little by little, though, the cheers subsided as the outcome became obvious. One by one, the boys in gray clandestinely pulled out their packets of White Company True-Life Blood, smeared themselves, went into violent death seizures and fell sprawling in the dust. But they had done some damage! The Union men bloodied themselves and fell, too, until the field was a mess of bodies and blood and moans and that by now familiar White Company special smoke, and not a man was left standing upright. A red spotlight was turned upon the lower level of the stage, where Lee (played by Leonard Lipscomb, pastor of the First Baptist Church) surrendered his glowing, jeweled sword to Grant (F. F. Parker, head of the YMCA). The slow, sad strains of "My Old Kentucky Home" swept across the gory tableau of carnage.

Then three portly men with large, fake noses and pieces

of Samsonite luggage covered by shag carpet came bustling through the bodies, to be hissed and booed by the audience. They opened their bags and proceeded to take out various boxes with stenciled words such as MACHINE and LUMBER on them. (Of course the effect of these boxes was lost upon those who sat up past midway in the stands, and these viewers strained vainly to make out the words.) The mournful notes of "My Old Kentucky Home" switched briskly to a jazz version of "Swanee," and all over the field fallen Confederates popped back up and reconstructed themselves.

Except for one. Lloyd Warner lay, grinning in spite of the pain, in a pool of the only real blood on the field. So he had fucked it up. So he had *missed*. Too drunk to shoot, he reckoned. But still, he had really meant to do it. He knew he had. So. Now he would not have to do it again, was free of it, was free. He tried to grin again but his shoulder hurt like hell. He grimaced and passed out.

Meanwhile, a vast, fidgety confusion had set in among the audience. They were not sure what to do after the battlefield scene. It sure was a funny ending for such a good scene. You couldn't tell if it was over with that one Confederate still laying out there on the field. What was he still laying out there for? Then several men went out to look at him (was this part of the pageant, too?) and started waving their arms, and after a minute Ron-the-Mouth said, "Excuse me, ladies and gentlemen, is there a doctor in the house? A doctor in the house, please. Come down front to the control booth, please. Thank you."

A last-minute change was made in the program, and a group of flappers were hustled onto the second level of the stage. They immediately began flapping away to the tinny beat of "Five Foot Two, Eyes of Blue." Despite the flappers' flashing knees, the audience was not diverted from the circle of men on the darkened field. Now they were bringing a stretcher. People craned to see. Several people, thinking it was all a part of the show, clapped at the brisk entrance of the men in white who carried the stretcher. "Well, if you *run* into a five-foot-two, covered in fur—diamond rings, and all those things, you bet your life it isn't her!" The flappers winked outrageously and did the Big Apple. Their long beads jostled and flew. The audience was confused. What did flappers have to do with the Confederacy? Some men left their seats and went down to the restraining wire around the field to see what was going on.

Then the flappers began screaming and jumping from their platform down onto the lower level. To the audience, the flappers' scream sounded faraway and artificial, the windup screams of tiny dolls. But the reason for the screams was soon apparent, as the first-level stage suddenly split and a column of flame and smoke shot up into the air. Flimsy dresses flying, the flappers fell like leaves and scurried safely onto the field, showing a lot of leg. Yellow spotlights frantically roamed the stage, focusing on nothing. Abruptly they were cut off, and everybody saw that the fire was real fire, and not merely a White Company special effect.

"Ladies and gentlemen, please keep calm," advised the smooth voice of Ron-the-Mouth. "'The Song of Speed' will continue following a short intermission. Please remain in your seats, ladies and gentlemen. Remain in your seats, please." But the beautiful voice of Ron-the-Mouth had no more effect now than a radio playing softly in an apartment where a murder is taking place. Fire raced across the patriotic bunting and leaped to the next level, outlining the tiered stage. But perhaps it was the wailing siren of the departing ambulance that caused the final panic: sirens affect some people that way. No White Company effect could ever be so real. The bunting, which covered the fence that half circled the football field, now caught on both sides of the burning stage; and tiny flames fanned out to the right and left of the main blaze. The crowd was in an uproar. People jammed the aisles, climbed down across the bleachers themselves. People fought toward the exits and their cars. Women screamed.

Buck Fire was at the control-booth phone, frantically trying to get the fire department, when a costumed football player grabbed the phone from his hand. "I got to make a call," the player panted, as if he were in a phone booth.

"Listen, man, I'm trying to get the fire department," Buck said.

"Hell, buddy, I'm the fire chief!" the beefy player exploded. "We're all volunteers anyway, and just about all my men is football players."

"You mean there's nobody at the fire department?"

"I can't get nobody to answer. Ed Bucker is supposed to be over there but his wife is expecting any time and—" The fire chief's explanation was interrupted as a wedge of people from Section F poured across the restraining wire and overturned the control table. The fire chief, giving up, joined them in their race across the field and the last Buck saw of him was his disappearing jersey, No. 44, as it was swallowed by the crowd.

"Holy shit," Buck said. He had never seen anything like it. There was no real danger, he judged: the stage would burn, the bunting would burn on the fence, and the bleachers would probably catch—but the gravel lot separated the gym from the fire, and the field itself was dirt. The real danger seemed to be that people would trample each other to death. Yet Buck saw that a number of them were climbing the fence, throwing children over, so maybe the exits would not be blocked. Buck stood in the nearly vacant center of the field, watching the confusion, and repeated, "Holy shit" at intervals to himself. The drive-in screen behind the burning stage, which had said WAR in big red letters during the War Between the States, now said RAW. Someone had knocked the projector, dislodging the letters. Then, as Buck watched, RAW disappeared too and the screen itself caught fire and curled. Buck hoped the White Company had some goddamn insurance.

The more he thought about it, the more he thought that maybe it might be a wise move for him to get out of here himself and keep right on going out of town. Lomas Cartwright rushed headlong into Buck, carrying his billy stick, and muttering about niggers and Communist conspiracies. Two men seemed to be following Lomas—two Confederates—and they had their guns. Buck didn't know if the guns were real and loaded or not but he got out of their way and headed off the field.

"Listen, *let go*, will you, I don't even know where my kids are," Sandy DuBois was screaming at Bob Pitt, near one of the exits. "Let go, I'm telling you!" Her blond hair glowed in the red light above her Indian headdress, and she had never looked better to Bob.

"Damn you, you must be crazy," Sandy screamed.

Behind the glasses, Bob's eyes showed red and slightly mad as he mumbled of Pompano Beach.

"You better leave, go on now," Sandy shouted, trying to push him away. "Listen, Johnny B. *knows* and if he sees you he'll kill you, you know Johnny B. Now go *on*."

Johnny B. himself, clad as a pioneer, suddenly appeared beside them. He was grinning hugely and he said, "I hear you all are taking a little vacation, ain't that nice?"

"Don't kill him," Sandy said.

But Johnny B. threw back his head and laughed. "Kill him!" he said. "Hoo-ha!" Sandy stared at him, furious— she had never been so mad, she thought—and then she started laughing, too. "Hoo-ee," they yelled, doubled over.

Bob stepped gravely back, staring at them. He did not understand them, but it was just as well. He didn't mind, really. He really didn't mind at all. He walked back into the crowd and allowed himself to be jostled and shoved. He would leave that night, immediately. As soon as he could get his car out of the lot. He had known he would leave ever since he wrote the first letter. He had known too, he thought, that he would go alone. In his mind's eye he saw a stretch of white, deserted beach and himself in his black Bushy Brothers top hat, dancing on the shore.

The fire's roaring was drowned out now by the tremendous din of car horns. It was the biggest traffic jam in the history of Speed. Many people simply abandoned their cars for the time being and began walking home. No car could have gotten through; the road was a river of people.

Caroline Pettit was finding it suddenly difficult to breathe and walk at the same time. An iron cummerbund seemed to encircle her girth, pressing in. It was only after she had stopped several times, to try to breathe, that she realized what was happening. She was in labor. She grabbed Ronald, in his Kop costume, to tell him the news. "Well, you just take it easy," Ronald said, infuriatingly smug. "We've got plenty of time. We can stop in your Aunt Grace's house and call the hospital." Like everyone else, the Pettits had left their car back at the junior high parking lot.

"But Dr. Johnson was in the pageant," Caroline wailed. Everything was awful, everything was over.

"Well, we'll just go on over there as soon as we can. Somebody will be on duty. Don't you worry, honey," Ronald said.

"Don't you think you ought to carry me?" Caroline said.

"Are you kidding?" said Ronald. He had said it just that way, with that particular inflection, ever since they were both in Mrs. Anthony's home room in the ninth grade. Caroline started to cry.

"Now, honey." Ronald patted her shoulder. "Indian women used to go out in the woods and have them all by themselves."

Caroline drew back from him in horror. "You don't seem to understand, Ronald," she said, her voice rising. "The whole point is, Ronald, that there is a little live baby inside of me trying to get out." She felt sickened and excited all at once at the thought of the real little baby, but looking at Ronald's face she realized that he didn't have, couldn't have, the faintest idea what she was talking about.

"You're just too excited," Ronald said. "It'll be all right."

Manly and Monica got out of the police car in the square, thanking Bill Blevins, the policeman, profusely. The crowd from the pageant was beginning to trickle into the square now, upset and a little wild, looking for someone to blame. A lot of people thought he was mean, but right now Bill Blevins was mainly worried. He had a radio in his patrol car, but there was no one to talk to. He didn't know what to do. If he drove around the square, he was likely to see somebody doing something they shouldn't do and then he would have to do something about it. Bull looked back toward the junior high, where the sky glowed red, and from that direction he saw a bunch of black boys running fast and low to the ground. Now Bull didn't like a nigger any better than anybody else, but he wasn't about to fool with a whole bunch of them. They might break up his car, and Bull really liked his patrol car. Bull mumbled something to Manly Neighbors and that black-headed wife of his and spun on out, spewing gravel. Bull didn't like the looks of things, so he turned on his siren and kept it on, and it wailed, and the red light went around and around on top of his car as he drove around the square.

Manly and Monica were jostled by the running blacks. She dropped the overnight bag containing her Indian costume. "Hey, man." Manly reached out a hand for Theolester Hodo, whom he knew as Suetta's nephew. "What's going on?"

"Hoo-ee," yelled Theolester. "Now they have gone and shot our lawyer, man. Now what do you think, man?" Theolester spun like a dervish, trying to free himself of Manly's hand.

"You mean that man was Lloyd Warner?" Manly asked. "The accident?"

"Accident hell," Theolester said. He seemed more joyful than concerned. Twisting on his heel, he jerked the iridescent stuff of his shirt free and ran on down the sidewalk, spinning and ducking as if he were dodging flying missiles, smashing windows wonderfully with a length of pipe. Suddenly the square seemed full of the sound of breaking glass. Splintering fragments hit the sidewalk and sounded like those handpainted tinkling wind chimes which Manly hadn't seen since he was a child. He had won one once at a fair.

"Is this a riot?" Monica asked, holding his hand. Her old dreams of rape had often included riots but they had invariably taken place in large Northeastern cities.

"Looks like it," Manly said. He had cheerfully worded his first paragraph by the time he got the door unlocked and pulled Monica inside the Speed *Messenger* office. It wasn't likely that they would break in here—there wasn't anything to take except a typewriter or two—but anyway he locked the door behind him and pulled Monica up the stairs in the dark. He turned on his desk light, put Monica in a chair, and sent out an understated story over the AP wire. He was totally absorbed in the story, and when he was through he was satisfied with it. He had been right to come back here and take this paper; this was the thing he could do. Let all his old classmates make *Harper's* with long intimate recitals of their own feelings about sex or racing or whatever. Who gave a damn? When he had to, Manly could write good, straight news. Later, of course, he would follow up the short piece with a longer, analytical story. Whenever anybody sorted out what the hell was going on.

He turned to Monica but—as usual—she had failed to stay put. She had opened the frosted door to Miss Iona's office and stood reading a pile of papers, with her back turned to him.

"Manly," Monica said in an odd voice, "look at this."

"What?" Manly said, going over to stand and watch the turmoil in the square.

"This is your obituary," Monica said in a stranger voice still.

"I'll be damned," said Manly, her husky, red-cheeked Manly. He went over to Miss Iona's father's desk and stood looking over his wife's thin shoulder.

"It doesn't even say where I went to school," Manly said after a while. "I've told her and told her to stick to the facts."

"But, *Manly*," Monica said.

"Well, the old girl is obviously getting senile, that's all," Manly said. "I guess she means this for a resignation."

Monica's head was reeling. Outside in the square, about thirty feet below that window, a riot was taking place. Apparently, at the pageant, someone had been shot. There was a fire. And Manly appeared not only to take these things in stride but to write them up, type them out with his stubby fingers, and send them out to the world over mysterious, humming wires. And she had had a real affair. When she thought of that affair now it seemed as though it had happened a long, long time ago. Years and years. She felt worn out and empty and suddenly brittle and just a little bit old. The image of a bottle came to her, a bottle with a note in it. The noise in the square intensified. It was as though Manly had found her, picked her up off a beach someplace where she had drifted, and dusted her off and kept her carefully among his most prized possessions. But he couldn't read the note, Well, that was all right. There were worse crimes than that. Having an affair was probably worse if one were to think in terms of morals. Monica didn't intend to think in those terms. And she had to admire someone who was capable of reading his own obituary without even batting an eye. Of course there was something insensitive about it, too. But there was something admirable as well.

"I think we'd better cut off the lights in this front office," Manly said. "No sense in advertising the fact that we're up here." He thought of his crank, prowling, but his crank didn't frighten him now.

Visions of rape danced in her head but Monica didn't need them any more for a while. Manly cut off the light in Miss Iona's office and they both went to stand by the window and look out. It was not going to be much of a riot after all. A lot of people seemed to be making off with a lot of merchandise, but the breaking glass had stopped and the looting went on quietly, almost mechanically. People struggled through the streets with TVs and clothes and chairs.

"Where are the police?" Monica asked.

"Probably still at the junior high, directing traffic," Manly said. "Most of those people out there right now weren't over at the thing, anyway. When Lomas Cartwright and some of those get back here, there might be some real trouble, but it looks like everything will pretty much be over by then anyway. If I know Higgins, though, he'll have troopers in here before morning, just to put on a good show. He's probably got them on the road right now."

Manly crossed over to his desk and picked up the phone but it was dead.

Monica was still looking out the window. "I can't recognize anybody," she said. She wished she would see Suetta, committing a heinous crime.

"They all look alike anyway," Manly said, a reflex.

Monica laughed and he looked at her, surprised, but couldn't see her face through the long dark fall of her hair. He didn't see anything funny.

"Come here," Monica said.

"I'm right here," Manly said in his eminently practical voice.

"No, come over *here*," Monica said. "Do this."

"Come on, Monica," he protested.

"Don't be stupid."

"For God's sake, Monica," Manly said. "This office is a hundred years old."

Manly didn't understand, himself, exactly what he meant. It had something to do with the fact that you might mess around in your office with your secretary, or somebody like that, but surely not with your *wife*. Not when you have your own bed right at home. He kept glancing at the door, so finally Monica relented. There was no sense in making him nervous. At least he can always get it up, she thought. Manly held her close and they looked out the window and breathed in heavily the sweet, smoky air.

"Well, let's go home, then," Monica said.

"I'll come back after while," Manly said. "I can't do much with the phone dead, anyway."

Manly pulled out his keys. He will always do what I want him to, Monica thought. He will do whatever I say. But she thought she had learned to accept that now, and she picked up her purse and they left.

THIRTY-SEVEN

A lot of people were gathered there, quietly, on the front lawn of the junior high school across from the still-smoldering stage. For the most part, they sat silently on the grass and watched the fire. Some mothers and fathers wandered among the seated ones, calling names. They looked black and flat against the fire. Nobody, it seemed, was hurt.

Bevo's Mamaw, telling everybody that she had fallen off the bleachers when the fire started and like to broke her leg, skittered like a waterbug from group to group, pulling sleeves with her little hands to make them listen. Finally she passed close to Bevo, who leaned against a tree.

"I been wondering where you was," she yelled at him over the noise of the fire, mad because she had been worried about him.

Bevo just laughed and laughed while his Mamaw glared at him, her eyes red as a rabbit's from the reflection of the fire. He wouldn't be surprised if his Mamaw knew all about it.

The fire hissed and sent up sprays of sparks that looked

like fireworks, and the fire department arrived at last. Bevo leaned against the tree and watched all the action. The field was full of people again, all yelling and doing things with hoses. All of a sudden everybody was there, separating from the crowd into real people: Mrs. DuBois and Sharon and Red, Anne, Ruthie, and Ron-the-Mouth. Ruthie squealed and held Ron-the-Mouth's hand.

Anne acted exactly like she attended a big fire every day of the year, Bevo thought. Nothing could shake her.

"Are you all right, son?" she asked Bevo quietly, her large blank eyes going back and forth across his face.

"Sure," he said, and even to himself he sounded insolent. He was elated. Anne looked at him the way she sometimes looked at Lomas.

Bevo went over and stood behind Sharon DuBois and put his arms around her from behind and covered his eyes. "Guess who," she said.

"Red," said Sharon.

It occurred to him then that she would never be able to guess, not even in a million years, so he took his hands down and let her look for herself.

"Bevo," she gasped, "I think that is a downright peculiar way to act after what you did." Bevo kept his arms around her waist and didn't say a thing. He knew she wouldn't tell. If she hadn't already, then she never would. He rubbed his cheek back and forth on the nubby number 70 on the back of Red Hawkins' jacket.

"Hey," said Red suddenly, but when Bevo turned to look at him, all Red did was walk away. Bevo could smell her hair.

"Well, I never," Sharon said.

"Let's go down close and look," Bevo said, pulling her along by the hand. His Mamaw and Mrs. DuBois were behind them. He thought as they reached the edge of the field that he probably wouldn't do it again, although for the life of him he could not feel sorry. It was almost out, and nobody was hurt, and the only thing that had really burned was the stage. Not much, considering. There were a lot of people on the field and the lights came back on. Bevo felt like he was throwing a party. "I'm so glad you could come," he said politely to Sharon.

"What?" she yelled above the noise.

"Nothing," Bevo said.

Bevo's daddy, Lomas, came through the crowd, hollering about conspiracies.

"Huh!" Mamaw said to nobody.

Ruthie said, "Isn't this fire the wildest thing?"

"This is nothing," said Mamaw. "When I was forty I was attacked by a house cat."

That one gave Bevo kind of a jolt but he could take it. He could take anything. Inside himself he felt all new; his mind ran free in his head; and throughout his whole body, he had come into possession.

So Bevo didn't pay any attention to his Mamaw. Bevo turned away from all of them—from his mother and Mrs. DuBois and his daddy, Lomas, going around like a fool, and from Ruthie, who was flirting with Ron-the-Mouth—turned away from them all to watch the last of the fire, and to hold his true love's hand.

THIRTY-EIGHT

MISS Iona sat alone in the front parlor of her big house, wearing a fancy dressing gown which she had kept in its box for fifty years. It had been special-ordered for her from Marshall Field's in Chicago by her father years ago, and it was made of soft, flame-colored silk embroidered with fanciful Oriental creatures. It was imported. For years she had thought it too fine to wear, but now she took it from its tissue wrappings and put it on, and it felt good. It felt slippery and rich and good, and she sat by the window and watched the commotion outside.

The whole pageant had been a mockery of her heritage and the Southern way of life. It had been diametrically opposed to her own Ideal Pageant. Instead of an exalting theatrical experience, it had been nothing more than a medicine show, a carnival, pandering to the lowest possible tastes. It had deserved to be struck by fire.

Miss Iona's head went round and round. She remembered when the land where the football field now lay had been an orchard, sun-dappled and green. While she was attending the Presbyterian School, her sketching class had often met there, and while the others sketched, the better scholars were often asked to read poetry aloud. She remembered reading "Thanatopsis" in her high, clear voice, with perfect phrasing, over the artists' bent, beribboned heads. Once Bell Hudgins, long since dead, had come up to her afterward, shyly, and said, "Iona, I just don't know how you do it! *I* never know when to breathe!" Ah, yes, she had known when to breathe! Breathing seemed hard now, here. She felt a vast relief and a shortness of breath. She felt brave and humane and tragic, as if she were a nurse in the Crimea.

She saw the people go by in the street on their way home from the pageant, and she watched them curiously. They were strange to her. They had been strange to her for a long while and she had not really known it, but now she knew it and she didn't care. She closed her eyes and imagined how Mrs. Pitt and Mrs. DuBois and Manly Neighbors would look when they read their obituaries.

Miss Iona sat so that the light from the Tiffany lamp fell on her face. If she opened her eyes just a little, a very little bit so that they were not really opened but slitted, she found that she had a peculiar sort of double vision and she could see the individual pieces of color in the light, all the colors that made up the white light, whirling and whirling in tune with the tune in her head, and beyond the individual points of whirling color she could see the whole turning earth as faster and faster it went. It was lovely. She had been wise, Miss Iona reflected, to stop trying to cure an illness for which there is no cure. When she slitted her eyes again she could see them behind the moving lights: the darkling plains and the loud black armies riding, riding across them, but something about the particular way in which she had learned to slit her eyes kept everything in its place, the circling colors, the turning earth, and the dark armies beyond the edge of the vision.

Miss Iona lifted her head as the fire trucks went by. She smiled at them, a sweet open smile, and stared still smiling at the Oriental peacock on her flaming gown. She did the trick with her eyes and kept the peacock in focus at the front of the vision, and said right out loud in the still house, "Speaking of fancy strut!" as he moved slowly at first and then faster, doing double time across the brilliant, buckling earth.

About the Author

Twice winner of the prestigious O. Henry Award, Lee Smith is the author of five novels including FAMILY LINEN, ORAL HISTORY, and CAKEWALK. She has published stories in *Redbook, McCall's, Carolina Quarterly*, and other magazines. She teaches at North Carolina State University in Raleigh and lives in Chapel Hill with her husband James Seay, the poet, and their two sons.